MARSHAL'S DILEMMA

BOOK 2 - GRANT'S CROSSING WESTERNS

JM JOHNSEN

Quirled Toes Publishing books may be ordered from your favorite bookseller.
www.quirledtoes.com

Hardcover: 979-8-9921908-4-7
Paperback: 979-8-9921908-5-4
Kindle also available.

Library of Congress Cataloging Number and Cataloging in Publication data on file with publisher.

Printed in the United States of America
10 9 8 7 6 5 4 3 2

To all my friends and family who have supported
my quest to bring these stories to life.

CHAPTER 1

IT'S A MORGAN

The gunman lay sprawled halfway off the boardwalk, the trigger guard of his pistol barely clinging to his index finger. The man had fancied himself one of the fastest gunmen in the West, but United States Marshal William Jacobs was faster. The marshal, known by most folks as Jake, kicked the weapon from the dead man's hand and sat on his heels beside the body, checking his pockets for identification. He found none.

The marshal stood and looked across the gathering crowd. "Anyone know him?"

Ross Meadows, owner of the saddlery shop, pushed his way forward. "I don't know him, Jake, I mean Marshal Jacobs, but I saw him ride in. He stopped and sat on his horse, staring at your office. Then, he went into Kat's Place. That's his horse over there."

Jake looked to where Ross motioned and slowly walked to the animal. He spoke softly to the chestnut horse, running his hands down his neck. The horse had bloody cuts and scars covering his body, which helped quell any remorse Jake was feeling about killing the bastard.

Sam Watkins, Jake's deputy, heard the pop of gunfire and came running. "What happened?" He said. "You hurt, Marshal?"

"Nope. I stepped out of the office, heard a holler from across the street, looked over, and he drew on me."

Jake gently removed the dead man's saddlebags from the horse while Sam examined the horse's injuries. "How could anyone mistreat an animal like this?" Sam checked the horse's withers and legs and ran his hands down his neck and chest. "Jake, this is a Morgan," Sam said, looking across the saddle. "You find anything?"

"A wad of money and the usual stuff. Nothing to tell who he is. There's no bill of sale for the horse, and our four-legged friend isn't wearing a brand...probably stolen before the owner had time to mark him."

Sam walked to the boardwalk, where the dead man hung halfway off the side. Blood oozed from the bullet hole in his chest and dripped from the rough edge of the boardwalk into the street. He touched the man's neck, checking for a pulse. "Someone, get Doc Cooper. Might as well get Bones, too."

Most of the curious onlookers had moved away, and Jake suggested to the stragglers that they do the same.

"We have a dodger for this man," Sam said as he stood. "I don't remember his name, but I remember the face. He's a hired gun."

"That could explain the wad of money in his saddlebag. Think he was after me?"

"Probably. I'm inclined to think he wanted to take down the man who out-gunned Russel Fitz and Graham Bryson. That would add a lot of value to his gun hand."

"Could be," Jake said, remembering having to shoot the men when challenged to a gunfight. He had never killed anyone before that. Fitz and Bryson were the first, and it had taken a toll on him.

"Like it or not, Jake, you've got a reputation."

Jake's skill with a gun came from years of practicing. He and Sam had been sworn enemies until they were ten, but as they grew up, they became friends. As teens, they were always trying to outdraw, outshoot, and out-twirl one another. Sam still pivoted his gun into his holster out of lifelong habit.

Sam unhitched the Morgan. "I'll take him to the livery and have John check him over. You want the saddlebags and bedroll?"

"Yeah, leave those here."

Leading the horse up Bridge Street, Sam met Doctor Cooper. "Heard gunfire. Since you're here, I'm guessing it was Marshal Jacobs. Hope Jake's in better shape than that horse."

"Jake's fine, but the gunman needs Bones."

"I appreciate your diagnosis, Doctor Watkins, but I'll be the one to say if he needs the undertaker or not." Coop grunted sarcastically. "Everyone thinks they're a doctor." Sam smiled, listening to Coop grumbling as he walked away.

Up the street and across from the marshal's office, Russel Walters, President of Fair Valley Bank, watched from his office window... disappointed. He hated wasting all that money.

CHAPTER 2

HER BIRTHDAY

Jake had finished flipping through the wanted posters by the time Sam returned. He had singled out the one identifying his attacker and tossed it in the middle of his cluttered desk. Sam picked it up. "Douglas Marten. That's him, all right," Sam confirmed. "At least Bones will have a name to put on his headboard."

Jake went to the table in the middle of the cramped office where he had left Marten's saddlebags and bedroll. He overturned the worn leather saddlebags, spilling their contents onto the battered tabletop. Sam joined him. They discovered a second gun and a box of ammunition, a rumpled change of clothes, a hairbrush, and a well-worn, crumpled piece of stationery—a letter from his girl. When they opened the bedroll, the musky scent of sweat and gun oil was almost overpowering—a testament to the rugged life Marten had led. But there was nothing else. The only thing of any consequence in Marten's possession was the neatly bundled greenbacks that Jake had found earlier.

"We can use some of this money to pay Bones for the burying and some to care for the horse," Jake said. "I'll keep the rest in the safe. Someone may turn up with a legitimate claim on both. If not, it'll be a generous donation from Marten to the town treasury."

"If no one shows up to claim the Morgan, we should buy him for the Circle G. He ain't worth a plugged nickel the shape he's in, but once he's had time to recuperate and get some meat on those bones, he'll make a fine mount for Lorene."

"Great idea, Sam." Jake nodded. "Grant's been searching for the perfect horse for her for weeks. So far, she hasn't taken to any of them." Jake knelt before the small safe behind his desk and placed Marten's money on the top shelf.

"She can be plenty persnickety," Sam said, "but I'm betting she'll want to nurse that injured beast back to full health. That Morgan has been through hell, but he'll be in heaven if Lorene takes a shine to him."

"For a fact," Jake said, smiling as he closed the safe with a sharp click. "Guess spring is over, not that it was much cooler then," he said, wiping sweat from his brow.

"It's always hot and stuffy in this closet we call an office," Sam said, taking a seat in front of Jake's desk.

"You still sulking about not having a desk of your own?" Jake's blue eyes sparkled with devilment.

"No," Sam snorted. "And it just got a whole lot stuffier in here. I need some air. Think I'll take a walk."

Marshal Jacobs watched as Sam bumped headlong into Deputy Edward Logan on his way out.

"Lookout, you old mossback," Sam barked.

"Well, excuse me," Logan said, bowing theatrically with a sweeping gesture of his arm. He stepped inside, glancing at Jake with a frown. "What's wrong with Sam? He's not his usual cheery self."

"It's his mother's birthday."

"Oh." Logan sat in the chair Sam had just vacated. He wiped his thumb and forefinger down his oversized, salt-and-pepper mustache.

"Sam doesn't say much about it, but he carries a chunk of guilt on his shoulders. Thinks he should have done something sooner to protect his mama. That husband of hers was a mean one. The bastard used his fists and belt on his wife and on Sam."

"There was nothing Sam could have done," Jake said. "He was just a kid, and Mort Watkins was a bad apple. I've never seen anyone like him. I was at Sam's one afternoon after school…we couldn't have been more than thirteen or fourteen. Mort came tearing in all liquored up and hollering for Sam. We ran and hid in a closet under the stairway before he saw us. He scared the stuffing out of me…yelling and knocking things over. I was afraid of him and afraid for Sam. I took Sam home with me that night."

"I remember," Logan said. "I'd been out to the ranch for supper. Never did turn down an invite to Lorene's table. Grant 'n me was on the back porch enjoying some fine brandy when we saw you sneaking across the lawn toward the barn. When we caught up to you, you said the plate heaped with roast beef, potatoes, gravy, and half a loaf of bread was for Herald." Logan chuckled, "Grant said he didn't think mules liked gravy on their tatters, and we all went into the barn."

Jake smiled at the memory. "Grant was sure surprised to find Sam asleep in one of the stalls. After that night, Sam had a permanent bedroom across the hall from me. We were both lucky to have Grant take us in like we were his own."

Logan flicked his hat toward the wooden peg behind Jake's desk. "Dang; missed again. Grant tried to convince Sam's mom to leave Mort. Said she could stay at the ranch, he'd give her a job, and she could earn her own way. But she wouldn't leave. Why she stayed with such a violent man is beyond me."

Logan motioned to the cellblock. "Mort was a regular here at the jail back when I was sheriff. Course, there were only two cells along that wall and no door separating us. Mort would caterwaul all night long. He didn't have the common decency to pass out like most drunks."

"I don't remember much about him," Jake said. "Except for that one time at Sam's and the tales I've heard. Was he as mean when he sobered up?"

"Don't know as I ever saw him sober. Close to it once when I had him in jail for whalin' on Sam."

Logan shook his head, recalling the incident. "Mort beat on Sam right out there in the middle of Bridge Street. Mort was yelling like a madman. He got louder and louder until it drew everyone's attention. I got there just in time to see Mort swing his empty growler at Sam's head. He hit him square in the face with it. That's how Sam got that scar on the side of his chin. When Sam fell, Mort jumped on him like a maniac, fists flying. It took two of us to pull him off the boy. I kept Mort in jail for two days."

"Bet that was pleasant."

Logan shook his head. "Arresting him turned out to be a mistake. All the while, he ranted about how it was Sam's fault and how he would make the bastard and the whore who birthed him pay. I was afraid Mort would kill them when he got out. I warned Mort I wouldn't tolerate him whackin' on them, but there wasn't anything else I could do. I couldn't hold him forever. Not that I wanted to. When I let him go, he told me what went on between him and his was none of my concern, and if I knew what was good for me, I'd butt out. Then he grabbed his growler and went straight to the Schooner."

Jake leaned back, his chair squeaking in protest. "Maybe it was Mort who made Sam such a bully back then. I'm just glad Sam got big enough and strong enough to finally kick him out."

"I never did see Sam fight back. Sam always took it and ran away. Guess he had a lot of built-up anger cause Sam didn't just kick him out. He beat him something fierce," Logan said with a smile. "Old Doc Thorn said it was a wonder Mort survived. Of course, anyone in Doc Thorn's care was lucky to survive." Logan snorted. "Wouldn't have torn me up none if Mort had died."

Jake nodded in agreement. "The town's a better place without him. Wonder what ever happened to him?"

"I got no idea where Mort is, but I do know that as young as he was, Sam was on a dangerous path. I don't know what might have happened if Grant hadn't taken him in. Like I've said at least a dozen times, I always thought that boy would end up at the end of a rope." He rubbed his fingers down his mustache. "Glad it didn't turn out that way."

CHAPTER 3

SANCTUARY

Sam removed his hat as he ducked through the vine-covered archway and entered the cemetery. A sense of serenity and hushed reverence surrounded him as he passed between two marble angels standing watch on either side of the entryway. Although he wasn't a religious man, Sam nodded respectfully to the silent guardians.

The small cemetery was a tranquil sanctuary tucked behind the Lutheran Church at the top of Bridge Street. Towering fir trees protected it on the north like a shroud wrapped around its shoulders. To the south, the church muffled the noises from Bridge Street, and stately elms and oaks created a canopy of shade.

Sam walked past a dozen granite markers, following the stone-lined path to his mother's grave. He recognized most of the names etched into the markers: *Beatrice Long, Beloved Mother; Pvt. John Smith, 1st Battalion, Company A; Lydia Finn, My Wife My Love; Lawrence Jones, Rest in Peace Father; Baby Jensen.* Each was a somber monument to how fragile and fleeting life can be. Some had slipped away peacefully in their sleep, while others had fallen victim to illnesses. Few of Grant's Crossing's finest had met a violent end. The unknown drifters and gunslingers whose lives ended in gunfire and violence were laid to rest under wooden headboards in Pauper's Field.

Sam sat on a bench near his mother's headstone and dropped his hat beside him. "Happy Birthday, Mom," he said softly.

Sam leaned forward, staring at the ground between his boots. "You died too young," he whispered, thinking how unbelievably rough their lives had been. He cherished his memories of her and the good times they had shared—but those moments had been far too few.

He looked up at her headstone. "Did I ever tell you how much I loved the times when we were together? I remember complaining a lot, but I can't recall ever saying I love you—and I'm sorry for that."

She had been gone for nearly six years, and the sharp pain of loss had subsided, but his guilt was as intense as ever. "You'd be alive today if it hadn't been for the beatings you suffered at Mort's hands. I should have done something sooner to stop him, but I was too much of a coward." Sam wiped his hand across his face. "I failed you."

A heavy sigh escaped his lips, and his voice lightened. "If you were here, I'd take you to the Dirty Mug tonight to celebrate your birthday. This guy, Albie, came to town a few years back and transformed the Mug into one of the best eating places in the territory. It's nothing like you'd remember, but then, everything has changed around here. With all the new people and businesses, you wouldn't recognize the place. Over a thousand people live here now. They've even added a new street south of our house." Sam grinned. "Heck, a fella could get lost in a town this size."

A small gray squirrel, unhappy with the intruder, furiously flicked his tail and scolded Sam from the branch of an elm tree. Sam ignored the disapproving chatter.

He leaned down, pulling a weed from the base of the shade-dappled marker. "There's gonna be a big to-do here at the church in a couple of weeks. Jake and Winnie are getting married, and I'll be standing up for Jake. I've even got a fancy new suit. For a while, I didn't think they'd make it to the altar, but they sorted everything out. I can't help thinking there'll be some earth-shaking battles, with Winnie winning most of them."

Sam rose to leave and dropped his hat on his wavy blond hair. "Happy birthday, Mom. I miss you. I'll always think that if I had acted sooner and kicked Dad out, you'd be alive today." Sam's brown eyes glistened. "I hate him and what he did to you. I hope Mort Watkins is long dead and rotting in hell."

CHAPTER 4

LAWTON, OKLAHOMA

It had been a scorching day, Texas-hot. After twelve hours in the saddle, a bone-weary Mort Watkins rode into Lawton, Oklahoma, searching for a quiet corner where he could crawl into a bottle of whiskey and make the world disappear. He passed rowdier establishments, choosing the Black Bull Saloon. Four cowboys leaned against the bar, and a dozen more were scattered at tables across the room. A poker game was in progress, and he could hear the murmur of voices calling and folding and the shuffling of cards. *Perfect,* he thought as he approached the well-worn bar.

The barkeep, a man with a pasty, weasel-like face, nodded to him. "What's your poison, mister?" He motioned toward a hallway. "There's a woman in the back if ya got the need."

"Whiskey," Mort said. He grabbed the bottle and a chipped glass, and made his way to a table in the far corner of the room. It had been a while since he'd enjoyed the comforts of a woman's body. *Tempting,* he thought. *Maybe after a few drinks.* But for now, the warming burn of the whiskey was all he needed.

Mort rolled up his shirt sleeves and leaned back, relaxing, as he sipped from the battered glass. Through a thin haze of smoke, he watched the poker game. The game had turned serious, with chips and crumpled bills piled in the center of the table. He could see the tension on their faces even from where he was seated. Mort scrutinized each player with idle curiosity. He wasn't interested in the game or in the outcome; he was just curious.

One of the players, a farmer, wore a desperate look and was sweating bullets. Mort figured he'd wagered his feed and seed money or even put up the deed to his farm. Whatever the case, he was in over his head. The stakes were too high for a man of his means.

The man next to him was a greenhorn. Mort smiled, faintly amused by the man's bravado, and failed attempt to look like he belonged. His unsoiled Stetson and slick-heeled boots, with not a lick of wear on them, told everyone that he was a greenhorn. But his biggest mistake was the iron leathered on his hip. It would likely get him killed.

Then there was the cattleman. Mort's sharp eyes assessed him from the crown of his hat to the tips of his boots. He was obviously well-off—no pretender. He was a man who could afford to lose three times what was in the pot and then some without a worry. But he also looked to be a hard man—one who wouldn't like to lose at anything. The rancher intently eyed the fourth man at the table.

Mort's gaze followed the rancher's unwavering glare to the fourth player. He did not appear to be a gambler, but his assurance and calm demeanor told Mort the man was a professional, and Mort suspected he was talented. Mort's eyes lingered on the man's slender fingers as he dealt, deftly slipping a card from the bottom of the deck. Mort smiled. His suspicions were confirmed. *Things could get interesting,* he thought.

It came as no surprise to Mort when the poker-faced gambler—the one with fast fingers—won the pot amid groans and curses from the other players. "I'm in too deep," the farmer said, slapping his pasteboards on the table as he rose to leave. "My wife's gonna feed me my balls for supper."

The tenderfoot pulled a wad of bills from his pocket. "My luck is bound to change," he proclaimed with conviction.

The cattleman continued to glare at the card slick "Nobody's that lucky, mister," the cattleman growled, pushing back from the table threateningly. "You're cheating."

The man who didn't appear to be a gambler, also pushed away from the table. Slowly and cautiously, he extended his arms, showing the rancher he was unarmed. "I ain't toting and I ain't cheatin'. Honest, mister. I usually leave with empty pockets, but Lady Luck has roosted on my shoulder tonight."

"Bar dog," the cattleman bellowed, slamming his fist on the table. "Bring us a fresh deck of cards." His scowl drilled into the cheater. "I'll deal."

The cattleman and the bottom dealer cleaned out the wide-eyed tinhorn in three hands. Mort watched with a smile as he scurried off, limping and wincing. *He needs to get them boots broke in.*

"Ever since you called me out for cheatin', the cards have turned against me. I can't catch a decent hand. Guess you broke my streak, friend," the four-flusher grumbled as he rose from the table. "Think I'll call it quits."

"Think again," the rancher growled. "Sit down. Maybe I broke your lucky streak, or maybe you stopped cheating because you were about to get caught."

"I told you, I ain't cheatin', and I don't cotton none to playin' two-handed poker," the professional insisted.

"I don't give a hoot what you cotton to. Sit down." His booming voice left no room for discussion.

The man who didn't appear to be a gambler sat, leaving only the two intense players in the game. No one else showed any interest in joining them, and most men, sensing the escalating tension, had cleared out.

They played hand after hand, the tension around the table thick as the smoke. First, one would win, and then the other. Then, the man who didn't seem to be a gambler began winning more often.

Mort noticed three cowpokes sauntering in, leaning with their backs against the bar, intent on the game. They lingered but weren't drinking, and even though their bodies appeared relaxed, their sharp eyes never strayed from the poker game. If Mort had to guess, he'd say they rode for the rancher and were three of his enforcers. Someone had probably told them about their bossman getting fleeced. He hoped the gambler had noticed them.

Mort estimated the pot to be well over a thousand dollars, and that wasn't chicken feed for anyone. The man who didn't look like a gambler won, and as he reached to rake in his winnings, one of the cowpokes leaning against the bar grabbed for his iron. Mort jumped to his feet, drew, and shot the man between the eyes.

Blood and brain matter splattered the other two enforcers. Caught by surprise, their moment of hesitation cost them their lives. They grabbed their guns but were too late. Their irons had barely cleared leather when Mort's bullets tore into one, then the other.

With his gun still smoking, Mort wheeled toward the rancher, who had a gun pressed against the head of the bottom dealer. Mort scrutinized the cattleman for a moment before pulling the trigger.

The man who didn't look like a gambler screamed, "By all that's holy, you crazy son-of-a-bitch. That bastard had a gun pointed at my head. He could have killed me."

Mort smiled and holstered his revolver. "The hammer wasn't eared back. Get your money, and let's get the hell out of here." Mort squatted beside the rancher's body, going through his pockets. There was over two thousand dollars in the cattleman's wallet. He took half and handed half to the gambler.

They froze at the sharp, unmistakable racking of a shotgun. Slowly, they turned. The barkeep had a fierce-looking double-barreled shotgun aimed at them.

"You killed a mighty important man, and the sheriff ain't gonna be happy. You'll swing before the night's over." The barkeep sounded gleeful at the thought of a lynching, but his hands were shaking.

Mort had sized up the barkeep when he first entered the saloon and doubted he had the starch to shoot. Mort spoke to him calmly as he side-stepped away from the card sharp. "We were defending ourselves. You saw that. I don't think you're the sort who could shoot a man in cold blood or watch an innocent man get lynched."

A bead of sweat trickled down the barkeep's forehead and hung from his nose. His eyes darted between the two men and then stalled on Mort. "Drop your gun, mister, and stop moving, or I'll shoot. I know you're fast. Those others didn't even clear leather, but I can pull both these triggers faster than you can hook and draw."

Mort stopped for a moment, then took another small step to the side, putting more distance between him and the other man.

Then, the four-flusher spoke. "Put the damned shotgun down, or I'll splatter your brains," he bluffed. He had no gun, but it distracted the barkeep, who had been focused on Mort. The moment the barrel of the shotgun swung away from him, Mort drew and fired. The bullet tore through the barkeep's chest. He was dead before he hit the ground. Mort scrambled to the back of the barroom and grabbed his bottle before running through the blood-soaked sawdust and out the front door.

People were gathering, and the gambler was already mounted. "Where you headed?"

"Damned if I know," Mort said, jumping into his saddle.

"Follow me."

After a half-hour of hard riding, they left the main road and descended into a rock and boulder-strewn gorge in the Wichita Mountains. They splashed through a shallow, fast-running creek for a mile before emerging on a narrow wildlife trail.

Cyrus reined to a stop. "We'll need to rest the horses before we go on. The rest of the way is a bit of a climb. I'm Cyrus Long," he said, extending his hand. "Thanks for saving my ass back there."

"Mort Watkins," Mort said, taking Cyrus's extended hand.

"Where were you headed before this?"

"The Dakota Territory. I got business there, collecting a debt that's owed me."

"My men are encamped further up the mountain," Cyrus explained, motioning toward the rugged incline to their right. "That's where we're headed. It's remote enough that no one will find us, and by morning, it should be safe for us to move out."

Cyrus looked at Mort with a frown. "Mort, I've been looking for another man. I need someone with guts and gun savvy, and I like the way you handled yourself back there. You didn't panic and didn't hesitate to pull the trigger. I could use a man like you. Would you be interested in joining up with my crew?"

"I don't know," Mort said, surprised by the offer. "I've always worked alone, and besides, I have things to take care of in Grant's Crossing."

"Perhaps me and my men can help you with your— things."

"Four men need killing. Two of them are important ranchers, not unlike the man I killed back in Lawton, and two of them are lawmen. One of the lawmen is my son." Mort smiled. "Still interested in helping me?"

"Killing a lawman wouldn't bother me or any of my men. Come on, we should get moving. Think about my offer."

The horses struggled up the slope, making their way slowly along a treacherous, nearly unrecognizable path. Rocks and dirt tumbled down behind them as the horses dug in to gain footing. Climbing higher, rugged granite cliffs and rock formations jutted above them, towering toward the sky. The path ended abruptly on a granite ledge that seemed to go nowhere. Cyrus pointed to the right and rode through a narrow opening between two large boulders. "It's just a little further," he said.

Mort followed him through the opening and along a wide ledge for no more than a hundred yards to a deep recess in the mountainside that sheltered a thicket of Wooly Buckthorn trees and several tents. "How did you ever find this place?" Mort asked.

"We were chasing after a wounded buck," Cyrus responded. "He led us here. The mountainside protects our backs, and we can see for miles in any direction." Cyrus dismounted. "And no one could track us through those rocks. Come on, Mort. I want you to meet the gang."

CHAPTER 5

WICHITA MOUNTAINS

Four men rose to their feet as Cyrus and Mort came into camp. Cyrus introduced Mort and told them how Mort had saved his life.

Red dished up plates of deer meat stew. "My turn to cook," he said, handing a plate to Mort and one to Cyrus. The other men were already seated around the fire with plates and spoons.

The talk around the fire that evening was mainly of robberies they'd pulled and war stories. "We grew up together back in Wisconsin," Cyrus said, taking a bite of stew and chewing noisily. "When the war broke out, we volunteered. Being from Wisconsin, we joined up with the Northern Army. We didn't know what we were fighting for, but it was war, and we were young. We wanted to fight."

Mort looked from one face to another. None of them looked to be past thirty. "You don't look old enough to have served."

"I was sixteen," Cyrus said, wiping his plate clean with a chunk of biscuit and shoving it in his mouth. "The rest of these yahoos were younger still. We thought we were escaping our hard work lives."

Mort scoffed. "It didn't take us long to realize we'd made a mistake. We were at Groveton at the end of August and then at Antietam in mid-September. After that battle, we were done. Everyone in our regiment was dead or missing, and we figured we were living on borrowed time."

Red collected the empty tin plates. "I got pulled out of our regular unit and put in with Berdan's Sharpshooters. I thought I'd have it easy, hiding behind a rock and taking potshots at the enemy, like a turkey shoot. But they sent us ahead, behind enemy lines, and those green coats they made us wear that were supposed to keep us hidden in the brush." He shook his head and frowned. "It was more like having targets painted on our chests. Two of the men I was with on my last mission got picked off. I've always suspected those Rebs had to be using scoped Whitworths, but I didn't stop to check. I ran for my life, the Rebs whooping and hollering behind me like banshees. I thought I was done for. I wouldn't be here today if it hadn't been for a hollowed-out tree trunk I hid in. After that, I ditched that green coat and hunted down Cyrus, belly-crawling most of the way."

Cyrus grinned. "I had just bedded down for the night, wondering how we'd managed to survive the day when I heard footsteps coming up behind me. If it was a Rebel, it was too late to do anything, and I was too damned tired to care. Thankfully, it was Red."

"I told Cyrus how bad things were up ahead, and he said it was time for a strategic withdrawal. He says to us, 'If anyone asks, we're on a secret scouting mission for the general himself.'" Red chuckled as he headed toward the stream.

"We were tired of stepping over the dead and slogging through the blood, especially after Antietam. Death was everywhere. It was time to get out." Cyrus stood and stretched. "Enough of the war stories, men. It's time to hit the bedrolls. We move out at dawn," Cyrus turned to Mort. "Think over my offer. We could use you, and I promise it will be a profitable partnership."

"I'll think on it," Mort said. "I'll have an answer for you in the morning." He'd always been a loner and wasn't sure if being part of a gang would work for him. Would he fit in? Would the others accept him?

Before dawn the following morning, Mort was up. Using his sleeve to pick up the dented, tin coffee pot, he poured himself a cup of thick, bitter coffee leftover from the night before. He returned the pot to the flat rock that sat among the embers and stoked the fire. The embers had kept the coffee hot, and steam curled up into his face as he took a careful sip. The morning was cold, and the warmth from the tin mug felt good on his hands. Mort walked the short distance to the edge of a cliff overlooking a narrow valley. Leaning against a large boulder, he didn't notice the distant peaks silhouetted against the faintest hint of morning light. His thoughts were on Cyrus and his offer.

If the stories they told the previous evening around the fire could be believed, they had pulled off some daring heists and walked away with significant rewards. They were a tight-knit group with a long history. Would they accept him?

Struggling with his decision, he failed to notice the brilliant colors of the sunrise, which limned the trees in oranges and golds. He missed the dark sky slowly turning to indigo blue and then to the bright blue that indicated the start of a new day. Gazing into the valley below, he didn't see the winding river or the rolling hills surrounding it, and he didn't see any of the beauty.

A rock on the ground in front of Mort sparked in the early sunlight and caught his eye. He stooped to pick it up and turned it around in his fingers, studying it. It looked like a thousand shards of sparkling glass packed together, like a snowball.

Mort turned at the crunching sound of footsteps coming up behind him. "Just me," Cyrus said. "So, what do you think?"

Mort's eyes returned to the small stone in his hand. "A rock is just a rock—no expectations, no disappointments. Men are different." Mort's eyes cut from the rock to Cyrus's face. "I've been thinking about your offer," Mort said, flinging the rock into the canyon. "Before I decide, I need to know what kind of plans you have. I don't want to join up to hang around a fire, telling war stories and swilling whiskey. I don't want to be *disappointed*. I have a mission."

"I know you do, and so do we. We're headed to Dallas. There's a bank there that's practically begging to be robbed, and afterward, we'll head north. To Dakota? To help you with your business." Cyrus smiled. "We could use you, Mort, and I think you'll fit right in. I've talked to the men, and they think so too. What do you say?"

Hell, why not, Mort thought. My business in Grant's Crossing has waited this long; it can wait a little longer. Mort nodded to Cyrus. "Count me in."

CHAPTER 6

OGDEN HOTEL, DALLAS

Mort yanked his watch from his vest pocket for the tenth time in ten minutes. He hated waiting. He unbuttoned his shirt collar and joined the other men gathered around the small, rickety table near the window. Their attention was fixed on a detailed layout of the Atherton Bank of Dallas, one of the country's newest and most secure banks.

The hotel room was hazed with smoke, sweltering hot, and not nearly large enough for the six men who crowded around the table. Tension hung heavily in the unmoving air as their leader reviewed the details of their plan. "We meet in front of the bank in two hours." Cyrus Long looked from man to man as he stubbed out his cigarette. The overflowing tin ashtray wobbled under the pressure of his tobacco-stained fingers.

"We've been watching the bank for over a week. We've studied the routines and should have no trouble pulling this off. That pompous president runs his bank on a strict schedule, making it easy for us." Cyrus paused, scanning the anxious expressions of his crew. "At precisely one o'clock, the vice president, his secretary, five bankers, and the guard nearest the president's office leave the bank for their noonday meal. At one-fifteen, the president calls his secretary into his office and closes the door."

A ray of sunlight from the grimy window illuminated blue whorls of smoke rising from the extinguished cigarette. "We move in at one twenty," Cyrus said in a commanding tone. Dragging his finger across the wrinkled map, he outlined their method of entry. "Red and Wes will stay outside with the horses, and the rest of us will enter the bank. Me and Bobby will take care of the guards and head straight to the vault. Patch, you and Mort will handle the remaining banker, the teller, and any customers. We'll be in and out in minutes."

"Does everyone understand what they're to do?"

The men nodded. Cyrus once again looked from man to man. "If there are any questions, now's the time."

Red spoke hesitantly, wiping sweat from his forehead with his shirt sleeve, "Do you have to kill the two guards? Couldn't you just knock them out?"

Cyrus glared at the man. "We've been through this, Red. I don't want to worry about those guards trying something stupid and getting one of us killed. Better them than us. You got a problem with it?"

Red shook his head. "No sir, no problem, Captain." Red understood that sometimes things could get out of hand, and people could get killed. It went with the job, but this was different; it was a planned execution, an out-and-out murder. At least he'd be outside the bank with Wes, watching the horses and keeping folks out of the bank.

"Anyone else got a problem?" No one spoke.

Cyrus put his hand on Mort's shoulder. "Mort Watkins is new to our crew. Maybe he didn't ride with us in the war, but I expect you to treat him as if he did." He looked from man to man for any disagreement. There was none. Mort nodded to them, acknowledging their acceptance.

"Spread out, men, as we planned. Wes and Red in the saloon across the street, and Bobby and Patch a block down at the city park. Me and Mort will stay here." Cyrus shot Bobby a knowing look. "And Bobby, stay out of trouble. If we stick to the plan and don't lose our heads, we'll be wealthy men by the end of the day."

Mort sat on the bed, the worn mattress sagging beneath him. He pressed his back against the wooden headboard and scrubbed his face with his hands. He pinched the bridge of his nose between his forefingers, trying to remain calm. He never did like waiting. He checked his watch again and leaned back, clasping his hands behind his head.

Cyrus stood by the window, his gaze turning toward the bank. The light from the window emphasized his sharp profile as he checked the streets with hawk-like scrutiny. He was a planner and tactician, and Mort admired him. Mort suspected Cyrus was mentally reviewing every step of the bank robbery, looking for any flaw in the plan.

Turning abruptly from the window, Cyrus pulled the makings from his pocket and, with hands steady as a rock, quirled a cigarette. He eyed Mort with a frown. "Why are you set on killin' your boy? You said he was one of the lawmen you wanted dead."

Mort's body stiffened. The question surprised him. He didn't know how to answer or if he wanted to.

"Tell me it's none of my business if you want. It won't change nothin'," Cyrus said, seeing Mort's hesitation. He grabbed a bottle of whiskey from the dresser and took a swig. He held the bottle out to Mort.

Mort gazed at the amber-colored liquor and shook his head. "A few years back, I was the town drunk. Stumbling down the street, begging for drinks, making a fool of myself—the butt of every joke." Mort took a ragged breath. Even after all these years, the memories of humiliation and ridicule ignited a fire of anger that burned in his belly.

"Me and the boy didn't part on good terms. The last time I saw him, I was drunk and having a row with my woman—one that involved a belt. When I was done with her, I planned to adjust his attitude as well. I wanted to remind him who the man of the house was, but he surprised me. He grabbed me and beat the shit out of me. I didn't realize how strong he'd become. If I'd been sober, I might have noticed that he'd grown into a man.

"He left me in the street like a pile of garbage." Mort's words were twisted with bitterness, and he could feel a cold sweat crawling down his back as he spoke. "My nose was broken, my ribs were cracked, and my eyes were nearly swollen shut. I had a knot the size of a goose egg on my forehead, and my lip was split open up to my nose. I reckon I was as close to dead as I've ever been."

"He hammered you good," Cyrus said.

"Yeah. I could use that drink now," Mort said, taking the bottle from Cyrus and tipping it back. "I still drink, but back then, it was a gnawing need, a hunger that was never satisfied. Nothing else mattered."

Mort's voice was edged with the stinging memory of pain and humiliation. "When I came to, that was the first thing I wanted—a drink. I couldn't stand, so I crawled to the hitching rail and pulled myself up. I hung there like a rag doll, limp and barely able to draw breath." "I must have looked pathetic hanging there, too frightened to go into my own home."

"What did you do?" Cyrus asked.

"What did I do?" Mort snorted. "I crawled across the field behind my house to the Night Owl Saloon. I could barely make out the barkeeper's voice asking me if I'd got caught in a meat grinder or a stampede. My head hurt, and when I rubbed my ears, my hands came away bloody. Hell, I could barely hear my own voice when I told the barkeep to pour a drink for Mort Watkins."

Mort's chest tightened, and he cringed at the memory. "I never got my drink. Four overnight drinkers surrounded me, laughing and asking who this Mort Watkins fellow was. Guess I didn't give them the right answer. The next thing I remember, I was waking up in the doctor's office stitched, wrapped, salved, and begging for a drink and something for the pain."

"When I was able, I slipped out of town with my tail between my legs—running from my boy." Mort scowled and ran his hand down his face. "Every time I tried to settle down, there was always some stinking lawman telling me to move on, so I wandered. It was whiskey and vengeance that kept me going."

"You ain't the butt end of any joke now, Mort. You're a man to be reckoned with. How'd you get shed of the whiskey pull?"

"Can't say. I woke up one day, and instead of drinking, I started practicing with my gun. I got odd jobs and built some muscles. It felt good—I felt good."

Mort raised his chin, his jaw tight. The memories were devastating, but he cherished them. They fueled his hatred, and he longed for the day when he would confront those who had wronged him and set things straight.

CHAPTER 7

ATHERTON BANK OF DALLAS

At precisely eight-forty-five each morning, Mr. Walter Green unlocked the doors of his opulent new bank. Although the bank belonged to his father-in-law, Percival Winston Atherton, Mr. Green felt as if it were his. One day it would be. Back East, the name Atherton was synonymous with old money and deep pockets. Mr. Green didn't care a lick about the name; he was only interested in the money, and he had struck it rich. He wooed and married Percival's only daughter, Penelope—a plump and rather uncomely woman. Walter easily convinced Penelope that what she wanted was for her husband to be the president of the Atherton Bank of Dallas, Texas.

To Green's surprise, Percival came through and appointed him president, but with the understanding that the vice-president, who was knowledgeable about the banking business, would make all the decisions and run the bank. Walter held a position of power and prestige with minimal responsibility. It was his perfect job, a perfect arrangement.

He strutted into the bank, admiring the dark oak chairs and benches flanking the entryway. He adjusted the angle of one—he'd have to speak with the janitor. He smiled in approval as he continued past the three bankers' desks on his right and the four ornate tellers' cages on his left, all of which were top-of-the-line.

The high ceilings were adorned with intricate moldings, and classic chandeliers gave the space an air of stately grandeur and elegance. He loved the echo of his footsteps as he strode confidently toward his office. He took a deep breath, immersing himself in the moment. "That's the scent of wealth and power," he murmured, his words softly echoing back to him across the empty bank. Both his office and the vice president's were tucked into the bank's farthest corners, though his was larger and more ornate, which pleased him. Even though he wasn't in charge, he was, after all, President of the bank.

He passed his secretary's desk on his left and, with lustful thoughts, dropped a small package on her chair. A token of appreciation for services rendered.

Unlocking the door to his office, he paused to admire his lavish surroundings. The rich dark wood of his oversized mahogany desk gleamed in the morning sunlight streaming through the windows. Luxurious leather chairs and a sofa were invitingly arranged around an ornate fireplace. The fireplace was a work of art crafted from the finest Italian marble, and above it hung a beautiful oil painting of a tranquil countryside. Every detail of the room reflected his sophistication and success. From the artwork to his gold-plated pens, he had selected only the best and most expensive items for his office. It took his breath away.

He realized he was ridiculously full of himself but couldn't help it. The opulence was making him hard. It surprised him, and his self-deprecating laugh echoed off the marble walls. The sound sent shivers down his spine and aroused him even more. *And why shouldn't I feel this way?* he thought. *I have everything a man could want: a respectable wife from an influential family, more money than God, and a mistress perfect enough to make a goddess weep with jealousy.*

Pulling a gold watch from his pocket, he checked the time. It was nearly nine o'clock, and his employees would soon begin taking their places. He ran his bank on a strict schedule and required his employees to be at their stations, attending to business at precisely nine o'clock. He was particularly eager for his secretary to arrive. Glancing at her empty desk, he cupped the bulge in his trousers and whispered, "Miss Harring, I shall have urgent dictation for you this morning."

He snapped his watch shut with an officious click, but before slipping it back into his vest pocket, he ran his fingers along the smooth gold chain leading to the diamond-studded medallion. *There's nothing like the soft glow of gold and the sparkle of diamonds*, he thought as he settled behind his desk. He stroked the butter-soft leather of his chair and fiddled with his gold-plated pen, listening and waiting for the flourish of his employees taking their places. Then he saw his secretary arrive, and a smile spread across his face. He watched her every movement as she shed her jacket and draped it across the back of her chair. He moved to his office door, admiring her as she bent down to put her things under her desk. "Miss Harring, I have an urgent letter to dictate this morning," he said.

She turned to him with a smile, holding the package he'd left for her. "Yes, Mr. Green, of course."

Miss Harring knew what he wanted.

She was a competent secretary and could easily find another job, but Mr. Green was a vindictive man. Despite his bootless arrogance, he had enough power to ruin her. If she quit him, she would never find another job in Dallas.

Miss Harring did not find Walter the least bit attractive. His body was soft and flabby from his decadent lifestyle of overindulgence, and he was an inconsiderate lover. His lips were narrow, and his kisses too hard and sloppy, and he never worried about pleasing her. But he had money and a lot of it. He kept her in style, paying for an elegant apartment in the best part of town and showering her with gifts and money. Even this morning, he had left a token of appreciation. Mr. Green could be a very generous man. All she had to do was spread her legs, tolerate his grunts, and moan his name, and he would give her anything.

But she didn't plan on tolerating him much longer. She had money saved and would soon have enough to leave Mr. Green and Dallas behind. She would find a new life and a new job in a town where Mr. Green couldn't hurt her. That knowledge kept her going.

She took a breath, fortifying herself, and entered Mr. Green's office. He immediately closed the door behind her and pulled up her blouse to fondle her breasts. Miss Harring moaned for him as his hands wandered. She wondered if this morning's dictation would take long and if it would be on his shiny desk or in front of the marble fireplace. She hoped for the soft rug or on the sofa, but it was his desk. He was clumsy and crude, grunting as he banged his body against hers, but she played her role and gasped with pleasure. She had learned that the more noise she made, the sooner it was over.

"That will be all, Miss Harring," Walter said with a self-satisfied grin.

"Yes, Mr. Green." She straightened her clothes and hair before leaving his office, thinking how she hated lying back on his desk. She always got poked with something. She choked back a laugh. Yeah, she always got poked with something.

Returning to her desk, she felt awkward and self-conscious. Everyone was looking at her, silently judging. She had heard the whispers and snickering of the other bank employees. They knew it wasn't dictation that went on in Mr. Green's office. She sighed, trying to prepare herself for the day. All the while knowing he would call her into his office again at exactly one-fifteen, as he did every day.

The vice president's secretary, Mrs. Warner, had a desk next to Miss Harring's. They seldom spoke. They had no reason to.

"Is it worth it?" Mrs. Warner asked.

Miss Harring turned in her chair to face Mrs. Warner. "Excuse me?"

The older woman wore a smug, judgmental look. "We all know what you do for him. Is it worth it?"

She heard Mrs. Warner's mocking chuckle as she turned away. Miss Harring's face burned bright with embarrassment. A wellspring of pent-up emotions threatened to break free, but she blinked rapidly, forcing back the tears. She wasn't about to let that dried-up old biddy see her cry. It was then she made her decision. It was time to quit.

She didn't have as much money saved as she wanted, but she had enough to leave town and start fresh. She would have to spend wisely, but she could manage. After picking up her check at the end of the day, she'd never be back.

She glanced at Mr. Green, who sat behind his imposing mahogany desk. A wry smile spread across her face. After today, she would never have to endure him again. She saw Mr. Green check his watch, and knew he was about to take his usual morning walk through the bank to make sure everyone was working.

Green rose and left his office. As he walked by, he brushed his fingers across Miss Harring's shoulders. It was a possessive touch—not one of affection. He nodded to the uniformed guard stationed near his door and glanced toward the lobby, confirming that the two additional guards were at their assigned posts inside the front door. He expected that if he looked outside, he would find two more uniformed guards flanking the ornate entrance.

Green strutted past the tellers' cages and returned to his office, his gleaming shoes tapping on the marble floor. He was satisfied that all employees were busy with the day's work. Returning to his desk, he opened the top drawer and pulled out a small silver compact. He examined his pencil-thin mustache, smoothing it with his forefinger. Holding the mirror at arm's length, he turned his head from side to side, admiring his reflection. *Quite dapper*, he thought, curling his lips to admire his straight white teeth. Satisfied, he snapped the compact shut and returned it to the drawer.

He surveyed his office, ensuring everything was perfect. He grimaced at the bulky mass of black steel embedded in the wall to his right. The enormous vault was an eyesore that belonged in a back room, not in the president's office. The fact that it was reinforced with steel doors and equipped with the best security features available did not impress him. However, Mr. Atherton insisted that the vault's presence conveyed strength and security to their customers, and it would remain in the president's office. Green wasn't pleased at being forced to endure its displeasing presence, but there was nothing he could do. Old man Atherton had spoken.

CHAPTER 8

SORE FEET

everal blocks up the street from the hotel where Cyrus and his men were meeting, Deputy Sheriff Davis was thinking about the rough start to his morning. He'd had a mind-numbing argument with his wife, and when he got to work, he was sent out to find the Arends girl—again. This was the fourth time she had run away in four weeks, and she was getting to be a real burr under his tail, but it was his job to find her.

Because her parents couldn't control her, he ended up walking all over the neighborhood, asking if anyone had seen her. His feet hurt, and he replayed the argument he'd had with his wife over and over in his head. He wished she wasn't so damned independent, and what good could possibly come from giving women the vote? She had a knack for getting him all riled, but he loved her, and the thought of making up with her brought a smile to his tan weathered face.

Then he spotted the Arends girl slipping around a corner two blocks away. He hurried to the corner and looked up and down the street, shaking his head in frustration. She was nowhere in sight. He figured she must have ducked into one of the stores or maybe into the bank. He sighed, knowing he'd have to check them all. If only his feet didn't hurt and it weren't so dang hot.

***

Melody Arends ducked into the bank and crouched down in the corner. She peeked out the front window and saw the deputy checking the stores across the street. He was watching for her and would eventually get to the bank. She didn't want to be found. She didn't want to go home. Tears clouded her eyes. She had learned to endure her stepfather's attentions, but last night, he brought a friend. Her mother did nothing to stop them. She never did. She hated them. She hated them all, and she hated her life. She had no place to go and nothing to look forward to if she went back.

CHAPTER 9

ALWAYS BE POLITE

At precisely one-fifteen, six men approached the Atherton Bank of Dallas. The two outside guards had been well paid to take their nooning at that time—and to keep their mouths shut. Cyrus smiled as he watched them walk away.

Wes Talbot and Red remained outside with the horses. Their job was to make sure no lawman would surprise them and to prevent any unsuspecting customers from entering the bank. Since the building was new, their story was that construction issues made it unsafe until appropriate repairs could be made.

Cyrus and Bob entered first, appearing as regular customers heading for the teller cages, with Patch and Mort just behind them. But as Cyrus and Bob passed the guards, they turned back, grabbing and killing them quietly, each with a knife between the ribs.

Mort herded six customers into a corner of the lobby, and Patch motioned with his gun for the one remaining teller and banker to join them. "Everyone cooperates, and no one gets hurt," Patch said, returning to the teller cages to empty the drawers. Mort passed a leather poke among the hostages, demanding their money and jewelry. Everyone cooperated. No one wanted to be hurt.

After killing the two guards, Cyrus and Bob charged to the back of the bank, bursting into Mr. Green's office. They surprised him and his secretary. She was sitting on the edge of a big fancy desk, naked, leaning back on her elbows, and Mr. Green stood between her legs, his mouth on her breast and his pants around his ankles. They froze, staring wide-eyed at the two men with guns.

Cyrus yelled, "Don't move an inch, or you die."

Mr. Green stood up to his full height. "What? Who…"

"Shut up. I told you not to move." Cyrus glared at Green. "All we want is the money in that vault over there. Cooperate, and we'll leave quietly, and no one will get hurt."

"Wish I had your job, Mr. Green," Bob said, ogling the naked woman. "Yes, sir, I do."

"Shut up, Bob," Cyrus said with a scowl. "Mr. Green, you need to open the safe—now."

Mr. Green's pulse pounded so loudly in his ears, he barely heard his own voice. "I can't."

"If you don't, I will have to start shooting people, beginning with her." Cyrus motioned to Miss Harring with his gun. "And that would be a real shame."

Miss Harring looked at Mr. Green, pleading with her eyes; she didn't want to die. Mr. Green looked at the robber with horror and confusion. He wasn't a brave man, but maybe he could stall until his guards—his guards? Where were they? Why hadn't they stopped this? He mustered all the courage he could. "Look, Mister, I can't. I can't…"

Whatever he was going to say was stopped by the explosive sound of a gunshot, ending the life of his precious Miss Harring. The crack from the gun echoed through the bank, bouncing off the walls and floors, causing the hostages who were cowering in the front corner of the lobby to huddle even closer together.

Mr. Green tried to back away from his desk and his secretary's body but tripped over the pants still around his ankles. He fell backward onto the floor like a turtle on its back.

"Dang, Cy, why'd you have to go and shoot her? What a waste."

"Shut up, Bob," Cyrus said, his voice laced with exasperation. "Get Green on his feet and over here in front of the vault."

Mr. Green was in shock. His lips trembled, and drool dribbled down his chin. He struggled to form coherent thoughts. What would he tell his father-in-law? How could he explain the dead woman on his desk and the blood? There was blood everywhere, ruining everything.

Bob grabbed the front of Mr. Green's shirt, yanking him to his feet. He looked down at the trembling man's shriveled member with a snort and a chuckle. "If she was moaning and screaming, Walter, she was faking."

Cyrus shot his partner a glare. "Shut the hell up, Bob."

Mr. Green let out a high-pitched yelp as Bob dragged him roughly to the safe.

"The combination, Mr. Green. Or should I start bringing your customers back here one at a time and shoot them?"

"No. No, please, you can't," Mr. Green whimpered, his voice trembling with fear.

"I can, and I will." Cyrus turned, fully expecting to find Bob standing beside him, but Bob was by the desk fondling the beautiful but lifeless Miss Harring. "Bob," Cyrus yelled, his voice rife with anger. "We don't have time for that. Leave her alone and bring me one of Mr. Green's customers."

Glancing at the wall clock, Cyrus felt a bead of sweat trickle down his back. They were behind schedule, and the minutes were ticking away.

Bob returned with a gray-haired lady, and Cyrus put his gun to her head. "It's all up to you, Mr. Green. I don't want to kill Grandma, but I will if you make me."

Mr. Green was trembling from head to toe. Tears streamed down his face as he spoke, "But you don't understand my father-in-law, he - he'll kill me."

A single gunshot rang out. Mr. Green wet himself, and Grandma fell to the floor.

The pungent smell of blood and gun smoke filled the air. Mr. Green's knees collapsed. *How the hell is this happening? Where are my guards? Why isn't someone coming to rescue me?*

Bob grabbed Green by the arm and pulled him to his feet.

"Don't you faint on me, you son-of-a-bitch. You made me kill Grandma," Mort snarled. "And I'm starting to get a real dislike for you. Quit stalling and open the safe."

From the corner of his eye, Cyrus saw Bob moving toward the desk. "Damn it, Bob. I told you to leave the dead girl alone."

Bob reluctantly moved to stand beside Cyrus. "I was just gonna—"

"I know what you were gonna do," Cyrus cut him off. "You got no respect for the dead? Hold Mr. Green's left hand up against the safe."

Grinning, Cyrus pulled a hunting knife from the sheath on his belt and ran his thumb along the blade, testing its sharpness. Mr. Green's face was drenched with sweat, and his eyes were as wild and crazed as an evangelical preacher at a tent meeting on a hot August night.

"Mr. Green, since you don't seem to care about the lives of your employees or customers, I will give *you* my full attention. We'll start with your fingers and then move south of your belt buckle."

Mr. Green's head bobbled crazily up and down as Bob flattened his left hand against the safe. Laughing at Green's futile efforts to free himself, Bob shifted his gaze to Mr. Green's crotch with a sneer. "Mr. Tiny's next after your fingers."

Mr. Green screamed as Cyrus drew the knife, still wet with the guard's blood, across his little finger, cutting it to the bone.

"No," Walter shrieked, snot streaming down his perfect mustache. "Please, no more," he sobbed. "No more. I'll open it." He shook like an aspen in a windstorm, but in less than a minute, the vault was open, and he watched Cyrus and Bob shoving money into gunnysacks. With his pants still around his ankles, Mr. Green backed away from the safe like a hobbled horse. He jumped when his back met up with the cold marble wall, but he leaned back, thankful for the support. He glanced at Miss Harring and quickly turned away as nausea overwhelmed him. What would Mr. Atherton say? How could he ever explain this? His life had been destroyed.

As the two bank robbers hurried toward the door, the relieved bank president closed his eyes and relaxed. He was thankful to be alive, even if his life was ruined.

Mr. Green didn't see Cyrus turn and level the gun at him, but he did hear the crack of the gunshot and had enough time to wonder who they'd killed.

The jarring noise of gunfire and the two men running from the back of the bank sent a new wave of panic through the huddled hostages. A young, fresh-faced boy grabbed onto his father's arm with both hands, letting a small bag of coins he'd been hiding under his shirt fall to the floor with a thud and clatter. Mort stooped, picking up the pouch. "Holding out on me, huh, kid?" he snarled.

The boy lunged for the bag, but before his fingers could close around it, Mort swung. The gun cracked against the boy's face, sending him crashing into the wall. His neck snapped with a sickening crunch. The boy's father went for the gun, and Patch shot him.

Patch stared in disbelief. "Mort… he was just a kid." His voice was tight with anger. "You didn't have to kill him."

"He reminded me of my bastard son back home. Come on, let's get out of here."

Bob was the last one out of the bank. He turned to the hostages. "You know we mean business. Anyone sticks their head out this door, they'll get it blown off."

Everyone nodded except for the young girl cowering in the corner. She came up slowly off her haunches and looked him in the eyes. "Take me with you," she said in a small voice. "Please, mister? Take me with you."

Well, hell. She wasn't bad-looking, and she did say please. Bob smiled and motioned her toward the door.

CHAPTER 10

DEPUTY DAVIS OF DALLAS

The bank robbers mounted their horses and rode slowly out of town. Cyrus, Red, and Mort headed east, while Bob, Wes, and Patch rode west. Each group carried two money bags, and the girl rode behind Bob. No lawmen were in pursuit, and no alarms were sounding. They were getting away without a hitch. They would meet later at their rendezvous point. It was a well-hidden campsite they had found earlier in the week and stocked with supplies in anticipation of a victory celebration.

Coming out of the dry goods shop two doors down from the bank, Deputy Davis saw three men riding west. It was a normal enough sight, but what drew his attention was the girl riding behind one of the men. At first, he couldn't tell who was on the horse, but then he recognized her. Melody Arends was sitting behind one of the men with her arms wrapped around his waist.

Davis shook his head in frustration, wondering what she had gotten herself into. She had a tough life at home, but riding off with strange men was a mistake. She had never done anything like this before, and he was concerned. She wasn't a runaway any longer. She'd been kidnapped.

He started toward the station house to report to his captain. Then, he would round up some officers to ride with him. Three men had taken Melody, and he didn't relish riding after them alone. He had only taken a few steps when he stopped abruptly. There were no guards in front of the bank. Mr. Green took bank security seriously and would be hopping mad when he found out his guards were slacking.

Davis hated dealing with Mr. Green and his pompous attitude. Any other day, he would have enjoyed putting a hole in the bottom of Green's tightly run little ship, but not today. He didn't have time. He'd let Green know about his missing guards and then go about finding the Arends girl.

Opening the door to the bank, Deputy Davis intended to deal quickly with Mr. Green, but what he found shook him to the core. Two of the bank guards lay dead in a spreading pool of blood, and a huddle of people cowered in the corner of the lobby, crying and whimpering in terror. He showed them his badge. "The robbers are gone, and you're safe," he assured them. Then he saw the bodies of the young boy, a man who was probably his father, and those of the two guards. Bile rose in his throat at the brutality, and he was even more concerned for the welfare of the Arends girl.

Davis glanced toward the back of the bank where Green's office was located. He needed to find Mr. Green but also needed to keep the witnesses from wandering off. He decided that his best option was to take them to one of the offices in the back. He put the iron bar across the front door to lock out unsuspecting customers and motioned for the group to follow him. He led them behind the tellers' cages to avoid the pool of blood that covered most of the lobby and the aisle leading to the back.

He gingerly pushed open the door to the vice president's office and was relieved to see everything was in order, but what he saw out of the corner of his eye sent a shiver down his spine. He turned his back to Mr. Green's office and quickly put himself between the gruesome sight and the witnesses. Even with his back turned, he could still see the blood-spattered wall and feel Miss Harring's lifeless eyes staring at him.

Thank God this is the sheriff's problem and not mine, he thought. He was preparing to question the witnesses when a forceful pounding on the front door caused him and all the others to jump.

"Let me in. What's going on in there? I demand that you open this door immediately."

The pounding and shouting continued as Deputy Davis hurried to the front door, dodging the pooling blood. "Who are you?" Davis demanded through the closed door.

"I'm the vice president of this bank. Who the hell are you?"

"I'm Deputy Sheriff Davis," he said, drawing his gun. He took the bar from the door and opened it slowly.

The vice president stepped inside, looking suspiciously at Davis, and was about to speak when he saw the bodies and the blood. Davis grabbed him in time to lower him to the floor.

"Your bank has been robbed," Davis said, slapping the vice president awake. "There are seven dead, including Mr. Green and his secretary. Three hostages were killed, and a young girl was kidnapped. Are you with me?"

The bleary-eyed vice president nodded. "Yeah. Yeah, I—I'm with you."

"I need you to go to the station house and explain to them what's happened. Can you do that?"

"I'm not feeling well," the dazed vice president mumbled, making no effort to get up.

"Look, pal, your bank has been robbed, and seven people are dead. I need you to buck up. I'll stay here to take care of the witnesses and make sure no one comes in. Unless, of course, you would like to stay here with the bodies?"

The horrifying thought of being left alone with the bodies sent the vice president scrambling for the door. Deputy Davis barred the door behind him and began interviewing the witnesses.

Arnold and Bertie Peterson had come by train from a Podunk town up north. According to Mrs. Peterson, they had come to the bank straightaway to put their money somewhere safe. "If we'd gone to the hotel like I wanted, we wouldn't be in this mess. But no, my husband had to come to the bank first. He always has all the answers—never listens."

The couple continued to bicker, and the deputy gave up trying to get any worthwhile information from them. He was glad his wife wasn't anything like Bertie.

Next, he talked to the farmer, who was sitting quietly in the corner, staring into space. "Can you tell me what happened?"

The farmer looked at him with glazed eyes. "My damn plow broke."

Deputy Davis smiled. "And then?"

"Oh, I'm sorry. I'm Abraham Peters. Folks call me Ab."

"Too bad about your plow, Ab, but I need you to tell me what happened here at the bank."

"I never saw anything like it, Deputy. I didn't get tangled up in the war. I've never seen any killin'. The noise and the blood. And that poor little boy."

"We need to catch them, Ab. They took a young girl with them, and I'm afraid of what might happen to her."

"I can describe them all, Deputy, and I remember their names. I can even tell you what they were wearing. I tried to memorize everything I could, hoping I'd be around to talk to the law."

"I stopped here to get some money to pay for fixing the plow and to buy a drink or two down at the Lamp Post. My wife told me to stop there but said I should leave the painted ladies alone."

Davis smiled. Now, that's the kind of woman a man wants for a wife. He focused on Ab's detailed recounting of the robbery, but his mind kept returning to the Arends girl. She was in a peck of trouble.

CHAPTER 11

THE DANCE

Bob liked the feel of the girl's arms around his waist and the feel of her breasts rubbing against his back. He wanted to stop and take her right there in the middle of the road—it wouldn't take long. But with a posse likely on their trail, he didn't dare risk it. He pulled one of her hands down to the bulge pushing against the front of his trousers. He was pleased when she didn't pull away and surprised when she unbuttoned his pants and slid her hand in to stroke him.

As much as he hated to, he pulled her hand away. "You are a surprise, aren't you? And in such a hurry to get to my goods." He laughed as he buttoned his britches. "For now, I'll have to disappoint you and keep my mind on business. It wouldn't pay to get caught with my britches down. Besides, sweetheart, we'll have plenty of time tonight. Once we get to the campsite, we can relax and take our time."

Earlier, Bob had sent Wes backtracking to check on the posse. Hearing the hoofbeats of a fast-approaching horse, he rested his hand on his gun until he recognized the rider.

"They're less than a mile behind us," Wes said, imparting his disagreeable news. "They must have one heck of a tracker riding with them."

Bob shook his head. He wasn't surprised there was a posse, but he didn't understand how they could be so close. "He must be good. We've used all the tricks Cyrus taught us and still haven't fooled him."

"Now what?" Patch said, taking off his hat and wiping the sweat from his forehead and hatband.

Bob thought for a moment. "We can't go to the campsite until we lose them. Let's circle back and get behind them. There was some rough ground and a stream back a ways. We'll stay in the rough as long as possible and then work our way upstream. If we do it right, we'll lose them."

It was late when they finally rode into camp. Cyrus and the others were already there, and a fire was roaring. "Posse?" Cyrus asked, approaching the three men as they dismounted.

"Yeah, we had trouble shaking them. They've got a bloodhound riding with them." Bob said, pulling Melody from his horse. "But it'll be a while before they pick up our trail."

"What's this?" Cyrus demanded, nodding at the girl.

Bob saw a flash of anger in Cyrus's eyes and quickly slung an arm around the girl's shoulder. "Loot from the bank," he offered, his tone smooth and conciliatory. "She asked to come along, Cy. She even said please, and we could all use something to take the edge off. You know what I mean. This is a celebration."

Cyrus snorted and turned away from them. Bob was a womanizing fool, but tonight was a celebration, and that gal looked like a fun time for his men.

Patch threw a bottle of whiskey to Bob. He snagged it, took a long pull, then shoved it toward the girl. "Drink," he commanded, circling her like a predator. He shoved the bottle to her lips. "Go on. A few long pulls, and you'll start feeling nice and friendly. And that's exactly how we want you—real friendly."

Six men inched closer, eyes gleaming in the firelight, hunger twisting their faces into something monstrous. The flickering firelight reflected on their dirty, sweat-streaked faces, contorting them into masks of carnal lust. Fear soured her belly. These men were murderers. She'd seen what happened in the bank and had no doubt they would kill her without a second thought. Riding away with them was a mistake, but what was done was done. *Maybe I should make a run for it*, she thought. *A bullet in the back, and it'd be over*.

She took a drink from the bottle Bob kept shoving against her lips, choking and coughing as the whiskey burned its way down her throat. Bob pulled the bottle from her hands and grabbed her from behind. Pulling her close, he thrust his hips against hers. His hot breath defiled her neck as he nuzzled against her ear. Bob laughed as the men egged him on, taunting him with obscenities and foul language.

He ran a finger down the neck of her blouse and tugged on it. "Take your clothes off. We wanna see what you've got under them duds." He held the bottle of whiskey over his head with a yell, "Let's get this party started," he whooped and pushed her toward the fire. "Shuck them clothes, bitch."

Her back to the fire, six men formed a half-circle around her. She undressed slowly and clumsily as the men watched, taunting her. When she stood naked, trembling, trying to cover herself with her arms and hands, one of the men approached her. His trousers were open, and his erection bobbed toward her. She closed her eyes. Her stepfather and his friend had been liberal with their attentions, but this was different.

She opened her eyes as Bob shoved the man away from her. "She's mine," he snarled at the man on the ground. Then he turned to the girl with a lustful smile on his wide, sweaty face. "Dance," he said, eyeing her body. She grabbed the bottle from him and took a long drink, coughing and sputtering, but the fiery liquid warmed her, and she drank deeply.

Bob grabbed the bottle from her. "I said dance."

The men laughed and chanted, "Dance, dance, dance."

She stood frozen, listening to the men jeer at her. One threw a rock, and Bob backhanded her, sending her to the ground. He grabbed a handful of hair and yanked her to her feet. "I told you to dance," he growled, "now dance."

Trembling, she locked eyes with him—then yanked the bottle from his hand. She drank, slowly twirling and dancing around the fire. The men grew louder and bolder. She drained the whiskey and hurled the empty bottle into the flames with a shattering crash, sending sparks flying. The men cheered as she danced dizzily around the fire.

Naked in the firelight, she danced with wild abandon. She had never felt so free.

Hands snaked out from the darkness, grabbing and groping for her, but she twirled away from each attempt to catch her—dancing ever closer to the fire and out of their reach. She saw her distorted shadows, multiplied and flashing across the trees, dancing with her, undulating to a beat only she and the shadows heard. It was exhilarating.

Exhausted and breathless, her knees gave out. Hairy arms grabbed her and threw her down, breaking the spell.

Cyrus leaned in; his breath hot against her ear. "I'm first."

CHAPTER 12

ON THE RUN

Despite their night of celebration, Cyrus and his men got an early start. Cyrus figured the Dallas posse would pick up their trail as soon as the sun came up, and he didn't want to get ambushed. They broke camp quickly, leaving the girl to fend for herself. Cyrus doubted she would live out the morning. He considered putting her out of her misery but didn't want to waste a bullet or announce their whereabouts.

Cyrus sent Wes to scout their backtrail and keep watch on the posse. They rode hard, and Wes didn't catch up for two days.

"There ain't no posse behind us, Captain," Wes reported, "but there's still two men dogging us. The one doesn't look like law, more like a preacher or an undertaker, and the other, I would guess to be a Ranger."

"They ridin' together?"

"No, Cy. The bloodhound preacher is several hours ahead of the Ranger."

Cyrus rubbed his chin. "If we push hard, we can make Wichita in under a week—but I'd rather not ride my ass raw gettin' there." Doubling back to shake those hounds would be a better plan. It'll take longer, but it'll be easier on us and the horses." Cyrus looked at Mort. "You in a hurry to get up north?"

Mort shook his head. "Another week or two won't make no difference."

"The Chisholm Trail winds into Wichita," Mort said. "We could run into a herd or two along the way—bury our tracks under thousands of hooves."

Cyrus laughed. "How would you boys like to play at being drovers for a while?"

Cyrus's suggestion was met with groans and colorful language from his men. "We ain't no drovers, Cyrus."

"I'm only joshing you boys. I can't see myself eatin' dust, either. Wes, you ride back and keep an eye on that hound dog. You know where we're headed. Catch up with us when you can." Cyrus mounted. "Let's see how good that tracker really is."

On the first day out of Fort Worth, as the sun sank below the horizon, they found a herd of over a thousand beeves heading to Wichita. They rode past the herd before bedding down. The smell of roasting meat drifted from the drovers' camp, making their mouths water. But Cyrus insisted on a cold camp.

The following morning, Cyrus and his men were up and out of their bedrolls before the cattle moved out. Cyrus's men groused about no coffee, but Mort moved them along. He was confident the trackers behind them would be lost in the dust, but he wasn't a man to take chances.

At midday, they stopped at a shady spot at the edge of a lake to rest. The men stretched out on the cool grass while their hobbled horses grazed nearby.

Mort jumped to his feet. "Rider. Coming in fast."

They scrambled to their feet, filling their hands.

Wes dismounted, arching his back with a groan. "Thought I'd lost you."

Cyrus hurried to Wes's side. "They still following us?"

"Half a day behind us. The one who looks like a preacher is who's dogging us, and he's leaving a trail for the ranger. Who do you suppose he is?"

"I don't know, but if he's tracked us through the cattle dust, he's definitely part bloodhound." Cyrus removed his hat and ran his hand through his straight black hair. "I'm tired of running. It's high time we turn the tables on this preacher-man. We'll have a surprise waiting for him in Wichita."

CHAPTER 13

WICHITA

Wichita was a town of five thousand residents, but that number exploded when the trail herds arrived. Thousands of noisy cows and dozens of cowboys eager to cut loose descended on the town.

"We need a rest," Mort said as they rode into Wichita. "And if the man tracking us is human, he'll have similar needs."

Bob got into a row over a woman that night, and the whole place went wild. They managed to smooth things over and kept Bob from getting thrown in jail.

The next morning at the Brass Parrot, Cyrus and Mort had breakfast while the four partiers passed around a whiskey bottle, hoping to dull the pounding in their heads. Cyrus chuckled, watching them and listening to their bellyaching. "You men will never learn. I keep tellin' you, moderation in all things, especially gambling, whiskey, and women." His advice was met with scowls and silence.

Cyrus pushed his empty plate away and pulled out his tobacco pouch. Waiting for his men to quiet, he leaned back and rolled a perfect cigarette. He ran his tongue down the length of the seam and placed the homemade between his lips. Red popped a match with his thumbnail and held the flame out for Cyrus.

"I reckon our shadow is already here and looking for us." Cyrus took a long drag and blew the smoke out through his nostrils. "With all the drovers in town, he'll have a tough time finding us."

Mort spoke up. "We could arrange for him to find us." All eyes cut to Mort. "Bob's experienced at stirring things up. He causes a row, we get kicked out, and ride off with pistols blazing. That will draw enough attention that we'll be remembered. Then, we wait outside town for the bloodhound to follow us—right into a trap."

"I like it," Cyrus said, stubbing out his cigarette. "Bob, you up for this?"

Bob smiled and headed in the direction of a buxom redhead he'd been eyeing.

Cyrus cracked his knuckles. "Let's belly up to the bar and make some noise."

CHAPTER 14

KNOW YOUR PREY

A tall, slender man in a long black coat stood outside the Wichita Telegraph office, watching six men ride noisily out of town. Their performance was clearly for his benefit, but they had overplayed their hand. They'd be waiting for him somewhere along the trail. He liked that they were waiting. He didn't like that they had set a trap.

Watching their dust settle, he pulled a slender cigar from his vest pocket. Earlier in the week, he had wired the home office for information on the men he was tracking. He never pursued a man blind. Caution had served him well over the years. He lit his cigar and stepped inside. "I need to send a wire," he told the man behind the counter.

"Yes, sir. What you wantin' to say?"

"Arrived in Wichita. Send requested information."

"How should I sign it?"

"Scott. I'll be at the Boardwalk Saloon."

"You'll get plenty a food there." The lightning-gobbler motioned to a tow-headed youngster behind the counter. "I'll send the boy with your reply as soon as it gits here."

Alexander Scott sat at a corner table in the Boardwalk Saloon, enjoying his first decent meal since leaving Dallas. He hadn't expected the hunt to take him so far and hadn't packed enough provisions for an extended time on the trail. He slathered butter on the last bite of muffin. These men knew how to cover their trail, the best he'd ever run into, and he was tired of tracking and backtracking. He smiled as he popped the last bite of sweetness into his mouth. Now they were waiting for him.

Alex leaned back and relit his cigar. Since his quarry was waiting for him, he considered getting a hotel room. He was used to sleeping on the ground and napping in the saddle, but the thought of a soft bed and one or two hours of serious shuteye was tempting. It would set him straight.

A young, fresh-faced waitress came to his table with a pot of steaming coffee. The buxom blonde wore a sheer low-cut blouse that left little to the imagination. She leaned over, close to his ear. "Will you be having any dessert?" she asked in a husky voice. The sight of her impressive cleavage and her inviting manner had him thinking more seriously about that hotel room.

A tow-headed lad ran up to his table, squelching his lustful thoughts. "Here's your wire, mister."

Alex threw the boy a shiny new silver dollar. The boy's eyes popped, and his smile split his freckled face. "Ohhh, thank you," he exclaimed loud enough for all to hear.

Alex looked from the boy to the busty blonde with a sigh. "That's how I figured I'd be feeling after dessert, but business first."

The blonde looked disappointed as she turned to walk away. Alex watched until she disappeared behind the kitchen door, then unfolded the telegram.

Based on the witness descriptions Alex had provided, the agency managed to track down five of the men who had served together in the Union Army. One with Berdan's Sharpshooters. All had been listed as missing and presumed dead, except for Robert Jenkins, who had at least a dozen dodgers plastered across the territories. The sixth man was a ghost. No record of him anywhere.

What concerned Alex most was the sharpshooter. Berdan's men had to place ten shots within inches of a bull's eye from six hundred feet. That was impressive, but in Alex's experience, most were even better—country boys used to hitting turkeys on the fly.

Alex mulled over the information. *I'd be foolish to ride into a trap. But when will I get a better chance?* He studied the smoke from his cigar twirling toward the ceiling. They'll rely on their sharpshooter. He'll only need one shot. Nothing noisy to bring curious cowboys or lawmen sniffing around. Just a hunter bringing down a deer or a farmer shooting a varmint. The sharpshooter might go for his head, but with his target on horseback and on the move, he'd likely make a chest shot to guarantee a kill.

A plan began to take shape, and he hoped his reasoning was correct, especially since he was the target.

After a stop at the blacksmith shop and one at the saddlery, he was as prepared as he could be. The saddlery owner helped strap him into his armor and onto his horse. It was heavy, awkward—but might just save his life.

"Good luck, Sir Knight," the owner of the saddlery shop said with a chuckle as the man in the long dark coat rode away.

CHAPTER 15

THE AMBUSH

People scattered for cover as six men on horseback galloped out of town, firing their guns.

Mort feared they had overdone the exit. The man dogging their trail wasn't a fool and would likely suspect a trap.

They found the perfect spot for an ambush and set up camp. It was closer to town than Cyrus liked, but Red only needed one shot. The single crack of a rifle wouldn't alarm anyone or bring the law.

Red slid his Sharps from the boot on his saddle and leaned against a large boulder. A mustache of perspiration formed across his upper lip. Cyrus came to stand at his side. "You good with this?"

"Yes, sir. I don't care none for killin'. Had my fill of it wearin' that damned green coat. But this guy won't quit, and I ain't lookin' to hang. He needs killin', Captain." Cyrus nodded and walked away, wondering how long it would be before their target showed up.

It was hours later when a lone rider in a long black coat came into view. "It's him, Captain," Wes said, coming down from his lookout higher up in the rocks. Cyrus motioned Red into position, and everyone scrambled to find a place to watch. Red chambered a round and raised the rifle to his shoulder. He sucked in a deep breath, aimed, and squeezed off a perfect shot.

The bullet hit the man in the chest. They watched the rider jerk with the impact of the bullet and topple into the brush at the side of the road.

"Fine job, Red," Cyrus said, slapping him on the back. He turned to the others. "Time we split up. We got rid of the bloodhound, but we still got a Texas Ranger doggin' us. Patch, you take Red and Wes and head north through Omaha. Mort and Bob, you come with me. We'll head west through Ogallala, and we'll meet in Grant's Crossing."

CHAPTER 16

DANG THAT HURT

The shot came sooner than Alex expected. The bullet slammed into his chest, and he slid from his saddle. He landed wrong with the wind knocked out of him. He lay still, his hand on his gun, hoping they wouldn't check.

Alex heard them ride away and sat up slowly, struggling out of his coat. He released the buckles holding the leather-covered lead plate in place across his chest. He'd fallen on it awkwardly, and his chest and side were on fire. He grunted in pain and called out to his horse, "Mooch, over here, boy."

Mooch trotted obediently to Alex and lowered his head. The white blaze on his dark chestnut face stood out against the evening light. "What're you lookin' at?" Alex growled. "No need to rub it in—you were right. Stupid idea. But at least it wasn't a headshot." Mooch pawed the ground and nosed Alexander's shoulder. Alex slowly got to his knees and unbuttoned his shirt to inspect the damage. His side was bright red and already swollen.

"It was worth it, Mooch. We're closer now than we've ever been." He buttoned his shirt, eased into his coat—and toppled over unconscious.

CHAPTER 17

HEADING NORTH

It had been three long weeks of hard riding and little sleep since they'd left Wichita. Cyrus, Mort, and Bob were tired, ill-tempered, and grating on one another.

They stopped a few times in small towns along the trail for supplies, fresh horses, and a night in a comfortable hotel bed. But every time they stopped, Bob got drunk, flashed money around, and stirred up trouble. He was big and loud and drew unwanted attention. If the Texas Ranger was on their trail, Bob was making it easy for him. So, they avoided towns and slept on the ground.

Bob was becoming increasingly difficult to control, and Cyrus's patience was wearing thin. He credited Mort for never complaining but suspected Mort was equally as frustrated with Bob's wild behavior.

After one particularly upsetting incident, Cyrus and Mort were on their way to bail Bob out of jail. Before they got to the sheriff's office, Cyrus stopped and turned to Mort. "I owe him, Mort. If it were anyone else, I'd let him rot in this podunk town or put a hunk of lead in his belly. He's saved my life more than once, and he's always got my back. You can't buy that kind of loyalty."

They bailed Bob out and the next day were back on the road to Grant's Crossing. They were a few hours out of town when Mort reined to a stop.

"If memory serves, my home place is just over that rise." Mort nodded toward the east. "I doubt anyone is living there. It was a dump when I was a kid, but the house might still be standing. It'd be a good place to bed down and rest the horses."

The sun had disappeared below the horizon, leaving only a soft glow of light. The brightest stars could be seen sparking to life as Cyrus arched his back and stretched. He leaned forward with a sigh, resting his forearms on the pommel of his saddle. "I'm dead tired, Mort. Lead the way. It can't hurt to check it out."

Mort's home wasn't abandoned. Gray smoke curled from the chimney, and a light flickered in one of the windows. Cyrus surveyed the area and spotted six or seven horses in a corral near the barn. "It ain't deserted, but looks like we can get us some fresh mounts." Cyrus dismounted, wrapping his reins around a tree branch and grabbing the rope from his saddle. Bob and Mort followed suit. "Bob, check behind the barn—make sure we're alone out here. Mort, we'll work our way up to the corral and catch three of those beauties."

Their plan went sideways when one of the horses sensed their approach. He pawed the ground, and a warning neigh caused the other horses to mill noisily in the corral. The commotion alerted the people inside the house, and the door flew open. A man and a woman rushed out, outlined by lamplight, it was obvious they were carrying shotguns.

Cyrus and Mort quickly retreated to their horses. As they mounted, they heard the boom-crack of two scatterguns. Cyrus grabbed the reins of Bob's horse, and they urged their horses toward the back of the barn, where they met Bob, injured and limping. Cyrus tossed him his reins and both he and Mort spurred their horses into a gallop. Running alongside his horse, Bob grabbed the pommel and leaped into the saddle.

Once they were sure no one was following, they veered off the trail and took refuge in a thick stand of trees. Cyrus inspected Bob's wounds. "I figured I'd find buckshot, but you're full of splinters," Cyrus grimaced, yanking a long, splintered chunk of wood from Bob's arm. Bob flinched. "It hurts, Cy. It hurts bad. I need a doctor and some of that laudanum stuff."

"Don't be a baby, it's not that bad," Cyrus said, tossing the bloody splinter into the brush. "We're going into town in the morning, and you can see the doctor then. I don't see as how it could do any harm. Besides, I don't wanna listen to any more of your whining." Mort had already led the horses to a patch of green grass away from the camp and hobbled them. He collected firewood and tinder as he headed back to where Cyrus and Bob were talking and set about building a fire. He pulled out what beans and hardtack they had left and used most of their Arbuckle to make a weak brew. It was barely worthy of being called coffee. He shook the bag, eyeing the few remaining coffee beans. Barely enough for morning coffee.

After a sparse meal, Cyrus pulled out a nearly empty bag of tobacco and rolled a thin cigarette. He sucked the hot smoke deep into his lungs and let it drift from his lips.

"First one since breakfast," Cyrus said, holding the cigarette reverently between his thumb and tobacco-stained fingers. He watched the smoke twirl toward the canopy of leaves above them and disappear on a breeze.

He took another long pull on the cigarette and blew the smoke through his nostrils. "Okay, men. We need to get our plan together." Mort and Bob grunted their agreement. "Tomorrow, we go to Grant's Crossing and do some reconnoitering. Mort, how do you think your favorite ranchers would take to getting some of their prime cattle shot and left on the range to rot? And maybe a few buildings burned to the ground?"

"They wouldn't like it."

"We'll get some fresh horses while Bob is with the doctor, and then we'll ride out and survey the ranch houses and barns. Then, we'll find the herds and do some target practice. It'll be like shooting fish in a barrel."

Mort looked across the fire. "One thing, Cyrus, remember. When the time comes, no one touches Deputy Sam Watkins but me."

CHAPTER 18

GRANT'S CROSSING

Cyrus, Bob, and Mort rode into Grant's Crossing at dawn. Cyrus claimed dawn was the best time to scout out an enemy encampment. Most folks would be asleep, and no one would be awake to recognize strangers or grow curious.

The town was eerily quiet. They watched a lone man leave the hotel and head up Bridge Street. He walked like a man with a purpose. Hearing the horses, he turned, his face catching the soft glow of the gas lamp in front of Kat's Place.

Mort reined in his horse and locked eyes with the man, but the man turned away and, continued up the street. "You'll never turn your back on me again," Mort whispered.

He drew and fired three shots, hitting Thomas Grant in the back.

One down. Three bullets well spent.

CHAPTER 19

CHADWAY

Jake bolted from bed at the sound of gunfire, or maybe it was the feeling in his gut that woke him. He knew Grant had been shot and was in serious trouble. Shirt hanging open, he strapped on his gun belt as he raced down the hotel stairs and out the front door. His eyes quickly scanned the street. He saw Grant on the ground and Sam kneeling at his side. He raced to them. "What happened?"

"I don't know. He's been shot. We need to get him to Coop's."

"Hang on, Grant. You'll be fine," Jake said the words, but he didn't believe them.

Deputy Logan came running up the hill from Murphy's Boarding House. "I heard the gunshots. I'll get Coop," he said, turning.

"No need. He's on his way," Jake said.

"Hunch?" Logan asked.

"You could say that. Help us get him up to Coop's office."

Grant's eyes rolled open. "Three men," he wheezed through gritted teeth.

"Did you recognize them?"

Grant's lips parted, but before he could speak, his head fell to the side.

Coop had heard the shots and came running. He was winded as he followed Jake and Logan into his office. "Take him to the operating room. What happened?"

"He was backshot," Sam said. "Before he passed out, he told us there were three men."

Coop cut away Grant's shirt and examined the wounds. "It's bad. But I won't know how bad it is until I start digging. Jake, you all right? You've gone white as a ghost."

"I've never seen Grant helpless," Jake said, looking from Coop to Sam.

"Take a deep breath, Jake, and go get Jenny," Coop said, hoping it would give Jake time to calm down. "Tell her it's an emergency—no time to dawdle with her hair. Logan, you should go to the ranch and get Lorene. Bring her back here as soon as possible. Sam, help me get Grant situated and ready for surgery."

"Just tell me what to do," Sam said, a chill running down his back.

Jake caught Winnie at the door, her eyes wild with panic. "How is he? What did Coop say?"

"Coop's in there." Jake hesitated, pulling her close. "It's bad, Win. We need to prepare ourselves."

"No, Jake. No."

"I have to go. Coop wants me to get Jenny. I'll be right back."

Coop heard Winnie. "Jake," he hollered. "Sam, will go get Jenny. You need to stay with Winnie."

An hour later, Doc Cooper emerged from the operating room, wiping his freshly washed hands on a spotless white towel. Winnie, Jake, and Sam stood with their eyes riveted on him.

"Grant was shot three times. One bullet grazed his upper arm—barely needed stitches. I removed a second bullet that was lodged in his side. It did no internal damage that I can find." Coop exhaled slowly, rubbing a hand across his face. "It's the third piece of lead that's the problem. It's lodged against his spine, and as far as I can tell, he can't feel anything below his waist. It may be temporary. I'll know more when he wakes. But the bottom line is the bullet needs to come out. The sooner, the better, but..."

"Then why aren't you in there?" Jake asked, an angry edge to his voice.

"I don't have the skills, Jake. Even with the best surgeon, there's a good chance the surgery could kill him or leave him paralyzed. With me wielding the scalpel, he'd have no chance at all."

"Then there'll be no operation," Winnie said, her voice shaking.

"That's the tricky part, Winnie. If we leave the bullet where it is..." Coop wiped his fingers across his splotchy beard with a long sigh. "If we leave the bullet where it is, even riding a horse could cause it to shift. Though, I doubt he'll ever walk, let alone ride."

"Damned if we do, damned if we don't?" Sam asked.

"That's pretty much the dilemma. It's a risk either way, but he's strong and healthy, and his odds are much better with the operation."

"And being bedridden or in a wheelchair wouldn't suit him. Can I see him?" Winnie asked, blinking back tears.

"Sure. He should be waking up soon."

"What do you think, Sam?" Jake said as he watched Winnie walk to her father's room.

"I can't imagine Grant paralyzed, and I know he wouldn't want to live that way, but I guess it's up to Lorene and Winnie."

"I know what needs to be done," Coop said, "but I can't be the one to do it. I wish I could, but I know a surgeon who can give Grant the best chance. He's a very sought-after doctor, popular with Chicago's elite. Coming to the backwoods might not appeal to him."

"What's his name?" Jake asked.

"Whitney Chadway," Coop replied with a wry smile. "Doctor and pompous ass supreme."

"If this Chadway fellow won't come here, why don't we take Grant to him?" Sam asked, resting a hip on the edge of Coop's desk.

"The jolting and jostling of a train ride might be all it takes for that bullet to move. Heck, the buckboard ride to the depot might kill him. No, Sam, we can't take the chance. Whit has to come to us."

"You know him?" Jake said, more of a statement than a question.

"We went to school together. We were good friends back in my former life. I haven't seen him since, but I keep tabs on him. He's in the Chicago paper often enough. Usually, the society pages."

"And he's the best?" Sam asked. "Not just a reputation?"

"In Grant's position, I wouldn't want anyone else."

"That's good enough for me," Jake said, standing. "Come on, Sam. Let's get to the telegraph office. We might as well get things moving."

Coop nodded. "The sooner the better."

Lorene and Winnie agreed with Jake and Sam's decision to go ahead and contact Chadway. "Grant's life is at stake, boys," Lorene told them. "You do whatever it takes to get that doctor to Grant's Crossing. Kidnap the jackass if need be."

After a flurry of telegrams and a sizable transfer of funds to his bank, the doctor agreed to travel to Grant's Crossing. Even before Chadway had agreed to make the trip, Winnie had sent Grant's private car to Chicago so it would be waiting for him at the station. If all went smoothly, the doctor would arrive in two days.

For two long days, Lorene and Winnie took turns watching over Grant as he drifted in and out of consciousness. Coop gave him medications to relieve his pain and make him as comfortable as possible. Jake and Sam visited several times a day, and during one of those visits, they made it a point to question Coop about his friendship with Doctor Chadway.

"He'll know who I am," Coop admitted. "The mistaken identity story won't fool him."

Jake pushed his hat back. "Would Chadway turn you in?"

"I doubt it. "We were close. Five grand wouldn't tempt him."

Jake sighed, "I don't think we can take the chance, Coop. Doctor Lloyd Templeton is buried in Pauper's Field, and we need to keep him that way."

Doctor Lloyd Templeton, now known as Doctor Franklin Cooper of Grant's Crossing, had killed a man back in the States. A bounty of $5,000, dead or alive, brought a relentless bounty hunter to Grant's Crossing, causing serious chaos and several deaths.

When the dust settled, the few who knew Coop's true identity had to make sure no one ever came searching for him again. They buried an unclaimed body in a grave marked Lloyd Templeton. Marshal Jacobs claimed to have tracked Templeton down and killed him in a struggle. Doctor Cooper, Marshal Jacobs, and Deputy Watkins filed all the necessary bureaucratic reports to attest to the fact that Lloyd Templeton was dead and buried. Only a handful of people knew Lloyd Templeton was still alive and practicing medicine in Grant's Crossing as Doctor Franklin Cooper.

"Even if he doesn't turn you in, he could let it slip to the wrong person that you're alive, and our ruse will have been for nothing. I don't want your old friend catching even a glimpse of you. Lloyd Templeton needs to remain dead and buried."

"You're right," Coop grudgingly admitted.

"I don't want you anywhere near town when he gets here. I'm sure you have some out-of-town calls to make, and when you're done with those, go to the Circle G and stay there until we send word that it's safe to return."

Doctor Chadway arrived early on the morning of the third day, and as Coop had warned, he was smug, rude, and condescending. With Grant in such a serious condition, Winnie and Lorene didn't understand why Coop had left town. At the same time, Sam, Jake, and Jenny were on edge, knowing they had to be careful not to say anything that could give away Coop's true identity.

Jenny Young, Coop's fiancée and medical assistant, saw to Doctor Chadway's needs during the operation that lasted well over two hours. The bullet was successfully removed, and Chadway guaranteed them there was no damage to the vertebrae or spinal cord. Grant would have a long recovery, but he would heal and return to an active life.

On hearing the news, Winnie hugged Doctor Chadway, thanking him for saving her father's life. He bowed extravagantly and kissed her hand. "I didn't expect to meet such a gracious, green-eyed beauty out here at the end of nowhere. Return with me to Chicago, Miss Grant, and I will escort you to parties and teas and…"

"Doctor," Jake said. Putting his arm around Winnie's shoulders. "She already has an escort."

"Ahh, I see," he said, releasing Winnie's hand. "Marshal Jacobs, before I go, would you take me to see Templeton's grave?"

Jake and Sam were surprised at his request but escorted him to Pauper's Field, where Templeton had supposedly been laid to rest. When they got to the cemetery, Chadway knelt by the grave and removed his hat. All bluster and snobbery gone,

"I read about how he got killed out here running from the law and some bounty hunter. He made big news back in the States." The doctor pulled weeds from around the base of the simple wooden marker. "I could never figure him for a killer. We had a couple of beers together earlier that evening. Maybe if I hadn't told him what a tramp his fiancé was, none of this would have happened. He had it bad for that gal, and she was nothing but a whore. I had to say something."

He looked up at the two lawmen. "LT caught her with another man. Cora kept screaming it was murder, and maybe it was. I always figured it had to have been an accident, but who knows? Love and jealousy can make a man do foolish things. Too bad it turned out the way it did. He was one of my few friends. Hell, he was my only friend, and Templeton was a fine doctor. Graduated at the top of the class.

Chadway got nimbly to his feet. "You would have liked him. Almost everyone did. He worked hard, and all he ever wanted was to help people." Chadway shook his head and let out an audible sigh. "The world lost a damn fine doctor. Yes, sir, a damn fine doctor, but not a surgeon." He shook his head and laughed. "Not a surgeon. Lloyd puked up his guts more than any student the professors could remember, and we never let him live it down. We called him Upchuck."

He faced Sam and Jake, the bluster missing from his words. "I'm sorry I missed meeting your Doctor Cooper, but I didn't need him for the surgery. His assistant did a fine job. Doctor Cooper has instructed her well." He checked his watch. "I must get to the depot. I don't want to miss my train. There are sick people back East who need me, and I would hate to be stuck here any longer than necessary." He started to walk away but turned back to look at the grave. "Wish I could tell you how much I admired you, LT."

Sam and Jake escorted the doctor to the depot and watched him get on the train. Chadway turned back to them as he boarded. "LT always enjoyed telling me what a pompous ass I was every chance he got. He was trying to keep me humble. Imagine how bad I'd be if it hadn't been for LT."

They heard his chuckles fade as he entered Grant's private car for the trip back to Chicago. Jake snorted. "How could he be any worse?"

"Hard to imagine," Sam replied. "But maybe it's a facade. His bluster was all gone out there at the cemetery. Too bad we couldn't have trusted him to meet up with Coop."

"Too risky. But all in all, a good day, Sam. Chadway has been and gone, Grant is out of the woods, and Coop is safe."

CHAPTER 20

POWDER MONKEY

Louis Woods hurried toward Mr. Grant's office but hesitated at the door. He was used to seeing Mr. Grant's imposing figure behind the large mahogany desk. The sight of Grant's daughter, Winnifred, gave him a moment's pause.

Winnie looked up and witnessed his hesitation. "It's okay, Lou. I do the same thing every time I walk in. I'm trying to fill some mighty big shoes," Winnie said, motioning Lou to a chair in front of her father's desk. "What brings you all the way in from the mine?" Even as she asked, she could tell by his face that he had terrible news.

Lou remained standing, turning his hat in his hands.

"There's been a cave-in at the mine, Miss Grant. The whole front of the mine collapsed, covering up the entrance."

Winnie leaned forward, a frown wrinkling her forehead. "How is that possible?"

"I don't know, Miss Grant. We were blasting but nowhere near the entrance. The only thing we can figure is that one or two of the support timbers near the entrance gave way. The tremors from the blast must have caused them to buckle."

Winnie sat up straighter. "Anyone hurt?"

Lou swallowed hard. "I'm afraid we may have one casualty buried under the rubble." He balled his fists, crushing the brim of his hat. "It's Luke," he said, wishing his words were a lie.

Luke was a young boy he had hired to run errands. He wasn't a day over fourteen, and Winnie couldn't help but think he should have been in school instead of working to support his family.

"What was Luke doing in the mine if you were blasting?" Winnie's eyes turned hard. "You didn't have him setting the charges, did you?"

"No, ma'am. Of course not. Uncle Ferd is our powder monkey and has been for years."

Winnie was relieved but concerned that the safety protocols her father was so unyielding about were not being followed. Still, Lou was a stickler about safety, just like her father. "So why was Luke in the mine?"

"Uncle Ferd came out, and we were all clear. Then Luke ran in to grab the stinking cat that's been hanging around the camp." Lou wiped his forearm clumsily across his eyes. "The men tried to stop him, but he shook them off. I guess he figured he had time before the fuse ran out."

"What are you doing to get him out?" Winnie's voice was calm. She refused to consider anything but a successful rescue.

"The men are working around the clock in shifts, but it's gonna be slow going. There's tons of rock and rubble to be removed, and we're afraid there could be another cave-in if we go too fast. Getting him out won't be easy, but no one is giving up."

"I didn't expect you would. How about dynamite, a small, well-placed blast?"

"We considered it, but after inspecting the area, we decided any explosion might make things worse." Lou sighed, "Maybe as a last-ditch effort."

"Tell me what you need."

"Timbers and hardware for reinforcing and bracing as we clear the rubble." Lou scoffed, "What we need is time."

"I'd turn back the clock if I could. But the timbers and hardware, that I can do. Let's find Clark. Give him a list of everything you need, and we'll get him on his way to the lumber mill. Do you need additional men?"

"No, I've got plenty of workers, and they're all determined to get Luke out." Lou let out a sharp breath. "I'm responsible for this. I should have shot that mangy cat." Lou said, his voice thick with guilt.

Winnie came from behind her father's desk and put her hand on Lou's arm. "This isn't your fault, Lou. You couldn't know Luke would take off like that? Let's find Clark and get you on the road back to the mine. You have a boy to rescue."

As they walked out the front door and down the porch steps, Winnie asked a question that had been nagging her. "Lou, how could those support timbers fail? We use the strongest materials. A timber giving way like that seems odd, especially one that far from the blast area."

"I've been asking myself the same question, Miss Grant. But what else could it be? Unless—they were tampered with?"

"That's what I'm thinking. Dad gets shot, we have cattle massacred up on the north range, and now this."

They found Clark in the bunkhouse, and Lou gave him a list of what they needed. Winnie followed Clark as he headed out to hitch up the wagon. "When you get to the lumber mill, tell Mr. Norton I want him to check all the equipment and make sure nothing has been tampered with, and tell him to put someone on guard around the clock. I don't want any more incidents."

"On it," Clark said, catching the urgency in her voice.

Lou looked at Winnie, his forehead furrowed. "You honestly don't believe this was an accident, do you?"

"No, I don't. Will you stop in town to see Luke's grandparents?" Winnie asked.

"Yes. I hate to worry them, what with their health problems, but they need to know."

"His grandparents are good people. Leave them with hope, Lou."

He nodded. "I will."

"If you need anything else, let me know. Find him, Lou—find him alive."

"We'll do our best, Miss Grant." Lou settled his hat on his head and mounted his horse.

Winnie watched him ride away, wondering what had gone wrong. She took a deep breath and walked slowly back to the office. All she could think about was her father, slaughtered cattle, and the mine accident. She was sure that it was all somehow connected.

She frowned at the papers scattered across her father's desk, relieved that soon he'd be well enough to take back the reins of Grant Enterprises. But for now, she was responsible, and the last thing she wanted was to disappoint her father. She had to keep the wheels turning, but there was so much she didn't know.

The ranch was easy. Their foreman, Linc, had been in charge for years and seldom needed her. As a child, she had often traveled with her father when he visited his other various holdings and was frequently scolded for her many questions and interruptions.

Looking back, she wished she had asked more questions.

CHAPTER 21

THE EYES OF A HAWK

Winnie sat behind her father's desk, absentmindedly twirling Jake's ring around her finger, unable to concentrate on the papers in front of her. The responsibility of protecting the ranch and all the other businesses owned by Grant Enterprises fell heavy on her shoulders. She had enough men to secure the ranch and the freight and stage offices in town, and the loggers could take care of themselves—they just needed to be warned. However, the grist and lumber mills, along with the mine and brickyard, would still be at risk. If she brought men in from the north range, she'd have sufficient manpower, but that wasn't a wise move. She'd only recently sent additional hands out to watch the herd.

She needed help, and Chief Adahay was the first person who came to mind. More than anything, she trusted him. She was mulling over how to approach the chief as she strode to the stable to saddle her horse. Ember nickered a greeting and lipped at her pocket. Winnie smiled and held out a lump of sugar for her. "You're such a beggar, but you'll earn your treat today. We're heading for Two Rivers and then to the Lazy W."

Winnie led Ember from the stable, but before heading out for the encampment at Two Rivers, she went in search of the ranch foreman.

She found Linc in his office at the main bunkhouse, talking to two of their ranch hands. Linc motioned for her to come in as he sent the men off. They tipped their hats to her as they hurried out the door.

A warm smile spread across Linc's face as Winnie entered.

She smiled back at the man she had known all her life and told him what had happened at the mine.

"I'm sorry, Linc. I should have checked with you before sending Clark off to the mill."

Linc's booming laugh shook the rafters and caught her off guard. "No apology needed. It's downright scary how much you take after your father."

His deep, rumbling laughter was infectious, and Winnie couldn't help but join in. "I'll leave you in charge for the next three days," Winnie said, her smile fading. "I'm riding to Two Rivers to talk with Chief Adahay and then to the Lazy W to see if our neighbors are having any problems."

"You think Gus is having problems?"

"They had a number of cattle shot around the same time we did, and it makes me wonder if anything else has been going on." Winnie shrugged and shook her head. "I don't know what I expect to find, but I can't just sit here waiting for something to happen. If my meeting with the chief goes well, you can bring the men back from the north range. Then we'll have enough manpower to guard the mills, brickyard, and ranch."

Linc looked at Winnie with a frown and a raised eyebrow. "You expect trouble here?"

"I don't know, Linc, but we need to be prepared."

"What about the freight wagons and the stages?" Linc asked.

"The freight wagons always have a second driver and a guard on all the stages, but you have a point. An additional armed rider couldn't hurt. I'll stop in town and make the arrangements."

Winnie mounted and headed toward Two Rivers. The encampment was located between two rivers at the lower edge of the foothills. Years ago, her grandfather had granted a small group of peaceful Lakota sanctuary on his ranch. Grandpa respected the people and formed a strong alliance with them. When issues arose with the army, Grandpa stood his ground. The army finally backed off and agreed that as long as the tribe members remained on the ranch and caused no trouble, they would leave them alone. Winnie's grandfather had kept the army at bay and had prevented them from relocating the tribe to a reservation.

Winnie rode up to the encampment and dismounted. Gray Wolf, the chief's son, greeted her with a welcoming smile. "How was your great adventure across the vast waters?"

"It's a different world over there, Gray Wolf. A different world. I like ours best."

"Little Bug," Chief Adahay called as he approached. "How is my brother, White Eagle?"

"Stronger every day, and Doc Cooper says if he behaves, he'll be home soon."

"White Eagle would be hard to keep down, and I'm doubtful he will behave."

"I'm doubtful of that, too. How are you and your people?"

"The Great Spirit has been kind to us. We have bountiful crops, and the game is plentiful."

Winnie nodded, unsure of how to proceed. She had often been with her father when the two men talked, but this wasn't White Eagle. It was Little Bug. She took a breath. "Chief Adahay, I need your help."

"What is it you need? I will help in any way I can."

"You know we had some cattle shot up on the north range?"

The chief nodded.

Winnie filled him in on her concerns. "I'd like to pull my men off the north range to take care of the ranch, but I don't want to leave the herd unprotected." Winnie paused, hoping she wasn't asking for too much. "I don't want to put any of you in danger, but it would be a great help if some of your men could watch over the north boundaries and keep an eye out for anything unusual."

After hearing what had happened, Chief Adahay became deadly serious. "Any man who stands against White Eagle stands against me and my people. What you ask of us is done."

"Thank you, Chief Adahay, and please be careful. If your men see someone who doesn't belong, don't confront them. Send word to the ranch. I hope I'm wrong, but it could be dangerous."

"We will watch with the eyes of the hawk and stealth of the fox," the chief said with a faint smile. "When you see your father, tell him I'm waiting to finish the chess game we started the last time he was here."

"I'll tell him."

Chief Adahay and Gray Wolf stood side by side, watching as she rode away. "Little Bug was smart to come to us for help. Get word to the war chiefs to meet us in the council lodge. We have plans to make. We will watch the north range *and* the house that White Eagle and Little Bug call home."

Winnie rode from the encampment, intending to go straight to the Lazy W. However, a longing to see Jake and her parents made her detour to town instead. It had been days since she'd seen them. Besides, she needed to hire extra guards for the freight wagons and stages. Tomorrow would be time enough to ride to the Lazy W.

CHAPTER 22

SERIOUS MEETING

Russell Walters, President of Fair Valley Bank, and Boyd Tate, his sharp-suited attorney, had settled into the plush leather chairs across from Emmet Richards, the mayor of Grant's Crossing. The mayor's office, situated in the east wing of City Hall, was dimly lit; the westerly sun no longer streamed through the windows.

Emmet's anxious gaze darted between the two men and then to the wall clock across from his desk—it was almost half past five. "I thought you said the boss would be here at five," he said, a slight tremor of uncertainty creeping into his voice.

With a casual air, Walters opened the humidor on the mayor's desk and helped himself to a cigar. "Stop worrying, Emmet. He's got a business to run. Something must have come up." In a smug gesture, he bit the end off the cigar and spat it across the desk at Emmet. It landed unceremoniously in front of the mayor, who brushed it away with a scowl.

"Yeah, and try not to look so anxious," Tate smirked, holding a lit match to the tip of Walters' cigar. "The boss doesn't like nervous men on his payroll."

Mayor Richards pulled a handkerchief from his pocket and nervously mopped the sweat from his forehead. "Why do you think he called this meeting?"

"Guess we'll all find out together." The words had barely left Walters's lips when there was a sharp rap on the door.

A slender, well-dressed man stepped inside and closed the door behind him. He leaned casually against the doorframe, but his voice was biting. "I just saw Jacobs, and he looked mighty healthy for a dead man. I thought you hired a gun to take care of him?" The man's eyes burned into Walters. "You said he'd be dead by now."

"Marten assured me he could handle the marshal. I never should have hired him. He was just too young." Walters' voice wavered, "It was a mistake."

"What are you doing to fix the situation?" The boss's voice was soft yet menacing.

"I had another man lined up, but when he heard that Jacobs had outgunned Fitz in a fair fight, he backed out." Walters added quickly, "But I found someone who isn't afraid to face Jacobs, and he's said to be faster than lightning. I'm expecting him any day now."

"I hope so, Walters. What's his name?"

"Drake Jefferies."

"I hope he can get the job done. I want Jacobs dead. He and that deputy of his strut around town like they own the place." The slender man snorted. "Comes from growing up around Thomas Grant. That whole family makes my skin crawl."

The man turned to leave but glanced back. "And don't forget, I'm counting on you to get the Town Council's approval for the bridge project on Elm Street. I've got the engineers and vendors all lined up, and they're eager to proceed. We all stand to make a killing on that project—don't let me down."

"No problem, sir. The bridge project will go ahead just as you've planned, and Jacobs won't live out the week."

The slender, silver-haired man fixed each man with a slow, deliberate glare. "Don't disappoint me."

CHAPTER 23

HAND'S UP

It was early evening when Winnie got to Grant's Crossing and tied Ember to the hitching post in front of the marshal's office. She opened the door and found Sam behind the marshal's desk, chewing on the end of a pencil with papers scattered all around him.

"Don't ask," he said, looking up and motioning to the cell block. "He's in the back."

Winnie opened the heavy door that separated the office from the jail cells, her face breaking into a smile when she saw him. "Hands up, you no-count sidewinder," she teased, her green eyes sparkling with mischief.

Jake obeyed, with a smile.

"Wipe that grin off your face, you troublemaker. You're going to jail," she taunted as she approached. Raising her hands she intertwined her fingers with his and pushed him back against the cell. Amidst the rattling of cell doors, she leaned her body against his, her lips hovered inches from his. "But first," she said, pressing her lips against his.

With a smooth and gentle motion, he brought their hands down and pulled her into his arms. His blue eyes clouded with a long-denied need.

"I do like a forceful woman," he said, leaning down and brushing his lips against hers. "Will you marry me?"

"Sorry, Marshal, but someone beat you to it."

"Tell me who, and I'll shoot him," Jake growled, playfully.

"You're silly," Winnie said with a flirtatious smile. "Mary says my dress is finished, and Pastor Emil is chomping at the bit for you to make an honest woman of me. He thinks you've already had your way with me, you know."

"Not for lack of trying—on your part," Jake said with a smile as he leaned down for another kiss. Then he took her hand and led her out of the cell block. "All I can say is, I'll be glad when it's all over and we're finally married."

Winnie changed the subject. "Anything new on Dad's shooter?"

"Nothing yet, Win. We've talked to everyone in town and rode to the homesteads and ranches outside of town. No one remembers anything, and no one has come forward to claim the reward we posted." Jake gently squeezed her hand. "I wish I had better news for you."

Winnie let out a sigh. "Jake, you have to find those men."

"We're doing our best and we won't stop looking."

"I know you won't," Winnie said, starting for the door with Jake following her. He pulled her into his arms and kissed the top of her head, "How'd I get so lucky to be marrying you?"

"You are lucky," she said with a smile. "So am I." She glanced around Jake's shoulder. "Bye, Sam."

"Go see your dad and mom, and meet me at the hotel for supper."

"See you there." She opened the door but stopped and looked back. "Sam, you want to join us?"

Sam looked up from his paperwork. "Thanks, Winnie, but I'll pass."

Jake closed the door behind Winnie and stood at the window, watching her walk up the street toward Coop's office.

"Thanks, Sam," Jake said, turning from the window. "We haven't had much time together lately."

Sam motioned to the pile of papers on the desk. "I've plowed through enough paperwork and reports for one day. Probably not a good idea to put them off the way we do. I need to get some fresh air. I think I'll make the rounds and then head home for the night. I'll make sure Logan can take the last walk-through."

Deputy Watkins checked his gun and adjusted his hat. "See you tomorrow," he said, closing the door behind him. It was quiet. Most of the stores and shops were closed and locked up for the night, and the streets were mostly deserted. The General Store was still bustling, and the saloons were still doing a booming business. He could hear the distant, tinny plinking of a piano as the man behind the keys pounded out "Camptown Races," accompanied by a chorus of off-key voices singing along at the top of their lungs. He was glad it was peaceful. He wasn't in the mood to deal with any belligerent drunks.

When he finished his rounds, he returned to the marshal's office and found Deputy Edward Logan sitting by the front door with his feet up and his hat pulled down over his eyes. "I'm headed home," Sam said in a voice louder than usual.

Logan sat bolt upright, chair legs thumping on the boardwalk. "I – I knew you were there."

Sam unhitched his horse with a smile. "Sure, you did. You good with taking the late rounds?"

"No problem," Logan said, chuckling at being caught napping. "I'll take the last round and head home myself. If you need me, that's where I'll be."

Edward Logan had retired as Sheriff of Grant's Crossing but had never retired from the law. It was Logan who had suggested Jake as a candidate for the post of U.S. Marshal. Jake had just turned eighteen at the time, but Logan had no doubts Jake would make an outstanding lawman. When the territorial governor gave Jake the appointment, Logan stayed on as a part-time deputy.

"See you in the morning," Sam said, turning toward home, with Pal close behind. The striking dark golden Palomino, with his flowing white mane and tail, neighed softly and nudged Sam. Sturdy, high-spirited, and fast, Pal was the perfect mount for him.

"I know, Pal, I've got to shed this mood." Pal neighed in agreement and gave Sam a harder shove in the back.

Sam walked beside Pal, his hand on Pal's neck as they loafed toward home. "Growing up, it was always me, Jake—and Winnie. Now, Jake and Winnie have a different kind of connection. I'm happy for them, but I feel like the odd man out. Dang, Pal, I guess I don't like the idea of things changing." Sam opened the door to the small barn behind his house and led Pal inside. "Sorry, Pal. I don't mean to bend your ear, but you're a good listener."

Sam pulled the saddle from Pal's back. "I have strong feelings for Kat. We've come close to being more than friends once too often," Sam said, hanging up the saddle and grabbing a curry brush. "She's an amazing woman, and sometimes I think we'd make a fine couple, but I don't love her the way Jake loves Winnie or Grant loves Lorene. I guess I feel about her the way I feel about Winnie. I'd fight to my last breath for her, but neither of them is my future." Sam stopped brushing and leaned against Pal. "I wonder if I'll ever love someone as wholeheartedly as Jake loves Winnie."

Pal shook his head and pawed the stall floor. Sam laughed and patted Pal's neck. "Of course, I love you. I'll bring you an apple later to prove it."

Sam closed the barn door and headed toward the house. He stopped and, squatting low, ducked into the shadows. Someone was inside his home, moving about in front of the kitchen windows.

CHAPTER 24

GOOD TO GO

Winnie left Jake at the marshal's office and headed for Coop's to get the latest news on her father's condition. She didn't trust her father to tell her the truth, and she figured her stepmother, Lorene, would agree with anything Grant said.

Winnie knocked on the door and stuck her head inside. "Busy?"

"No. Come on in. I'm unpacking some supplies that came in on the train this morning."

Winnie watched him pull two bottles from the crate and check each against the invoice. "Where's Jenny?"

"Within moments after this crate was delivered, she decided to take the rest of the day off." Coop pulled another bottle from the crate, inspected the label, and checked it off the invoice. "She said she had urgent business that needed tending to." Coop stopped what he was doing and looked at Winnie. "I'm guessing her urgent business was a shopping trip."

"She probably didn't want to hear you bellyaching about how they always mess up your order."

Coop scowled. "They usually do." With a grunt, he pulled a small white box from the crate.

"When are you and Jenny getting married?" Winnie smiled.

"I could ask the same of you and the marshal," Coop said, his eyes scanning the invoice.

"Well, that's up to you, Doc." She knew he hated being called Doc, but sometimes she couldn't resist. "I can't get married until Dad can walk me down the aisle."

Doctor Cooper shot Winnie a withering look. "You'll be married soon, then. Your dad is doing great and healing up faster than we could have imagined. He's well enough now that I might as well turn him loose before he tries to make a break for it."

"When can I take him home?"

"He's all yours."

"I can take him home tomorrow?"

"Tomorrow is fine. But no stress, Winnie. Keep him calm and relaxed." Coop paused for a moment before adding with a smirk, "Doc's orders."

Winnie laughed but quickly sobered. "I hope you're not serious about no stress. I know firsthand there are no stress-free moments in Dad's world. I've been trying to stay on top of things for the past month, and I'm near frazzled."

"Well, whatever goes on in your dad's world, you'll have to keep him un-frazzled." Coop put on his best doctor face. "Look, I know this is tough on you, but you must stay strong for your dad. He needs at least another month of rest for everything to heal properly. Your father is an active man—and stubborn. If he does too much too soon, he could undo all the work we've put into his recovery."

Coop saw the dismay on her face. "Tell you what. I'll give you a list of what he can and can't do. You and Lorene will have the thankless task of getting him to follow my instructions." Coop smiled. "I've gotten to know your father fairly well these past few weeks, and I do not envy you trying to keep him on a tether."

"We'll do our best," Winnie said, smiling at Coop. "It would be easier if Jake could be at the ranch more often, but he has his job to do, and part of it is to find the men who shot Dad. I hope he finds them soon."

"Me, too," Coop said absently, his attention already back on the crate of supplies. "See you tomorrow."

CHAPTER 25

DEPUTY PUMPKIN

The short walk to Murphy's Boarding House gave Winnie time to think before seeing her folks. Her father had been taken to Murphy's as soon as he could be moved. It was more comfortable than Coop's accommodations and still close enough for Coop and Jenny to easily check on him daily. Between Lorene and Mrs. Murphy, Grant had been hogtied into behaving, but he was getting restless.

Deputy Logan had lived in the boarding house for years and readily agreed to give up his cherished main floor room for Mr. Grant. He was sleeping elsewhere in the house. No one asked where, but everyone suspected Mrs. Murphy had discreetly made room for Eddie in her room.

Winnie knocked, sticking her head in the door, and Mrs. Murphy motioned her in. "Come on in, dear. They're in the parlor. Lorene's doing stitchery of some kind, and Grant is reading."

"I'd like to talk to you and Logan before seeing my folks. Is he around?"

"Eddie." She hollered down the hallway toward the back of the house.

Deputy Logan stuck his head out of one of the rooms. "What is it, Rachie?"

"Come here a minute, Pumpkin."

Winnie smiled at the nickname, wondering about a pet name for Jake. He didn't seem like a pumpkin.

"Winnie wants to talk to us," Mrs. Murphy said as Logan kissed her cheek.

"Coop says I can take Dad home tomorrow, but for tonight, I'd appreciate it if you'd keep this place locked up tight and keep an extra watchful eye on Mom and Dad. They may be in danger."

"What's up?" Mrs. Murphy asked, concern wrinkling her brow. Winnie shared her suspicions. Mrs. Murphy was horrified. "You can count on us, Winnie. We'll keep them safe."

"Thank you. And please don't say anything to Dad or Mom. I don't want Dad getting upset about this."

"It's our secret, Winnie," Mrs. Murphy said, taking Logan by the arm and starting down the hall. "We need to check all windows, Pumpkin, and that cellar door. And we need to get a stronger lock on our back door. It hasn't been working. You were supposed to fix it a week ago. We don't have…"

Winnie smiled as Mrs. Murphy's words faded down the hall. She entered the parlor and found her dad napping, *The Adventures of Tom Sawyer*, lying across his chest. His gentle, rhythmic breathing was a reassuring sound. Her mom sat by the window with an embroidery hoop in one hand and a tiny needle in the other.

Winnie felt a moment of horror as she envisioned the chaotic condition of her mom's kitchen. Her mom would not be happy, but there was no time to do anything about it.

Lorene looked up from her sewing and put down her embroidery hoop. "Did you talk to Coop?" she asked, standing to hug her stepdaughter.

"I did, and he says Dad can go home tomorrow." Winnie picked up Lorene's embroidery hoop, admiring the tiny stitches that transformed a regular flour sack into a lovely tea towel. "Wish I could do this."

Lorene chuckled at Winnie's remark. "You haven't the patience, my dear. But if you decided on it, I know you would do a fantastic job."

Grant woke with a snort. He got out of the chair without a cane or any help and walked steadily to Winnie for a hug. "Look at you. No wonder Coop says I can take you home tomorrow."

Grant grinned and hugged his daughter again. "He stopped by to see me earlier and said I was cleared to go." Grant wrapped an arm around his wife's shoulders. "Can't wait to get home and back to work."

"Dad, I know for a fact that he did not say you were cleared to go. Did he?"

"Well, maybe not in so many words," Grant acknowledged. "But I feel great." Both women rolled their eyes at the impossible man.

Grant and Lorene had been married for only a brief time when he was shot. The ink in the family Bible was barely dry. Lorene was terrified of losing the man she loved and ending up widowed for a second time. But Grant beat the odds.

Grant moved slowly but confidently back to his chair. "Chris and Pete stopped by to see how I was doing. They were in town to pick up the mail. Those two have been getting lots of letters from those mail order brides they advertised for in the Eastern papers. Can you imagine that?" Grant chuckled. "How's things at the ranch?"

"Everything's fine."

Grant nodded, watching her closely. There was something she wasn't telling him. He knew her, and something in her voice and eyes gave her away.

She smiled innocently at her father, trying to keep from blinking; Jake told her that was her tell. "You have a well-oiled machine, Dad, with knowledgeable people in all the right places. They ask for my opinion now and then. Otherwise, I seldom hear from anyone." Winnie shrugged. She was lying to him, but not totally. It was a well-oiled machine, but somebody was busy trying to bring it down.

Grant frowned, his head slightly tilted, studying his daughter. "Winnie, there's something you aren't telling me."

"Everything's fine, Dad. Honest. I'm tired and maybe a bit stressed trying to juggle everything. I have lots of questions for you, but they can all wait. Coop says you need rest."

"Well, I can't wait to get back in the saddle."

"Don't get ahead of yourself. Coop's giving us a list of dos and don'ts, and I doubt getting back in the saddle is on the list."

"We'll see."

"I can guarantee you that Mom and I will ride roughshod over you, and you will follow Coop's instructions to the letter."

"Well, I don't see what's to be gained by arguing about it since you're ganging up on me. I'll go quietly for now, but I don't have to like it, and you can't watch me all the time."

Winnie hugged her parents. "I hate to leave, but I'm meeting Jake for supper at the hotel. Remember, you'll walk me down the aisle two weeks from Saturday." Winnie stopped at the door. "Love you both," she said over her shoulder as she hurried out and down the steps.

CHAPTER 26

A CHICKEN AND A COWBOY

Winnie hurried her steps, making it a quick walk to the hotel. She hadn't eaten since breakfast and was hungry and eager to see Jake. When she arrived, he was already at a table. She went straight to him. He stood to hug her and pulled out her chair.

"Such a gentleman," Winnie said, her green eyes sparkling.

"Always am," Jake said, his smile melting her heart.

She smiled back, the mischievous smile that always made him wonder what was next. "Well, I guess you are at that, Pumpkin."

"Pumpkin?" he said, one eyebrow cocked.

"Pumpkin is Rachie's pet name for Eddie."

Jake laughed. "Thanks, Winnie, I'll have fun tomorrow razzing Deputy Pumpkin." He reached across the table, gently taking her hand, his eyes lingering on hers.

"Pumpkin doesn't work for you, but I'll come up with something."

They ordered their meal, and while they waited, Winnie told him about the incident at the mine. "I don't believe it was an accident, not with everything else that's going on."

"It does seem suspicious, "Jake said with a frown. "I don't know much about mining, but if you want, I'll ride out in the morning and take a look around." Winnie nodded. "I'd like that."

Will you ride with me?"

"No, I'm going to the Lazy W to see if Gus has had any problems."

"You think they're having similar problems?"

"I don't know," Winnie shrugged, "But it's worth the trip to check it out."

"Keep your eyes on Matthew, Winnie. I've seen how he looks at you."

Winnie rolled her eyes.

"Sam and I have been chasing him off ever since you two were kids."

"You and Sam ran him off?"

"Yes, we did."

"I can't believe you did that. I liked Matthew.

I'm serious about Matthew. He's persistent, and I don't care for the way he looks at you. He's like a wolf salivating over a chicken— and my girl is the chicken he's drooling over. Why don't you go with me to the mine, and then we'll ride over to the Lazy W together? That way, I'll know you're safe."

"You don't need to worry about me, Marshal. I can take care of myself, and I'm nobody's chicken. I'll get an early start in the morning, and we can meet here tomorrow night for supper, and compare notes."

Jake gave up, knowing it was pointless to argue. "Fine, but be careful. I don't want anything happening to my little chicken."

Two large plates of food were brought to their table, and between bites, Jake continued warning Winnie about Matt.

"Jake, are you jealous?" Winnie said playfully, her green eyes sparkling.

"I am not jealous—maybe a bit," Jake said with a smile.

"I'll be fine, Jake. Don't worry about me."

Jake put down his fork, his blue eyes narrowed. "I'll always worry about you, Winnie, always."

After supper, Jake and Winnie wandered out to the hotel's front porch and settled close to each other on the swing. Jake's arm casually encircled Winnie's shoulders. He hooked his finger under her chin and turned her face up to him. He leaned down for a kiss, but before their lips touched, Clark came tearing down the street.

"Miss Winnie, Jake," Clark hollered, huffing to a stop on the hotel steps. "Oh, uh, sorry to interrupt, but it's important. I need to talk to you."

The tone of Clark's voice had Winnie and Jake on their feet, meeting him on the steps.

"I told Mr. Norton what you said about wanting him to check the equipment and keep a close eye on things. That squinty-eyed, scrawny-necked weasel shook his head at me and said it'd be a waste of time. He'd just checked everything the night before. I told him you would not be pleased when I reported back."

"So, did they check?" Winnie asked, a frown wrinkling her forehead.

"They sure did, and it's a good thing, too. While I was still there, they found a big problem." Clark chuckled. "You wouldn't believe the look on Norton's face when he told me." Clark leaned over and spat a long line of tobacco juice into the hotel flower garden.

"What did they find?" Jake asked.

"Heck, I don't know. Something about some nuts and bolts on one of them big, high-falutin' saws they got. Norton said he'd checked it himself the night before. He was in a tizzy and had workers running all over the place, checking out the equipment. He did tell me that if they hadn't caught it, it could have caused some major damage. That's all I know. I didn't hang around for any details. I hightailed it to the mine with the lumber and then came straight back here hoping to catch you."

"How's it going at the mine? Any word on Luke?" Winnie asked.

"Nothing yet, but they're digging round the clock."

"Have they found any sign of tampering?" Jake frowned, pushing the hair from his forehead.

"Lou says they're getting close to the supports in question. It's a mess out there, Jake."

"Knowing that the mill was tampered with tells me that the braces at the mine were also sabotaged. I can't believe it," Winnie said, "but it's the only thing that makes sense, and I'm right about someone coming after us."

Jake nodded his agreement. "And whoever's behind this isn't worried about who gets hurt."

"Clark, I don't want you riding out to the ranch alone. I don't want anyone riding alone until this is cleared up. From now on, we ride with partners. Get a room here at the hotel for tonight, and plan on riding out with me at dawn. I want to talk with Mr. Weisenberger. And, Clark, please keep all of this quiet until we know what's happening around here."

Clark spat a second glob of tobacco juice into the flower bed and wiped his sleeve across his mouth. "Yes, Miss Winnie. You can trust me not to say a thing."

Winnie pulled her shawl closer around her arms and leaned against Jake. "We'll meet in the hotel cafe for breakfast and get an early start."

Clark nodded. "I think I'll wander down to Kat's and grab a bite and a few drinks. Maybe even a dance or two. See you at breakfast." Clark ambled down the boardwalk toward Kat's, wondering what storm clouds tomorrow would bring.

Standing on the porch unmoving, Winnie and Jake watched Clark vanish into Kat's.

"Why, Jake? Why would anyone do these things? Is it revenge? I hate that they're endangering innocent workers with these accidents."

"It could be revenge or it may be leading to blackmail. Either way, this is a lot more complicated than we thought." Jake paused momentarily, breathing in the cool evening air. "I'll stop at the mill on my way to the mine and talk with Mr. Norton. How long has Norton worked for your dad?"

"He's been around since the start-up, and honestly, I can't imagine him being behind any of this. He's as dependable as the sun coming up in the east. He sends in reports twice a month with updates, and occasionally, he'll contact Dad if he runs into a problem he can't handle. Dad trusts him, and, for the most part, Norton calls the shots."

"For now, he's off my list." Jake said, looking at her with a soft smile, "Who will be my partner tomorrow? I'm hurt. I offered to ride to the Lazy W with you, and you turned me down cold. And now you're partnering with Clark."

Winnie turned to face him. She smiled and flicked his shiny badge. "You're a big, tough United States Marshal. You can take care of yourself." Then she turned serious. "Get Sam to go with you. You and Sam are associated with the Grants up to your eyeballs and are in as much danger as any of us." She put her hands on his cheeks and guided his lips down to hers. "Go find Sam, and I'll see you at dawn, Cowboy."

Jake looked at her with what he hoped was a frightening scowl, "Cowboy, huh?"

"Yeah. If I'm your chicken, you're my cowboy. Now go—and leave me alone."

He wrapped her in his arms and murmured, "I'll always be here, no matter what. You're stuck with me."

"I'm just fine with that," Winnie said with a smile, as his lips covered hers.

CHAPTER 27

SAM'S VISITORS

Jake didn't find Sam at Kat's Place, but Kat was in her usual spot at the far end of the bar. He headed to his customary table near the door, nodding to her as he dropped his hat on the chair next to him. Kat came to the table with two glasses of whiskey and sat down. "I thought you would be at the hotel with Winnie, gushin', holdin' hands, and moonin' all over her."

Jake laughed his warm, throaty laugh. A laugh seldom heard. "Am I all that obvious?"

"You know you are. And you don't care who knows it."

Jake acknowledged Kat's words with a smile. Dark hair fell across his forehead. "You seen Sam?" he asked, pushing the hair back into place.

"I saw him earlier. He said he was headed home."

After his drink with Kat, Jake wandered to the marshal's office, where he found Logan sitting at the table cleaning his gun. "Everything's quiet tonight," Jake said, glancing down at the dismantled gun.

"You know you jinxed us," Logan scowled.

"Let's hope not. Seen Sam?"

"Yeah, he left for home not more than ten minutes ago."

"You got the watch tonight?"

"Yep, I'm doing the late rounds, and then I'll head home. I hope Rachie waits up for me," Logan said, pushing a cleaning cloth into the barrel of his revolver. "I'm feeling frisky."

Jake shook his head. "Can you watch the office tomorrow? I need Sam to ride out of town with me."

"Sure, what's going on?"

"I'm riding out to check on the accident at the Big Dipper Mine, and I have a feeling it would be smart to have someone watching my back."

"It's wise to pay attention to those feelings of yours. It's paid off more than once."

"I'm heading to Sam's. Would you like me to stop by the boarding house and tell Rachie you're feeling frisky?"

Logan grabbed one of the bullets from the table and threw it at Jake. Jake snagged it out of the air. It scorched his fingers, and he dropped it as a vision flashed through his mind. He saw men—men without faces and empty holsters on their hips. The vision disappeared as quickly as it came and left him wondering what it could mean. Looking at his fingers, he expected to see burns and blisters, but there was nothing. He gingerly picked up the bullet, half expecting it to be hot. It wasn't. Turning the shell in his fingers, he wondered what the vision meant. It wasn't threatening, but it left him feeling uneasy. He tossed the bullet back to Logan with a frown and left.

Jake wandered toward Sam's house, puzzling over the vague vision. If a burning hot bullet had caused it, he doubted it was a good omen. Still, it was clear that the faceless men weren't packing any weapons.

It was a pleasant evening, lit by a starry sky and the soft glow of an enormous moon. Thoughts of Winnie pushed any worry about questionable visions from his mind. He wished she were with him. It was a perfect night to be holdin' her hand, moonin', and gushin' over her. Remembering Kat's words made him smile.

Sam lived at the far end of Jefferson Street on the outskirts of town. That end of town was building up fast, with new houses popping up seemingly overnight. The overwhelming sweet smell of lilacs drifted to him on the breeze. He thought he might pick some for Winnie on the way back. It was funny how often she was in his thoughts these days. He had trouble keeping his mind on anything else. He wanted to hold her, to feel her lips on his. And whenever he was close to her, it was difficult to suppress his overwhelming desires. He wanted to wrap her in his arms and...

Jake was a few yards from the walkway leading to Sam's front door when his amorous imaginings were interrupted by someone darting into the shadows at the side of the house. He stopped, his eyes searching, but he couldn't tell where they had gone. There was no other movement outside, but two men were moving around inside, and neither of them was Sam. Jake moved to where he had seen the man dart into the shadows and crouched behind a large bush for cover. "Sam?" he whispered as loud as he dared.

"Jake?"

"Yeah, what's going on?"

Sam scurried to the bush and crouched beside Jake. "I got home a few minutes ago and noticed movement inside. I've only seen the two of them. I was trying to figure out what to do and wishing I had some backup."

"Deputy Watkins, your backup has arrived."

"Thank you, Marshal Jacobs. I'll take the front of the house if you cover the back?" As Sam moved away from Jake, he brushed against him.

"Sam, wait." Jake paused. The same vision he'd had earlier flashed before his eyes. "Those men are dangerous, but not tonight." Jake rubbed his eyes.

"You sure?" Sam asked.

"Sure as I can be."

"Then I'll walk in like I own the place, since I do. You got my back?"

"Always."

Walking to the door, Sam removed the safety loop and loosened his gun. Behind him, Jake melted into the shadows. Sam pushed the door open. The aroma of freshly brewed coffee filled the air, assaulting his adrenaline-spiked senses. He stood in the doorway scrutinizing the intruders. The man at the stove turned, and a surge of anger shot through Sam. It was his father. Sam's hands balled into fists, and his chest tightened as he struggled to contain the raging hate he felt toward the man.

The man he had called Father was at the stove with a pot of coffee in one hand and a mug in the other. A man he didn't recognize was sitting with his feet up on the kitchen table.

"Hello, son. You're just in time for coffee. I didn't think you'd mind if I made myself to home."

"I do mind. This is not your home. Take your friend and get out," Sam said, jerking his thumb toward the door. "You aren't welcome here."

Sam walked over and shoved the man's feet off the kitchen table. The man jolted off his chair, reaching for his revolver, but Sam's dad walked between them, still holding the coffee pot and mug.

"Now, Sam, is that any way to greet your father and his pal?"

Sam turned to the man he had hated his entire life. "I won't repeat it," he glowered. "Get out and take your friend with you." Sam took a step toward his father. "If I have to throw you out, I'll finish the job this time. You won't crawl away."

"The badge hanging on your shirt says otherwise," Mort sneered, setting the coffee pot and cup on the kitchen table.

"I'll make an exception for you," Sam seethed and backhanded his father, knocking him off balance.

The man Sam didn't know turned on him and again started for his gun but backed off when Jake stepped out of the shadows. "You need any assistance, Deputy?"

"Nope, Pop and I were just having a father-son talk, but I think we've come to an understanding." Then he turned to his father, his jaw clenched. "We do understand each other, don't we, Father?"

Sam breathed heavily, struggling for control. "Marshal Jacobs, do you have any questions for my visitors before they leave?"

"Why yes, I do, Deputy. Thank you."

Jake stepped forward, looking at Sam's father. "I know you, Mort Watkins, but I don't know your friend."

The second man answered, "Name's Cyrus Long, Marshal."

"Hmmm," Jake said, sizing him up for the owl-hoot he was. "Where you from, Long?"

"Down south. Texas."

"You don't sound like a Texan." Jake was sure he'd seen his face on a poster.

The man's beady rat-like eyes bored into Jake as he spoke. "Moved there recently."

"What's your business in Grant's Crossing?" Jake returned the man's intense gaze with steely blue eyes.

"Mort wanted to see his son. He feels bad about how they've been at odds for years and wants to make it up to him." Cyrus Long was a mean, rangy-looking man. His greasy, coal-black hair hung in uneven clumps, and his dark, close-set eyes scanned the room like a rat in a granary. His skin was pale, waxy, almost sickly, and he never quite stopped smirking.

"Marshal," Mort said, looking innocently at Jake. "We are not here to cause any trouble. I wanted to see my son and make things right." Mort held his hands out, opening himself up as if embracing his lie.

Mort Watkins shifted his gaze to Sam. "I'm a changed man, Sam. I want to make amends."

"You killed my mother—your wife. Do you think you can make up for that? The last beating you gave her killed her, and if I could prove it, I'd see you hang." Sam took a deep breath, denying the urge to kill. "If you came to make amends, forget it. Now get out of my house and out of my town."

Jake had been watching Cyrus closely and now turned to Sam. "Anything else?" he asked.

"Nope."

"Your business here is finished, so I'll ask you nicely to leave town. There's an eastbound train leaving in the morning, a westbound stage in the afternoon, and several trails leading out of town. Your choice but be on one of them."

"Now, Marshal, you're not being very friendly. Me and Mort planned to stay for a while, maybe even settle down here."

"That would be a mistake. If I see you or Mort here after tomorrow, I will be your worst nightmare, and that is a promise."

Jake noticed the slight twitch in Cyrus Long's fingers and saw it in his eyes. Long wanted to go for his gun. "I wouldn't," Jake said, his gaze steady. "There's nothing to be gained by it except a wooden marker in Pauper's Field."

Cyrus backed off. The last thing they needed was trouble with the law. He forced a grin that didn't reach his eyes and gave Jake a stiff nod. He wasn't sure he could take the marshal—but he'd sure like to try one day.

Sam shoved Mort and Cyrus toward the door. "Don't ever come back," he snarled, his voice low and threatening. One hard push sent them stumbling outside, and he slammed the door behind them.

Jake let out a long, deep breath. "There, for a minute, I thought you were going to kill your old man."

"I was, but I didn't want you to have to hang me."

CHAPTER 28

A PLAN FOR THE DAY

Jake strolled into the hotel cafe as the sun peeked over the horizon. Sam, Clark, and Winnie were already gathered around a table. They looked up as he came in.

Clark cackled as Jake approached. "Good morning, sunshine. You're late, but it's nice of you to join us."

"It's barely light out." Jake yawned, his voice gravelly. He ran his fingers through his hair. "I smell coffee. Where is it?" he grumbled.

"It's on its way. We ordered two pots when we got here." Sam motioned in Clark's direction. "Clark and I brought the horses down from the livery earlier. They're out front and saddled."

Jake stopped to kiss Winnie on the cheek before sitting beside her with another yawn. Two pots of coffee were delivered to the table, and the talk turned to the previous night and Sam's visitors.

Winnie shook her head. "Why on earth would your father come back here? I can't believe he thinks he could set things straight."

Sam nodded, sipping from his coffee mug. "He's up to something. He always had a scheme, but in the past, he was too drunk to do anything about it. Last night, he was sober as a judge, and that friend of his looked to be a bad case."

Jake glared at the empty table in front of him, his stomach growling at the smells of breakfast drifting from the kitchen. He sighed and took a drink of coffee. "I stopped by the office last night on my way back to the hotel," Jake said, his voice still gruff with sleep. "I thought I'd seen Mr. Long's face on one of our wanted posters, but I didn't find a thing. When do we get our food? I'm hungry."

Sam looked at Winnie with a grin. "You certain you want to marry this man?"

"I'll be careful not to wake him too early," she said with a smile. "How long has it been since you kicked Mort out?" Winnie asked.

"I was seventeen or so. Six years, maybe. I should have ended him then."

CHAPTER 29

AN EPIC FIGHT

"It's gonna take us the rest of the morning to get to the Lazy W," Clark said, stuffing a chaw of tobacco in his cheek and shoving it into place with his tongue. "My backside is already complaining, and we ain't halfway there."

Winnie smiled at Clark and his bulging cheek. "You look like a chipmunk."

Clark grunted and was about to reply, but his head snapped up, and he twisted in his saddle. "I thought I heard a rider."

Winnie turned, looking behind them, her eyes scanning both sides of the road. "I don't see a thing. You?"

Clark shook his head. "Me neither. With all what's going on, I'm a little jumpety," Clark grinned, looking across at Winnie. "You think Gus has trouble at the Lazy W." More a statement than a question.

"He and Dad are close friends, and if Dad is being targeted, maybe he is, too. Gus did have a number of cattle destroyed like we did." Winnie stood in her stirrups. "I thought I saw smoke."

Clark's eyes searched the horizon, and he sniffed the air like a bloodhound on the hunt. "Can't see or smell nothin' amiss," Clark said.

"Guess I'm a bit jumpety, too," Winnie said with a shake of her head. "Do you know why Gus's father and my granddad were at odds?" Winnie asked, half wondering if their historic feud had anything to do with the current situation.

"Don't reckon I ever knowed exactly how it started, but it was Gus's father, Joseph, who was always stirring up trouble and had his nose out of joint about something," Clark shifted the chaw, putting some teeth marks in it before spitting.

"Joseph and Caleb, your granddad, settled here about the same time. It wasn't long before they was pawin' the ground, snortin', and lockin' horns. Joseph was a hard man and stubborn down to his toes. He was always crawling up somebody's back. The man had no give. But your granddad was cut from the same cloth. He was a peaceful sort, but he didn't know how to back down. They had plenty of set-tos over land, water rights, women, cards, and anything else you can think of." Clark chuckled, "Them two kept things interestin'."

"What do you think? Could any of their arguments be the source of what's happening now?"

"Nah. Heck, there was only one fight 'twixt them that amounted to anything, and it was somethin'. It was over that tract of land out by Dead Ox Seep. According to the land office, they both had legal claim to it."

Clark shifted in his saddle. "The way I heard it, things came to a head one day when they both showed up at the land office at the same time. Some say that old man Weisenberger was bribing the clerk, and Caleb caught him in the act. But I know that ain't so. Joseph Weisenberger was too much of a penny-wiser to bribe anyone."

Rubbing his whiskered chin, Clark continued. "Old timers say that the argument got so loud it shook the windowpanes. The clerk tried to defuse the situation by suggestin' they split the land equally." Clark chuckled and shook his head. "That riled things even more since Gus and Caleb figured it was likely the clerk who had made the mistake. They turned on him and started shootin'."

"Did they kill him?" Winnie asked.

"Nah. When the sheriff got there, the clerk was cowering under the counter, and Caleb and Joseph were all calm and collected, discussin' how they would settle the issue once and for all—permanent-like. No one knows how he managed it, but the sheriff talked them out of killin' one another in a shootout. He suggested a winner-take-all fistfight. The parcel of land would go to the man left standin', and no one would have to die. I always figured they agreed because the winner would have the victory to hold over the loser's head—a lifetime of gloatin' rather than a one-time buryin'."

"I remember Dad telling me and the boys about a fistfight Granddad had over a piece of land. I was too young to pay much attention. But Jake and Sam ate it up."

"It wasn't your typical fistfight, Miss Winnie. Folks called it epic, and the old-timers still talk about it."

"Seems to me a fistfight is a fistfight. What made it so epic?"

"I'm gettin' to it," Clark said. He leaned over, spitting a line of tobacco juice in the weeds, sending a dozen grasshoppers whirring into the air. "The sheriff took them outside, shucked them of their guns and knives, and told them to have at it. The bettin' started before the fight had even begun. It was an even fight. No one was willin' to give any odds."

"The fight went all the way up Bridge Street to Miller's Livery. They clouted each other without mercy. Right fists, then left fists, but no one ate any dirt. Joseph almost drowned your granddad in that wooden trough in front of the general store. He was thrashin', and water was flying. Don't know how, but Caleb managed to get away from Joseph's chokehold."

"They punched their way down Bridge Street. They threw punch after punch, pummeling each other. One was down, then the other. They fell through windows, broke down hitchin' rails, and all but destroyed old Cooty's Saloon. When they couldn't stand any longer, they rolled, wrestled, and tumbled right to the edge of the river down where the old ferry used to tie up. They were on their knees in the mud, throwin' punches and swaying. Then Caleb seemed to get a second wind from somewhere and threw a wicked punch into Joseph's face. Them closest said you could hear Joseph's nose crunch under that haymaker. Joseph went down, and Caleb fell on top of him. For a moment, folks thought they was both out cold or dead. But Caleb got to his feet, covered in mud. Battered and bleeding, he leaned over Joseph, gasping air into his lungs. "I beat you, you son-of-a-bitch. The land is mine." That's what Caleb said, or so they say. Then he staggered to the Schooner."

"Interesting story. How much of it is true?" Winnie asked with a smirk.

"Every word is true. Even Steven Wagner can't gussie it up any."

Winnie had her doubts on both counts, but she did know Dead Ox Seep was part of the Circle G Ranch. "How did Joseph take it, losing the land?" Winnie asked, still thinking the feud could somehow be at the root of their problems.

"He didn't like it one bit. It was hard for him to swallow his pride, but he was a man of his word. He signed away his claim to the disputed land and stalked from the land office. It's said that Caleb offered Joseph his hand, but he wouldn't take it and never gave up his personal feud. It was because of Joseph that your granddad sent his daughters to school in England."

"What?"

"Joseph was a widower and tryin' to get friendly with Grace. Caleb would have none of it. He didn't know what Joseph's intentions were, and he wasn't takin' any chances with his young daughters."

"I didn't know that's why they were sent abroad. Dad always told me his sisters were sent off to school, but he never said why." Winnie shook her head. "I'll bet Joseph didn't like it when Dad and Gus became friends."

"You could say, but there wasn't anything he could do about it. Gus and Tom were determined men like their daddies. Joseph was livid when Gus asked Grant to stand up for him at his wedding. One day, he caught Grant alone at Miller's Livery and thought he would voice his opinion of dislike with his fists. I doubt Joseph wanted to kill your father, but your pa turned the tables on him and gave him a serious drubbing. When Gus and Sylvia married the next day, Tom Grant— black eye and all—was his best man. Joseph stayed home. Said he never wanted to see Gus again."

"Did he ever see his grandchildren?"

"Nope, he carried the grudge to his grave. His loss. They're great youngins, hardworkin' and polite."

"Matthew and Joshua were in school with me, but the girls were a lot younger. I didn't pay them much attention."

Clark chuckled, "Them chubby little girls are turning into fine-lookin' young women. All three of 'em got eyes for Sam."

"I had eyes for Matt," Winnie said. "He was handsome and shy, and he didn't pick on me like Jake and Sam did. He was nice."

"No one needed spectacles to see that Matt was pie-eyed over you or that Jake didn't like it."

"We had a silly tradition at school. On Valentine's Day, the girls brought box lunches for two. Some of the boxes were wrapped in plain brown paper, and some were decorated with hearts and bows."

"What did yours look like?"

"If it'd been up to me, it would have been in a plain brown wrapper, but Lorene insisted on going all out. It was always the fanciest one on the table. I figured it was what was inside that counted."

"Can't disagree with you."

"Mr. Terrance would number the boxes, and then the boys would gather around his desk to draw a number from his hat. It was always exciting—waiting to see who you'd eat lunch with. I always hoped Matt would be the one to win mine, but it only happened once. When Mr. Terrance drew his number, Matt's face turned bright red, and he was so tongue-tied he could barely say a word."

"I take it Lorene's fried chicken was wasted on him."

"Yeah, but he held my hand under the desk. I liked him a lot back then. I still do. He's grown into a good man."

"Should Jake be worried?"

Winnie smiled at Clark and coaxed Ember into a gallop, leaving Clark to wonder.

CHAPTER 30

I SMELL SMOKE

As Winnie and Clark neared the Lazy W, they caught sight of a dark column of smoke billowing toward the sky. "You thought you saw smoke earlier," Clark said, his brows knitted together with concern. "It ain't spread out like a brush fire, and it don't smell like one. I'd say it's a buildin', and I'd bet my hind leg it's coming from the Lazy W."

Winnie's heart raced as they urged their horses into a gallop. When they reached the ranch, they found the source of the smoke. One entire side of the main stable was engulfed in flames, and fiery tongues were rapidly spreading across the rest of the structure.

A number of ranch hands had formed a bucket brigade. Sylvia manned the water pump, furiously pumping water into the horse trough, while Josh and his sisters splashed buckets into the water, filling them and handing them off to the men. But despite their frantic efforts, the fire continued to devour the stable. Amidst the swirling smoke, horses screamed, and men shouted—it was utter chaos.

Several horses bolted from the building, their eyes wide with panic and nostrils flared. Gus and Matt were right behind them, hollering and waving their arms, chasing them to safety. Then, they turned and ran back into the inferno.

"No!" Sylvia screamed, her voice a piercing cry as she watched them disappear back into the smoke. She grabbed the pump handle with a determined look on her face and worked it even faster, water splashing into the trough.

The flames licked up the side of the building and jumped to the roof as more horses escaped the conflagration. Clark leaped from his horse before it had come to a stop. "We got to get them out of there. It's spreadin' fast, and that roof ain't gonna hold," he hollered, running toward the stable. He stopped long enough to dunk his neckerchief into the water trough and dump a bucket of water over his head.

"I'll get them," he said to Sylvia, tying the soaked neckerchief over his face. Then he raced into the smoke, dodging six horses that came charging out of the flames.

Winnie ran to help Sylvia and said a silent prayer as Clark disappeared into the smoke-filled building.

Choking on the smoke and heat, Clark hollered, "Gus! Matt! This whole shebang is about to go. We got to get out of here!" There was no response. "Where are you?"

"I'm over here," Gus yelled. "Who's there?"

"It's Clark," He coughed. "We need to get out. The roof just caught, and it's spreading fast."

"Matt!" Gus screamed.

"There's two more horses," Matt hollered.

"Can't you get out the back way?" Clark hollered.

"It's blocked." Matt's muffled voice sounded miles away.

"Leave them!" Clark rasped.

The roof above them seemed to heave as blue flames licked the inside of the roof. Two horses ran past them as one of the walls collapsed. Part of the roof screeched and whooshed as it fell between them and Matt. Fire and burning embers flew in every direction. Clark and Gus were knocked off their feet, and a fair-sized chunk of burning wood landed on Gus's chest. Clark knocked it away, using his hands to put out the fire on Gus's shirt.

"Come on, Gus. We got to get out of here while we still can."

"I ain't leavin' without my boy!"

Clark doubted the boy was alive, but if Matt were his son, he'd feel the same. He'd do anything to save him. Smoke and heat blurred Clark's vision as he searched for a way to get to Matt. He was familiar with building construction and knew they had only minutes before the whole thing came down.

The fire wasn't as intense on the one side of the building—that wasn't saying much. Blinking and squinting, Clark could just make out what appeared to be braces on one of the stalls that were still intact. It was risky, and the odds weren't in their favor.

Beneath his neckerchief, Clark's face was scrunched into a frown. They might be able to get to Matt, but there was no guarantee they'd make it back. He hadn't planned on dying in a fire, but at least he'd go out all heroic-like. Maybe it'd make up for some of the bad decisions he'd made in his life.

"This way, Gus. Stay right behind me."

They managed to get through the fire and found Matt pinned under a smoking beam, his shirt and pants smoldering. Gus fell to his knees and began slapping away the fire. Clark pulled his shirt off over his head and used it to lift one end of the beam.

"Quick, Gus! Pull him away!"

Gus picked Matt up and started back the way they came, but the fire had advanced, cutting them off. Gus stopped and hung his head. "Sorry, Clark."

"Don't be a sorryin' me yet. We got us one chance," Clark said, his voice barely heard above the roar of flames licking across the beams overhead. "I'm hopin' that's mostly smoke and not so much fire."

Even as he said it, a flashing tongue of flame shot across their path. Clark placed his shirt over Matt's face for some protection. "Hold your breath and run. Run like the fires of damnation are burnin' your ass." *Cuz they are*, he thought to himself.

Ducking beneath charred timbers that threatened to crash down at any minute, glowing embers raining down on them like fiery snow-flakes, searing their skin and flames shot out licking at them with burning tongues.

As they barreled from the stable, the entire frame gave way and the building collapsed with a thunderous crash sending sparks and ash flying in all directions.

Clark cast his eyes skyward and, with a solemn nod, thanked the Man in Charge.

Sylvia ran to Matt's side, "Oh, my God! Is he alive?"

"He's alive, Syl, but we need to get him to Coop. Someone bring the buckboard!"

Taylor, the ranch foreman hollered back from the corral, "The horses are riled up a bit, but we'll get the team hitched."

The three Weisenberger girls were huddled together, watching, not knowing what to do. "Girls, go to the house and get some blankets for the back of the buckboard," Gus commanded, then gentled his voice. "It'll make Matt more comfortable." Glad to have something to do, they rushed to the house.

"Matt," Sylvia whispered, kneeling beside her eldest son. Tears filled her eyes— she didn't need a doctor to tell her how bad his burns were, and she was afraid.

Gus stood as the foreman brought the buckboard. "Help me get Matt in the wagon." Taylor jumped over the seat and into the back. He took Matt from Gus's arms, laying him gently on top of the blankets the girls had hurriedly brought from the house.

"Josh, you get up there and grab the lines. Girls, you get in the back with Matt. Sylvia, you ride with Josh." Gus helped Sylvia up and onto the bench seat. "I'll come soon as I can," he said, giving her hand a comforting squeeze.

"Get on your way, Josh, and don't waste any time. Get Matt to Coop's and take care of your mother. I'll be right along." Josh nodded to his father and whipped the team into a frantic run.

"Taylor, have a couple of the men round up any strays and get the rest of the hands guarding the place. Then get Klaus and Earl and ride with my family. Make sure they get to town in one piece. Then hightail it back here."

"You belong with Matt and your family. I can handle things here," the foreman protested.

"I know you can, Taylor, but right now keeping my family safe is the most important thing and you're the best man for that job. And I got somethin' that needs doin' right here."

Gus, Winnie, and Clark stood with their backs to the smoldering remains, watching the buckboard veer around the corner and disappear from sight. Behind them, charred wood snapped and cracked, sending showers of cinders into the air.

"I need a drink, and I'm betting you do, too," Gus said, glancing at Clark, "And I've got a shirt I can lend you."

"Wouldn't turn down either."

The air was thick with acrid smoke and the sharp tang of charred wood, as Winnie and Clark fell in behind Gus, walking slowly toward the house.

When they got to the front porch, Gus turned and stared for a moment at the burning shell of the stable. Clark and Winnie turned, following Gus's gaze. Winnie's heart skipped a beat thinking of Matt. She quickly turned back to Gus. "Looks like you need to see a doctor yourself."

"I suppose I do," he hesitated. "Later. I figure the kids will be safe in town. Come on inside. There's always a pot of coffee on the stove."

Clark chuckled, "When you said drink, I was thinkin' of somethin' a mite stronger."

Before entering through the shiny black screen door, Winnie glanced back over her shoulder at the burning rubble with a frown. *Another accident?* She doubted it.

CHAPTER 31

GUS TALKS

Gus led them to the kitchen and went straight to the sideboard where he pulled out a bottle of whiskey and held it out to Clark. "Will this do?"

Clark replied with a grunt, "Sure enough."

Gus grabbed two glasses from the cupboard and then looked at Winnie. She shook her head. "Thanks, Gus. I'll pour myself some coffee if that's all right."

"Of course. Help yourself." He looked down at his scorched and tattered shirt with a grimace. "I'll get Clark a shirt, and it looks like I need one for myself." Gus put the bottle and glasses on the table and headed toward the front of the house and the stairway to the second floor.

"This wasn't an accident, Clark. I'm sure of it," Winnie stated as she settled at the kitchen table with her coffee.

"Whoever it was started the fire on the far side of the stable so they wouldn't be seen from the house or the bunkhouse." Clark splashed whiskey into the glasses.

"I can't believe how fast that fire spread. It took only minutes before the whole place went up."

"All the hay and straw helped it along," Clark said, taking a long swig from the plain glass. Gus was more pennywise than Grant and didn't find it necessary to have fancy glassware or china.

"It did, for a fact," Gus agreed, returning to the kitchen wearing a clean shirt. It hung open, exposing the burn on his chest. It looked painful, and he winced as he tossed a shirt to Clark. "Clark, I'm in your debt. I could never have gotten Matt out of there by myself. I'm glad you didn't get hurt."

Pushing his arms through the sleeves, Clark grunted a reply. "Can't say as much for my beard. It's singed right up to my chin."

"So are your eyebrows. What little is left of them." Winnie said, with a grin that turned into a smile. Then she turned serious. "What's going on, Gus? Why aren't you headed to town with your family?"

"You know about the cattle being slaughtered and left for the vultures?"

Winnie nodded.

"Three days ago, one of our grade bulls was shot and killed right out there in the corral in broad daylight. We couldn't find any trace of the shooter. He left no tracks of any kind. We figured it had to have been a long shot—someone with good shootin' skills." Gus shifted in his chair, wincing in pain.

"Then, yesterday, one of my hands was shot when he ran across some coyotes up north working a branding fire and using a running iron. Mark managed to get back here, and we patched him up, but he'll be taking it easy for a few days." Gus took a swig of whiskey. "I rode out with Taylor, but we couldn't pick up a trail."

"We've had some troubles, too," Winnie said, concerned with the severity of Gus's burns and thinking he should be on his way to town. "There was a cave-in at the mine and a near accident at the lumber mill."

"What's your dad say?"

"I haven't talked to Dad about any of this. Coop made it clear that Dad is not to be stressed. Did you see anyone lurking around the stable before the fire started?"

"After everything that's happened, I've had men patrolling the place, and no one saw a thing."

Winnie studied her father's long-time friend, tapping her fingers on the tabletop. She couldn't imagine the worry he must be feeling about his son. And the physical pain of the burns had to be excruciating. "Gus, I can't help but think all these incidents are related."

"Why would you think that?" Gus asked.

"Why wouldn't I? You and Dad have been friends forever, and now you're both being targeted. Do you know anyone who would want to create this kind of trouble for you and my dad?"

"No," Gus answered, but Winnie saw a slight hesitation.

"Gus?"

"It's not my story to tell, Winnie. Ask your dad or Logan. Yeah, ask Logan."

"Logan?" Winnie tilted her head, her brow furrowed. "What's going on, Gus?"

Gus shook his head, and a tear trickled down his face, cutting a furrow through the soot and grime. "Winnie, for God's sake, I can't deal with this right now."

"Terrible things are happening, Gus. Tell me what you know before someone else gets hurt or killed."

"Ask Logan."

Winnie saw Gus flinch and wondered if it was from physical pain or something else. "No, Gus, I'm not going back to town to pry the answer out of Logan when you're sitting right in front of me. We need to stop this, Gus. People are getting hurt, and if you know why, you need to tell me."

"It happened a long time ago, and it's hard to believe it could have anything to do with any of this." Gus took a long drink of whiskey before continuing.

"Your dad, Logan, and me took our fishing poles and three jugs of whiskey to Raccoon Creek. We planned on spending the day fishing, but we spent most of it drinking." He stopped and squeezed his eyes shut as if in denial.

Winnie gently urged him to continue. "What happened, Gus?"

"We lynched a man."

CHAPTER 32

THE LUMBER MILL

From Grant's Crossing, it was a twenty-minute ride north to the lumber mill. It was early when Jake and Sam rode in and found Lester Norton unlocking the doors. He waved them to the front door. "Good morning. You men are out and about early."

"Good morning, Mr. Norton. We want to talk with you before your workers arrive. I understand one of your machines was tampered with. Can you show us where and what you found?" Jake said, getting quickly to the point.

"It was definitely tampered with." He motioned for them to follow him.

As they walked through the cavernous, equipment-crowded building, Mr. Norton explained the equipment and different processes. The sweet, overpowering smell of pine made their noses burn and stung their eyes as they listened to Norton's litany of production procedures.

"This one." Norton stopped and pointed to a complicated-looking machine with an enormous circular saw attached to it. "That iron brace that extends down to the floor below holds this big fellow in place. If that were to come loose, the blade's stability would be compromised."

"And that means?" Jake looked at Norton with a raised eyebrow.

"It means there's a good chance someone gets hurt or killed." Norton inspected the machine as they spoke. "At the very least, it would shut the mill down for a significant amount of time." He shook his head. "Marshal, I inspect these machines every night after everyone goes home, and all these nuts were tight as ticks on a dog's ear. I'd swear to it."

Sam walked around the towering machine. "How familiar would someone have to be with your operation to do this?"

"Anyone who's worked in a sawmill or factory."

"Any unhappy workers who might have a score to settle with you or the Grants?"

"Not off hand, Deputy. Most of the workers here are grateful for their jobs. They earn a good wage, have a safe environment, and aren't asked to work unusually long hours."

"Most of the workers?" Sam said with a quizzical tilt of his head.

"Those who aren't thankful are at least happy to have a job, despite their grumblings. Deputy, there isn't one person here I wouldn't vouch for."

Jake strolled around the imposing machine, impressed with the massive saw blade. He leaned in to examine the iron braces that supported the behemoth. "Did you post a guard last night?"

"I didn't have time to make the arrangements, but we're covered starting tonight. I stayed here until after midnight and came in early to inspect the equipment before the morning shift. I'll be doing morning and evening inspections from now on."

"We'll get out of your way and let you get back to it." Jake took one last look at the machine in question. "If you see anything suspicious, anything at all, let us know. Thanks for your help."

Jake and Sam walked out of the mill and mounted. "I doubt Norton's behind any of this, and it sounds like he's made the necessary changes."

"He seems genuine enough," Sam said. "But then, Grant always finds the best people."

"I agree, Sam. He found us, didn't he?"

"No, Jake, he didn't find us. Fate dumped us on the poor man."

"Guess that's a fact, but he's never complained—much."

CHAPTER 33

LITTLE DIPPER MINE

It was a long road to the mine, and they stopped midway to rest the horses. They found shade under an oak tree and unpacked the lunch Sally had fixed for them at the Carmichael Cafe. They were hungry, and it was time for a stretch.

"Sam, I never officially asked you, but I want you to stand up for me at the wedding."

"Thought you'd never ask," Sam replied, a grin spreading across his face.

Jake stretched out on the grass, his hands laced behind his head, gazing up at the cloudless blue sky.

Sam was sitting nearby, his arms resting on his knees, chewing on a blade of grass. "Maybe they'll have found Luke by the time we get to the mine. I hate to think of him being crushed under a pile of rocks."

"I'd like to see those timbers they think could have been damaged by the blast. Winnie says it shouldn't have happened. Not without some help."

"Wonder if Winnie found anything at the Lazy W?" Sam said, tossing away the blade of grass.

Jake smiled. "I don't envy Gus if Winnie is interrogating him. She can be like a dog with a bone." Jake's smile faded. "I just hope Matt stays away from her."

"That boy has been stuck in your craw ever since you found him and Winnie behind the schoolhouse. Even back then, I thought you were too protective."

"Me?"

"Yeah, you," Sam said with a grin. Getting up, he kicked the bottoms of Jake's boots. "Time we got on the road. Let's go."

They found Louis Woods and a dozen of his men stretched out under a large canvas canopy that flapped noisily in the wind. Their hands and arms were bruised and bleeding, and their clothing in tatters. They also saw at least six men at the mine entrance removing debris.

Lou got to his feet, his sweat-soaked shirt sticking to his chest. "I suppose Winnie sent you out to inspect the site."

Jake nodded. "No sign yet of Luke?"

"No. We thought we broke through earlier this morning, but it was a void with another pile of rocks behind it."

"Can we see the supporting timbers that are in question?" Jake asked.

"You can, and there's no doubt that two were tampered with. Come on and I'll show you." He led the way toward the mine entrance. "We use the square set timbering system to ensure the mine is safe. If it hadn't been for the tampering, there wouldn't have been a problem. Why would anyone want to do this?"

Climbing over piles of debris, Jake and Sam followed him to the mine entrance. It was plain to see where an axe had been used. The axe marks were fresh and obvious—deep grooves chewed into the beams like a beaver with bad intentions. The damage had weakened them enough to allow the whole structure to collapse and fold in on itself.

"It could have collapsed at any time. We could have had a dozen men trapped inside or killed."

Walking back toward the tent, they heard jubilant yells. "We're through. We broke through."

Everyone ran toward the mine, watching as one of the miners squirmed his way into the small opening. It was minutes, but it seemed like hours until they heard him call out. "Luke's alive. I need help in here—his legs are buried."

A cheer went up as another miner scrambled through the opening. The sheer exhaustion Jake had seen on their faces was replaced with excitement and relief. It was hard for Jake to stand back and do nothing. He wanted to help but figured he'd get in the way. He looked over at Sam.

Sam returned a knowing look. "They've got this well in hand, and besides, I'd never fit through that opening."

Jake and Sam watched as Luke's limp form was carefully passed through the opening to the waiting men outside. They carried him gently to the tent and laid him on the grass. His legs were torn up and bloody, but he was alive. Lou yelled at one of the men to get the buckboard. "We need to get Luke into town." Lou pointed at three men, telling them to ride along and make sure they didn't run into any problems.

Watching them leave, Lou smiled. "I didn't think we stood a chance of finding him alive. Damn, it's a great day."

"When you get back, tell Miss Grant that the mine is secure, and we'll be up and running by the end of the week with guards on duty around the clock."

CHAPTER 34

HE HAS FANGS

It was late when Sam and Jake rode into Grant's Crossing. From the front of the hotel, they saw lights on in the doctor's office. Sam leaned forward, resting his arms on the saddle horn. "Looks like Coop is in his office. You go on in and find Winnie. I'll take the horses to the livery and let Coop know the miners are on their way with Luke."

"Thanks, Sam. We'll meet you in the dining room." Jake bounded up the steps and into the hotel, eager to find Winnie.

Inside the hotel cafe, he found Winnie and Clark already seated at a table with a pot of fresh coffee in front of them. He leaned over and kissed Winnie's cheek before sitting down beside her. "They found Luke. He's alive."

A smile lit up Winnie's face. "Oh, thank God! How is he?"

"His legs are severely injured, and he's unconscious. They're bringing him into town, maybe two hours behind us." Jake changed the subject. "How was your ride out to the Lazy W?"

"Someone set fire to their stable."

Jake reached across the table for the coffee pot. "Not an accident?"

"No, it wasn't. Gus and Matt were inside when part of the roof collapsed. Matt got pinned under a beam and it took both Gus and

Clark to get him out." Winnie glanced at Clark. "They just made it out the door when the whole thing burst into flames and collapsed. Sylvia, Joshua and his sisters brought Matt into town. Coop says Matt is in bad shape."

"How are Gus and Sylvia?" Jake asked.

"Worried sick, and Gus is badly burned. He should be at Coop's too, but he didn't want to leave the homeplace." Winnie sighed. "It was tough talking with him, but he told me some things."

Jake tipped his head to the side, one eyebrow raised, waiting.

"It's a long story, Jake, and you and I need to talk before it totally unravels. It involves Logan, Gus, Dad, and Mort Watkins."

"Mort?"

"Yeah, Mort. I'd bet the ranch he's behind all of this, including shooting Dad in the back. I want to see that bastard dead."

Jake took her hand gently in his. "Mort and his partner were supposed to leave town this morning. Wonder if they did."

"It's doubtful," Winnie sighed, calmed by the warmth of Jake's hand encircling hers.

"So spill the beans, Winnie. I want to hear your story."

Clark cackled, "It's a humdinger, Jake, and that's a fact."

Sam and Logan walked through the door and took seats around the table. Deputy Logan looked at Clark. "What's a humdinger?"

"Nothing," Clark said, shooting Logan a frown, which Logan returned along with a questioning gesture.

Sam poured himself a mug of coffee and filled the one Logan held out to him. "I stopped at Coop's to let him know the miners were bringing Luke in, and he told me about Matt. Coop said he doubts he'll make it till morning. Dang shame."

After a momentary silence, Jake gave Winnie a questioning look. "We're all here, Winnie. Now tell us this humdinger of a tale and why you suspect Mort."

Sam looked at Winnie. "Mort?"

"Yes, Sam. I think he's behind all of this."

"It can't be." Sam shook his head. "He's nothing but horns and rattle."

"Jake glanced across the table at Sam. "What about that partner of his, I got a hunch he's got fangs."

"But why would Mort want to cause trouble for Grant and Gus?"

"You'll understand once you hear Gus's story."

Winnie quickly filled them in on the problems Gus had been having. And then added, "Gus told us about a fishing trip that ended in a lynching."

Logan's eyes darted to Winnie. "I'd like to tell the story if you don't mind."

Winnie nodded. "It's yours to tell."

"It all happened right before Sam was born." Logan took a swig of coffee and cleared his throat. "Me, Gus, and Grant went on a fishing trip. We got an early start and headed north out of town, following along the Raccoon—looking for a good place to set up for the day. We had our fishin' poles, a pouch of big fat worms, and plenty of whiskey. We hadn't had much luck fishin', and it was gettin' on toward evening. We'd nearly finished off the three jugs of squeez'ns we'd taken with us and were well-oiled and so tangle-legged we had trouble staying afoot."

Logan paused, letting memories of that day wash across his mind. It had been almost twenty-five years, but the shame of what they'd done had never faded.

"We was chewin' on the idea of headin' home when we saw a lone rider herdin' a dozen unbranded calves right down the middle of the road, whistlin' like a carefree fool." Logan sighed and swallowed hard before continuing. "We yanked him off his horse and saw that it was Ralph Watkins—Mort's brother. Neither of them was ever any good. Ralph told us he'd found the strays, but we knew he was lyin'. The only cattle for miles around would have belonged to the Grants or the Weisenbergers. Then we spotted the Circle G brand on the horse he was ridin'. We had caught ourselves a horse-thievin' cattle rustler, and there was only one solution. He needed a strong dose of Dakota justice."

Logan glanced from face to face, lingering on Sam's. "We arrested Ralph, tried him, and *executed* him. We were so roostered, it was a tussle gettin' him strung up, but we finally managed it." Logan wiped his hand across his face.

"It took him a good while to die, and we just sat there and watched him dance. When he quit kickin', we rode back to town. We left him there, hangin' in the tree. The next day, I couldn't find my badge. I figured it came off in the struggle the night before and rode out to search for it. The body was gone, and I never found my badge."

"Gus said no one ever reported the lynching," Winnie added.

"No. No one ever did. But there never have been any secrets in Grant's Crossing." Logan refilled his coffee cup and leaned back with a sigh. "My badge did turn up years later—in the middle of my desk with a scrawled note. "You'll pay."

Logan sighed. "Ralph was a horse thief and a rustler and would have been hanged anyway, but that's no excuse for what we did. I was the Sheriff. I never should have let that happen."

"I never knew I had an uncle, but it doesn't sound like he's any better than Mort," Sam said.

Everyone was quiet. Logan looked at Winnie, wondering if he should continue. Winnie shook her head with a frown.

The food was delivered, and everyone but Sam dug in. "Logan, tell me about Ralph. How is it that I never knew about him?"

Logan sputtered, "He – uh – he was the black sheep of the family and quite a bit younger than Mort. He - died before you were birthed."

Winnie changed the subject before Sam could ask any more questions. "How's your food, Jake?"

"Fine?" he answered with a frown. "Like always." Jake put down his fork and smiling he took Winnie's hand. He realized she had redirected the conversation. He wondered why but decided to help her. "We need to take a hard look at Mort and Cyrus. They were supposed to leave town today, but I doubt they did. We know they aren't at either of the hotels or at Murphy's. Sam, do you know if Mort has anyone who would put them up? Maybe an old friend?"

Sam shook his head. "I don't recall Mort ever having any friends, at least none I can recall. He had enemies. One in particular that he bellyached about all the time—Tug. Tug hung out at the Night Owl and picked at Mort all the time.

"How about the Watkins home place? Could he be holed up there?"

Sam shrugged. "I have no idea, Jake. I know where the farm is, but I was never there. I never knew my grandparents. They never wanted anything to do with me."

"Let's check at the land office in the morning and see if anyone has moved in. It might be worth a trip out there to investigate." Jake paused and looked around the table. "I don't think there's anything we can do before morning. Anyone?" There was no response.

"We'll meet here for breakfast, but let's wait until the sun is up."

Clark excused himself and shuffled up the street toward Kat's.

"Jake, would you stop by my room before you leave for Kat's "

Logan frowned. "How'd you know that's where we were going?"

Winnie rolled her eyes. "That's where you always go, and if I wasn't dead tired, I might join you."

Jake stopped Logan as he started down the steps in front of the hotel. "Logan, wait. The story you told tonight happened a long time ago, and it was different then. You didn't break any laws. You did what any rancher would have done if they'd found a rustler and a horse thief. What you did doesn't change the respect I have for you. Or for Gus or Grant."

Sam nodded in agreement. "This whole town respects you, Logan. We couldn't ask for a better lawman."

"What you're saying means a lot, and I thank you. But I'll never get that rooster off my shoulder. I was Sheriff, and I shouldn't have let that happen."

Jake slapped him on the back. "See you guys for breakfast. Hey, ask Kat if Mort's been around lately."

Halfway down the steps, Logan stopped. "Thought Jake was coming with us?"

Sam looked at him, shaking his head. "Did you not hear Winnie invite him up to her room?"

"Oh," Logan said with a chuckle. "Let's get down to Kat's and see if she's got something for us to drink."

Jake knocked on Winnie's door, wondering why he'd been invited to her room. He knew it wouldn't be what he envisioned.

Winnie opened the door, and let Jake kiss her senseless before wiggling from his arms. "We need to talk. There's more you need to know."

Jake sighed, his eyes lingering on the bed. He didn't want to talk but knew this wasn't the time or the place for what he had in mind.

"Sam's dad isn't Sam's dad."

Jake's eyes darted from the bed to Winnie. "What are you talking about?"

"Sam's dad *isn't* his dad."

"Well, that certainly clarifies everything, " Jake said with a scowl.

"Ralph was his father."

"What? His uncle—that he never knew was his father?"

"Gus told us that Ralph was about fifteen or so when he kidnapped Sam's mother and held her captive in the barn. When his dad found her, he turned her loose and confronted Mort and Ralph. Ralph admitted to tying her up and then boasted about what he'd been doing to her. He got the hide peeled off his backside. When Sam's mom turned up with child, old man Watkins made Mort marry her. Ralph was too young."

Jake whistled softly. "That's why Mort's dad and granddad didn't want anything to do with Sam?"

"Yeah, those god-fearing men wanted nothing to do with Ralph's bastard son. Sam was too much of an embarrassment for them good Christians to deal with. So, they ignored him and tried to keep it quiet. Most of those who knew are long dead and gone."

"We have to tell Sam."

CHAPTER 35

CORSETS

When Logan and Sam entered Kat's Place, Steven Wagner and Charlie Rose were already settled at a table with Clark. Steven had come to Grant's Crossing from Virginia after the war, searching for a fresh start, and had opened the General Store. Charlie, his face etched with the hardships of a cattle drover, had trailed cows until he was severely injured in a stampede. Unable to handle the rigors of a trail drive, he retired in Grant's Crossing. When he and Steven met at Kat's, they became instant friends and eventually partners in the General Store.

Logan and Sam pulled up chairs and joined them.

"What are we talking about tonight?" Kat asked as she sat down next to Sam.

Sam laid his arm across the back of Kat's chair. "Settle back. I think Steven is about to spin us a yarn," Sam said, affectionately stroking her shoulder with his thumb, a gesture that spoke of the close bond between them.

Everyone knew that when it came to storytelling, Steven had a talent for throwing bull better than anyone in Grant's Crossing, and they could tell from his posture that he was about to burst at the seams.

"We got a package this morning that wasn't ours Steven's eyes darted dramatically from table to table as if searching for anyone who might be eavesdropping. "We had a big delivery, and the depot manager must have thrown it in with the rest of our crates and packages by mistake. I didn't pay any attention to the address. I just figured it was one of ours, and I tore into it. You won't believe what was in that parcel."

Steven's eyes again scanned the room with exaggerated concern. Then he leaned forward. "There were two unbelievably risqué corsets in that package." Steven giggled. "The kind that cinches tight around a gal's waist and pushes everything up and over. There was a red one and a black one—all trimmed in lacy ruffles and delicate little rosettes. Well, we hadn't ordered any such revealing finery. I checked the label, and guess who they were addressed to?"

Steven paused for effect. "Prudence Purdy, that's who. Yessiree, those corsets were addressed to that puckered-up old prune-face Prudence."

Charlie put a hand on Steven's arm, "Steven, it isn't nice, calling Miss Purdy a puckered-up old prune."

Steven shrugged and shot Charlie a look. Then, forged ahead with his story. "If the parcel had been addressed to one of the working girls at the Slipper, I wouldn't have given it a thought. Heck, we've ordered such finery for some of those saloon hall girls. But Prudence Purdy, of all people. Now, my question is this—what would a dried-up, goody-two-shoes old spinster like Miss Purdy want with them?"

Charlie scolded, "Now, Steven, be nice. Maybe she's got a feller who likes how she looks in those git-ups. My mama always said there's a lid for every pot, and I suspect it's true. Hell, I'm turning into a withered old prune myself."

"But you ain't ordering fancy lace corsets for yourself." The final straw was the thought of Charlie's scrawny body cinched in one of those lacy corsets, and the laughter that had been percolating burst out.

The laughter faded, and Steven continued. "I rewrapped those corsets and sent word for Miss Purdy to stop by. When she came in this afternoon, she had a nose full of snobbery. Like always, but I knew what was in that package, and it was hard not to let her know how shocked we were."

Steven looked at Charlie for agreement. Charlie shrugged. "I was shocked," he said, but he didn't sound convincing.

"I still can't fathom what she wants with them. I swear that old spinster is like a dried-up waterhole. If she smiled, her face would crack like mud in the sun."

When Steven finished his story and everyone had quieted down, he spoke to Sam. "Your dad was in the store this morning with another guy, buying supplies. Have you seen him?"

"Yes, unfortunately. You're sure you saw him this morning?" Sam asked.

Steven thought for a moment, "Yeah, it was this morning. Charlie, it was this morning when we saw Mort, wasn't it?"

"Yep, him and his pasty-faced friend bought a bunch of supplies, packed them on a mule, and rode to the east. I reckon it was about nine this mornin' when they left. Appeared to me like they was settin' up camp."

Bear was walking past, delivering a bottle to another table, and heard part of the conversation. "Sam," he said. "Mort was in here, too. Archie waited on him and another dark-haired guy. I didn't pay any attention until I heard Mort's voice as they were leaving.

"You sure it was my dad?"

"I didn't get a close look at him, but I'd know his voice anywhere. I did get a good look at the other man. He had the palest skin I've ever seen and shorter than Steven—but not as round."

Steven shot Bear a scathing look and nodded to Sam. "Mort's friend had the palest face and greasy, slicked-back hair—black as a raven's wing."

Sam got up to leave and Clark and Logan stood to follow him. "At ease, men. I'm only going to the hotel to let Jake and Winnie know what my dear old dad is up to."

"It only takes a minute, Sam. Think about what happened to Grant."

"I'll be fine."

But Logan followed Sam out the door. He lit a quirly, scanning the street and watching until Sam disappeared inside the hotel. Something in Sam's stride didn't sit right with Logan. He flicked the match away and waited, just in case.

CHAPTER 36

WHO AM I

The buckboard from the mine jostled up the street on squeaky springs as Sam started up the steps to the hotel entrance. He'd seen how bad Luke's legs were and wondered if the boy would walk again. If his father was behind all of this, he'd pay.

Sam stopped at the front desk to get Winnie's room number and climbed the steps to the second floor. He hesitated before knocking softly. "Winnie, it's Sam."

Jake opened the door. "Come in, Sam. Winnie and I need to talk to you."

"Sounds serious," Sam said, throwing his hat on the dresser. "The men from the mine just rolled into town."

"We'll check on Luke later,"Winnie said, "but right now, Jake and I have something to tell you. When Logan told his story at supper tonight, he left out part of it at my request. I wanted to talk to Jake first."

Sam frowned. "What's going on?"

Jake didn't sugarcoat it. "Sam, Mort is not your father. Ralph was."

Sam blinked. The words didn't land right at first. "What? What are you talking about?"

"Ralph Watkins was your father, not Mort."

"So, the man I just found out existed—my supposed uncle—is actually my father?"

"Yes."

"Oh, this just gets better all the time."

Jake put his hand on Sam's shoulder. "Buck up, buddy, there's more you should know. Ralph kidnapped your mother and kept her in the barn. He did terrible things. When old man Watkins found her, he set her free, but she was already carrying Ralph's child...you. Since Ralph was only a kid, your grandpa forced Mort to marry her."

Sam's mind wrestled with what Jake had told him. "Oh great. I thought a wife-beating, worthless drunk was bad. Now I find out my father was a kidnapper, rapist, rustler, and horse thief who got himself lynched." Sam snorted. "I'll have to do some serious thinking about all of this later, but for now, there are more important things to deal with than my lineage."

"Are you all right, Sam?" Winnie said.

"I'm fine, Winnie. I have to be. When it comes down to it, whether Mort or Ralph is my father, it doesn't change anything." Sam shrugged and shared with them what he found out at Kat's. "It seems *Uncle* Mort and his friend are setting up camp somewhere east of town."

"Sam, did Mort ever work at the mill?" Jake asked.

"He worked there shortly after Grant got it up and running, but he was always late and hungover. Grant finally fired him."

"Interesting, isn't it?" Jake said.

Sam didn't know what to feel—rage, shame, grief—but none of it mattered tonight. Not yet. "Another nail in Mort's coffin," Sam said with a smirk.

CHAPTER 37

LUKE AND MATTHEW

They were quiet for some time. The stillness made Winnie uncomfortable. "Come on," she said, picking up her shawl. Let's get out of here. I want to find out about Luke."

As she picked up her shawl, Jake stepped forward, his hands wrapped around hers taking it from her grasp. He draped the soft fabric over her shoulders and leaned in, pressing a warm, lingering kiss against the delicate curve of her neck. His unexpected gentle touch and the warmth of his lips sent a shiver down her spine.

Sam looked at his two friends with a grin. "You two don't have time for that. Come on, let's go."

The town was quiet as they walked up the street toward Coop's office. Yellow light spilled from open windows and doors, and a distant piano accompanied by the harsh twangs of a mouth harp could be heard. An occasional bust of laughter broke the quiet, but there were no gunshots or screams, no breaking glass or shouting. There was nothing that would send the marshals running.

Opening the door to Doc Cooper's office, Jake poked his head in. Coop was sitting at his desk. "Come on in, Jake," Coop said, slapping shut a leather-covered journal.

Jake stepped aside, letting Winnie enter, and then he and Sam followed. "How's Luke?"

"He's doing remarkably well. There'll be some scarring, but he'll be walking and running in no time."

Winnie's smile faded. "How's Matthew?"

"Not what you want to hear, I'm afraid. He's failing, and there's nothing I can do for him. It's not only the burns. Those are bad enough, but when the roof collapsed, something struck him on the back of his head. There's a nasty gash, and he lost too much blood before they got him here. I doubt he'll make it till morning."

"Should we get his parents in here tonight?"

"His folks can't do anything more for him than what his siblings are doing. He won't die alone."

"Where are they?" Winnie asked.

"Jenny took them home to feed them. They didn't want to go, but they were about to drop."

"Can I see him?"

"Of course, but he's burned something terrible, and the smell is overpowering. Be prepared."

Winnie took a deep breath and crossed the threshold into Matt's room. Coop beside her, she walked to his bedside. "You can take his left hand gently if you want to." Then Coop stepped back and joined Jake and Sam in the doorway.

Winnie picked up Matthew's left hand and gently squeezed it. "Matt, it's Winnie. Fight, Matt. You hear me, you fight." A tear ran down her cheek. "I was always sweet on you, you know. Remember the Valentine boxes? I always thought of you when I was fixing mine." Her voice broke. "And that day behind the schoolhouse? I thought you were going to kiss me. I wanted you to. Maybe if we hadn't been interrupted—" She shot a look at Jake. "—you would have." Winnie kissed his hand. "I don't want you to die, Matt," she whispered and gently lowered his hand to the bed. Her hand lingered on top of his for a moment before turning away.

She stood still for a long moment, her back to the bed, forcing her feet to move even as her heart begged her to stay.

Jake stood in the doorway smiling the tenderest smile she had ever seen. "Is it true, Winnie? Were you really sweet on Matthew?"

"I was. I wanted him to kiss me more than anything, but he never did. Maybe he was too shy or afraid of you—and Sam."

She melted into Jake's arms, willing back the tears. "We have to get the men responsible for this," Winnie said, looking up at Jake with a firm set to her jaw. "I want to see them hang for what they've done."

"We'll get them, Winnie," Jake said, stroking his hand gently up and down her back. "I promise you, they'll pay."

The walk back to the hotel was quiet. Sam stopped at the marshal's office, and Jake and Winnie walked the rest of the way alone. Jake walked Winnie to her door and opened it, placing the key in her hand. The hallway was deserted, and Jake took advantage of the privacy to kiss his girl. It was a tender kiss lasting longer than it should have, and his hands strayed to places they shouldn't have.

"I wish I could stay with you tonight," Jake whispered, "but I can't. There are too many eyes and ears in a place like this."

"I'd like for you to stay," Winnie whispered back.

She watched Jake start down the hall toward his room. "Jake?"

He turned, his eyebrows raised in question.

"I love you."

Jake went back to her, wrapping her in his arms. "I love you, Win, and we'll get through this. We'll figure out what's going on, and we'll get through this."

He hungered to hold her and make love to her, but not here. He heard the laughter of two hotel guests as they turned the corner and came down the hall, and not now. He stole a brief kiss and doffed his hat to the couple who opened the door next to Winnie's.

CHAPTER 38

THE BECKS ARRIVE

Early the next morning, Winnie and her crew met for breakfast to plan the day. They were deep in conversation when Coop came in, looking tired and haggard. Jake got up to get him a chair. "Here, have a seat and some coffee."

"Thanks. I'd prefer a stiff drink, but coffee will do. I wanted to let you know that Matthew passed about an hour ago. I hate losing anyone, especially one so young. He should have had a full life ahead of him instead of a cold, dark grave." Coop rubbed his hand down his face and took a sip of coffee. "I overheard Matt's brother and sisters talking, and it sounds like the fire wasn't an accident. Is that true?"

Jake nodded. "Neither was the cave-in at the mine."

"Whoever is behind this needs to hang." Coop took another swig of coffee and rose from the table like an arthritic old man. "Well, folks, it's been a hell of a stretch. I'll be at home getting some shuteye—emergencies only, please."

After breakfast, Jake and Sam walked to the train depot to talk with Calvin Johansen, the station manager. As they suspected, no tickets had been sold to anyone resembling the two individuals they described.

"Well, we know they didn't leave town on the train," Jake said.

Sam nodded. "From what Steven and Bear told me, I'm not surprised. It sounds like they're setting up camp."

"And if that's the case, they could be anywhere?" Jake pushed back his hat.

Thanking Cal, they started down the steps to the boardwalk, but the piercing sound of a train whistle split the morning air—one long and two short blasts. "Hey, Cal," Sam said, turning back toward the depot. "What train is coming in at this hour?"

"It's yesterday's train from back East. The one that usually comes in around ten in the morning. Got stalled this side of St. Paul, waitin' for parts."

Sam and Jake made it a habit to meet the trains and stagecoaches, when possible, to check out any strangers stopping in Grant's Crossing. Jake pulled his hat low against the morning sun and gazed down the track. "The land office isn't going anywhere. Let's wait and see who gets off the train."

The train chugged into the station, spewing steam as it squealed to a stop in front of the depot. The engineer rang the bell and pulled the cord, one long and two short blasts of the train's whistle, signaling to his wife that he was home.

He greeted Sam and Jake. "I gotta get home fast and see if I can catch my wife being naughty with the neighbor." He winked and pulled a dark blue hanky from his back pocket. Laughing, he wiped the soot from his face. "If she isn't being naughty, I plan to correct the matter."

Sam and Jake watched as he hurried down the depot steps. "Think he's serious about the neighbor?" Sam asked.

"Nah. His closest neighbors are you and Lavinia Kent. You know Lavinia. If anyone so much as moves a whisker, the whole town will know about it."

"She is nosy," Sam agreed, watching the passengers step off the train.

Most of them were greeted by family or friends. There were several drummers, but no one appeared to be a threat or a possible addition to Mort's crew. The last passengers to depart the train were a well-dressed dandy and his wife. Tired and bedraggled from their long trip, they looked lost standing in front of the depot.

The lawmen approached the newcomers and introduced themselves. "You folks meeting someone?" Jake asked, noticing that each carried only a small valise.

"No, Marshal. We're just visiting for now, but we'd like to stay for a while to see if we like it. I'm Quimby Beck, formerly a newspaperman in Chicago, and this is Hannah Beck."

Jake scowled at the man. He wasn't keen on newspaper reporters and the brand of the truth they trotted out for everyone to read, but he remained polite. "If you're staying for a spell, I recommend Murphy's Boarding House. Lower rates than the hotels and the meals are included."

"But be warned," Sam added. "Once you've sat at Rachael Murphy's table, you'll never want to leave. Do you have any luggage?"

"No." Jake and Sam exchanged looks at Quimby's reply. "This is all we have for now. Our belongings are in storage until we decide where to settle."

Sam nodded. "Well, if you like, you can follow us. We're headed for the land office, and the boarding house sits right behind it on Jefferson Street."

Quimby smiled as he and Hannah followed the lawmen down the depot steps. These were the very men he wanted to find and interview. He thought it had to be fate that these men were the first people he met when stepping off the train. As they walked toward the boarding house, Quimby took in his surroundings with a reporter's eyes. The town was more expansive and cleaner than he expected. The streets were wide, buildings were in good repair and well-marked with colorful signs, and most of the folks were well-dressed and polite. It wasn't anything like he'd expected, but he knew from experience that there was always more beneath the surface. Every town had a story buried beneath its surface. He intended to dig it up.

CHAPTER 39

SHARPE'S EDGE

The Chicago afternoon was hot and humid, and Horace Sharpe's office was sweltering. Isaac Beck peered across the expanse of Horace Sharpe's enormous desk, patiently waiting for his response to his revised proposal. This was his third run at Sharpe, and he hoped this option would meet with his approval.

As Sharpe studied Isaac's document, he hummed an unrecognizable tune, tapping his baby-sized front teeth together with the rhythm. Most annoying, Beck thought. Almost as irritating as the sprinkling of snow-like flakes on Sharpe's shoulders and the ridiculous comb-over that failed to hide the fact he was nearly bald. Beck pegged Horace as somewhere in his late seventies, but stinking old codger or not, the man was sharp as a whip and a very powerful man. Isaac looked away from the unpleasant man, studying the office instead. The room was large but too dark for Isaac's taste and smelled old and sour, like Sharpe. The windows were small letting in little light, and the Chicago skyline was barely visible. The furniture was extravagant and overpowering but comfortable. The artwork he thought was the most interesting part of the office. The paintings appeared to be ancient and of Oriental origin, but the subject matter was what held Beck's attention. It wasn't what one would expect to find in an office. The paintings were of naked men and women in various positions of fornication. They were explicit and quite erotic. The artwork was too magnificent for a saloon or a brothel and would perhaps be more appropriate in a bedroom or a fancy parlor house rather than here. Each to his own, Beck mused.

A large bookcase stood along one wall, its dark shelves full of books. Isaac suspected it was mostly for show, but perhaps the subject matter followed along with that of the artwork. Nestled in a dark corner beside the bookcase was the sculpture of a nude woman. The white marble statue glowed from the darkness, while the dark pedestal it stood on disappeared. The enigmatic goddess appeared to float on air.

Horace closed the file and leaned forward, looking intently at Isaac. "Dang it, Beck. I thought you were bringing me something new. I'd like to do business with you, but this is the same old pitch in a new pair of britches. I can't see enough of an upside for me in what you're proposing, and your numbers are pie in the sky. Besides, everyone knows you have a, shall we say, cloudy reputation."

Sharpe removed his glasses and threw them on the desk. "Hell, I'm not judging you. Goodness knows I'm not above reproach in my dealings, but I don't relish being out-Sharped by you." Sharpe chuckled at his cleverness, pushing the proposal back across the desk.

Isaac scoffed inwardly. He figured Sharpe had used that line countless times before. He sat quietly, his fingers steepled in front of him, his eyes fixed on the weathered old man. "Mr. Sharpe, how close are we to making this happen?"

"Like I said, this isn't a bad deal, but you're greedy, Beck. You insist on a 70-30 split of profits in your favor, which I find unreasonable since you need my foreign contacts to pull this off. I can't do business with you under these terms. If you want to do business with me, you have no choice but to sweeten the pot and clarify those vague phrases hiding in the fine print. We can each make a substantial profit, but you need my foreign contacts…Horace rasped out a phlegmy cough…and that's my ace."

Beck got up and reached across the desk to shake hands. "Let me see what I can do." The hand Sharpe extended was bony and covered with age spots and bulging blue veins. It held no physical strength, much like the man himself. "I'll meet with my lawyer and get back to you next week."

"Next week, then," Sharpe said, pulling a file folder from his drawer and opening it. He wiped his thumb across his tongue and began flipping through the documents with deliberate care. He looked up as if surprised that Beck was still there. "Remember what I said. Sweeten the pot, or don't bother wasting my time."

Beck was on his way out but paused with his hand on the doorknob. He turned back. "My daughter has returned from Europe, and we are having an informal get-together on Saturday to welcome her home and to celebrate her seventeenth birthday. Drinks on the terrace and a light lunch. It would be nice if you and Mrs. Sharpe could join us, say around eleven."

Sharpe nodded slightly. "I'll check with the missus," he replied with only a hint of interest. Then, with a quick wave of his bony hand, as if brushing away a fly, he dismissed Beck.

Isaac pulled himself up straighter and quietly shut the door behind him. He tamped down the anger boiling in his gut. Sharpe wouldn't see it—Beck knew better than to let blood scent the water.

CHAPTER 40

THE MAKING OF A MONSTER

Isaac was livid. He had been dismissed. Walking briskly down the street toward his lawyer's office, he fumed. He wanted to wrap his hands around Sharpe's scrawny neck and squeeze the smugness out of him, but he had swallowed his anger. There were smarter and legal ways to hurt the man.

Beck was intelligent and clever. Physically harming the insolent old bag of wrinkles was not the answer. He would destroy him financially, and that would hurt him more than anything else. He had brought a money-making deal to Sharpe that would mean millions, and he had been dismissed with the wave of a hand. Beck seethed. He didn't plan on meeting with his lawyer to hammer out a proposal giving Sharpe more control, and he wouldn't sweeten the deal. He would bring the man down. He would *out-sharp* Sharpe.

Isaac Beck was all about pursuing money and the influence and power that came with it. Using his charm, cunning, and unique blend of blackmail and intimidation, he secured favorable regulations and lucrative contracts for his company. He grew his modest railcar repair shop into the largest manufacturer of railcars in the country. Subtle flaws integrated into the manufacturing process guaranteed inevitable breakdowns and the continued profitability of his many repair shops.

Standing on the corner, waiting to cross the busy Chicago street, his mind drifted back to his youth. He'd grown up on the streets and in the alleys of Chicago, scavenging, stealing, and hanging on to life by a thread. It was dangerous for a young boy alone on the streets. He'd been beaten up for meager scraps he'd pulled from a garbage can and stabbed for his boots—boots he'd killed for only the week before.

Tattered and weary, he had watched the gangs holding court on street corners and learned how the hierarchy of the streets played out. And how a pack was able to thrive. They didn't ask for handouts from passersby. They demanded them with threatening words and posturing that sometimes turned violent. They stole from storeowners, roughing them up and terrorizing their customers.

Belonging to a gang seemed to be the answer, but his only attempt to join one had ended in a severe beating, with him running for his life. Whipping around a corner and into an alley, he lost the four thugs chasing him and met Saly. Salvador was a large foreigner of some sort who shared Isaac's fears and commiserated with him.

Despite his size, Saly was no match for a gang of toughs. But together, Beck and Saly became partners and recruited other loners. That was the beginning of a brutal gang that would become known as Beck's Boys. Beck was street-smart, and Saly was tough, and they offered loners protection. They also provided protection to the stores in the neighborhood. No one dared hit one of the stores under Beck's protection or cross into their territory.

The corner where he stood had been Beck's corner, and their territory stretched for blocks. He'd come a long way from that filthy, under-fed urchin on the streets of Chicago, but he still had the same instincts, and Sharpe would feel his wrath. Mr. Sharpe had three weaknesses he could play on. His greed and his deviant sexual appetites, but most importantly, Sharpe didn't think he could be beaten. *Underestimating your enemy is a fatal mistake,* Beck thought as he waited to cross the street.

Beck and his lawyer spent over an hour reviewing possible strategies, but he couldn't hang his hat on any of them. "I need more information on the man. I need someone inside Sharpe's organization. There must be a weak link. Someone who can be bribed."

"I'll see what I can find out, Mr. Beck. My secretary is good at ferreting out information. I'll send her over and see if she can get a read on Sharpe's personal staff."

Beck left his lawyer's office, wondering if Sharpe had any weak links in his tightly run ship. He crossed the street to stand again on the corner that had once belonged to him and his gang. He thought about the strange art collection that adorned the walls of Sharpe's office and the marble statue of the naked woman floating in the corner. He had wanted to touch her and to rub his hands over the cold marble. Now, thinking about it, he was feeling lusty and needed attention. The kind of attention he didn't get at home. Unless, of course, he insisted.

Beck owned dozens of buildings throughout the city. He had built a real estate empire after the Chicago fire, which destroyed thousands of buildings and left tens of thousands homeless. He had seen an opportunity and quickly grabbed up building sites. Some had been abandoned, and sometimes, he used persuasion. His buildings went up quickly, using substandard materials and unskilled workers. By bribing city inspectors and blackmailing those who couldn't be bought, he avoided having to deal with any of the new stricter building codes.

Some of his buildings were in the choicest parts of town, and some in the seamy, unsavory areas. He didn't ask or care what his tenants did as long as they paid their rent. Some of the buildings he'd kept for his own use. Turning them into brothels. Peddling flesh was a prosperous business and an investment that he found utterly enjoyable.

He never used his downtown brothels. The women there were not up to his standards, and the premises were not as pleasant or clean as his parlor houses. He owned four such fancy establishments on the edge of town, but The Taylors was his favorite. That was where he headed with a smug, self-satisfied grin on his face. He preferred women who feared him—who knew he didn't need to pay. He owned the house. He owned her. That was what gave him pleasure. There was nothing like owning the whore who serviced you.

CHAPTER 41

THE TAYLORS

The Taylors was an establishment run by Ruby Taylor, one of the most talented and smartest whores he had ever had the pleasure of enjoying. He had made a wise decision when he put her in charge of his bordellos. She not only knew how to please a man but was a shrewd businesswoman as well. She liked working the sheets, even though she no longer had to, but the men who got her on her back paid dearly for the privilege. She didn't come cheap.

Isaac thought about the paintings on Sharpe's wall as he bounded up the steps of the ornate building that housed The Taylors. Sharpe was obviously a sexual deviant to display such renderings for all to see. Perhaps he would like a free pass to one of his parlor houses. One that would include access to any new meat that was brought in, a treat he usually claimed for himself. Maybe that was one way to sweeten the pot, but how would you write that into a contract? Could Sharpe be blackmailed, caught with his pants down? He doubted it.

Ruby met him at the door with a smile. "Good afternoon, Mr. Beck"

"Ruby, I need a drink, and I have a problem that needs to be taken care of."

"I have a special surprise for you, Mr. Beck, and I think she will solve your problem. She's fresh as driven show and big breasted just the way you like."

"Ruby, you know me so well." Isaac crooked an eyebrow and smiled at her. "Where is it?"

"Right now, she's chained to the wall in the back room—as a precaution. She was feisty when the men delivered her. She's stronger than she looks, but I gave her some of my special candies to calm her down."

"Not too many, I hope."

"Just enough to make her more—agreeable. She needs to be taught her place. I don't want her having any doubts about what her life will be like from now on."

"Sounds like I have my job cut out for me. Have her brought to my suite," he said, pushing away from the bar and heading upstairs.

Ruby instructed two of the house servants to deliver the farm girl to Isaac. She almost felt sorry for the wide-eyed innocent girl, but she would be a good moneymaker once she learned her trade. She went to the bar and poured herself a generous drink, congratulating herself. Over the years, she had worked her way into Beck's empire. Through charm and subtle manipulations, she had ingratiated herself with Isaac, and he had come to trust her, giving her more and more responsibilities until he had turned over all of his brothels to her. One day, he would ask more of her, and she would be ready. Savoring her drink, she leaned against the shiny bar, envisioning the day when she would be at the head of Beck's empire, and he would be an unpleasant memory.

CHAPTER 42

A SON OF MY OWN CHOOSING

It was early evening when Isaac Beck rode onto his estate. He loved the mansion and the grounds he called home and admired the well-kept property. He rode straight to the stable, dropping his reins in front of a livery boy. Pausing, he looked the boy up and down. "Are you new?"

"Yes, sir, my name's…"

Isaac left the boy standing with his mouth agape and staring after him as he crossed the lawn toward the main house.

Old Hack, the stable master, came to where the boy stood. "He's an odd stick, Timmy, but don't let him worry you none. He doesn't come down here often, and when he does…" The man paused, rubbing his fingers across his scarred cheek. "When he does, keep your head down, stay busy, and out of his way."

Beck strode quickly across the well-manicured lawn and into his mansion. He crossed the large foyer, passing the butler and two house servants who were busily preparing for Saturday's party. Deep in thought, he barely noticed them. He went straight to his den and poured a drink. Sitting ramrod straight, he stared out the large window overlooking the expansive lawn that ended on the banks of a small stream. It was an exquisite view, and it usually soothed him. But his jaw grew tight thinking about Sharpe.

Three figures darted back and forth outside the window, bringing him abruptly out of his reverie. It was his wife and his daughters, Amelia and Margaret, chattering as they prepared for the party. Irritated by the interruption, he turned from the window. Tapping the knuckles of his loose-fisted hand on his desktop, he replayed the meeting with Mr. Sharpe. "Every man has a weakness to be played, and so does Sharpe," Isaac said aloud, his mind going back to the artwork in Sharpe's office. "Is hedonism his Achille's heel?"

He had been the passive player in this farce for long enough. It wasn't a position he was comfortable with, but perhaps it could work in his favor. The old man was arrogant and wouldn't be expecting an all-out assault. But he needed a plan and more information on the old coot before he could make a move on him.

Hannah, one of his three daughters, came running into his office, sweet innocence radiating from her face. She was as perfect and seductive as any woman he had ever seen. She ran behind his chair and, wrapping her arms around his shoulders kissed his cheek. "Thank you for the party, Father. I can't wait. I know it is going to be wonderful."

He patted her hands, "Let's hope it doesn't rain."

"It wouldn't dare," she said with a laugh and whirled around, landing in the chair in front of his desk.

"I can't believe you're turning seventeen. It seems like yesterday that all three of you girls were toddlers, bouncing and playing in the yard." He smiled at the memories. "You looked like a litter of puppies; now, you've all grown into beautiful women."

Hannah giggled at her father's memories. "I have to help with the party," she said and was gone as quickly as she had appeared.

Isaac looked out the window at his other two daughters. Amelia and Margaret had grown up arrogant, greedy, and ill-tempered, not becoming traits for women of marrying age. That was probably why they weren't being courted. Hannah was the opposite of her sisters. She was his wild child, and he had difficulty keeping her out of trouble. Her natural beauty, along with her penchant for excitement, made her irresistible, and there was no end to clumsy young and untried boys wanting to woo her.

But Isaac had seen the way men looked at Hannah. They undressed her with their eyes, wanting more than to woo her, and he couldn't blame them. He wasn't immune to her charms and had to remind himself repeatedly that she was his daughter. If only Hannah had been a son. He wanted the name Beck to mean something. He wanted a dynasty, but none of his daughters had a head for business, and they would never understand about the brothels and parlor houses.

His ire flared, this time at the wife he hated. He hated her for failing to give him a son and for disappointing him in so many ways, the least of which was her performance in their marriage bed. She didn't like his rough ways, and it was only by force that he had managed to sire his daughters. He still frequently bedded his wife even though there would be no more children. The doctor said she was too torn up inside, but he didn't care. Now, when he took her, it was her fear that stimulated his lust, not the need to sire a son. He enjoyed hurting her.

He poured another drink, thinking back to his afternoon at The Taylor's. It had been most satisfying. As Ruby had warned, the new girl was a handful, but bringing her into submission had been absolutely delicious. He had been sated, but now, thoughts of Sharpe and the failure of his wife to provide him with a son were causing the tension and pressure inside him to grow again. He needed an outlet. He smiled, thinking of his wife. Later, he would seek her out and remind her that she was his wife and that he could do with her as he pleased.

Watching the women working on the terrace, he wondered what kind of a son he might have had. He would have been sorely disappointed if he had a son like his brother's. Acie was a handsome lad and clever enough, and he did have a way about him. But he had no business sense and not a responsible bone in his body. Acie used all his charms on loose women and at the poker table. Isaac's older brother had been killed in the war, and with Acie as his heir, he would have no decent legacy.

Isaac's two youngest daughters had grown into decent-looking women. They didn't have Hannah's beauty, but perhaps he could parlay their comely looks into fruitful marriages. He would pick appropriate husbands for each of them, men who could run his businesses and sire him grandsons. Arranged marriages weren't unheard of, and he could choose men he would be proud to call son.

He smiled, one problem solved. Now, he would concentrate on how to own Sharpe and his empire.

CHAPTER 43

SWEET HANNAH

Georgia Beck snuck quickly past the door of her husband's office and up the stairs to her bedroom. She was afraid of her husband and didn't want to draw his attention. Over the years, he had made it all too clear to her that she was nothing more than a possession, one to be used for his pleasure whenever he wanted. He demanded things from her, acts she was loathe to perform, but the punishments if she refused were worse. Regardless, she always ended up bruised and swollen for days after one of his *love* sessions. That's what he called them, but no love was involved. The last time, he cracked two of her ribs when she refused to do his bidding.

When Isaac opened the door to her bedroom, she jumped. It was late and she wasn't expecting him. He was rough, but he didn't hurt her this time, at least not so anyone would be able to tell. There was the party to think of, and it wouldn't do for his wife to be bruised and limping.

Later, when Isaac left his wife's bedroom, he stopped to look in on his girls. He lingered at Hannah's door before entering. He looked down at his sleeping beauty, watching her breasts rise and fall in the rhythm of a sound sleep, her lips slightly parted. He needed to touch her. He covered her with a light coverlet, letting his hands brush across her breasts, lingering, feeling the warmth and softness of her flesh through the thin material of her nightgown.

Isaac sighed quietly and left her room. He wanted her and knew no shame in the wanting, but she was bait for the perfect son, and his ideal son would want a virgin.

CHAPTER 44

HANNAH'S PARTY

The morning of Hannah's party dawned calm and clear with a light breeze that gently rustled the leaves. It was going to be a perfect day. Guests began arriving, all fashionably late, while uniformed servants carried silver trays of drinks and hors d'oeuvres through the crowd. Based on the chatter and laughter, the party was a resounding success. He had invited a senator, a congressman, and two judges, who had all arrived with their wives. But it was nearly noon, and Mr. Sharpe had yet to show.

The butler was about to call everyone to dinner when a buggy came up the front drive. Beck was pleased to see Mr. Sharpe climb from his carriage, but wondered why he hadn't brought his wife. He motioned for the butler to hold off as he watched the man hobble across the lawn. He didn't fawn over Sharpe but made him feel welcome. He was holding on to his passive role without groveling. He had to be believable and keep him on the line until he could set the hook.

"My wife came down with a headache," Sharpe huffed, trying to catch his breath. "She sends her regards." Sharpe motioned to where four couples stood chatting. "I'm impressed, Beck. A senator, a congressman, and two judges. Can you fit them all in your pocket, or could you use some help?"

"I have no one in my pocket, Mr. Sharpe," Beck said, motioning to the butler for the food to be brought out.

After the meal, a game of croquet blossomed into a best two-out-of-three tournament. As the third game heated up, those not playing became the gallery cheering for one or the other of the teams. Hannah's team won amidst cheering and booing. Some claimed the game was rigged in favor of the birthday girl. The losing team groaned in defeat while Hannah's team bounced up and down in a group hug of celebration.

Mr. Sharpe spent the afternoon watching Hannah. He spoke to her several times, marveling at her perfection. Hannah was aware of his preoccupation and thought it creepy. The smelly old man was the only blemish on her otherwise perfect party. She wished he would leave, but he was still hanging around when the last guests disappeared down the front drive.

Isaac returned to the terrace after sending off the last of his guests. Sharpe pulled him aside. "I want to talk to you, Beck."

"So, talk."

"Let's sit over here at the table." Sharpe limped the few steps to the table and sat down with a grunt. "I want your daughter, Beck. I want Hannah." Sharpe said it as if asking for a cookie. I'll give you the 70-30 split you want and access to my foreign contacts."

Isaac nearly choked but answered calmly. "No." Isaac's mind was racing. "Besides, what would your wife think?"

"My wife's approval or disapproval doesn't mean shit to me." Sharpe's cloudy, red-rimmed eyes bored into Isaac. "I know who you are, Beck, and what you do. You have that little railcar thing going on, but you peddle flesh every day of the week, like beef to market. This is no different. I'm willing to accept your original proposal with all its fine print. The price for my signature is Hannah."

Isaac frowned for Sharpe's benefit but wanted to laugh out loud. "I'll have to think about it." Isaac felt his heart racing. He had the man hooked, and the hook was set deep, but he couldn't appear too eager.

"You moved quickly from no to I'll think about it." Sharpe's chuckle turned into a coughing fit. Sharpe pulled an embroidered handkerchief from his pocket and spit a wad of phlegm into it. He stuffed it back into his pocket. "I'm sure you understand the wisdom of such a transaction. Unless, of course, you would prefer having one of those pimple-faced youngsters deflower her. It's only a matter of time, you know. Five of them were falling all over themselves today, vying for her attention."

"Perhaps a pimple-faced youngster would be better than an incontinent old man."

Sharpe wheezed out a laugh, "Better for who? You or your daughter? Besides, I've seen the way you look at her. She's your daughter, but you'd have your pecker inside her in a heartbeat if it served your purpose. I'll tell you what, Beck, once Hannah and I have gotten to know each other, I'll invite you over to watch or perhaps to join in."

"I said I'd think about it, Mr. Sharpe."

"Bring her to me on Saturday, next. That will give you a week to break the news to her and get her used to the idea. And I know you will convince her to be agreeable to pleasing me." Sharpe's eyes searched the lawn and terrace for his prize. "Unless I could have a taste today?"

Isaac struggled to keep his breathing in check and his voice calm. "I'll have to get back to you."

Sharpe smirked at Beck. "See you Saturday." He turned and limped across the lawn to his buggy.

Beck watched until Sharpe was out of sight, then went to his office. This was a coup. He'd been thinking about marrying his daughters off to men who would be an asset to the family, and as far as giving Hannah to Sharpe out of wedlock, it didn't matter. Hannah didn't have to love him. All she had to do was satisfy him. And he still had Abigail and Margaret to marry off to men who could provide him with heirs.

He'd wanted to get someone inside Sharpe's inner circle. Someone who could help bring him down. Hannah would be perfect. Pillow talk had sunk more than one ship, and he could trust his daughter.

The contract he and his lawyer would draw up on Monday would give him total control of the project and a significantly larger share of the profits. Sharpe would pay dearly for the privilege of bedding his daughter. Hannah would fetch an outrageous price and, at the same time, serve as his spy. Isaac rubbed his hands together, barely able to control himself. He was giddy with excitement over the unexpected turn of events.

Laughing, he left his office in search of his wife.

CHAPTER 45

TILL SATURDAY

Georgia was exhausted after the party and on her way to her room for a rest. She passed by a window that opened onto the terrace and was surprised to hear voices. She thought all the guests had left, but she heard her husband talking with another man. Their words sickened her. Her heart raced, and her breath came in gasps as she hurried from the window. She shut herself in her room, horrified at the thought of Isaac using Hannah as payment to close a business deal. She couldn't catch her breath. The panic rose into full sobs.

She remembered when Hannah was little, how Isaac used to lift her onto his shoulders at parades, how he once said she was the light of his life. Now he'd trade her like a sack of flour.

Georgia had noticed a change in Isaac. He was no longer the doting father he'd once been. His daughters had turned into lovely women, and she saw how he looked at them. The way he eyed Hannah was despicable, but all he understood was pleasing himself. He had no sense of right or wrong, but to think that he would pimp Hannah out like one of his whores to seal a business deal was beyond belief.

"I have until Saturday," she sobbed into her lace-edged hankie. "I won't let you use my precious daughter as chattel, you stinking bastard. And Hannah will never lay with that filthy old toad of a man." She paced the floor, shaking with anger and fear. "I'll send her far away where you'll never find her. I need help, but who would dare to help me?"

The door to her room slammed open, and Isaac stood in the doorway, a smug smile radiating from his face. He saw the fear in her eyes as he slowly pushed the door shut behind him.

CHAPTER 46

QUIMBY BECK, NEWSPAPERMAN

Quimby Beck sat at his desk in the newspaper office, working on an article. Frustration gnawed at him—he couldn't focus. He was an experienced writer, a tenacious reporter, and had excellent horse sense when it came to ferreting out stories. But lately, any story ideas he presented to the editor were then given to the editor's twin sons. They were young boys with no experience. The ideas were his and should have been his stories to write.

Over the years, he had written hundreds of front-page stories, but now he had been relegated to lesser pieces. It was tearing him up, and he had to make a change. But he didn't know what kind of a change he could make. He needed the job to keep a roof over his head and food on the table.

Quimby was resting his face in his hands, trying to imagine how he could improve his lot, when he heard his sister-in-law's voice as she approached his desk.

"Quimby, there's no need to cry. Tell me what's wrong, and I'll fix it if I can."

Quimby got up from his desk and offered her a chair. "Georgia, you're looking positively lovely," he said as he hugged her.

"Don't lie to me, Quim," she said with a smile. Taking a seat, she removed her gloves. "How's my favorite reporter?"

"Don't ask."

"Why, Quim, what's wrong?"

"You really want to know?"

"Of course I do."

He told her in detail how the editor had undermined his job by giving his sons all the best stories and assignments.

Georgia picked up a pencil and rolled it slowly between her fingers, her knuckles tight. "If you could do anything you wanted, what would it be?"

"I would take my charming sister-in-law to dinner, and then I'd go to the train station and get a ticket to this place way out West. There are two lawmen out there I'd like to interview. As sure as my chin bleeds red every morning when I shave, there's a story waiting to be told."

"Taking your sister-in-law to dinner is a wonderful idea. But tell me why you aren't already on a train headed for this God-forsaken place you're talking about."

"The editor won't approve the expenditure for my travel. He doesn't think what I'm looking at is newsworthy." Quimby sighed, his shoulders slumping. "And I don't have enough money to do it on my own. If I had the money to get out there, I could free-lance the story and make some folding money."

"How can you be so different from your brother?" She paused as tears welled up. "I desperately need your help. I wouldn't ask, but I have no one else to turn to. No one else I can trust."

"Anything, Georgia. Has he hurt you again? He has, hasn't he?"

"It's not for me, Quimby. It's Hannah. I must get her out of town before Saturday."

Quimby froze at the desperation in Georgia's voice—she'd risked everything just to come here. Whatever was going on had to be serious, or she wouldn't have risked Isaac's wrath by coming to him. Isaac didn't allow her to leave the estate unless he accompanied her. And Quimby knew that over the twenty years Georgia had been married to his miscreant brother, she had taken beatings and betrayals without a complaint.

"I have a household account and some money saved back. You can use it to buy train tickets for you and Hannah to wherever you want to go. If you're careful, there's enough to make a new start somewhere."

"What's going on, Georgia?"

"Your brother plans to use his daughter as a bargaining chip in one of his business deals." She snapped the pencil in half. "He's trading her—to some shriveled old man—as if she were livestock, just to close a deal."

Quimby's face flared crimson red. "My God, Georgia. How could he even consider such a thing?"

Georgia held up her hand as a tear spilled down her cheeks. "It doesn't matter, Quimby. It's the way he is. He used to dote on those girls, but now, he sees them differently. They've become assets, pawns to be used to get what he wants. Amelia and Margaret are at risk, too, but Hannah is in the most danger. Please, promise me you'll take her away."

She had taken Isaac's beatings in silence, but this—this was a line she couldn't let him cross.

"Yes, of course. I'll leave with her as soon as it can be arranged. Please, please don't cry," Quimby said, jumping to his feet. "Come on, let's go." He took hold of Georgia's arm and hurried her toward the door. He didn't know how they'd do it or where they'd go, but none of that mattered. She'd asked, and that was enough.

"Quim, what about your job?"

"I quit," Quimby yelled over his shoulder as the door to the newspaper office slammed shut behind them.

CHAPTER 47

HE'S DIFFERENT

Hannah and her friend Amanda had been riding all morning, exploring. They'd ridden farther than they ever had before. They'd have gone even farther, but hunger pangs stopped them.

"This is a good place to stop," Amanda said, dismounting and pulling the drawstrings of her lunch bag from around the saddle horn. "What did you bring?"

Hannah opened her lunch bag and looked inside. "Looks like fried chicken, radishes, and a half loaf of bread."

"I've got a roast beef sandwich and potato salad," Amanda said, spreading a small tablecloth on the ground. "Let's share."

"It's good to be home, Amanda. I missed you and my mother and father." Hannah nibbled on a fried chicken leg. "But Father is different since I returned from Europe. I can't put my finger on it, but he's changed. Did you notice?"

"The only thing I noticed was how Charles Whiting looked at you and not at me."

Hannah giggled. "It was nice seeing him again. I think he may be the one, Amanda. I get all tingly whenever I'm close to him."

"He'll be at the party tomorrow night. You have to come. Say you will. You have to."

"Father will never let me go to an unchaperoned party, but maybe I could sneak out. I want to see Charles. I liked the special attention he gave me at the party, and he was so close the one time I could almost feel his lips on mine." Hannah sighed, "I want him to hold me and smother me with his kisses. The thought of it is almost more than I can bear."

"Sounds like you want more than hugs and kisses," Amanda said, her mouth full of roast beef sandwich.

"Would I be evil if I let him do more? Have you ever—been with a man?"

Amanda almost choked, "No," she said with a giggle, "but Oliver and I did move things along a bit while you were away. I let him see my breasts."

"What?" Hannah gasped.

"And I let him touch them with his hands and his mouth," Amanda giggled. "It was wonderful."

"Mother told me all men are savages. But you liked having him touch you."

"I did, it was very—stimulating, and Oliver wasn't the least bit savage. Just determined. I shouldn't have let him. I mean, goodness knows what he'll try tomorrow night." Amanda winked at Hannah. "And who knows what I'll let him get by with." She sighed. "I wonder what it would be like to make love to him."

Hannah tingled at the thought of Charles' athletic body and imagined his hands and mouth on her breasts. She let out a long, shaky sigh. She'd be at that party if she had to walk barefoot over nails to get there.

On the ride home, they talked about the party and who they expected to see there. They reviewed the attributes of all the boys they knew and discussed whether Margie Summers had let her boyfriend go all the way. They suspected she had and were dying to hear all the juicy details.

When Hannah arrived home, she went straight to her room. She changed from her riding clothes and slid into a nice warm bath that had been prepared for her. She knew her father would forbid her going to an unchaperoned party, but she would sneak out. She had already arranged with the new groomsman for her horse to be saddled and waiting.

She stepped from the bubble-filled tub and looked at her reflection in the full-length mirror. A smile tugged at the corners of her mouth, wondering if Charles would think her beautiful. She touched her hands to her breast and felt the nipples harden. She jerked her hands away and slid into her robe without a glance back at the mirror.

Sitting at her dressing table, Hannah brushed her strawberry-blonde hair, counting one hundred strokes. All the while imagining what it would feel like to be in Charles' arms and, wondering if he would be so bold as Oliver. She put the hairbrush down and fluffed her hair over her shoulders. Yesterday had been such a wonderful day, but after the party, her father seemed distant and angry with her.

She wondered if she had done something to disappoint or displease him. Had he noticed Charles getting too familiar? She thought her father would approve of Charles. He came from old money, studied law at a respected ivy-covered university, was on the rowing team, and would graduate at the top of his class.

Hannah crawled into bed, wondering about her father. She plumped her pillows and turned off the lamp. That's when she saw him standing in the doorway, silhouetted by the light from the hallway. She hadn't heard him open the door and wondered how long he'd been watching her. He approached slowly and looked down at her for the longest time before sitting on the bed beside her. He stroked her cheek with his long, slender fingers and kissed her forehead.

"Hannah, it's time we talked. I've made some difficult decisions."

She remained silent. Something in his demeanor and how he looked at her was frightening, and she was afraid to speak. She had seen him look at her mother with those same dead eyes, and it sent chills up her spine.

"Hannah, you've come of age, and it's time you marry. I've arranged for you to marry Horace Sharpe Saturday at his estate."

Hannah sat bolt upright in bed. "I will not. He's at least a hundred years old, and he smells. Besides, he's already got a wife."

"It will be the same as being married, Hannah. There won't be a preacher or a wedding ring, but there will be a wedding night."

"I won't," she screamed. "You can't make me."

"You're my daughter, and you'll do as I say." He watched the rise and fall of her breasts under the lacy nightdress she was wearing and wanted to reach out and touch her.

Hannah saw the lust in his eyes and jerked the covers around her neck. "Get out. Get out of here now."

Isaac backhanded her. "Wedding or not, you will belong to Mr. Sharpe, as your mother belongs to me, and you will please him in all ways." He smiled, thinking about the artwork on Sharpe's office walls. If those drawings were any indication of his intentions, Hannah would be pleasuring him in many, many ways. A smile teased his lips, and his pulse quickened, thinking of Sharpe's invitation to join them.

He rose from the bed. "I'll expect you to be civil at breakfast. Understand this, Hannah, you will go to Sharpe, and you will make him happy, or I shall take you for myself." He left the room, closing the door quietly behind him.

Hannah sat clutching her knees to her chest, rocking back and forth. The man she'd once tried so hard to please no longer existed. In his place stood a monster. His parting words had her shaking so hard her teeth chattered. She jumped at the gentle tap on her door and cowered against the wall. The door opened a crack, and she heard her mother's voice. "Hannah, are you alright?"

Hannah's sobs were answer enough for Georgia. She hurried to her daughter, taking her in her arms. "Hannah, I'm so sorry. I should have done something sooner, but I'm here now, and you are leaving this place. You're going with your Uncle Quimby. Get dressed in traveling clothes." Georgia handed her a money belt to wear around her waist and pushed her unmoving daughter toward the closet. "Hurry, child, hurry."

With sobs still racking her body, Hannah dressed while her mother packed her valise. *This has to be a nightmare*, she thought. But she wasn't asleep.

"You'll have to buy appropriate clothing when you reach your destination, but this will do for now," her mom said as she snapped the valise shut and pushed it into Hannah's hand.

"We don't have a moment to waste. Go down the backstairs and out the kitchen door. Your Uncle Quimby is waiting for you." Georgia's love-filled eyes looked at her daughter. "I have to get back to your father before he comes looking for me. I love you, Hannah." She didn't know what Isaac would do if he discovered what she was planning, but she feared she wouldn't survive it. She kissed her daughter's cheek and hugged her goodbye before hurrying away.

Hannah raced down the stairs and out the back door where Quimby waited. He hustled her into the buggy and took the back way off the estate to avoid being seen or heard as they left. He wouldn't fail Georgia, and he wouldn't fail Hannah.

CHAPTER 48

SMUDGE

Hannah and Quimby had been on the train for two days, and Hannah still couldn't believe her father's words. She muffled a sob. The whole thing was too horrifying to think about, yet his words echoed in her mind, and she found she could think of little else. Her gloved fingers tugged viciously at the folds of her skirt, and she struggled to hold back the tears.

"How much longer before we get there?" she asked.

"Sometime early tomorrow morning, or so the conductor says. It isn't much further, but between the breakdown and stopping at every cowtown, it's taking longer than I had anticipated."

"Sorry, I haven't been better company. I can't seem to think of anything but my father's parting words, and I can't stop worrying about Mother."

"I'm worried about her, too. I hate to think of what he might do to her if he finds out she helped you run away." Quimby snorted, "I used to envy my brother's success and his happy family, but I didn't know then how he treated your mother. I never could figure out why she stayed with him. I guess it was to protect you and your sisters."

Quimby looked over to Hannah and, seeing the tears about to spill down her cheeks, took her hand in his. "I'm sorry, Smudge, I shouldn't have said those things, and I'm sorry you had to go through all of this, but we have new lives to look forward to, and we'll be safe."

A smile softened Hannah's face at his use of the nickname he'd given her the first time he saw her. He said she was no bigger than a smudge of ink on a newspaper.

"We'll never be safe, Uncle Quim," Hannah said, her smile quickly fading. "He'll send men to find us. He'll never give up." Her words settled between them like a stone dropped in water. Quimby didn't argue—he couldn't.

Quimby didn't say so but had to admit that Hannah was right. No matter what they did, they could still be found if someone looked hard enough.

"He'll find us, and he'll kill us."

Quimby squeezed her hand. "We'll be all right, Smudge. I promise." Even if he didn't quite believe it himself.

CHAPTER 49

TUG

Jake and Sam stood in front of the Land Office, watching Quimby and Hannah Beck as they walked to Murphy's Boarding House. Sam knew what Jake was thinking. No luggage, no plans, and Quimby Beck was lying through his teeth. There was a whole lot more to those two than met the eyes. But there was little chance they were involved with Mort or what was going on in Grant's Crossing.

Sam was about to open the door to the office when the owner of the of the Night Owl Saloon came rushing up to them. "Marshal! Marshal, you need to come with me. There's been a murder! It's awful."

Jake and Sam stood in the middle of the Night Owl Saloon, looking at the bloody body hanging on the back wall. Forks and knives from behind the bar had been used to pin the body in place. Some had been poked through the man's clothing, but several had been jabbed through the palms of his hands. Knives protruded from various parts of his body and more littered the floor beneath him. It was obvious that the man had been used for target practice.

Logan rushed through the door. "I heard there was a murder." He saw the body and went still.

What happened?" Jake asked.

"I don't know, Marshal. He was like this when I opened up this morning. I locked up and came to get you right away. This ain't good for business, Marshal."

"You know him?"

"That's Tug Bertleson, Marshal. He drinks here most every night. I've never known him to cause any trouble."

"Tug his given name?" Jake asked.

Logan grinned. "Don't know as anyone ever knew his real name. You?" Logan asked, looking at the bartender.

"No. I know his wife died a few years back but never heard him talk about any other family.

"Mort did it."

They all turned abruptly to stare at Sam.

Mort had it in for Tug. He was Mort's worst tormentor—always needling him. One time, Tug told Mort he'd buy him a bottle if he'd drink the troubled water from the lunch table. Mort would do anything for a drink. So he took all the forks and spoons out of the glass and drank that dirty water right down. Tug pulled out some coins like he was gonna buy Mort a drink but instead tossed them into a spittoon. Mort fished them out and got his drink and everyone had a good laugh"

"You almost sound sorry for Mort," Jake said with a grin.

"Never. I just remember how Mort would rant about getting even with Tug.

"Sam's right, Jake. This is Mort's work. When I was sheriff, the worst thing Tug ever did to Mort was to pin his arms to the wall with forks from the lunch table. Then he threw knives at him—Tug wasn't that good of an aim. Doc Thorn sent word to me and I hightailed it to his office. Mort had lots of cuts and gashes, but only one or two needed stitches. He told me it was Tug who'd done the dirty work, but I couldn't find anyone willing to backup what Mort was saying."

"I remember that night," Sam snorted, "Mort came home all patched up and madder than a hornet. He cut a swath down my back."

Jake pushed his hat back with a deep breath. "Let's get this poor man down."

Bones came through the front doorway with a smile. "Heard you had a body for me and it don't look like we need Coop to verify he ain't breathing. What name do I put on his marker?

"Tug Bertleson," Logan replied.

"Why'd they call him Tug?" Jake asked.

Sam, Logan, and the barkeeper grinned at Jake's question. "Well, Jake," Logan said. "It wasn't unusual to find him back of the saloon – uh – tugging one out."

Jake frowned at the smiling faces. "What? Oh."

CHAPTER 50

AN ANGEL

Amid grumbling and groaning from Logan, Jake and Sam left him and Bones to finish up at the Night Owl. It was mid-morning, and the streets were busy as they made their way toward the Land Office. "Wonder if the Becks are all settled in?"

"They didn't have much with them, so I doubt it took much settling in." They stopped on the corner in front of the Land Office. "I have a strange feeling about them, Sam. And it's more than my dislike for newspapermen. If that's what he is. That dang poker game at Kat's draws lots of no-goods into town."

"You think they might be gamblers?"

"Yes. No. Maybe. All I know for sure is they have trouble trailing after them."

"I'd be glad to keep an eye on her, I mean them." Sam said with a smile. "She sure ain't hard to look at."

"She's married, Sam."

"Don't hurt to window shop."

A cowbell tied to the door clanged and rattled as Sam opened the door to the Land Office. The officious-looking clerk glanced over his wire-rimmed glasses and greeted them with a grunt. Ignoring them, he continued working on the document in front of him.

Jake scowled at the imperious little man. "We need some information." Jake's voice boomed in the small office.

The clerk jumped. "What is it, Marshal? I'm a busy man," he said without looking up.

"Has anyone purchased the old Watkins place?"

"I don't know." He looked up and met Jake's gaze. Seeing the look on Jake's face, he added, "Give me a minute. I'll check the records." He shuffled through file drawers and, after several minutes, found documents showing that Burton Corning had purchased the Watkins property over two years ago.

They left the Land Office and headed to the General Store. If anyone knew about the Corning's, it would be Steven and Charlie. The store was quiet, and the two owners were playing cards at a small table behind the counter. "Don't know as I've ever seen it this quiet," Sam said.

Steven got up from the card game and met Sam at the counter. "Lots of people in the street, but no one stopping in for shopping. Doesn't often happen, for a fact." Steven tilted his head slightly to the side and looked questioningly from Sam to Jake. "You boys are wearing your lawman faces. Charlie! It's an official visit." Charlie rose slowly his bones stiff from sitting too long.

Sam chuckled, "Guess you could call it an official visit. What do you know about Burton Corning?"

Jake popped a peppermint stick in his mouth and threw a penny on the counter.

Steven stuffed two more sticks in Jake's shirt pocket. "These are for Winnie. You make sure she gets them. The Cornings. Charlie, do we know a Burton Corning?"

"Sure we do. Burt and Molly are real nice folks. They always pay with cash."

"Now I remember. An older couple with no kids. They come into town two or three times a year. They got patched clothes and all, but clean and polite, and it is nice to have a customer who pays with folding money."

Sam was fiddling with a fancy bridle hanging on a post near the counter. "What does Mr. Corning look like?" he asked.

"Looks to be in his late forties, balding and thinner than most. Wears red stripped suspenders to keep his britches up. He stopped in a few weeks back and bought new boots for himself and a frilly dress and bonnet for his wife." Steven leaned forward on the counter, his eyes wide with curiosity. "What's going on with the Cornings?

"Nothing. We're grasping at straws, trying to figure out what my dad is up to. I doubt they can help us, but it can't hurt to ask." As Sam finished speaking several men and their wives entered.

"That's right. They took up on the old Watkins place. If you see them, give them regards from me and Charlie." Steven shifted his gaze to Charlie. "Looks like our quiet time is over."

Jake thanked Steven for the extra peppermint sticks for Winnie, and they hurried from the crowded store. Stopping on the boardwalk, Jake turned to Sam. "What do you think? Is it worth the trip to visit the Cornings?"

"It's under two hours, and we don't want to miss something important. If we hurry, we can be out and back by midafternoon and still have plenty of time to get Winnie and her folks home."

"Let's hit the leather."

CHAPTER 51

SHE'S GOT A SHOTGUN

As they approached the Corning property, a woman with a double-barrel shotgun greeted them from the porch of a somewhat ramshackle house. It was evident that some repairs had recently been made, but it was still in need. "What do you men want?"

"Good morning, Mrs. Corning. I'm United States Marshal William Jacobs," Jake tipped his hat. "And this is Deputy Marshal Sam Watkins."

Sam doffed his hat and nodded. "Morning, ma'am."

Jake wished she would point the shotgun in a different direction. "We have some questions. Is it all right for us to get down?"

"Do it easy, Marshal, if that's who you are. This shotgun has a hair trigger, and I'm not afraid to use it."

Jake and Sam dismounted and approached Molly, removing their hats. "Is your husband home?"

"Is that one of the questions you came all the way out here to ask?"

Jake was amused by her sassy comeback. "No, Mrs. Corning. No, it isn't."

Burt Corning rounded the corner of the barn, leading a bay mare, and Molly introduced the two men to her husband. "They say they're the law from Grant's Crossing."

"Put the gun down, Molly. I recognize them. They're who they say they are."

Molly slowly lowered the barrel of the shotgun until it pointed at the ground, but she held on to it.

Burt continued, "Sorry, but we've been jumpy lately. Molly, apologize to these men and get out that custard pie you baked this morning. We've got guests."

Mrs. Corning watched Sam duck his head as he entered her home. "Deputy, you sure was made from some long, tall timbers."

"They were knotty timbers, too, ma'am," Jake said, earning a glare from Sam.

Seated at the kitchen table, Sam couldn't help but look around, inspecting the house his grandparents had lived in. A place he had never seen before. He wondered if his life might have been different had he known them.

Molly noticed his scrutiny and scowled. "You looking to buy the place, shorty?"

"No, ma'am, sorry. I was curious. This was my grandparent's home place."

Molly's face and voice softened. "Fond memories from your childhood?"

"Yes, Mrs. Corning." Sam didn't care to explain. He didn't want to talk about how much he'd missed out on—how many nights he'd wondered if he had family out there who would've loved him, if things had gone differently.

Jake swallowed a bite of pie. "You said you'd been jumpy lately. Why's that?"

"A few weeks back, three men rode in late in the evening and tried to steal our horses right outta the corral over there by the barn. We've worked hard on this place, and we wasn't about to let them get away with robbing us. The first year we lived here, we had a raggedy-ass, shirt-tail outfit—barely making it. But we held on. Good thing we did, cuz I got lucky."

Mr. Corning took a bite of pie, chewing slowly, savoring the creamy sweetness. "Best pie ever," he said, winking at his wife.

"I got real lucky. I went to town to ask that banker man, Mr. Walters, for an extension on my loan, but he was hard-fisted and wouldn't budge. He's a piece of work, that one. Said we had two weeks until the bank took over. We'd have lost everything. Our land, our stock—our home. All our hard work would have been for naught. I can tell you, it was a bitter pill to swallow, Marshal."

Burt poured cream into his coffee. "There's little a man can do in two weeks. When I left the bank, I was desperate and thought if I went to the church and did some serious praying, it might help. I hadn't been in God's house for a good spell. I never seemed to find the time for it, but I figured he'd listen to one of his stray lambs. I guess most folks get religion of some sort or another when the chips are down."

"How about another piece of pie, Deputy?" Mrs. Corning offered, filling Sam's coffee cup.

"I can't say no, ma'am," Sam said with a dimpled smile. "It's the best custard pie I've ever had." Mrs. Corning beamed as she slid a second piece of pie onto his plate.

Jake looked at him, shaking his head. "Careful, Mrs. Corning, or he'll eat the whole thing. He doesn't have a bashful appetite."

Mrs. Corning scoffed at Jake's remarks. "How about you, Marshal, another piece? Coffee?"

Jake covered his cup with his hand. "No, thank you. And delicious as it is, one piece of pie is enough for me."

Mrs. Corning's husband was eager to continue his story. "As I said, I was on my way to church to bend my knees when this stranger came barreling up to me. He shakes my hand and slaps me on the back, greeting me like a long-lost buddy. Then he puts his arm around my shoulders and drags me into the Schooner Saloon, insisting he buy me a drink for old-time's sake. I ain't a drinking man, Marshal, but considering my troubles, I didn't see how a free drink could hurt anything, and the church would always be there."

Mrs. Corning was puttering around the kitchen but interrupted her husband's story. "This is where it gets spooky. You won't believe what happened next."

"This stranger leads me up to the bar and tells the barkeeper to set us up with whiskey and to leave the bottle. I watched the barkeep fill two glasses and walk away, leaving the bottle in front of us. I got to looking at all the bottles behind the bar and, sorry, Molly, but I got to studying pretty intense on a picture. It was a buxom woman—stark naked. I took a swig from my glass and turned to thank the stranger, but he wasn't there. There was no bottle on the bar and only one glass of whiskey. The one I was holding in my hand. I asked the barkeeper if he had seen where my friend had got to, and do you know what he told me? He said, Mister, you came in here alone. Well, I couldn't believe it. I knew I wasn't crazy, and I'd had only one sip of whiskey."

Burt looked from Jake to Sam, waiting for a comment, but there was none. They were listening intently, waiting for him to continue.

"I asked the soldier standing on the other side of me if he had seen the guy I came in with, and he told me the same thing, you came in alone, pal."

I reckon he thought I was drunk, but he was friendly, and we struck up a conversation. That's how I met Major Shepherd, a man looking to buy horses for the army." Jake and Sam exchanged a glance. They'd heard tall tales before—but something about the man's conviction, the timing, the eerie vanishing—it didn't feel like a tall tale.

Jake leaned forward, his blue eyes intent. "You were the only one to see this, friend of yours?"

"For a fact, Marshal, I was the only one to lay eyes on him. Anyway, this Major Shepherd tells me the last herd of horses on its way to the fort had been rustled, and the army was desperate for mounts." Burt took a sip of his coffee. "He was looking for horses to buy. I couldn't believe it. I told him I had fifty solid horses for him to look at. He bought them all, and I had enough money to pay off the bank, restock, and even make some repairs around the place. The army liked the mounts they got from me, said they were exceptional, and we got us a deal now. Things are looking up. It was a miracle, and the only thing I can figure out is that stranger I met out front of the Schooner musta been an angel."

Jake sat back in his chair. "Your meeting, Major Shepherd, does seem to have been fated."

"You believe me, Marshal?"

"Of course I do." Jake had seen enough, unexplainable things of his own.

Sam swallowed his last bite of pie. "…wondrous strange," he quoted.

Jake shook his head, scowling at Sam. "Shakespeare?"

"Seemed appropriate," Sam said with a shrug. "I'm glad you saved your place, Mr. Corning. Too many outfits have been getting gobbled up by that bank."

"I can say one thing. Mr. Walters was most unhappy when I paid off my loan. That man tried to get me to renew it. He musta thought I'd just fallen off the turnip wagon yesterday."

Jake pulled the conversation back to the horse thieves. "What happened when those men tried to steal your horses?"

"We each grabbed a shotgun and ran out shooting. They high-tailed it, and we haven't seen them since."

"Can you describe the men?"

"It was dark, but I can tell you one of the men was kinda small with a pasty white complexion, and the other man was big, like you, Deputy."

"Do you know if you hit either of them?"

"Don't think we did, Marshal. We didn't want to shoot straight at them; they was too close to the stock, and we didn't want to hurt the horses or them. We only wanted to scare them away."

Jake got up from the table. "We appreciate your help and hospitality." He ran his fingers through his hair, pushing back the lock that had fallen across his forehead, and settled his hat on his head.

Mr. Corning rose from the table. "You're welcome, Marshal, and you're welcome here anytime."

"Yes, anytime," Mrs. Corning confirmed.

Sam grabbed his hat and followed Jake outside. "Thanks for the pie and coffee, Mrs. Corning." Sam nodded with a dimpled smile and a wink, causing her to blush.

Jake muttered as they mounted up, "Careful, Deputy. That second piece of pie might come with a shotgun wedding."

CHAPTER 52

WHERE'S SISSY

As they mounted to leave the Cornings, a horse with a young rider came galloping up to the house. The horse skidded to a halt, throwing dirt and rocks as the boy slid from the saddle. He ran to Burt. "Have you seen Sissy? Is she here?"

"Why no, Raymond, what's wrong?"

"We can't find her. We've looked everywhere." His young voice was breathless and shaking. "Dad told me to come and see if she had wandered over here."

Molly and Burt exchanged fearful looks. "She's not here. We haven't seen her."

"When did she go missing?" Jake spoke from the back of his horse.

The young boy looked up as if noticing the two men on horseback for the first time. "This morning, we couldn't find her after the morning chores."

Jake and Sam dismounted and walked over to where Molly and Burt were trying to comfort the boy.

Jake put his hand on the boy's shoulder. "Don't worry, Raymond. We'll find her. I find things all the time, especially people. Tell me what she looks like."

"She's five years old and short—real short, and she has blonde hair and blue eyes, blue like yours."

"That helps, Raymond. How far is it to your place?"

He pointed in the direction of the rise. "Just over there."

Burt untied his bay. "It's about fifteen minutes. Let's go." Burt jumped onto the back of his horse, and the four rode toward the Johnson farm with Raymond and Burt in the lead. When they got to the house, Raymond's father ran to meet them, hoping they had found Sissy. He looked at Sam and Jake, surprised to see the two lawmen.

They all dismounted and approached Raymond's father, shaking hands. Jake put his hand on Mr. Johnson's shoulder, telling him they would find her. He asked what she looked like, where she liked to play, and where they had already looked. Jake never took his hand away from Mr. Johnson's shoulder.

Sam stood nearby, watching, knowing Jake was trying to use his unique inner sense. The minute it happened, Sam saw the change in Jake's face. It was like a match flaring in the dark. Jake knew where she was.

"You wouldn't happen to have an old well somewhere on the property?" Jake said, his head tilted to one side. "One you never use?"

"There's one out back aways, been dried up for years and all boarded over."

"Did you check there?"

"No, but like I said, it's all boarded up. There's no way she could get in there."

"I'm sure you're right, but it couldn't hurt to check. When I was about Raymond's age, my sister dropped her favorite doll down between the boards of an old well. We never knew how she managed it, but she got a rotten board pulled off and fell in."

Jake had barely stopped talking when Mr. Johnson, Burt, and Raymond took off running around the house. Sam looked at Jake with a smile. "Your kid sister, huh?"

Jake shrugged. "Seemed like a reasonable explanation."

It wasn't long before the three returned. Mr. Johnson came back carrying a muddy little girl in his arms, who was sobbing with big tears only a child could produce. They were pouring down her cheeks, falling onto the muddy doll clutched to her chest.

Jake walked over to Mr. Johnson and smiled down at Sissy. He spoke softly, taking her small hand in his, "Sissy is a sweet name. My name is Jake. Did you hurt yourself when you fell?"

"No, I kind of bounced and splashed, but I was scared." She hiccupped and sobbed. "It was dark, and there was a snake, and there were bugs and spiders."

Jake motioned to Sam. "See that big guy over there? That's Sam, and he's scared of spiders. He screams like a girl when he sees one."

Sissy giggled and looked at Sam with a teary smile. "He wouldn't have liked the well."

"You were very courageous. But from now on, you stay away from wells, okay?" Jake showed Mr. Johnson the peppermint sticks he had in his pocket. "Can she have these?"

Mr. Johnson nodded, tears of relief still dampening his eyes.

"Thank you, you're nice," Sissy sniffled, clutching the peppermint sticks in her small dirty hand. She snuggled against her father's chest.

"Mr. Johnson, you have a beautiful little girl."

"I don't know how I can ever thank you, Marshal," Mr. Johnson said, holding his young daughter in one arm, the other around his son's shoulders. "These two are all I care about in the whole world."

"I'm glad I could help. Next time you're in Grant's Crossing, stop by the marshal's office and let me know how Sissy is doing, or better yet, bring her and Raymond in for a visit."

Young Raymond's eyes lit up. "Can we, Dad, can we visit the marshal's office?"

"You bet we can, son. We'll plan on it."

Mr. Corning watched the lawmen disappear behind a stand of pine trees, scratching his head. He had seen another miracle. What was it the big guy said, something about "…wonderous strange?"

As they rode away from the Johnson farm, Jake turned to Sam. "We need to pay a visit to Sheriff Waters over in Sparkston."

"A hunch?"

"No. I was thinking about a telegram he sent a few weeks back? Some guys traveling through killed a farmer. All I remember is that one of them had an eyepatch. It could be worth checking out."

"I'd forgotten all about Sheriff Waters's telegram."

"And you're supposed to be the smart one?" Jake taunted, urging Drach forward.

Sam heeled Pal into a gallop to catch up. "Let's stop in town first. I want to check with Coop to see if he's removed buckshot from anyone lately."

"And I need to let Winnie know we won't be able to leave for the ranch today. She won't be happy, but she'll understand."

Sam chuckled. Winnie would not understand, and neither would Grant.

CHAPTER 53

A LOVE SPAT

When they returned to town, they went straight to Coop's to check on any buckshot wounds he might have recently treated and to see how Luke was doing.

Coop bent over his desk, a book open in front of him and a pen poised over his journal.

"How's Luke?" Jake asked.

"He walked this morning. He didn't go far, but he's determined."

"That's good news."

Coop wiped his hand across his face with a sigh. "The kids are on their way home with Matt's body. They'll bury him in the family cemetery tomorrow afternoon. Pastor Emil is doing the service."

Winnie came tearing in just as Coop finished speaking. "I saw your horses outside. Where have you been? It's late. We'll need to hurry to get mom and dad home before dark."

"I'm sorry, Winnie, but Sam and I are riding out to Sparkston to talk with Sheriff Waters."

He saw the anger flair in her green eyes and rushed on. "Two strangers passed through there a while back. They hurt a young dancehall girl and killed her boyfriend, and there's a fair chance it's related to what's happening here. It's a long ride, and we won't be back till late. Too late to leave for the ranch." Jake saw the storm approaching and quickly continued. "It's important, Win, and I am sorry to disappoint you and your dad. You understand, don't you?"

"Oh, I understand, all right. Don't I always? But I'm not happy about it." Jake thought he heard her whisper a swear word under her breath. "Dad isn't going to be happy either. He's been chomping at the bit to get home, but I'll try to make him understand how you can't be bothered."

"It's not a bother, Win. I love Grant and Lorene, but this is important. I wouldn't be going if I didn't think I had to."

Winnie smiled at him innocently, batting her eyelashes. "I know it isn't your fault, *sweetheart*. It never is."

Jake shrugged. She was angry, alright. She never called him sweetheart, and the tone of her voice left little doubt.

"When I explain to Dad why he isn't going home today, I will blame it on you. All of it."

"I wouldn't have it any other way, darling," Jake whispered in her ear, giving it a nibble and a kiss.

Infuriated, Winnie was about to tear into him, but Sam interrupted her fury. "We need to do this, Winnie."

Winnie turned on Sam. "You! You always take his side. You – you – jackass!"

Coop cleared his throat. "If there's going to be any violence or bloodletting, I'd prefer you didn't mess up my waiting room. .

Winnie spun around to face Coop, "What are you smiling at?"

Coop held his hands up in surrender as she looked from him to Sam and then to Jake. "You're all three stinking jackasses," she said, storming from Coop's office.

Sam couldn't help but comment, "Dang, but she sure can stir up a storm when she's mad, but then, she always could."

Coop chuckled and rubbed his stubbly chin. "You've got your hands full with that one, Jake."

"She'll cool off."

Sam smiled, knowing it would be a while and remembered why they came to see Coop. "Have you dug buckshot out of anyone lately?"

"No. No buckshot, but I dug some splinters out of a guy a while back. He told me his girlfriend's father chased him with a shotgun. He was mostly interested in getting some Laudanum for the pain."

"What did he look like?" Sam asked.

"Big guy, nearly as big as you, but a mean-looking son-of-a-gun. Why? What's up?"

"We want to talk to him. If you see him again, let one of us know," Jake said, as he and Sam turned to leave.

But before they could mount, they heard yelling, the crashing of tables, and breaking glass coming from the Schooner Saloon. They ran into the Schooner with guns drawn.

CHAPTER 54

TOUGHER THAN HE LOOKS

A barrel-shaped man in ragged clothes stood in the middle of the room holding a bloody knife in one hand and a pistol in the other. He nodded toward the man, groaning at his feet, but kept his gun pointed at the two lawmen. "He got what he deserved," he told the lawmen as he easily slid the bloody knife into the scabbard on his belt. "I told him I'd gut him like a pig if he didn't stop cheating. He didn't, and I did."

The stranger's eyes were intent as he watched the lawmen. "Holster them guns, boys. I'm walking out of here and riding away. You'll never see me again."

Jake's eyes were riveted on the man. "Not going to happen. Sam, go get Coop."

The man lost his concentration for a split second. It was all Jake needed. His bullet ripped into the stranger's shoulder, and he fell against the bar.

"You shot me," he hollered, clinging to the edge of the new bar. "You son-of-a-bitch. You shot me." He brought the gun up, thumbing back the hammer. Jake fired, the bullet ripping a hole in the man's chest.

"Micah? You hurt?" Sam hollered.

"No," Micah said, peeking over the bar. "Am I ever glad to see you! Is it over?"

Coop hurried in carrying his doctor's bag. "Heard the shots, thought someone might need me." He checked for a pulse on the stranger's neck. "Bones can have him," Coop said, turning his attention to the other man.

The man on the floor was lying on his side, curled into a fetal position. When Coop pushed him onto his back, his insides didn't follow. Coop retched and lost the contents of his stomach on the sawdust covered floor. The man moaned, and Coop turned away, throwing up again. "My God. How can this man still be alive?" Coop gagged.

Jake crouched beside the killer's body, pushing long, dirty locks of hair off his face. "Micah, you know either of these men?"

"Never saw him before, and I'm glad I won't be seeing him again." Micah shivered. "He sliced that guy down the middle."

Sam motioned to the other man on the floor. "How about him?"

"He's been here before, but I don't rightly know his name or where he's from. Dang, that's a horrible way to die."

Sam pulled Coop away from his gory task. "He's gone, Coop."

"I know, but..."

"There wasn't a thing you could have done for him. He was as good as dead when you got here."

Coop fell into a chair, staring at his bloody hands resting limply on his lap. Sam handed him a glass of whiskey. "Here, drink this."

Coop took the glass, his hand shaking. "Sam, I helped bring a new baby boy into this world this morning, rejoicing in life and how sweet it is. Now, this. That man was gutted like an animal, and for what? A stinking card game? What kind of a world is this?"

"I don't know what causes a man to snap like that," Sam said with a shake of his head. "Maybe he was too long alone out on the prairie, or maybe he was born mean."

Sam watched his disheartened friend empty the whiskey glass. "This is a hard country," Sam said. "But it gets better every day—thanks to you and men like you." Sam paused, wondering what else to say. "I've got a question for you, Coop. You were born into a soft life back in the States. If you could go back, would you want to?"

Coop had never thought about it. Would he want to go back? After what he'd seen and experienced, both good and bad. He knew the answer. "No, I wouldn't. It would seem meaningless. This is my life now, and I can't imagine anything else."

Jake looked at the poor man on the floor. Micah was right. That was a horrible way to die. "I'll get Bones to come and clean up, but in the meantime, Micah, you got a place where Coop can wash up? We don't want him returning to his office covered in blood and vomit."

Micah guided the doctor to a back room. "You can borrow some of my clothes. I think they'll fit you."

Sam stood at the batwing doors, keeping away the curious folks who had heard the shooting. They didn't need to see the bloody spectacle on the barroom floor.

Jake returned from the undertakers and stood by Sam. "Bones is on his way with the bone wagon. Guess these two will go to Pauper's Field unless he finds someone to identify them."

Micah and Coop came from the backroom, chatting. The color had returned to Coop's cheeks, and he no longer looked like death. "I'm fine now," he said, not looking at the two dead men as he pushed his way through the doors.

Bones stopped his buckboard in front of the Schooner and pushed through the crowd congregated in front of the saloon. Sam and Jake pushed back the gawkers and held the batwings open for him. He stopped to survey the carnage. "I got some canvas, and a bucket, and scoop in the buckboard. I'll be needing them. Horrible way to die," he said, shaking his head.

Jake stepped inside as Deputy Logan showed up. "Heard the shooting," Logan said. The sight in front of him brought him to a stop.

"Micah, we have to leave, but Logan will stay and wrap things up."

"I will?" Logan scowled at their backs as they left. "No problem, Marshal. Yeah, sure. Thanks for asking. Logan'll wrap things up. No need for a 'please' or 'would you be so kind as to...'"

CHAPTER 55

THE ROAD TO SPARKSTON

"It was nice what you said to Coop back there," Jake said to Sam as they rode toward Sparkston.

"You heard?"

"Yep, but I didn't want to interrupt and spoil the moment. You're good at saying the right things to people—you'd make a good politician.

"I've thought about it, but right now, I like what I'm doing." Halfway to Sparkston, they stopped in a shady spot to rest the horses and let them graze. A spring near the road provided a cool drink for the horses and the men. It had turned into a warm afternoon, and they enjoyed the shade provided by Aspens clustered along the stream.

Sam stretched out on the grass, his hands behind his head, studying the fluffy white clouds slowly moving across a bright blue sky. "Jake, how do you know the things you know, and what do you see—when you see things?"

"It's hard to describe. Sometimes, I just know things and when I have a vision, they're usually hazy and vague."

"You used to have terrible headaches with your—knowing and visions."

Those headaches used to be the first warning that something was wrong, but I've learned not to fight it. Now it just happens. I think the pain came from me trying to deny my abilities.

"When Sissy was in the well, did you see her?"

"I saw her and I could feel the dampness and smell the stagnant water and rotten wood. She was frightened by the closeness of the walls and all the slithery, crawling things. I knew her fear like it was my own. But it was only a flash. It was the same when Winnie was kidnapped. I got a brief view of her shackled to a chair and the cavern where she was being held. That was the first time I had a vision, and I can't help but think it was Winnie's fear, or maybe mine that triggered it that first time."

Jake sat cross-legged on the grass, rolling the stem of a yellow wildflower between his fingers, watching the bloom spin as he talked.

"Jake, you've had these hunches since you were a kid. You could find the lost key, go right to where Lorene had hidden the cookies, or sidestep a rattler. When did you start sensing that someone close to you is in trouble, "

"I always assume it's you, and it usually is. The first time was when you and Monty Dirksen blew up that chicken house I knew you were hurt or scared. Boy, I thought for sure Grant was going to tan your hide.

"He didn't have to. When Logan brought me home, the look of disappointment on Grant's face was enough."

"Lately, I know who's in trouble and what kind of mess they've gotten into."

"How about that day we were out at the Humphreys? You knew Grandma passed before Coop had a chance to tell us."

"I felt her leave. I looked up and there she was—winking at me. That was the first time I saw a spirit."

"Seen any since."

"A few here and there. There was a rag-tag little boy hanging out behind the general store. I asked around and found out the littler fella got crushed by a runaway freight wagon in the alley. I told him his mom was waiting for him, and it was alright to leave. I haven't seen him since."

"Your powers seem to be growing—triggered by events, like the chicken house blowing up and Winnie being kidnapped. We'd have never found Winnie if you hadn't had that vision. We need to be careful, Jake. That little sister thing you came up with at the Johnson's was an acceptable cover story, and I think they bought it, but I don't want to see you burn at the stake."

"I agree, but you're the only one who knows about my—abilities. Logan has his suspicions. He's seen me pull things out of thin air once too often, but he'd never say anything." Jake sighed loudly. "If only I could control it. I'm just thankful it kicked in this morning."

Sam nodded, "Mr. Johnson was so certain Sissy couldn't be in that well that I doubt he would ever have looked for her there."

"Sometimes I feel like a freak," Jake said, leaning back, his elbows straight, the palms of his hands flat on the cool green grass behind him. "This whole thing scares me—more than I want to admit."

"You're not a freak, Jake. You have a strange and unique talent, but you're no freak." Sam frowned. "Did your mom see dead people?"

"Not that she ever said."

"So, you have hunches and visions the same as your mom. Plus, you can see people who have passed. Your mom was a healer, I wonder if you are."

"I doubt it. I tried it a couple of times, but it didn't work. Of course, it only works sometimes. Mom cured Logan's earaches once a long time ago. He told me she whispered something in German and blew in his ears. I don't know what those words were."

"Maybe it doesn't have anything to do with the words."

"Could be."

"Well, next time I get hurt, I want you to blow in my ear and whisper sweet nothings to me in German." Sam laughed and gave Jake a silly cross-eyed smile.

Jake snorted. "I don't think so."

They sat without speaking for several minutes. Sam sighed; his forehead wrinkled with a frown. "Have you told Winnie about any of this? About your gift?"

"She knows about my hunches. They're kind of hard to hide but I haven't told her the rest. It never seems to be the right time. And I don't know what to say."

"Jake, you need to tell her before the wedding. I understand your dilemma, but she needs to know. She needs to know that your children could inherit this—thing you have."

"I know, Sam. But I can barely deal with it, what if she can't?"

"Hey, we're talking about Winnie. There isn't much she can't handle, and she's as crazy about you as you are about her. Seriously, Jake, you need to talk to Winnie and soon. Your weirdness doesn't bother me, but we're not getting married, and I won't be bearing your children. Winnie needs to know, Jake, but you don't dare tell anyone else."

CHAPTER 56

SPARKSTON

Sheriff Waters was surprised and pleased when he saw Sam and Jake riding into his town. He stood on the boardwalk in front of his office with his thumbs hooked in his gun belt and a big grin plastered on his face. "Didn't expect to see you two back so soon."

Jake and Sam dismounted, shaking hands with the sheriff. "Come on in, boys. We've always got coffee on the stove, and it's guaranteed hot and strong enough to float a horseshoe."

Sheriff Waters poured three cups and joined Sam and Jake at a small table in the middle of his office. "I don't want to stir up bad memories, but I sure was glad when you caught that madman who killed the Carsons. I would have enjoyed watching him swing, but if anyone had a right to shoot him, Marshal, it was you."

Waters was referring to a man who had violently killed his friends, the Carsons, as well as Jake's parents, and many others.

Jake frowned and unconsciously touched his badge. "I dogged his trail for a lot of years, thinking of how I'd end his life." Jake looked at Sheriff Waters. "When all was said and done, I wanted to bring him in. I didn't want to be an executioner."

"You're a good lawman, Jake." Trying to lighten the mood, he smiled and nodded toward Sam, adding, "You and Shorty here make a great team."

Sam smiled at Waters. Over the years, he had gotten used to the handle.

"So, I doubt this is a social call. What brings you boys out to my neck of the woods?"

"Your telegram about a farmer getting killed and one of your saloon girls getting roughed up. Can you tell us what happened?" Sam asked.

"Sure thing, Deputy," Sheriff Waters said, stirring his coffee. "Two men rode into town and registered at the hotel. They spent most of their time across the street at the Watering Hole, trying to soak up all the whiskey in town. The one guy wouldn't leave Gretchen alone. This is a small town, and everyone knew what Gretchen did for a living. She was loose with her love, but she's a nice girl. Heck, most of the men around here have contributed to her reputation, but she was settling down, gonna marry a farmer from out south of town."

Jake wondered at the sheriff's sad smile but said nothing.

"When the guy with the eyepatch got rough with Gretchen, some local men tried to stop him, but he tore through them like they was nothing. Heinie, the owner, came running over to get me, and I did my best to defuse the situation. The galoot with the red hair told the other man to settle down. If he hadn't stopped him, I think he'd have killed me. I hate to admit it, Marshal, but those men were way outta my league."

The Sheriff looked down at his hands, folded on the table. "The redhead told the man with the patch that they had a job to do and didn't need any trouble. He said the captain wouldn't be happy. After that, things settled down. They got a couple of bottles and went to the hotel. I thought they were down for the night and went home. I didn't know anything had happened until the next morning. At least one of them followed Gretchen home, roughed her up, and killed Joe. I reckon Joe was trying to defend her honor. I rounded up a posse, but we found no trail to follow. Those boys knew how to cover their tracks. That's when I sent you the telegram. Figured you should know."

Jake took a swig of coffee and grimaced, swallowing hard. He put the mug down on the table and pushed it aside. "How's Gretchen?"

"She'll be fine, given a bit of time. I tried to talk to her, but she was too upset. She's left town. Went to live with an aunt in some small town in Iowa."

After seeing Jake's response to the coffee, Sam ignored the cup in front of him. "We need to talk to Heinie. Is he working now?"

"If not, we can track him down. He never wanders far. Come on. I'll buy you a drink, and you can talk to him."

Heinie was drying glasses when they walked into the saloon. "Hi, Sheriff. What'll you have?"

Sheriff Waters bellied up to the bar. "Three whiskeys, Heinie." The sheriff jerked his thumb at the two men by his side. "I don't think you've met Marshal Jacobs and Deputy Watkins. They have some questions about those strangers who killed Joe and hurt Gretchen."

Heinie leaned across the bar and shook hands with Jake and Sam. "Pleased to meet you, Marshal, Deputy. It's an honor to shake hands with you. The Carsons were nice folks, and they'll be missed. Everyone around here was relieved when we heard you killed the monster. You did us all a favor."

Heinie poured three drinks and set the bottle on the bar.

Jake threw back his head, slamming down the whiskey, hoping it'd kill the lingering taste of the sheriff's bitter brew.

Sam hooked his boot over the brass foot rail and leaned his elbows on the bar. "How about a water chaser for this whiskey?"

Heinie poured two glasses of water from a pitcher under the bar, talking constantly. "It was terrible what they did. Gretchen is such a sweet gal. Those men were as bad as I've ever seen. Of course, around here, we don't usually have any trouble. But I'll bet you two have dealt with plenty of toughs like them."

Sam took a sip of whiskey and chugged the glass of water, listening to Heinie's prattle. When Heinie took a breath, Sam took advantage of the opportunity. "Can you describe the two men?"

"You bet I can. The man with the eyepatch was the meaner of the two. He was about my height but skinny as a rail. He had black hair and swarthy skin like he'd been in the sun too much. And he had a tattoo on his forearm that looked like some military thing. He tried to force Gretchen upstairs. Some local men tried to stop him, but he went through them like a hot knife through butter."

"What about the other guy?" Sam asked, nodding his thanks as Heinie poured him another glass of water.

"He had the reddest hair I've ever seen, like a clown's, and a face full of freckles. Except for that, he looked average enough. He tried to keep the one called Patch in line. From what I could tell, they'd been on the trail for quite a spell.

"From their talk, I figured they'd been in the army together, blue-bellies. They were on their way to meet someone on what he called *their mission.* The guy with the patch wasn't happy about coming this far north and said it had better be worth it. He would have continued running his mouth, but Red shut him up. He warned him again that the captain wouldn't be happy if they caused any commotion."

Heinie leaned his elbows on the bar in thought. "I heard bits and pieces of their conversation. The word blackmail came up, and the names Mort and Bob. Based on what I heard, I'd be worried if I was

Mort. I don't think those two plan on keeping him around for long. Sorry, but that's all I can remember."

Sam thanked Heinie for his help and downed the second glass of water.

The three lawmen were at the door when Heinie called out to them. "Hey, wait a minute, I remembered something else. It could be important. The guy with the red hair did complain about having to sleep in a warehouse full of rats."

"Thanks, Heinie," Jake nodded. "You've been very helpful."

The three lawmen walked out of the Watering Hole, squinting in the bright sunlight. Jake shook hands with Sheriff Waters. "Thanks for everything, Sheriff, except for that coffee of yours."

Chad Waters laughed. "It's an acquired taste, Marshal. Stop by anytime. Always glad to be of help to you city boys."

Jake sprang into his saddle, waiting for Sam to mount up. "Come on, Sam, let's go. It's a long ride back."

Sam scowled at Jake and shook hands with the sheriff. "Take care, Chad. We'll let you know what happens."

CHAPTER 57

A PINKERTON

Riding home from Sparkston, the horses were restless. "Let's let 'em run off some steam," Jake said. "Race you to that big oak tree just this side of Pony Creek."

"You're on."

Both horses were natural runners. As they raced down the road, the riders leaned forward, gripping tightly with their legs. Anyone who met them would have thought they were running for their lives.

The run calmed the horses, but there was considerable disagreement over who had won the race. "All right," Jake said graciously. "I will concede—to a tie."

Sam smiled, "I can live with that. Although I still think Pal won, if only by a whisker."

Jake's tone shifted. "Looks like we're dealing with at least three more men working with Mort and his friend. The two we found out about in Sparkston and the big guy with splinters."

"But there could be more," Sam said as a dozen grasshoppers flew from the brush at the edge of the road, spooking the horses. One lit with sticky feet on Sam's arm. Jake watched Sam pull it off with his thumb and forefinger, holding it upside-down until it spit tobacco juice.

"I used to love to catch these bugs and watch 'em spit," Sam said with a grin and tossed the insect to the side of the road. "It shouldn't be hard to check out the warehouses. There are only two that are empty. The others have too much activity for anyone to hide there."

"We're going to need more help, Sam."

"We can recruit Bear. He knows how to handle himself. And there's Clark. He's handy with a gun, and he's fought his way out of plenty of tight spots." Sam thought for a moment. "What about Nate Daniels? His military experience could prove an asset."

"We can depend on Bear and Clark," Jake said, "but I'm not sure about Daniels. He tends to keep to himself, and I've never seen him toting a gun."

The sun sat low in the west when Jake and Sam rode up to the marshal's office and dismounted. Logan came out to meet them. "There's someone inside waiting to talk to you. He's a Pinkerton, rode in this afternoon."

When they entered the office, a tall, lanky stranger stood to greet them. Reaching out his hand with a slight grimace, he introduced himself as Alexander Scott, Pinkerton detective.

Jake shook hands. "William Jacobs, U. S. Marshal, call me Jake."

"Deputy Watkins, Sam," Sam said, shaking hands with the Pinkerton.

"Call me Alex. Most do."

Jake scrutinized the man. Alex's gray eyes were sharp and alert and held a hint of danger. He looked to be in his forties and was over-dressed in a long, dark, go-to-church kind of coat. Beneath the coat, a crisp white shirt was accented by a black string tie. Jake doubted that the overly refined look was typical of all Pinkerton detectives.

The engraved pearl-handled revolver holstered at Alex's hip held Jake's gaze. This was definitely not a standard Pinkerton issue. "So, what's a Pinkerton doing in Grant's Crossing?" Jake asked.

Alex sat in an oak, curved-back chair in front of the marshal's desk. "I'm here on behalf of a Dallas, Texas, bank. It was robbed, and I'm tracking the men who did it."

Logan wiped his thumb and forefinger down his mustache and looked the man up and down. "You're a long way from Dallas, Mr. Scott."

"I am, for a fact, and it's Alex." He leaned casually back in his chair. "I've been tracking these men for well over a month. Always on their heels, but they're good at covering their tracks."

Jake remained standing, hooking his thumbs in his gun belt. "They must have gotten away with a lot of money for a Pinkerton to be involved."

Alex Scott sat up a little straighter. "They did get away with an enormous amount of money, Marshal, but they also killed seven people and kidnapped a young girl."

Jake sat down behind his desk, his chair squeaking in protest. "What happened? A shoot-out?"

"No shoot-out. I'll give you the short version. They knifed two of the guards when they entered the bank. One of the outlaws pistol-whipped a young boy, striking him hard enough that it nearly split his face in half and broke his neck. The boy's father charged the killer and was shot. The bank's president refused to open the safe. They killed his secretary and a customer trying to convince him to cooperate. He finally opened the safe when his own life was threatened. Once they had the money, they killed him. Cold-hearted murder. Then, they rode off with a young girl."

Alex stopped to steady his voice. "The town sheriff took a posse out for one day and then hung it up. Not an impressive display of courage on his part. Deputy Davis was the only one wanting to pursue the outlaws. He was worried about the girl and what might happen to her, but the sheriff said the trail was cold and gave him a different assignment. Atherton, the bank's owner, contacted Mr. Pinkerton as soon as he found out about the robbery. I got the assignment, and here I am."

Sam was leaning against the wall with his arms crossed, listening. "Still haven't said why you're here."

Alex continued presenting the facts. "I was in Fort Worth working a different case when I got the wire from Pinkerton himself. I was on their trail that same day, but I didn't find their campsite until late the next morning. Like I said, they know how to cover their tracks. I found the girl's body. They left her hanging over the trunk of a fallen tree."

Jake could have sworn he heard the slightest break in Alex's voice. "She was brutalized and beaten, and when they finished with her, they rode away. I wrapped her in my slicker and laid rocks on her. Later, I met a rider and asked him to let Deputy Davis know where she was."

The smell of fresh coffee filled the office, and Logan poured a cup for each of them. Alex accepted the battered, grey enamel cup. "Thanks. It's been a long day."

Sam pushed away from the wall. "And you still haven't told us why you're here in Grant's Crossing."

Alex slightly tipped his head, giving Sam a sideways look. "I got close to them in Kansas. They bushwhacked me north of Wichita and nearly killed me. I was laid up for two weeks. After that, they split up, and it took a while before I picked up their trail. Three went west and three to the north. I stuck with the three that headed north and caught up with them in Omaha. I killed one when they tried to back-shoot me, and the other two hightailed it. After that, I thought I'd lost them." Alex shifted in the chair with a wince and took a drink of coffee.

"But I got lucky. I stopped in Sioux Falls to telegraph the home office and report my progress. While I waited for an answer, I visited with the man behind the key. He'd never met a Pinkerton and was overly impressed. One thing led to another, and he said he remembered seeing two guys in town who matched the description I'd given in the telegram. He didn't remember the contents of the message, but he remembered it was sent to Grant's Crossing. That's why I'm here, Sam. I believe this is where they plan on meeting up.

"Also, you should know there's a nasty-tempered Texas Ranger trailing the outlaws, and he'll be showing up shortly. I left him to straighten out the killing in Omaha. That won't have improved his disposition any. Nebraska lawmen don't appreciate Texas Rangers in their territory."

Jake couldn't help but feel bad for the man. Alex was right. A Texas Ranger would not be welcome in Nebraska.

Jake looked at the Pinkerton, wondering if he could trust him. His gut told him he could, and it was seldom wrong. "Your bank robbers are here, Alex. I have a hunch they may be the ones causing the trouble we've been having."

"What kind of trouble?"

"Listen, Alex, I've got some things to take care of before we can sit down and get into this. If I value my life, I need to find my girl. I'm betting she's hotter than a branding iron right about now."

"A pretty gal with big green eyes and long brown hair?"

"Sounds like her."

Alex smiled at Jake and shook his head. "She flew in here minutes before you did, and she's hopping mad."

Jake let out a sharp breath. "I figured as much. Okay, Logan, find Clark and meet us at Kat's. Have her set us up in one of the back rooms with food and drinks. We all need to eat. There'll be seven of us, including her and Bear. Tell her they need to be there. Alex, you go with Logan. You'll like Kat's Place, and you'll like Kat. Sam, you're with me. I am not facing Winnie and Grant alone."

Sam followed Jake out the door, and they walked side by side to Murphy's Boarding House, dreading the tongue-lashing they knew awaited them.

Back in the marshal's office, Alex looked at Logan with an amused grin. "Is he always so bossy?"

Logan chuckled, "Always, except with Winnie, that's his girl. Around her, he's meek as a lamb."

Jake stopped at the steps leading up to Murphy's front door. "I'm sorry to disappoint Grant. I know he's going to be upset, but that trip to Sparkston was worth it. I was thinking we could make our move on the warehouse tomorrow after Winnie and her folks leave town and are out of harm's way."

"Winnie won't like being left out, and neither will Grant," Sam warned.

"I know, but I'm the law hereabouts."

Sam laughed as they climbed the steps to the boarding house. "I'm going to enjoy seeing how *I'm the law hereabouts* works out for you." Sam motioned to the door. "You go first. I got your back."

The door flew open as Jake reached for the handle. Winnie stood in the middle of the doorway, her arms crossed. "Nice of you to stop by."

"Aw, Win, come on. You know we couldn't help it. I'm sorry."

Winnie turned her blazing eyes on Sam. "You got anything to say?"

"I'm sorry too, Winnie, but it was Jake's decision to go to Sparkston. I'm just a deputy following orders."

Jake glared at his friend. "Thanks, Sam, way to have my back."

"Sparkston was your idea," Sam said with a grin.

Jake turned to Winnie, using the sweetest voice he could muster. "Winnie, if you would let us in, I'd like to talk to Grant and Lorene and tell them how sorry I am."

Winnie reluctantly moved away from the door, letting the two men into the boarding house, her arms crossed and a scowl scrunching her face. Jake slinked past Winnie and headed for Grant's room. He knocked on the door. "It's Jake and Sam."

Lorene answered, "Come in, boys."

Grant was propped up in bed reading *Frankenstein,* and Lorene sat in a chair near the window knitting. Jake and Sam went to her, each kissing her on the cheek as they'd done since they were youngsters. Grant looked up from his book. It was a look Jake and Sam were familiar with. Winnie stood in the doorway smiling in anticipation of the tongue-lashing the two men were about to receive.

Grant slapped his book shut. "Glad you could make it." The two men wilted into little boys under Grant's forceful scrutiny. "Something is going on. Winnie won't tell me a damned thing." He shifted his glare to his daughter, the smile immediately fading from her face.

He waved a piece of paper at them. "According to this list from Doctor Cooper, item number one is, don't - let - him - get - upset. Well, I'm plenty upset. I'm not an invalid, and I'm certainly not a fool. If someone doesn't tell me what's going on, I'm going to bust a gasket and three bone-headed ingrates to boot."

Jake looked at Sam. "Two more for supper."

Sam looked from Grant's stern face to Lorene's. "Seems so."

Jake cleared his throat. "We're meeting at Kat's for supper tonight to discuss what's happening and to decide what to do next. A Pinkerton agent came into town this afternoon, and he'll be…"

"I knew it," Grant bellowed, looking at his wife. "I told you, whatever's going on is something big."

He turned his attention back to Jake and Sam. "A Pinkerton! There's a Pinkerton in Grant's Crossing, and you two…" He looked at Winnie. "No, you three have been holding out on me. What's going on?"

Jake and Sam had inadvertently stepped back, trying to avoid Grant's burst of anger and piercing eyes. Grant was a father figure to them and the only man who could set them back on their heels.

"There have been—incidents," Jake said, backing slowly toward the door.

"Incidents? What are you talking about? What incidents?" Grant scowled.

"We'll go now and let you get dressed." Sam and Jake hurried from the room, leaving Grant still blustering.

CHAPTER 58

THE MEETING

Jake and Sam escorted Winnie and Lorene through the alley to the side door of Kat's Place so they could slip into the backroom unnoticed. Grant went through the front door, motioning for Clark, Logan, and Alex to follow him.

Kat and Morgan had drinks and glasses ready on the sideboard, and Tank was in the kitchen, preparing their food. The billiards tables had been shoved aside, and the gaming tables were pushed together in a horseshoe shape.

Kat smiled at the group coming through the door. "Grant and Lorene are joining us," Sam said.

Kat nodded, giving Sam a warm smile. "There's plenty of food and drink for everyone." Her words faded as her gaze was drawn to a tall, slender man who was last to enter the billiards room. She couldn't recall ever seeing the dark-haired stranger, and he wasn't the kind of man a woman would forget. When their eyes met, an unexpected thrill quickened her heart. There was something about the way he carried himself and the way he smiled at her that captured her attention entirely.

Everyone had something to drink, and Alex was introduced as they gathered around the table. Alex made it a point to sit beside Kat.

Bear entered from the saloon and joined them. He put a closed sign on the large oak door before pulling it shut, closing them off from the noise and clatter of the barroom. His gaze shifted to Kat, and he nodded. "Morgan and Ethan got the bar covered," Bear assured her. Kat returned his nod.

Jake addressed the nine people seated around the table. "Everyone here knows at least part of what's going on, but after today, we all need to lay our cards on the table. We need to understand what we're dealing with before we go any further."

"Everyone here but me knows what's going on," Grant grumbled, shooting Jake a hard-eyed glare, still upset at being excluded.

"Sorry, Grant, but we thought it best to keep all of this from you. We didn't want to worry you." Jake's voice was strained. "I doubt you're going to like some of what we found. Some old skeletons have tumbled out of the closet."

Logan whispered to Grant, "They know what we did and think it's related to what's been happening."

Grant's eyes darted to Logan. "It was bound to come out eventually, but how is it connected to whatever is going on?"

"Excuse my interruption, Mr. Grant," Alex said. "I'd like to go first by giving everyone a short version of the bank robbery and how I came to be here. Then, the marshal can follow up on what's been happening here in Grant's Crossing. Then, Mr. Grant, you and I will both be all caught up."

Alex recounted the chilling details of the deadly bank robbery in Dallas and how he had trailed the bandits to Grant's Crossing. Then Winnie recounted the tragic events at the Weisenberger ranch. Her eyes glistening with emotion as she told of Matt's death, and described the sabotage at the mine and mill. Logan's story followed. He kept it brief, telling of a fishing trip that turned into a lynching. Jake was last, giving them details of what had happened in Sparkston and the information that Heinie had provided on the possible location of the gang of killers.

As Jake finished speaking, there was a knock on the door. Tank and Morgan brought in bowls and platters of food, set them on the sideboard, and quickly left, returning to their duties.

After supper, Jake recapped over brandy. "We know these men are killers. We believe we are dealing with five or six men who are likely holed up in an empty warehouse. If they served in the army, as we suspect, we can't ignore the possibility that they might have recruited additional men. With their military background, they'll know how to handle their weapons and how to protect their camp."

"How many men do you have?" Grant said, still reeling from the news of Matthew's death and worried about his friend Gus.

"There's me, Sam, Logan, and now, Alex. We're the ones who've signed up for this kind of mess. Then there's Clark and Bear, who I can deputize if they're willing."

Bear nodded. "I'd be pleased to help. I've had some military experience."

Jake nodded to him.

Clark hurled a gob of tobacco juice neatly into a spittoon Kat had placed nearby and wiped his mouth. "You can count me in," he said with a cackle. "Imagine me a deputy marshal. You're scraping the bottom of the barrel, Jake."

"I've seen you handle a gun, and you have a cool head. That's what we need."

Alex had always worked alone, and all the talking was wearing thin. "When do we start the search? I don't want these robbers slipping away."

"They won't. They don't know we're on to them, and they haven't finished what they started."

Alex drummed the tip of his index finger on the table. "So, when do we start?" he said again, pressing for action.

Jake recognized Alex's impatience and shared it. "We start tonight, Alex. We're going to find Zeke and see if he's noticed strangers hanging around the warehouses. He might be able to pinpoint the search for us, and that's enough for now. I don't want to try to take them tonight. It's too dangerous in the dark. One of them could slip away, or we could end up shooting each other."

"This time of night, Zeke will be over at The Schooner," Kat volunteered, her eyes darting from Alex to Jake and back. Distracted by the man beside her, she found it difficult to follow the conversation.

Logan spoke up. "What's the plan for tomorrow?"

"Tomorrow, Winnie, Grant, and Lorene will leave to attend Matthew's service. Once they've left town, we'll make our move." Jake stopped, looking at Sam and Alex for anything additional.

Grant, who had been quiet until then, spoke up. "Wouldn't it be wiser to hit them early in the morning before they get a chance to wake and scatter? Maybe it'll all be over by the time we leave for the service, and we can tell Gus and Syl we got the guys who killed their son."

Logan answered Grant. "We considered it, but we wanted the three of you out of town in case something went wrong. These men are cold-blooded killers. We want you safe when we go after them, and you'll be protected at the ranch."

"I think I'd feel as safe here in town. I might even be able to help. I can stay outside the warehouse and…"

"Absolutely not." It was Alex who stopped Grant. "I told you what these men are capable of. We met briefly today, Mr. Grant. I would like the opportunity to get to know you. You will not be accompanying us tonight or tomorrow, and that's final."

Grant gave Alex the glare that had earlier melted Sam and Jake's mettle, but it had little effect on Alex.

"I like your idea about moving on them in the morning," Alex said. "And as for staying in town, that might not be a bad idea. We'll need to find you a secure location and see that you have weapons and plenty of ammunition." Alex backed off, suddenly realizing he had overstepped. "Sorry. Jake, Sam, I guess I'm used to being in charge. You approve of Grant's plan?"

"We're fine with it," Sam said with a nod and then looked to Winnie. "You?"

"I'm fine with it, too," Winnie said. "We know how to take care of ourselves."

There was a lengthy discussion about the best place for the Grants to ride out the storm. Grant remained silent, thinking about the various options. "Alex," he said, "what will they do to the folks at Murphy's Boarding house if they come looking for me and my family, and we're not there? They must know where I've been staying."

Alex looked at Grant and nodded. "It could get ugly."

"Well, that answers the question. If they come for us, we'll make our stand at the boarding house, but we need to get the residents and Mrs. Murphy out of there before anything happens. Logan, any concerns?"

"Yeah. How do we get everyone to leave?"

"A big rat problem," Grant said. "Send everyone to the hotel and have Lars put it on my bill."

Grant looked at Jake. "Your decision, Jake. Are you good with this?"

Jake took a deep breath and nodded, then turned to Logan. "Logan, you and Clark escort Grant and the ladies back to the boarding house and make the rat thing happen." Grant and Logan got up to leave, waiting for Lorene and Winnie.

Winnie put her arms around Jake's waist. "Don't get yourself killed, Jake. I couldn't stand to lose you. I wish there were something I could do to help."

"You're helping by staying safe. I don't want to worry about you." He gave her a hug and a lingering kiss. "Sam and I will be roosting at Murphy's tonight. I'll see you later."

"I'll wait up for you," Winnie whispered in his ear. The soft promise in her voice sent tingles of desire through his body, and he didn't want to leave.

Jake brushed his lips over hers and whispered, "I love you, Win." Then he turned to Alex. "Care to join Sam and me for a stroll to The Schooner?"

"No, you two can handle it. I'll stay here for a drink if Kat will join me."

Sam turned to Jake with a knowing wink. He doubted anyone had missed the lingering looks Kat and Alex had shared over supper. "Come on, Jake. Let's get out of here and find Zeke."

CHAPTER 59

ZEKE

Zeke stood just under five feet tall and was somewhat plump. He had long ago appointed himself the town handyman. He was a street cleaner, lantern-lighter, and chimney sweep and, at any given time, could be found replacing creaky boards in the boardwalk or carting horse apples off Bridge Street. He slept in a corner of Miller's Livery, and grateful business owners provided Zeke with free meals and drinks for his unsung services.

The lawmen found Zeke at the Schooner bellied up to the bar thanks to the shipping crate he was standing on. His blondish, red hair spiked wildly from under his grey wool, flat cap that he'd worn for as long as anyone could remember. The sleeves of his hand-me-down shirt were rolled up to his elbows, revealing a set of surprisingly muscular forearms.

"What'll it be, Marshals?" Micah Payne said, throwing a towel over his shoulder.

"Evening, Micah. Pour Zeke a drink."

Zeke hooked his thumbs in the leather suspenders that held up his baggy gray pants and nodded, thanking Jake.

A shiny new oak bar had only recently replaced the old one, which had been nothing more than wooden planks laid over empty beer barrels. Micah took pride in his new bar and the respectability it brought to the place. The selection of drinks was limited and there were no women, but the prices were reasonable, enticing cowboys to make it their watering hole. When a fella wanted nothing more than to get tangle-legged, this is where he'd come.

The smell of fresh sawdust and a chip out of Micah's new bar were the only reminders of the unpleasantness earlier in the day. Jake asked Micah for another pour and motioned Zeke to a table.

"Thanks for the drinks, Marshal. What can I help you with?" Zeke followed Jake and Sam to a nearby table.

"We do need your help, Zeke. You know more about what happens in this town than anyone else."

Zeke chuckled. "You would be surprised at some of the things I see and hear. Heck, I probably know more than that nosy old Lavinia Kent, but unlike her, I'm discreet." Zeke sipped at his glass of whiskey, making a slurping noise. "Folks are entitled to their privacy."

"You don't need to be discreet about this. Have you noticed any unusual activity around any of the warehouses?" Sam asked.

Zeke puckered his lips and rolled his eyes, thinking. "Funny you should ask. About three weeks ago, I saw two strangers wandering around inspecting the warehouse north of Bridge Road. The one just over the bridge. I thought maybe they was lookin' to buy it."

"Did you see what they looked like?"

"Nah, I didn't get close enough to see their faces, and I didn't pay them much mind. I'm not snoopy or nothin' like that. I like to keep my nose clean, but I can't help it if I see things."

Sam and Jake got up to leave. "Thanks, Zeke."

Zeke saluted the marshal with his empty glass.

Sam and Jake nodded to Micah as they left. "Guess we know where to start," Sam said.

A lone gunshot came from The Dirty Mug two doors up from the Schooner. Jake and Sam sprinted toward the sound.

A man ran from the Dirty Mug, brandishing a pistol. He stumbled, trying to keep his balance. Jake hollered for him to stop and drop the gun. The man turned to face him, gun hand hanging at his side. Jake recognized him as a young farmer who came to town occasionally to drink away his woes. He'd never caused any real trouble before. He'd been involved in a bar fight once, but it had been a free-for-all. All issues had been amicably resolved, with everyone bellied up to the bar and sharing a bottle.

Jake doubted that Jim meant him any harm, but a man with a gun in his hand had to be considered dangerous. Jake stood, ready to draw if he had to. "Drop the gun, Jim. I don't want to shoot you. What happened? I know you, Jim. You're not the kind of man who wants to hurt anyone. Drop the gun and tell me what happened." Jake kept talking, giving Sam time to maneuver behind the farmer and disarm him.

"Marshal Jacobs?" Jim said, trying to focus. "I'm sorry, Marshal. I didn't mean to kill him, but he wouldn't leave me alone. He slapped me—spit in my face—and told me I was too yellow to fight. Said I smelled like hogs and that I should go back to the farm and belly up to the trough with 'em." Jim gulped back a sob. "I only wanted to scare him, Marshal. That's all. I just wanted him to leave me alone."

"Jim, I understand you were angry, but I won't tell you again—drop the gun."

The owner of the Dirty Mug, Albert Archambeau, came out onto the boardwalk, "Marshal, the man's alive. Jim didn't even hit him. Just scared him bad enough that he pissed himself and fainted."

"Albie says you didn't kill the guy, Jim. You didn't even hurt him. It's over. Put down the gun."

Sam came up quietly from behind Jim, wrenching the gun from his hand. Jim swung around drunkenly, winding up to throw a punch, but he ended up on the ground.

"Sorry, Jim, I didn't mean to wallop you like that, but I wasn't expecting you to come at me." Sam looked at Jake. "I didn't mean to hurt him."

Jim had his hand on his face, wiggling his jaw. He looked up at Sam. "That hurt," he said, slowly toppling onto his side.

"Come on, Sam. He'll be fine. Let's get him over to the jail and let him sleep it off."

Jake and Sam grabbed Jim under his arms and hauled him to jail, his boot toes dragging through the dirt. They put him in one of the cells and stopped long enough to grab three rifles from the gun rack before heading across the street to Kat's.

CHAPTER 60

SMITTEN

Alex and Kat were alone in the backroom. Alex observed Kat with evident interest, and Kat returned his scrutiny, her eyes bright with curiosity and amusement.

Alex broke the silence. "I haven't cared much for any of the women I've known. They served a purpose. It sounds harsh, but that's how it's been." He paused, weighing his words. "But there is something about you." He smiled, leaning forward. "You intrigue me, Kat, and I want to get to know you."

"I'd like that," Kat said, melting into his intense gray eyes.

"I can promise you one thing, Kat. Regardless of what does or doesn't happen between us, I will always be honest with you."

"That's a big promise, Alex. One that could be hard to keep."

He smiled at her. "I always keep my promises, Kat, always. I'll stop by for a drink later tonight, and I'd be honored if you would allow me to escort you to supper tomorrow evening. Providing, of course, everything goes according to our plan."

"Then, I hope to see you later this evening, and yes, I would be pleased to join you for supper."

"There is one thing, Kat," he said, rising from his chair and offering her his hand. He pulled her to her feet and into his arms. "I said I would always be honest with you, and right now, I want to kiss you."

"I wouldn't object," she said with a smile.

His lips were warm and soft, but the kiss was interrupted when Sam and Jake barreled through the door.

"What the blazes, Kat?" Sam said, tossing a rifle to Alex with a grin. "We can't leave you alone for a minute."

Jake was about to say something when Kat and Alex said in unison, "Mind your own business."

Jake checked his rifle. "Alex, if you're on board, we know where to start."

Sam quickly went over the configuration of the warehouse where they figured they'd find the outlaws. "The warehouse has doors on three sides. The door on the west, facing the river, and the one facing Mill Road on the east are tall and wide for loading and unloading of freight. The third door on the south side, that's where we'll go in. It's a smaller door that leads into a room previously used as an office."

Alex studied Sam with a darkening frown. "Those shoulders of yours will make a hell of a target out there, Deputy."

Sam laughed. "I may not be as fast or agile as Jake, but I manage. Come on, let's go see if we can find our outlaws."

The three men removed their spurs, checked their guns, and headed out the door with rifles in hand. Their goal was to verify they had the right building and to find out how many men they would face come morning.

They strolled along quietly, not wanting to draw any attention— Sam on one side of the street and Jake and Alex on the other. Their senses heightened as they neared the warehouse. A sliver of a moon in a clear, star-filled sky provided a perfect evening.

The sounds of Grant's Crossing seemed to echo in the still night air. The faint sound of piano music came from one of the saloons and the breaking of a glass followed by hoots and uproarious laughter from another. Nearer to the bridge, the sounds of rushing water, bullfrogs, and a chorus of chirping crickets took over.

They silently crossed the wooden bridge and slipped into the dark work-yard. Sam motioned toward a pile of broken barrels surrounded by weeds. Hunched over, they ran for cover and waited. There were no warning shouts and no gunfire. No one had seen them.

Jake peeked through the weeds. A faint, flickering glow emanated from the two windows on either side of the office door. "Looks like someone's home," Jake said, scanning the work yard and warehouse. The dim moonlight created shadows that blurred the building's edges, making the outer walls seem strangely out of kilter. The building was eerily foreboding and loomed larger than Jake knew it to be.

Sam removed his hat and peered over the pile of barrels. The wide-open area stretching from their vantage point to the building was littered with empty and broken barrels. A couple of the barrels might provide some cover, but the loose staves and hoops scattered about would make it difficult to approach quietly, and if anyone were watching, it would be almost impossible to cross the yard undetected. Sam ducked down. "It'll be tough to get across the yard if anyone's watching."

Jake leaned his rifle against one of the broken barrels and handed his hat to Sam. "Well, let's hope no one's watching. Cover me."

He sprinted across the open area, skillfully dodging the debris. He flattened himself against the building and took a deep breath, trying to calm his racing heart. The occasional sound of men's muffled voices told him someone was inside the office.

He moved slowly toward the window and peered in. The window was covered with a thin layer of paper, making it difficult for him to see anything. However, a small tear was enough for him to see inside. Four men were sitting around a desk playing cards, and six cots were set up on one side of the room. Two of the men were missing. The big blond wasn't there. Was he hiding somewhere, or was he watching the building? If so, he was a poor guard.

Slowly pulling away from the window, he turned back to Sam and Alex. He worried that one of the missing men might be patrolling. He looked from side to side and saw Sam give him an all clear sign. He flew across the open area, rejoining the other two men, crouching behind the barrels.

"They're in there. Six cots, but I only saw four men. The big blond guy isn't with them."

Sam handed Jake his hat. "I doubt he's on guard duty. We haven't seen anyone patrolling the area. Think we can take them now?"

Alex whispered, "Not without knowing where the other two men are. That sixth cot could be for the man I shot, or there could be someone else we don't know about."

The adrenalin rush was wearing off, and Jake's heartbeat and breathing were returning to normal. He brushed the hair from his forehead before dropping his hat into place. "Let's go see if we can find our missing guys. The saloons on Washington Street are close by. That's where we'll start."

CHAPTER 61

A WATER TROUGH

They left as quietly and cautiously as they'd come. Once across the bridge, Sam motioned for Alex to follow them as they turned down Washington Street to the Bear Paw, Scarlet Slipper, and Night Owl Saloons.

They stopped at the Bear Paw. Alex warned them about the blond man they were looking for. "He's mean and fast. He's proficient with a knife and gun and can beat you to a bloody pulp with his fists. He's not the smartest, but he is the most dangerous. If it comes to it, don't give him an edge. Shoot to kill."

Alex looked at Jake. "I respect that I'm in your territory, but two lawmen walking in could be very distracting. Everyone knows you. Me, I'm just another barfly. I'm the logical choice."

Jake looked at Sam and let out a sharp sigh. "You want the front or back door, Deputy?"

"I think I would prefer the front door, Marshal."

All right, I'll take the back." Give me a minute to get in place." Jake rounded the corner of the building and disappeared into the dark alleyway.

While they waited, Sam told Alex what to expect when he got inside. "There are five rooms at the rear of the saloon. The first one on the right is the office and storage room, and the others are for the ladies. If your man isn't at the bar, that's where he could be."

Alex smiled. "Good to know."

"Guess you've done this kind of thing before."

"Yeah, but getting up-front information is always helpful."

Alex leaned his rifle against the front of the building where Sam was standing, pushed his hat back on his head, loosened his tie, and put a goofy grin on his face before entering the saloon.

Jake was outside the backdoor. He didn't like it. He trusted Alex, but he hated not knowing what was happening. He wanted to go in, but he waited.

Sam listened intently, trying to hear what was being said. He heard Alex order a drink at the bar and offer to buy a drink for the man next to him. Sam could hear the murmuring and laughter of the two men as they became barroom buddies. Then Alex excused himself, and the next thing Sam heard was Alex saying in a drippingly sweet voice, "Oh my, if you ain't the loveliest lady I ever did see?"

Then, a woman's coarse laughter. "Honey, I ain't no lady, but I'd be pleased to show you that I am all woman. Come with me, handsome. I have a cozy, private place where we can get naughty."

Sam heard the guy at the bar holler. "Way to go, Al. Barkeep, send a bottle back with them. I'm buying."

She grabbed Alex's hand and the bottle and pulled him through the curtains and into a hallway. As Sam had described, there were rooms on either side. Passing by the second set of doors, he heard the frenzied squeaking of bedsprings and the practiced, almost believable moans of an experienced whore pleasing her customer. Was it the big blond?

Sam hadn't heard anything for some time and began to worry. Then, the loud pop of a gunshot echoed from the building, followed by the sound of someone running hard for the front door. Sam stepped to the middle of the doorway as the man barreled out of the saloon, knocking them both into the street.

It took a moment before either of them caught their breath. The man's gun had been knocked from his hand and was out of reach under the boardwalk. Unarmed, he stood facing Sam head-on with an intensity that sent a shiver down Sam's spine. Sam watched in disbelief as the man threw back his head and released a primal howl. He wondered if the howl was meant to intimidate him or if the man was simply insane. Or maybe it was the whiskey.

Sam's expression was intense as he surveyed the blond's hulking frame, wondering if he had any neck at all. He had no doubt that he could whip the man, but it wouldn't be easy, and win or lose, it was gonna hurt. Sam stood with his back to the boardwalk, his muscles tensed, as he waited for the blond's next move.

The man was drunk, and when he charged like a bull with his head down, it was easy for Sam to sidestep. The man ran headlong into the side of a concrete water trough, knocking him unconscious. Sam heard applause and looked over his shoulder to see Jake and Alex standing on the boardwalk.

Alex laughed, "I thought we were gonna see a real knockdown, drag-out fight."

"Turned out easier than I thought it would. Either of you got cuffs?" The man at his feet groaned as Sam cuffed his meaty hands behind him. "I wasn't looking forward to fighting this beast. I felt my ribs busting just looking at him."

Jake nudged Alex. "We'd have come to your rescue if you were in serious trouble. Honest."

"Sure you would. Come on, let's get this moose locked up. I don't want to fight him again."

"It wasn't much of a fight," Jake said, needling Sam.

Sam threw a bucket of water in his prisoner's face, thinking he might do the same for Jake. The large man woke sputtering and angry. He became even more enraged when he realized he was handcuffed. He managed to get on his feet and immediately wobbled toward Sam. Sam put his hands out, signaling him to stop. "Look, I can knock you out again, or you can go quietly. It's your decision, but I don't wanna have to carry you."

Ready to attack, the blond looked the lawman over. "You're a big bastard," he said, thinking the deputy would be hard to take down. He struggled momentarily with the handcuffs, then shrugged. "I'll go peaceful, but there ain't a jail built that can hold me. I'll be gone by morning."

When they got to the jail, Jake released Jim and handed him his gun with a warning. "Attempted murder is a serious crime, Jim. You're lucky no one was hurt, and no one is pressing charges. Don't let this happen again."

"I'm sorry, Marshal, I don't know what came over me. It won't happen again. I swear."

Jake watched him hurry up the street to his horse. He was relieved that the man Jim shot at had decided not to press charges. But what man wanted to go into a courtroom and tell the judge, jury, and spectators that he pissed himself and passed out.

Once Jim was gone, Sam took his prisoner into the cellblock and locked him up. The blond had remained quiet and cooperative. Now, he slumped onto the cot along the backside of the cell, his head in his hands. "What the hell did you hit me with?" he moaned.

Sam looked at him with a grin. "A water trough."

The prisoner looked up with a frown. "Oh."

Sam left the cellblock, locking the heavy wooden door behind him. "Alex, what's his name? I can't remember anyone ever saying."

"His name's Bob Jenkins, at least that's what his army papers say. I believe it to be his real name."

Jake turned to Sam with a wink and a nod in Alex's direction. "I could use a drink, Sam. How about you, Alex? Kat won't be there. She told me earlier she was meeting some guy at the Mug for a late supper."

Sam knew Jake was baiting Alex, and Alex, still unfamiliar with his new friends, took the bait.

"She said she'd wait for me this evening." Alex frowned, obviously puzzled. "I didn't figure her to be the double-dealing kind of woman."

"Alex," Sam said, casually hanging his arm around his shoulders. "You are far too easy, but I doubt your gullibility will last. So, you'll have to forgive us if we make the most of it while we can."

Alex understood immediately. He looked from one to the other with a smile. "Why are we still standing here? I've got a thirst and a hankering to see the lovely lady across the street."

Walking out the door, Sam chuckled. "Alex, what about the gal down at the Bear Paw? You two seemed to be hitting it off, and here you are two-timing her already?"

"Sam, you have no idea. That was one strong woman, and she was ever so determined to get me out of my pants. I barely escaped. Although, if she hadn't yanked me back into her room, I'd be getting fitted for a coffin right about now. That shot wouldn't have missed."

CHAPTER 62

PRISONER ESCAPES

Kat's Place was busy, but their regular table near the door was unoccupied. They sat down, and Kat approached with a bottle and glasses. Alex stood, politely holding a chair for her. Sam and Jake exchanged glances and rolled their eyes. Kat shot them a look, conveying an unspoken warning to keep their comments to themselves.

"What?" both said, acting confused and innocent.

"It's nice to have a man with manners around," Kat said to Alex. She turned to Sam and Jake, "You two have no manners, and there are times when you act like naughty, pimple-faced little boys."

"Ouch," they said in unison, looking at one another in disbelief.

The two men perplexed Alex. He had checked them out, and according to all reports, they were serious-minded lawmen, considered dangerous by some. Perhaps living in a peaceful place like Grant's Crossing gave them the freedom to let down when there wasn't a crisis. He had never known anything like that in his lifetime, and he'd never had a close friend. Perhaps this banter was a normal thing among friends.

Alex tuned back into the conversation, wondering what he'd missed. He smiled at Kat, who was trying to glare at the two lawmen but couldn't hide her smile. "It's not that you two grow on folks, Sam. It's that we've learned to tolerate you."

"Kat, that's downright hurtful," Sam laughed.

"I heard you got one of your robbers," Kat said.

Sam nodded. "We marched him right down the middle of Bridge Street and into the jail for everyone to see."

Some grumblings at the back of the saloon caught her attention. "Excuse me. I have some customers who need attending to."

Alex started to get up to follow her, but Jake touched his arm. "She can handle it, and she wouldn't appreciate your interference." Alex nodded and sat back down. "We offer assistance only when it gets ugly."

"Besides, we need to talk about our prisoner," Sam said. "Good news is, we have Bob in jail, one less to deal with in the morning. The bad news is that when they realize Bob is missing, it won't take them long to find out we have him locked up. They might try to break him out, or they may…"

"… skedaddle." Jake finished for him. "Sam's right. All they need to do is hit any saloon in town, and they'll find out we've got their man in jail. News spreads fast around here."

"What if we use the rumor mill to our advantage?" Alex suggested. "We let it be known that Bob escaped before we had a chance to question him. If the gang members think he got away without spilling his guts, they won't worry about him. Based on his history, they'll assume he's hiding from the law, whoring it up in some saloon."

"It's worth a try. Let's get Kat in on it," Jake said, standing and waving to Kat to join them.

Kat weaved her way back in their direction, greeting customers, and calling most of them by name. Alex rose from the table, holding her chair, giving Sam and Jake a fierce look of warning.

"Kat, we could use your help."

"You two always need something. What is it this time, Marshal?" she said, pretending to be put out.

"We need to let everyone think our prisoner has escaped, and we need to get that information out as quickly as possible." Jake motioned to Alex. "The Pinkerton here suggested we use the town's rumor mill to spread the news."

"If you want to spread a rumor, your timing is perfect. See that guy in the black bowler hat by the roulette wheel?"

"Yeah. It's Ira Terrel. I've seen him around."

"When it comes to carrying a tale, he's worse than Zeke, Steven, and snoopy old Lavinia Kent all rolled together."

Kat smiled wickedly at Alex. "I have a great idea. These two country bumpkins," she said, motioning to Jake and Sam, "were the ones responsible for allowing your prisoner to escape."

Sam and Jake both sat up straighter. "What?"

"I don't like that idea," Sam said, glaring at Kat.

"I do," Alex said with a smile.

Kat smiled innocently. "Alex, I suggest you nail their hides to the barn door. Make it memorable and loud enough for Ira and everyone else to hear. Ira will be eager to spread the news of the tongue-lashing, and the story will spread through Grant's Crossing like a prairie wildfire."

Getting up from the table, she leaned over and whispered in Alex's ear, "Make it good, Alex." Then, she went to the far end of the bar to await his performance.

Alex stood as he dramatically berated Sam and Jake, calling them brainless yokels and small-town idiots—morons who were the most incompetent lawmen he had ever worked with. Because of their inept bird-brained blundering, they had allowed the prisoner to escape before he could be questioned.

He regally strutted to where Kat stood and apologized for causing such a commotion in her establishment. He winked at Kat and whispered, "How'd I do?" The look on her face told him she approved.

He strode purposefully from Kat's Place. To maintain their ruse, he would have to conduct a mock search for the escaped prisoner.

Jake and Sam watched Alex leave, the batwings flapping noisily behind him. "He did a bang-up job of tanning our hides," Sam said, glaring at Kat.

"And at Kat's request," Jake said, scowling at the smiling woman.

"Alex sounded a lot like Grant that day when we pulled all the hay out of the barn and piled it up so we could jump from the loft." Sam's voice was nostalgic as he continued. "He used some of those same words to describe us."

"Don't think I've seen Grant any angrier," Jake said. "I thought he was going to bust a seam, and we'd be getting our backsides tanned for sure, but Grant never did whale on us for any of our antics."

"We did some stupid things. Didn't we?" Sam said with a smile. "Thankfully, Grant wasn't around to witness most of them."

Jake eyed his empty beer glass, then looked across the table at Sam. "The last stupid thing we did together was to put on these badges."

"Hey, that's all on you, Jake. That was your decision."

"You didn't have to pin on that deputy's badge," Jake said, a grin spreading across his face.

Sam bowed slightly in Jake's direction with mock seriousness. "You are my liege. Where you go, I follow."

"Quit using those big words," Jake shot back, amusement as well as annoyance evident in his words. "Besides, I'm not what you said,"

Jake sneered, getting to his feet. "Come on. We've spent enough time licking our wounds."

Jake pushed through the batwing doors. "Let's go help that uppity, Pinkerton," Jake said for all to hear. He didn't have to turn around to know Kat was enjoying herself at their expense.

CHAPTER 63

TEXAS RANGER MARK HILL

Sam and Jake caught up with Alex at The Schooner. Alex had already introduced himself to Zeke, who was perched on his shipping crate at the bar. Alex was explaining to Zeke and the barkeeper how the incompetent peace officers of Grant's Crossing had let his prisoner escape. Zeke, enthralled by the presence of a Pinkerton Detective, was soaking up every word.

Jake scowled at Alex. "Let's head for the Bent Ear next and talk to Malcolm Gardner, the owner. It's usually crowded this time of night," Jake said. "Lots of folks to hear your tale of woe."

As they pushed open the doors to the Bent Ear, they ran into Ira Terrel, who was leaving. Ira looked sheepish as he skittered past them with a nod.

Alex got everyone's attention and asked if they'd seen a big, tall, blond man. One man pointed to Sam and hollered, "Right there beside you, mister." Laughter filled the air as Alex, Jake, and Sam exchanged glances and left.

Turning the corner onto Bridge Street, they saw a short, stocky man trying the door to the marshal's office. "That's Mark Hill, the Texas Ranger I told you about," Alex said, halting in front of the newspaper office. "I'm serious when I say you can't take Hill lightly. He's a treacherous coyote who'll go to any lengths to get his man and doesn't care who gets hurt. If you get in his way, he'd like as not shoot you."

"Sounds like you've worked with him before?" Jake said.

"A couple of times. He's tough, and I can respect that, but after his wife and daughters were murdered, he changed. Two brothers who had sworn vengeance on him for killing their father went after his family. Hill was the one who found them. After that, he didn't care what happened to him or anyone else."

"Did they ever find the men who killed his family?" Jake hoped they had. He clearly remembered the rage and hatred he had felt toward the man who killed his parents and thought he could understand how Hill must have felt.

"He hunted them down and brought them back over their saddles. He claimed self-defense, and no one questioned it. I've always felt bad for him and cut him some slack, but mind my words; don't turn your back on him."

Jake approached Ranger Hill with his hand outstretched. "I'm William Jacobs, U.S. Marshal. Call me Jake."

Mark sneered, ignoring Jake's hand. "I see you're keeping questionable company," he said, nodding toward Alex. "I suppose he's told you all about me."

"Let's all go inside where we can talk. We need to bring you up to speed," Jake said.

Sam stepped up to the door. "Logan, it's me, Sam. Open up."

Logan unbarred the door and let the men in. Jake introduced Logan to an uninterested Mark Hill.

"I stopped for a drink when I got into town, and I understand you caught one of the men, then let him escape. Nice job, Alex," the ranger chuffed.

"We didn't exactly let him escape," Alex explained. "We want the remaining men to think he did. Jenkins is locked up in the back, and we know where the rest of the men are hiding."

"Why aren't you going after them?"

"We're waiting for morning," Alex replied, cutting a threatening look at Hill.

Jake looked at Mark Hill, studying him. Mark saw the undisguised assessment and growled, "Well, if you got something to say, Slim, spit it out."

"Name's Jake. We have a plan, and if you want, we'll include you when we go after them. Otherwise, you can join Bob in a cell. I'm not going to let you mess this up."

Texas Ranger Mark Hill doubled over with laughter. "You think you can put me in a cell? Lock me up?"

"I know I can," Jake said, leaning slightly toward the ranger, piercing him with ice-blue eyes. "You're in my territory, and you have no authority here. You either play nice and do as I say or go to jail."

"I won't go to jail here or anywhere else. Who do you think you're dealing with? I'm a Texas Ranger."

"I don't care who or what you are. I'll shoot you if I have to. My future wife is one of the people who's in danger, and I will kill you or anyone else who gets in my way. That's a promise." Jake paused, returning the ranger's glare. "If you agree to do things my way, we can work together. Otherwise, we might as well have it out here and now."

"You are a feisty one, aren't you, Slim?" Mark Hill laughed. "When are you gettin' hitched?"

"Two weeks."

"Congratulations," Mark said, evaluating Jake and the situation. It appeared the young lawman had a gizzard full of grit and two capable deputies backing him up. Alex was a wild card but seemed to be in cahoots with the local law. It was three against one. For the time being, he would play nice. "Okay, Jake, I'll do it your way."

"We can use another man," Jake said, nodding but doubted Hill's sincerity. "We'll meet at Kat's before dawn and be in position before sunrise."

"Where are they hiding?" Ranger Hill asked innocently.

"We'll fill you in tomorrow morning at Kat's." Jake didn't trust Hill and hoped he wouldn't try anything stupid between now and morning.

Hill shrugged. "See you at Kat's then." He left to check in at the hotel but planned to return to the marshal's office later to get his hands on Bob. He'd make him spill his guts. Bob would tell him where the gang was hiding, and he'd take them back home to dance at the end of a Texas rope.

Sam, Alex, Jake, and Logan stood on the boardwalk, watching the ranger saunter down the street toward the hotel. Jake pushed back his hat. "Not a personable sort, is he?"

"Not by a long shot, and I don't believe he'll cooperate." Alex let out a long breath, rubbing his hand across his chest. "It's been a long day and dawn comes early. I've got a room at the Carmichael calling my name."

"Go get a good night's sleep," Jake said. "We've got this."

"I haven't had a soft bed under my backside since Fort Worth."

"Did you meet Sally?" Jake asked.

"I did. A real looker and quite the flirt."

"Be sure to lock your door," Jake said.

"And hitch a chair under the doorknob just to be safe," Sam added. "Sally has a master key."

Alex waved goodbye to them as he headed out the door.

Sam volunteered for the first watch. "I'm not sleepy, but don't forget to have someone relieve me."

Jake nodded. "I'll be back. Be careful, Sam. I wouldn't be surprised if our new friend from Texas tried something."

Sam stood in the doorway, watching Jake and Logan cross Bridge Street heading to the boarding house. He smiled when he saw Alex disappear into Kat's Place.

CHAPTER 64

WAITING UP

All the boarders had been moved to the Carmichael Hotel to avoid the rat problem, and the boarding house was quiet. Logan said goodnight and went to his room, and Jake found Winnie asleep on the parlor sofa.

"Waiting up for me?" he whispered, kissing her cheek.

In the dim light, Jake could see the flicker of a smile.

"You're late," she whispered, looking up at him with sleep-filled eyes.

Jake sat down beside her. "I know I am, but we caught one of the robbers. One less to worry about tomorrow."

"What happened?" She said, sitting up.

"We found him down at the Bear Paw, Sam knocked him out, and we hauled him off to jail. Then, the Texas Ranger who Alex told us about showed up. He's a dandy, and I'm afraid he'll try to mess things up."

"Why would he?"

"He wants to take the robbers back to Texas to hang. Alex says he's a loose cannon, and after meeting him, I'd agree—I've got a bad feeling about him."

"Please be careful, Jake."

"I will," Jake said, leaning in for a kiss that Winnie eagerly accepted.

"Carry me off to bed," Winnie sighed, her voice thick with longing.

"Where is it?" Jake asked, raising an eyebrow.

"Upstairs," Winnie answered, her voice low and inviting.

Jake chuckled softly and whispered close to her ear, "Not likely, woman." The warmth of his breath on her neck sent a shiver down her spine, and the air between them was charged with an undeniable tension.

"Well, fine then," Winnie huffed, playfully shoving him away and getting up from the sofa. "You need to get some sleep, anyway. Tomorrow will come early. Mrs. Murphy fixed rooms for you and Sam. They're at the top of the stairs, to the right, second and third doors."

She cast a sultry look over her shoulder, issuing a playful challenge that was loaded with promise. "My room is the second door to the left if you're interested."

Jake smiled and took Winnie's hands, pulling her into his arms. "Oh, I'm interested," he said, capturing her lips in a kiss that left no doubt as to how he felt. "I want you, Win. I don't want to say good-night. I'd even carry you up the stairs, but..."

"I know," Winnie sighed, "It's not the time or the place."

Jake followed her up the stairs, the carpet muting their footsteps. Pausing at her door, he leaned down, his lips once again finding hers. The kiss lingered. "Soon, Win. We'll be together soon," he said, gently nudging her toward the door.

With a frustrated sigh, he watched as she closed the door behind her. Hearing the click of the latch, he reluctantly went to his own room.

CHAPTER 65

BAD RANGER

Jake's head had barely touched the pillow when a jolt of knowing brought him bolt upright. Sam was in trouble. He was hurt. Jake pulled on his boots, grabbed his gun belt from the bedpost, and ran hell-bent down the stairs and out the front door. Rounding the corner onto Bridge Street, he saw a shadowy figure limping down the boardwalk and into the alley. He didn't have to look twice to know it was Hill.

He wanted to give chase, but first, he had to find Sam. Jake flew through the open door and into the office. Sam was leaning against the desk for support, blood running down his arm and dripping from the desk, forming a pool at his feet.

"Evening, Marshal," Sam said with a strained smile. "I had a visit from our new friend, Hill."

Jake pulled the kerchief from around his neck and wrapped it tightly above Sam's wound. "How bad is it?"

"It won't stop bleeding." Sam winced as he tried to move his arm. "I tried to tie it off with my kerchief but couldn't get enough leverage. It hurts like hellfire."

"Hold still," Jake said, tying the scarf around Sam's arm and pulling it tighter.

"What's wrong with that butt-faced jackass?" Sam grimaced, sucking in a big breath.

"I saw him limping into the alley. Why'd you let him in?"

"I shouldn't have, but he seemed agreeable until I let my guard down. Then he turned into a wild man." Sam turned slightly with a muffled groan, picking up a bloody knife from the desktop. "I got his knife away from him before he could kill me. I couldn't get to my gun, but I cut a chunk out of his leg."

Jake was seething. Texas Ranger or not, he wouldn't get away with this, not in his territory.

Sam saw the fury building in his friend. "Jake, cool off and don't give me that look. I know what you're thinking, but we need to stay calm and make tomorrow's plan work. And in case you hadn't noticed, I'm bleeding like a stuck pig. Get Coop. I'll stay here with Bob." Sam weaved to the side, his face turned ashen as he tried to steady himself against the desk.

"Let me see your arm," Jake said, frowning as he reached for Sam's arm.

"What are you doing?" Sam protested, pulling away. "Go get Coop before I bleed to death."

"Maybe I can heal it. It never worked before, but let me try. We talked about this once, remember? You said if you were ever hurt…"

"Yeah, yeah, I remember."

Sam started to object, but Jake insisted. "Shut up, Deputy, and hold still. That's an order." Unsure of what to do, Jake closed his eyes and covered the wound with his hands. An odd tingling sensation ran up and down his arms as he focused on closing the wound. It wasn't an unpleasant feeling—almost euphoric.

Sam jerked his arm away. "Jake, stop. Whatever you're doing, stop it."

Jake opened his eyes. "No, Sam, I think it's working."

"It's working, all right, Jake. Look at your arm, and your face is pale as rice."

Jake looked at the blood on his left shirt sleeve, then at Sam. "What the…" He rolled up his sleeve and found a narrow gash oozing blood.

The gash on Sam's arm was visible, but the bleeding had stopped. Sam removed the scarf Jake had used as a tourniquet. "Jake, are you okay?"

"I feel a bit off-kilter, but it didn't hurt until I looked at it. Before that, it was a prickly feeling. You shouldn't have stopped me." Jake reached for Sam's arm. "Let me try again. I think I can heal it completely."

Sam pulled away. "Maybe you can, but now you're bleeding and I'm not. Let's not push it."

"Sam?"

"No, Jake. I'm not bleeding, and that's enough." Sam moved his arm and found there was hardly any pain.

Jake glanced back at his arm. He was no longer bleeding and only a thin red line remained.

"Guess you are a healer, but how did that cut get on your arm?"

"I don't know." Jake inspected Sam's wound. "It still looks a little weepy. Maybe it could use a few stitches. I'll get Coop. Unless…"

"No, go get Coop."

Jake left to get Doc Cooper out of bed, leaving Sam alone. Sam thought about Jake's new ability. He had been Jake's friend for many years, and even he found it difficult to rationalize all the strange things Jake could do. He didn't understand any of it but accepted it as part of Jake's unique being. He feared others would be less accepting or understanding.

Coop arrived and stitched Sam's arm, saying he had never seen such an odd wound. As he snapped his black bag shut, he noticed the blood on Jake's shirt, "You want me to look at your arm?"

Jake looked at his shirtsleeve in mock surprise. "I'm not hurt. I must have brushed against Sam when I tried to stop the bleeding."

Coop eyed them suspiciously and headed for the door. "You boys have to stop playing so rough."

Jake followed Coop to the door and slapped him on the back. "It keeps you in business, Doc."

Coop hated being called Doc. He scowled at Jake, grumbling as he left, "It might be in your best interest to be nicer to the man who holds your life in his hands on a fairly regular basis."

Jake called after him in a quiet voice. "Coop, you should get up early tomorrow morning. Your services may be required."

Coop waved without turning around.

Jake went behind his desk and slumped into his chair.

"You alright?"

"Yep," Jake said, brushing the lock of hair from his forehead. I've tried before but it's never worked. When Grant was shot, I thought maybe…I tried, I really tried, but it didn't work. If only I knew how to control it."

"Maybe there is no controlling it."

"Maybe. Why don't you get cleaned up and stretch out for a couple of hours? I'll take the watch. I doubt I can sleep now anyway."

CHAPTER 66

IT'S TIME

Jake catnapped in his chair throughout the rest of the night. He got up around four-thirty, stretched, and rolled his shoulders. "Sam, you awake?"

"Am now," Sam said, sitting up effortlessly and pulling on his boots. "Is there time for coffee?"

"Sure. How's your arm this morning?"

"Not even stiff," Sam said, getting up and moving to the washstand. He pulled up his sleeve to inspect the wound and found it completely healed. "You didn't do that healing thing again last night while I was asleep, did you?"

"No, why?"

"Take a look. There's barely a mark. Even the stitches disappeared. I can't let Coop see this. It would be hard to explain. And you know how he is. He'll want to take a look if only to admire his handy work."

Jake shrugged. "He wouldn't believe us if we did tell him the truth."

Sam poured water from the pitcher into the bowl on the washstand and splashed his face. "I still can't believe I let that evil little skunk get the drop on me last night."

"Wonder where he limped off to?"

"He knows we're meeting at Kat's," Sam said, toweling his face dry.

Jake grabbed two deputy badges from the top drawer of his desk and started toward the door with Sam close behind. They stopped at the door, both realizing they hadn't arranged for anyone to watch their prisoner.

Jake let out a sigh. "After last night, we can't leave Bob unguarded."

"What about Winnie?"

"That isn't the worst idea I've ever heard. She is a crack shot, and she'll be all right if she keeps the doors locked and barred. Plus, I know she'd like to be involved."

"Grant won't want to see Winnie alone with no backup. He and Lorene will both want to be included. We won't be gone for long, but Hill would have plenty of time to make a dumb play like he did last night."

"Still, they should be fine if they keep things locked up—like you should have," Jake said pointedly. "Hill wants Bob alive, and unless he's watching us, he won't know who's inside the jail guarding him. One way or another, I have a feeling Hill is gonna be a hair in our butter."

"While you talk to Winnie, I'm going to Kat's for coffee."

Jake sprinted across the dark street. The sun was still well below the horizon, giving him enough time to get his new guards settled before heading to Kat's.

When he got to the boarding house, the doors were locked. He knocked lightly, hoping Logan and Clark were up and fixing to head out. He heard footsteps stop on the other side of the door and called out softly, "It's Jake."

Winnie opened the door, smiling. "I heard you run out last night, and I couldn't get back to sleep. I got up and got dressed.

"We heard the commotion, too," Grant said as he and Lorene joined them in the foyer. "What happened?

Jake gave them a brief version of the confrontation with the ranger and asked them to guard the prisoner. Grant and Lorene hurried to their room to get dressed, and Jake took advantage of the moment to steal a kiss. Winnie moved gently against him, reaching her arms around his neck.

"Break it up, kids," Logan said, coming around the corner. "Thought we were supposed to meet you at Kat's?"

Before Jake could answer, Clark came around the corner from the kitchen and joined them. "Yeah, what's going on?"

Jake told them about Sam's run-in with the Texas Ranger. Leaving out any reference to Sam's injury and the healing. As he finished, Grant and Lorene returned to the parlor, eager to go.

Jake hurried Winnie, Grant, and Lorene to the jail, giving them firm instructions to keep the doors locked and barred. Although Jake didn't expect any trouble, he had misgivings about leaving them with the prisoner. It might be a bad decision, but it was too late to do anything about it.

Logan, Clark, and Jake entered Kat's Place and were joined by Sam, Alex, and Bear. There were six overnight drinkers and a dancer who had fallen asleep face down on a table. Art was busy cleaning and wiping down bottles behind the bar while Ethan and Riley were working as swampers at the back of the saloon, talking and laughing.

Jake spoke quietly, handing Bear and Clark each a badge. "We need to hurry. Bear, you'll take the east door on Mill Road. Clark, I want you on the west side by the river. Sam, Alex, and I will go in the office door, and Logan, that's where I want you…watching that door."

"Seems simple enough," Alex said.

"Let's hope it works." Jake had Bear and Clark raise their right hands, then shrugged. "Consider yourselves sworn in and be careful. I don't want anyone getting hurt."

Clark smiled like a kid in a candy store as he polished the badge on his shirt. "I'm a U.S. Deputy Marshal, and I got the badge to prove it. Yessiree, United States Deputy Marshal Clark," he said with reverence, then laughed. "No one back at the ranch is gonna believe me." He cackled and spat into one of the brass spittoons.

CHAPTER 67

RATS ATTACK

The deserted warehouse Cyrus had picked proved to be a perfect hideout. It was small, close to town, and there were lots of doors if escape was necessary. The horses were stabled inside the warehouse where they couldn't be seen, and cots for the men were set up in what had once served as an office.

Red sat on the edge of his cot, listening to the rustling and squeaking sounds of unidentified vermin coming from all around him. Sweat trickled down his face and back, and the smell of putrid flesh, moldy wood, and dead fish hung in the air, making his stomach lurch. He wished he could open a window or one of the big doors for fresh air but knew Cyrus wouldn't allow it. "This place gives me the willies," he said, wiping sweat from his eyes and trying to think of something besides rats.

Patch, Mort, and Cyrus were seated around a table playing poker. There were sounds of grumbling and laughter when Cyrus won a big pot. Patch stood to stretch and yawn.

"Hey, Red, why don't you sit in? We could use some fresh blood, and it'll give you something to do besides frettin' about them rats." Patch chuckled.

"Not tonight, Patch." Red doubted he could concentrate on the game.

Wiping sweat from his forehead and scratching his belly, Patch pulled a bottle of whiskey from his saddlebag. "Wonder what happened to Bob?"

Cyrus looked up from dealing. "He's in one of the saloons poking some working girl."

Patch smirked as he picked up his cards. "I hope it's a gal he's getting himself into and not trouble."

Red had no doubt where Bob was. He was in some saloon, drinking and looking for trouble. Bob was trouble on the hoof and getting more quarrelsome and unruly by the day. Red had been surprised when Cyrus let Bob go out, but Bob could do no wrong in Cyrus' eyes. It worried Red. There was a pile of money at stake here, enough that Red figured he'd leave the gang and retire when this job was finished.

Red took a long drink and settled back on his cot. He hated rats and tried not to listen to the scratching noises in the walls and ceiling. He fell asleep thinking the rats were displeased that their domain had been invaded. Close to dawn, he woke with a start. Droves of rats had organized, row after row of them, like troops in the field. They were attacking from all sides. They swarmed through the warehouse and up the side of his cot. Hundreds of them, thousands, smothering him, eating him alive.

Arms and legs flailing, he jumped from his cot, frantically beating the horde of nightmare rats from his body and face. Soaked in sweat, his heart racing, he panted for breath as the nightmare of ravenous rats began to recede. But the blind terror was still with him, lingering with a realness that shook his senses.

Cyrus raised from his cot with a frown. "What is it, Red?"

"Nothing. I need some air, that's all. Sorry, I woke you." Red sucked in a calming breath and grabbed his bag of tobacco with shaking hands.

Standing at the end of the dock, peeing into the river, Red thought it a minor miracle he hadn't peed himself back in the warehouse. The chilled morning breeze flattened his sweaty shirt against his back, and the coolness was refreshing. Only wisps of the nightmare remained. He shivered, remembering the part where the rats were feasting on his eyeballs and personals.

He sighed with relief as he emptied his bladder. He buttoned his britches and held out his hands. They were steady enough now to roll a cigarette, and he needed one bad. He lit up, pulling the smoke deep into his lungs and expelling it with a satisfied sigh. He finished his cigarette, sucking the crackling fire close to his fingers, then flicked the stub of a butt into the river. He couldn't wait to get out of this place.

CHAPTER 68

WAREHOUSE

They walked three abreast down the middle of the street. It was still dark, but a faint glow along the horizon told them they needed to keep moving. Alex walked between Jake and Sam, followed by Clark, Logan, and Bear. Anticipation and adrenaline heightened their senses.

The sound of their footsteps and the sharp chirping of the early-morning birds seemed louder than usual in the predawn stillness. This time of morning separated the loud noises of nighttime merrymakers from peaceful daytime activities.

"I haven't seen a thing of Hill," Alex said, "but I can't help but think he's following us. That's what I would do."

"He might not be able to," Sam said. "His leg has to be hurting and stiffer than a hickory stick."

"Maybe," Alex replied, his eyes shifting from side to side.

They quietly crossed the bridge over Mill River and snuck into the warehouse yard one by one, zigzagging to avoid the metal rims and loose barrel staves that littered the ground. The pile of empty barrels in the corner didn't provide enough cover for six men, but they would soon be on the move.

Nudging Jake's arm, Bear motioned to his left, whispering, "There's someone on the end of the dock."

Six men held their breath, not moving. Their eyes searched intently through the darkness, looking for additional movement, but there was none. Jake motioned for Clark and Bear to head to their assigned positions. They moved quickly and silently. Jake waited, giving them time to get into position, then hunched over, he started toward the building. Alex and Sam followed close behind. Logan hung back where he'd have a clear view of the office door.

Red had decided to stay outside. It was near dawn, and he didn't want to go back inside the warehouse. He stood at the end of the dock, trying to forget about the hoard of ravenous rats. He breathed in the cool air, calmer now. He caught a glimpse of movement from the corner of his eye. He stood perfectly still. If it was a varmint, it was a big one. Was he awake, or was this part of his nightmare? Was an oversized rat ready to pounce on him?

He watched silently, his eyes straining in the dark. He saw another shadowy movement, but there wasn't enough light to tell what he'd seen. It could be a bear or maybe a tumbleweed. Or had someone found their hiding place? He watched unblinking until his eyes began to hurt. Then he saw a man dart out from behind a pile of barrels, then another, and another. Three men were running for the office door. Red drew, firing as he ran down the dock, trying to warn the others and to make it to dry land and cover. Trying to aim and run was impossible, but he was a dead man if he didn't move fast.

At the sound of gunfire, the lawmen hit the ground. Sam's hat flew from his head as he flattened himself, hugging the ground. The bullet had barely missed him.

Almost to solid ground, Red heard the heavy sound of a rifle shot close by and felt a sharp sting in his side. The flare from Red's gun had given Clark a perfect target. Red stumbled forward, skidding on his face to a painful stop. *Oh, rats*, he thought, choking out a laugh.

Clark ran to Red's side and grabbed his gun. "You're clear on the west," he yelled to the others.

Jake, Sam, and Alex got up and ran for the office door, slamming in with guns drawn, but the men were gone. They crashed through the office and into the warehouse. Patch was about to mount his horse when gunshots erupted on the east side of the warehouse.

"Go on," Alex yelled. "I'll take care of this one," he said, pulling Patch down and taking his weapon. Patch tried to throw a punch, but Alex blocked it. One well-placed fist put Patch on the ground. Alex cuffed him to a steel ring in the wall and followed Jake and Sam.

Bear ran into the warehouse to meet them. "Two of them got away. Sorry, Jake, I couldn't stop them. They came at me too fast and knocked me down. But I got off two shots. Hit one of them with a solid body shot."

Jake gave Bear a once-over. "You okay?"

"I'm fine. But my pride and my Sunday face are smarting."

The four men headed for the riverside door to check on Clark. Standing over the man he'd shot, he turned to them, "He's in bad shape. We need to get him to Coop's."

Jake turned to ask Logan to go for the doctor as a buckboard rattled into the yard with Coop perched on the seat.

"You told me to be prepared for anything this morning, and when I saw you marching down the street, I followed along. Been waiting up the road. When I heard the shots, I figured that was my cue."

"Two casualties, Coop." Jake stooped to pick up Sam's hat. "That red-head over there and Sam's hat"

"Looks like the hat's a goner. Did he part your hair any?" Coop said to Sam.

"Close."

"Can't help your hat none, but let's see what I can do for this guy." Bending over to inspect his patient, he talked to Sam. "How's the arm?"

"Oh, it's, uh, fine. It hurts a bit, but you did a great job fixing it up." Sam stumbled over his words. He hadn't expected the question.

Coop looked up at Sam with one eyebrow raised, almost to his hairline. "Uh-huh," he said, shaking his head. "Grab his feet, Sam, and help me get him in the wagon."

The sun was up and shining bright by the time they finished searching the warehouse and surrounding area for the bank money or any sign of where Mort and Cyrus might be headed. Jake, Alex, and Sam paused on the bridge, leaning their elbows on the railing. Looking back at the warehouse, they couldn't help but wonder if they had missed something.

"I don't know about Cyrus," Sam said, staring at the water beneath the bridge. "But Mort is like a cockroach. He'll be back."

Alex turned, leaning his back against the railing. "I doubt the gang members are loyal to Mort, but they've ridden with Cyrus for a long time. It could be a task getting them to talk."

The three men left the bridge and caught up with the others who were escorting the handcuffed Patch to jail. The parade caused the town's early risers and business owners to leave what they were doing and gather on the boardwalk to watch. They wondered what had happened and what the man in handcuffs had done. Quimby Beck stood among the onlookers. He smiled, envisioning his front-page headline.

CHAPTER 69

TEXAS BARBEQUE

When they got to the jail with their prisoners, Winnie, Grant, and Lorene came out with the missing Texas Ranger at gunpoint. His right arm sported a bloody tourniquet, his hair and clothes were singed, and his face was covered with soot.

Grant shoved his rifle into the ranger's back, looking pleased. "He tried to burn us out, but Winnie shot him before he could throw the lantern. The only thing he set on fire was himself. He's got some nasty burns. Didn't know what you would want to do with him."

Sam stepped forward and unleashed a knockout blow to the ranger's jaw, that sent him to the ground. He beat Jake to it by only seconds. Sam yanked Hill to his feet and was about to swing again when he felt a hand on his shoulder.

"He's law, Sam, don't kill him." But Alex's voice did not sound all that convincing.

"You're lucky, Ranger—real lucky," Sam started to release him but hesitated. "I don't like it when someone goes after my family," Sam clouted Hill with another devastating blow that dropped him to the ground.

Logan had locked up Patch and stayed in the front office. Sam and Jake were leaning against the hitching rail with Winnie tucked between them, and Alex sat on the bench in front of the building, his legs stretched out in front of him, his ankles crossed. Clark excused himself and left for the livery to hitch up the carriage for the trip to Matt's service.

Bear tossed his deputy badge to Jake. "Sorry, I couldn't stop those two."

"You did fine, Bear. I'm relieved you didn't get hurt."

Bear nodded and gave the ranger, still out cold, a sharp kick in the ribs before heading to Kat's Place.

Grant leaned against the doorframe. "You got any ideas where Mort and that Cyrus fellow got off to?"

Jake looked back toward the warehouse. "Bear put a chunk of lead in one of them. I doubt they'll get too far."

"You going to question your prisoners to see if they know where they were headed?" Grant asked.

"I think I'll let Alex handle that."

Pushing away from the doorframe, Grant was about to protest, but Jake waved him off. "He's followed them all the way from Texas. Besides, Sam and I can always take a turn if needed."

Grant settled back. He trusted Jake's decision and understood the logic, but he didn't know Alex, and there was a lot at stake.

Alex read the mistrust on Grant's face. "Mr. Grant, I've been with Pinkerton since I was old enough to spit. I know not everyone has a high opinion of Pinkerton detectives, and I can't tell you that I have always been on the right side of things, but today I am. I'll find out what we need to know. I don't care where they hang, as long as they hang."

Grant gave Alex a half-nod. "If Jake trusts you, so do I."

Clark pulled up in the carriage. "Come on folks, I'll give you a ride to Murphy's so we can get your gear before heading to the service."

Jake kissed Winnie before she left and lingered with Alex and Sam in the warm midmorning sunshine. There was a comfortable silence between them.

"Bring Patch out. He's the only one I'll need to question," Alex said as he stood

Alex followed Jake into the office, which seemed dark after the bright sunshine outside. Jake brought Patch out of the cell block, and he and Logan joined Sam outside, leaving Patch and Alex alone.

Jake glanced in Sam's direction. "Any idea where Mort might have gone?"

Sam pushed back his ruined hat. "No, but he's close. He still has a score to settle with me."

Texas Ranger Mark Hill had been hanging halfway off the board-walk and into the street since Sam had dropped him there. He moaned and tried to move, falling into the street with a grunt. "What the hell hit me?"

"I did," Sam answered. "What were you thinking? Someone could have gotten hurt."

The ranger looked at the burns on his arms and chest and gingerly touched his jaw. "Someone did get hurt," he grunted.

"The doctor's office is up the street on the right." Sam held no pity for the man.

The ranger managed to get to his feet and hobbled up the street, groaning in pain.

Jake nodded toward the ranger. "Logan, you mind following him up to Coop's. We don't want Coop getting bushwhacked by him or that redhead."

Logan scowled. "Sure, Jake. I can't imagine anything that would please me more than spending time with that no-good Texas…" Logan's voice faded as he tromped up the street.

Alex came out of the marshal's office with a smug smile. "I know where they plan to meet up. They have fresh horses and food at a farm east of town. The money is there, too."

Jake frowned. "You didn't hurt him, did you?"

"Nothing that won't heal in a day or two."

Sam pushed away from the hitching rail, looking at Jake. "I'll go with Alex. You go to the service and get our family home safe. If Logan wants to attend Matt's service, I'll get Bear to stand watch for him."

Jake wanted to protest, but his gut told him Sam was right. He needed to be at the service to protect their family. "Well, that's how we'll do it, then."

Sam smiled at Alex. "I love it when he lets me be the boss. It happens so seldom."

"I have noticed he tends to be a bit of a boss bag," Alex said, surprising himself. He'd never been in one place long enough to make friends or find a girl. He never thought he needed them, but he liked knowing these two had his back and that a woman was waiting for him.

CHAPTER 70

DON'T MESS WITH KAT

Sam and Alex led their horses out of the livery and watched Jake ride toward the boarding house to join the group going to Matt's graveside service. "Let's stop at Coop's to see how Red is doing and then the General Store for provisions," Sam said. "You haven't met Steven and Charlie yet. They own the general store. Then we'll make a stop at Kat's."

Alex sneered. "For someone who doesn't drink, you spend an inordinate amount of time at Kat's."

"I like the company," Sam said pointedly. "And besides, that's the best place to find out what's happening in Grant's Crossing."

Sam knocked and opened the door to Coop's office. Logan nodded from where he lounged in the corner. He motioned to a door at the back of the room, answering the question before Sam asked. "No news. Coop is still working on him."

Jenny heard voices and popped her head out of the back room. "Coop is having trouble getting to the bullet. He says it's a tough one. He doesn't know if he can save him, and you know how he can get. Even over a bad man." Jenny started to close the door but stopped, "Oh, and speaking of bad men, I sewed up that ranger and took care of his burns. He left without a by your leave. Not the most pleasant man I've ever met." She shut the door with a firm hand.

Sam nodded to Logan. "If you want to go to Matt's service. I'll find someone to cover for you. If you hurry, you can catch them at Murphy's."

"Thanks, Sam. I'll be on my way."

Sam and Alex left the doctor's office and went to the general store. "All we have to do is tell Steven or Charlie how many days we'll be gone. They know how we travel, and they'll pack what we need. Any idea how long we'll be on the trail?"

"The farm isn't too far away. If we're lucky enough to catch them there, we'll be back tonight in plenty of time for my supper date with Kat. I would hate to stand her up." He paused with a grimace. "But just in case, let's plan for three days."

When they entered, the storekeepers were busy. Alex idly looked at the store's odds and ends, trying to hide his impatience. The trail was getting cold. Charlie finished ringing up a sale and turned to the two men.

"What's up, Deputy?

Sam introduced Alex and told Charlie they needed provisions for a three-day trip.

Charlie grunted, bending to retrieve two war bags from under the counter. "I heard you had some excitement down at the warehouse earlier. See you came away in one piece, except for your hat. I got some new ones in yesterday, Sam."

Steven came over to be introduced to Alex, then hurried away to help another customer. Charlie handed saddle bags and bed rolls to each man. "This should get you by."

Alex waved as they left the store. He looked at Sam as he tied down his bedroll. "I need to let Kat know I might not be back tonight."

"No problem. I need to talk to Bear."

Bear agreed to check on Coop, and he and Sam watched as Alex spoke with Kat, holding her hands in his. He kissed her cheek before turning to walk back to where Sam waited.

Sam frowned. "If you hurt her, I'll kill you, and when I'm done killing you, Jake will kill you, and then Grant will kill you."

"Put me on that list," Bear growled.

"I want to woo her, not hurt her. In fact, I have a feeling she could put a major hurt on me."

"Well, Romeo, if you want to be back in time for supper with your girl, we better stop jawing and get moving. Where are we headed?"

CHAPTER 71

DON'T BE LATE

Jake rode Drach toward the boarding house to meet up with his family for the trip to the Weisenbergers. He wanted to be on Cyrus and Mort's trail, but he knew Sam and Alex could handle them.

He dismounted to help Clark with Lorene and Grant's luggage, but Thad Barnes came charging up to the carriage. "Marshal," Thad gasped, out of breath. "Mal sent me to find you. There's a rough-looking man at the Bent Ear asking questions about you."

With a frown, Jake pulled Winnie aside. "Sorry, Winnie, but I need to find out what's going on at the Bent Ear. It won't take long. Wait for me."

Winnie glared at him. It seemed there was always something. "Make it fast, or we'll be late to Matt's service."

"I will, I promise."

Jake pushed through the swinging doors of the saloon. The air was heavy with the smell of stale beer, smoke, and other unidentifiable odors. The sounds of laughter and a dozen conversations morphed into an eerie silence as Jake stepped inside.

Jake went to the bar and ordered a beer. Mal leaned over the counter, his expression changing from laid-back to serious. He paused, then subtly flicked his gaze in the direction of an unsavory-looking polecat seated at a nearby table. "I think you've got the worst kind of trouble looking for you," he murmured quietly so as not to be heard. "Say's his name is Drake Jefferies. He's a…"

"I know who he is."

Jake didn't turn around or acknowledge the man's presence. "How long has he been there?"

"Half an hour or so," Mal said, risking a glance over his shoulder. "You want me to send for Sam?"

"No, he's busy. I'll handle this," Jake said, his voice low and confident.

The polecat was watching Jake, and with a self-satisfied smirk, he stood and sauntered to the bar. He positioned himself only a few feet away from Jake. The two men between them moved away to distance themselves from what looked like the beginnings of a violent confrontation.

"I hear you got yourself quite a reputation," the man said, a flicker of menace in his eyes. "And I'm planning to call you on it."

Jake didn't flinch or glance his way. He raised the beer mug to his mouth with his left hand while his right hand hovered inches above the grip of his gun.

"I ain't worried about your reputation, Jacobs. It's nothing. Taking down Fitz, an old worn-out has-been, and Douglas Marten, an inexperienced wannabe don't mean squat in my book."

Jake stared straight ahead, sipping his beer.

"I'm talking to you, Marshal," the man said in a friendly voice. "You're too young to be hard of hearing, so that means you're ignoring me. And that's just downright rude. Didn't your mother teach you any better?"

Jake bristled at the mention of his mother, but he didn't flinch. Turning to face the man, Jake smiled as their eyes met. "Sorry, mister. You're right. That was rude of me. Let me buy you a drink?"

"Oh, can't do that. It just don't feel right somehow, lettin' a dead man buy the drinks. Especially when I'm the one who's gonna kill him. Nice meetin' you, Jacobs," he said with a smile and turned to leave.

"Hey, mister," Jake hollered after him, "what's your name?"

"Don't matter none—you ain't gonna be around long enough to use it."

Jake shrugged. "I just thought it'd be nice to put it on your marker."

"You're a funny one, Jacobs. Real funny." The man pushed through the batwings, his laughter carrying back into the saloon.

The patrons who had backed away from the bar and nearby tables now returned to their drinking, all eyes on Jake.

"Thanks, Mal," Jake said, finishing his beer.

Mal placed his hand on Jake's forearm. "He'll be waiting for you."

"Probably."

"Don't it worry you none."

"Some, but I've got a funeral to get to. I can't run and hide from every threat. And slinking out the backdoor doesn't appeal to me."

Mal squeezed Jake's forearm. "Be careful, Marshal. We can't afford to lose you."

Jake nodded and left the Bent Ear. He paused on the boardwalk, scanning Jefferson Street in both directions. There was no sign of the gunfighter, but when he got to Bridge Street, he spotted him sitting in front of Ross's Saddlery.

When Jefferies saw the marshal, he got up and moved into the street.

"It's time, Marshal. Hook and draw."

"This is your dance, mister. You lead."

"I heard you was fast, so prove it. Or are you wearing yellow down your back?"

"I ain't dancing to that tune, mister. It ain't worth it. But if you wanna do this, you're gonna have to make the first move. It won't be me."

The street had cleared. Only intense faces peeking through windows and from doorways could be seen. In the bank, Walters watched from his window, nervously chewing on the stub of a cigar that hung from the corner of his mouth.

"I never heard you was yeller, Marshal, but I s'pose it's easy to imagine. You bein' able to hide behind that badge and throw your weight around."

"Look, let's be reasonable. I don't want to do this. Walk away and ride out of town, and we'll forget this ever happened." Jake's hand hovered near his .45, his eyes fixed on the man taunting him.

"Marshal," he laughed. Do I look like a reasonable man?" he was rapidly, closing the distance between them.

"Not from the front side."

Laughing again, the trouble-monger shook his head. "You know Marshal Jacobs, I'm beginning to like you. You're a standup kinda guy. If things were different, I'd have that drink with you and then ride out."

"That's still a possibility."

"No, Marshal, and as much as I've enjoyed our chat, it's time— reach." Jefferies's hand shot toward the gun strapped to his hip.

In one smooth, fluid movement, Jake drew and fired. In only a split second and with a flick of his wrist his .45 was in his hand, the muzzle smoking. The slug slammed into the man's chest before his gun had cleared leather.

Drake Jefferies's face was etched with pain and surprise. "You shot me. You bastard, you shot me." He fired his gun twice into the ground before falling to his knees and pitching forward onto his face.

Doctor Cooper heard the commotion and rushed to the scene. He pronounced the man dead, and Bones, who arrived only a few minutes later, called on some of the gathered men to help get the body up to his mortuary.

Coop wiped his hand down his clean-shaven chin. "Another gunman looking to build a reputation?"

"Seems so," Jake said, pushing his hat back.

"You know who he is?"

"Drake Jefferies. All he has in his pockets is a makings pouch. What I don't understand, Coop is how I got such a reputation. The drawdown with Fitz happened no more than two months ago, and Marten isn't cold in his grave."

Jake's eyes scanned the horses tied on either side of Bridge Street. One horse wore a saddle trimmed with silver that matched the studs on Jefferies's leather wrist cuffs and hatband.

Jake rifled through the saddlebags, finding a large roll of bills. "There's close to a thousand dollars here," Jake said with a frown. There was no longer any doubt in his mind. It wasn't his reputation they were after. This man and Marten had both been hired to kill him.

CHAPTER 72

LOOKING FOR THE BAD GUYS

"The Whitman place is about a two-hour ride from here," Sam said as they mounted." I've never been to the farmhouse, but part of the Whitman land butts up against the Johnson spread. I know where that is, and I know a shortcut. It's a bit rough in places, but it'll be mostly across pastureland."

They moved quickly, keeping up a steady pace. Both worried they'd taken too long to get on the trail and that Mort and Cyrus could have slipped away.

Sam reined to a stop in a copse of trees. "The Whitman farmhouse is just over that rise."

"I Wonder why they trusted some farmer with their money? Maybe he's related to one of them?" Alex posited.

"Could be," Sam said, "but I'm more worried about what they might have done to Mr. and Mrs. Whitman."

"That thought crossed my mind," Alex said, dismounting.

Let's go take a look-see from that rise over there," Sam said. "We should be able to see how the place is laid out before we head in."

Sam slid his rifle from the boot on his saddle and followed Alex to the edge of the rise where they could look down on the farm.

"They're here. Those horses out front of the house are theirs," Alex said, keeping his voice low. Then added with a frown, "Unless they've ridden off on fresh ones."

"Not much cover between here and there," Sam said, motioning to the chicken coop. "But if we can get to that coop without being seen, we'd be in a decent position."

"See that pile of rocks between here and the coop? It ain't much, but it makes for a little cover."

"Maybe for you," Sam snorted.

Alex smiled. "I'll go first and see if there's any gunfire before moving up behind the chickens. Then, if it's clear, you follow."

Alex ran hunched over and stopped, squatting behind the rocks. When no gunfire erupted from the house or the barn, he ran for the backside of the chicken coop. Sam followed using the same path. Still, there was no gunfire. They hadn't been seen. Sam motioned for Alex to go left, and they ran silently to the front corners of the house.

Alex looked at the worn and rotten boards of the porch floor with a scowl. They'd never make it to the door without being heard. He stepped gingerly onto the porch. There was no sound. On the second step, two boards rubbed together, creaking loudly.

"Who's there?" a woman yelled.

Alex looked at Sam with raised eyebrows and a shrug.

"It's Deputy Marshal Sam Watkins from Grant's Crossing."

"What do you want?"

"I'm looking for the men who rode in on these horses. Can I come in and talk to you? Are you alone?"

"Wouldn't be none too bright of me to tell you I'm all alone in here now, would it?"

Alex took a step closer to the door while Sam distracted her, but on his next step, a board snapped under his weight.

"I hear you. Don't come any closer. I got a shotgun pointed at the door, and law or not, I'll splatter you all over the porch."

Sam signaled to Alex that he was headed toward the rear of the house. Sam eased his way along the side of the house. Halfway to the back corner, he pounded his rifle against a window frame. At the sharp hammering sound, the woman spun toward the sound, and Alex made his move. He kicked the door off its hinges and went in low. The woman was facing the back of the house, and he caught her from behind, pulling the shotgun from her hands. Alex pushed her into a chair by the kitchen table and noticed bloody rags littering the floor.

"Where is he?" Alex asked, his face close to hers.

Sam entered through the front doorway and saw Alex leaning close to the woman's face. "I asked you a question. Where is he?"

She motioned to a room off the kitchen. A dark, heavy drape hung across the archway, serving as a door.

"Who you got in there?" Alex asked.

"My man, Cyrus."

"Is he alive?"

"No," she answered, tears in her eyes.

"I'll check on Cyrus," Sam said, moving toward the curtained doorway. "You keep an eye on her."

Not sure if the woman was telling the truth, Sam drew his gun and slowly pulled back the heavy velvet drape. A bullet whizzed through his hat and slammed into the kitchen wall, splintering the wood. Sam fired, missing as Cyrus spun from the bed. Crouching between the wall and the bed, Cyrus fired again, clipping Sam's arm. Sam jerked back, and the next bullet went wide, missing him. Sam waited quietly, flattened against the wall. He could only see part of the bed.

When Cyrus came up shooting, Sam dropped to his haunches, firing several rounds through the curtain and hitting Cyrus in the chest.

The woman screamed as Cyrus spun and fell backward onto the bed, blood fountaining from one of the wounds. Sam pulled the gun from Cyrus's hand. There was no need to check for a pulse.

"He won't be robbing any more banks," Sam said, picking his hat up off the floor and wiggling his fingers through the two bullet holes.

Alex turned back to the woman. Towering over her, his voice a low, rumbling growl, "What's your name?"

"Juanita. Juanita Velasquez."

"Well, Juanita, I have two important questions, and I don't have time to be polite."

Sam's head snapped up. Alex's voice held a menacing tone that would have scared most anyone spit-less.

Alex's mouth was next to the woman's ear. "Where's the money?"

"W-what money?" she stammered.

"You're gonna make me hurt you, aren't you? I told you I don't have time to be polite." He played with her hair as he spoke, wrapping it around his fingers. "Where's the money, Juanita?" His voice cut like a knife as he jerked her head back.

She gasped and pleaded with Sam, "Stop him, Deputy, you need to stop him. He's hurting me."

"That's not the way I see it, ma'am. He's simply asking you a question, and you might want to give him a straight answer. Myself, I don't care for the sight of blood, but it doesn't seem to bother him."

Alex pulled a long, slender knife from a sheath in his boot and trailed it slowly down her cheek.

"It's in the barn," she cried out. "It's in the barn—in the second grain bin—four bags, under the oats. I wish Cyrus had killed you both," she sobbed.

The woman started to get up, but Alex shoved her down. "We're not done. Where's the man Cyrus rode in with?"

"Cyrus rode in alone. I didn't see anybody else."

Sam came in with the four bags covered in oat dust and chaff. "I found the farmer and his wife in the first grain bin, both shot through the head."

"She says Cyrus rode in alone. What do you think, Deputy?"

"I think the horses hitched out front would call her a liar."

"Did you lie to me—again?" Alex asked, twirling her hair between his fingers. He made a small loop and sliced through it with his knife.

"He never came in," she blurted out, cowering away from the knife. She twisted, trying to get out of the chair and away from Alex. He grabbed her and shoved her down. "And?" he growled.

"I wasn't lying. I never saw him," she blubbered. "He saddled another horse and rode off."

"Which way did he ride, this man you didn't see? Don't lie to me."

She pointed toward the northwest, her hand shaking. "He rode that way fast. Now go away and leave me be."

Alex backed away, and Sam pulled Juanita to her feet. "Sorry, ma'am, but we're taking you back to town. You'll stand trial with the rest of them."

"Why? I didn't do anything."

"You're an accessory to murder, attempted murder, kidnapping, and robbery," Sam said, boosting her onto one of the horses at the hitching rail. He tied her hands to the saddle horn and her feet to the stirrups.

"What about Mort?" Alex asked.

"We don't have to track that cockroach. He'll be back." Sam shook his head, a frown creasing his brow. "Why do you suppose he left the money."

"Maybe Cyrus didn't trust him enough to tell him where he hid it."

"True. But leaving Cyrus and the money behind makes no sense. And where was he off to in such a hurry? He didn't know we'd be showing up."

"Maybe he's planning on coming back."

"Maybe."

They tied Cyrus, belly down, on one of the horses and covered him with a canvas tarp from the barn. They led the two horses carrying Cyrus and his woman back to the timber, where they'd left Pal and Mooch.

Mounting for the ride back home. Alex leaned back in his saddle, lighting a long, slender cigar. "It's been a bankable day, Sam. We got Cyrus, recovered the money, and I'll be back in time for supper with my gal. Let's ride, Deputy. I've got an appointment to keep."

CHAPTER 73

THE BURIAL

The trip to the Lazy W Ranch was a quiet one. Jake rode beside the carriage, wondering if Sam and Alex had caught up with Cyrus and Mort.

Arriving at the Lazy W, they saw people already gathering in the small family cemetery. The coffin had been lowered into the grave, and the service would soon begin. Clark helped Grant and Lorene down from the carriage, and they went straight to Gus and Sylvia. Jake and Winnie stood back, Jake's arm around her shoulders.

Winnie heard Gus's sobs, and this time, there was no stopping the tears. She turned her face into Jake's chest and wept silently while he gently stroked his hand up and down her arm. When she regained control, she looked up at him with a sniffle. "Sorry about your shirt."

"It'll dry."

"We need to pay our respects to Gus and Sylvia," she said. With a deep breath to steady herself, she moved to where her dad and mom stood next to Matt's parents. Jake stayed close, holding Winnie's hand. He liked taking care of her, something she seldom tolerated.

Pastor Emil gave a stirring sermon, and they sang two hymns. Jake noticed another flood of tears in Winnie's eyes as they sang Amazing

Grace, and in all honesty, he had to admit his eyes misted up, too. *What is it about that song*, he thought, as he handed Winnie a handkerchief?

Grant at his side, Gus threw a shovel of dirt onto the top of his son's casket. It was difficult listening to Gus's sobs as Grant led him back to his wife and children. Jake's heart stirred for the man. He and Matt had never been friends. But they were neighbors and had gone to school together. And even though he had always shown an inappropriate amount of interest in Winnie, he wasn't a bad kid. He didn't deserve to die.

Gus turned to Grant, tears running down his cheeks. "How do I say goodbye to my son? How can I go on without him?"

"That's why you go on," Grant said, motioning to Sylvia and his children. "You keep going for them, Gus."

Lorene walked with Sylvia to the open grave and steadied her as she tossed a handful of dirt onto the coffin. "You died too soon, my sweet, handsome Matthew. You never knew the joys of marriage or the incredible happiness of holding your newborn child in your arms." Her voice gave way to sobs. "We'll miss you," she choked out.

Lorene gently guided her back to her husband's side. "He's gone, Gus. Our boy is gone, and he's never coming back." Sylvia sobbed, clinging to her husband.

Matt's brother and sisters each threw a handful of dirt on their brother's coffin and, with tear-streaked faces and sobs, returned to huddle around their parents.

Winnie took a small white box with a lacy paper heart on top of it from her handbag and approached the grave. She crouched down and gently tossed the box on top of the casket. "I was always sweet on you, Matt." She tossed a handful of dirt onto the lid of the coffin. "Goodbye, my valentine." Winnie's words were a whisper, meant only for Matt.

Jake helped her up and tossed a handful of dirt. "We'll get them, Matt. We'll get the men who did this to you." They walked away from the grave and stood next to the grieving family as several people added items or tossed in a handful of dirt, saying their goodbyes.

As Pastor Emil began the final prayer, asking the Lord to comfort Matthew's family and friends, Jake's watchful eyes caught a glint of steel in the timber. He pushed Winnie to the ground and yelled, "Logan, get 'em down."

Logan and Clark tackled Grant, Gus, and their wives from behind, pulling them to the ground in a tumble of petticoats, screams, and curses. Bullets meant for Gus and Grant slammed into the side of one of the carriages. Everyone scattered, finding cover.

Winnie watched Jake streak across the field in the direction of the shots and disappear into the timber. Her emotions were raw, and her heart pounded heavily against the lump of fear lodged in her throat. "I can't lose you, Jake," she said in a voice that was barely a whisper. Then she ran after him.

Jake heard the screams and pandemonium behind him, but Logan and Clark were there, and he didn't have time to hesitate. He hoped he had reacted in time and prayed that no one had been hurt. Adrenaline surged through him as he pushed himself to run faster. He entered the stand of trees, focused on speed and dodging the outstretched tree limbs.

He heard someone thrashing through the underbrush just ahead of him. Jake was rapidly gaining on the man, yelling for him to stop.

Realizing that Jake was closing in on him, the man stopped and spun around to shoot, but Jake was fast and flew at the man, knocking the rifle from his hand as they both hit the ground. They got their boots under them and circled, facing one another.

"Mort Watkins," Jake said, his disbelief turning to anger.

"Yeah, it's me," Mort said, slipping his left hand into his pocket and sliding his fingers into a span of brass knuckles. "Nice to see you again, Marshal."

Mort launched himself at Jake, his brass-wrapped fingers aimed at Jake's jaw. Jake blocked it but took a solid punch to the ribs, then another. Jake backed away, gasping for air, and Mort came at him again. All Jake could see was the hunk of sharp brass wrapped around hairy fingers. Jake grabbed Mort's arm, holding tight, which left him open. Mort slammed his other fist into Jake's side, sending Jake to the ground. Mort kicked him in the ribs twice before turning to look for his gun. Jake grabbed his foot and brought him down with a grunt.

They rolled on the ground, trading punches, each trying to get a solid hold on the other while struggling to find the gun. Mort managed to get on top of Jake. Jake saw the metal knuckles heading for his chin and grabbed Mort's arm. Mort slammed his bare fist into Jake's face again and again. Then, it stopped, and Mort was gone.

Jake looked up through the one eye that hadn't already swollen shut to see Winnie standing over him. "I had him right where I wanted him. What happened?" Jake mumbled around a split lip and passed out.

He woke in a grassy field with his head in Winnie's lap. He tried to move, but the severity of the pain told him he had injured every inch of his body.

Winnie tried to smile at his bloodied face, glad to see a slit of blue peeking at her from under the swollen eyelid.

"Where are we?" he slurred.

"We brought you out of the timber. Gus and Grant have gone for a buckboard to take you to town."

Jake's brain began to function. "Where's Mort?" he asked, trying to get up but falling back into Winnie's lap with a groan.

"Lie still, Jake."

"Was anyone hurt—besides me?"

"No one was hurt. Mort ran when he heard us coming."

"Winnie, You're very beautiful."

"Thank you, Jake. I think you're very handsome."

"Will you marry me?"

"You already asked me."

"Umm. I did? What did you say?"

"I said yes."

"Good," Jake whispered and closed his eyes against the pain.

CHAPTER 74

JAKE NEVER WAS A FIGHTER

When Jake woke, he was in Coop's office. He had a bandage around his head, and his ribcage wrapped so tight it was hard to breathe.

"Where's Mort?" Jake mumbled, trying to sit up, instantly realizing it was a bad idea.

Logan's face appeared in his limited vision, a recognizable blur. "We don't know. He got away slick as a whistle. I'll get Coop."

Jake relaxed as he felt Winnie take his hand.

Coop came into the room and walked up beside her. Both their faces were a blur. "Logan told me you were awake. How do you feel?"

"Not too great." He spoke slowly, his words slurred.

"You look like something the dogs dragged out from under the porch and been fighting over," Coop said, listening to Jake's heart.

"Funny, Coop," Jake said, trying not to move his lips.

Coop frowned. "This time, it's cracked ribs, a split lip, bloody knuckles on both hands, swollen eyes, and nicks and cuts probably from tree branches and rocks. Your entire body is going to be one painful mess for the next couple of weeks."

"I can barely see you, Coop. Are my eyes damaged?"

"Not permanently, if that's what you mean. The swelling will take a few days to go down. The left eye is the worst, but you'll have two splendid black eyes to brag about."

"I'll live?"

"Yep."

Jake tried to sit up and again fell back in pain. "My head is splitting." Jake winced as he tried to raise his hands to his head, setting off even more pain. He hurt everywhere, and he didn't like feeling helpless.

"I'll make you some tea. It'll help with the headache and the rest of your aches and pains. It isn't too strong, but it'll take the edge off."

Coop prepared the tea and added a dose of sleeping powder. Without it, Jake would fight against staying in bed. It was wrong not to tell him, but he would heal faster if he got plenty of rest, behaved himself, and followed the doctor's orders. And if his doctor had to drug him, so be it.

Winnie sat by Jake's bed, waiting for him to finish his tea. Jake was restless, and Coop thought perhaps next time, he'd give him a more potent dose of sleeping powder. Finally, Jake's head rolled back against the pillow.

Coop took the cup from Jake's hand. "He should be out until morning. He took an awful beating this time, Winnie, but he'll be right as rain in no time. You might as well get a room for the night. When he wakes, I plan on giving him another dose of this tea. He needs his rest." Coop took Winnie's hand. "Don't worry, Winnie. I'll take good care of him."

"I know you will. Thanks, Coop."

Winnie was at the door when Sam and Alex came in. "We saw Logan and Clark down at the office, and they told us what happened."

Winnie hugged Sam. "Coop says he'll be fine. He gave him something for the pain and to help him sleep. Mort gave him a terrible beating."

"Guess we know where Mort was off to in such a hurry," Alex said, looking at Jake's battered face.

"Jake never was a fighter," Sam said. But even in jest, the relief in his voice was evident. Mort could have killed Jake and nearly did.

CHAPTER 75

LORENE AND FREDDIE

The next morning Sam went to the livery before checking on Jake. John Miller met him at the door. "Good morning, Deputy."

"How's our patient doing?"

"I doubt you'll recognize him," John said, leading Sam toward the corral.

The Morgan glared at them as they came to the rails. "He's still a mite skittish, but I can't say as I blame him. Not the way he was treated. You reckon it was that Marten fella that beat on him?"

"Don't know as it could have been anyone else, but those days are over. He looks well enough, that I'd like to take him out to meet Lorene."

"How soon you leaving?"

"I'm gonna stop in and see how Jake is doing and then head out."

"I'll have Pal and Freddie both ready by the time you come back."

"Freddie?"

"Yeah, I've been calling him Freddie."

"I'll tell Lorene, but naming him will be up to her."

Sam headed across the street to Coop's and found Coop at his desk. "How's your patient?"

"Uncooperative like always. Go on in—maybe you can talk some sense into him. He wants me to let him go."

Opening the door to Jake's room, Sam had to stop and shake his head. Jake was sitting on the edge of the bed, looking like a sad scarecrow who'd had the stuffin' kicked out of him. "His left eye was swollen shut, and the left side of his face was covered with red bruising that was beginning to show hints of a bluish-purple hue. His bottom lip was split and still looked red and painful."

"What are you looking at?" he barked through his split lip and then groaned in pain.

"I'm not sure, but whatever it is, it ought to be in bed."

"Very funny," Jake said, painfully trying to enunciate.

"You go back to bed and rest. I'm going to take Marten's horse out to meet Lorene. I'll let you know how it goes when I get back."

Jake got out of bed slowly and headed toward the door.

Coop met them. "Where do you think you're going?"

"He didn't say so, but I'm pretty sure he's decided to ride to the ranch with me."

"Jake nodded."

"Well, tell Lorene I wish her luck taking care of this mule-headed numbskull."

The ride to the ranch was slow, and Jake was in a great deal of pain, but aside from a few grunts and groans he never complained. Lorene spotted them coming down the hillside and met them in front of the house. She eyed Jake with a grimace, "Sam, get him off his horse and up to his room. Me and Winnie will take care of him." Her gaze shifted to the third horse. "Whose horse is that?"

"Yours if you want him." Sam smiled. "Be careful, he's a nervous one."

Lorene walked slowly up to the horse and held her hand out for inspection. "What's his name?"

"Don't know, but John's been calling him Freddie,"

Lorene walked to Freddie's side, stroking his neck and scratching him gently across his withers. Lorene smiled when Freddie turned his head and nibbled at her shoulder. "We'll get along just fine, won't we? I'm just not sure about the name Freddie. We'll have to talk about it later when we know each other a little better."

Sam was helping Jake up the steps and onto the front porch. "I think Freddie likes you."

"Who harmed that animal?"

"Probably his previous owner."

"Well, I hope he gets his just reward."

"He already has, Lorene."

CHAPTER 76

GRANT TALKS TO SAM

Three days later, in the early evening, Sam and Jake joined Grant on the back porch. They settled into white wicker rockers on either side of Grant and watched the sky's dramatic turn from blue to deep oranges and purples. While Grant and Jake sipped fine Tennessee whiskey, Sam had opted for Lorene's sweet lemonade. Knowing Sam didn't smoke, Grant only offered Jake a cigar.

Jake shook his head and flinched at the pain. "Thanks, but I doubt I could get it fired up. My lip is still sore, and my ribs hurt with every breath, but it's better than it was."

"Heck of a fight," Grant said.

"Sorry, I missed it," Jake mumbled. "It felt more like a beating than a fight."

Sam sat back in his chair. "Wish I'd been there. Nothing would give me greater pleasure than to slam a fist into Mort's face."

"I wish you'd been there, too," Jake said.

"When I saw him kicking you in the ribs, I figured you were in trouble," Grant said, puffing on his cigar. "Mort fights dirty."

"All I could see were those brass knuckles coming at me. He'd have made minced meat out of me with those," Jake said, gently pushing on the tender skin below his eyes. "He did a bang-up job with his bare fist. At least the swelling is going down, and I can see out of both eyes."

"You didn't protect yourself like I showed you last time we sparred," Sam said.

"I know I didn't, but all I could see were those brass knuckles. Mort sharpened them to points or had them special-made. I was so busy keeping them away from my face that I couldn't take care of the rest of me."

Grant looked at Jake with concern. "I hope you take it easy for a few more days. Coop says you need rest, but I know how stubborn you are."

"I'm supposed to see Coop in the morning and let him poke and prod." Jake took a sip of whiskey and winced at the sting on his lip. "Before this started, Steven had been after me to take some provisions out to the Caldwells and check up on them. I'm heading out that way after I see Coop."

"You going with him, Sam?"

"Jake says no, but he can't stop me from following him."

Jake tried to scowl, but it hurt. "I don't need a babysitter."

"Well, you have one," Sam said. "Besides, I might as well ride with you. There's nothing else going on."

"What do you mean nothing else? We need to find Mort."

"I keep telling you Mort will come to us. Besides, what could you possibly do if you found him? I doubt you can even draw your gun."

Jake gently flexed his fingers, recoiling at the pain. His hand was better, but Sam was correct—and he didn't like it.

Grant puffed on his cigar. "What's Alex up to now that his bank robbers are in jail?"

Sam and Jake looked at each other.

"What's going on?" Grant asked in a demanding voice.

Sam smiled. "Well, Alex and Kat are…um…getting acquainted. He has it bad for her. And as far as I can tell, she's smitten with him, as well. She isn't discouraging him any."

"She's been playing a lone hand for too long. She needs a decent man who'll watch her back. I've only met Alex twice. What's he like?" Grant asked.

Sam finished the last swallow of his lemonade. "He's tough. I wouldn't want to meet him face to face in a showdown, but I can't find any fault with the man. Besides, I think she's got him hamstrung."

Grant scowled, puffing his cigar and rolling the smoke around in his mouth before taking a swig of whiskey. "If he hurts her, I'll kill him."

Sam laughed. "I already warned him there would be a firing squad waiting for him if he did her any harm, but he's dead serious about her."

Grant cocked his head in thought. "Since you boys are heading south tomorrow, why don't you check on old Brownie—it's on your way? He's been out there all alone since his wife died two years ago. I've tried to talk him into coming to work here at the ranch, but he's determined to keep his farmstead going. Check with Steven or Charlie to see if he has been in lately for supplies."

Jake nodded. "Think I'll go to bed," he said, getting up slowly, fighting a yawn. "That whiskey seems to have knocked me for a loop. I'm feeling a little tangle-legged. Good night, all."

"Get your rest, Jake. You need it." Grant watched him limp into the house and then turned to Sam. "Is he all right?"

"He'll be fine. Coop gave me a vial of sleeping powder, enough for three nights. He told me to slip it into his evening drink. This was the final dose. Jake would be madder than a hornet if he found out what I've been doing, but I figure it's doctor's orders."

"I didn't realize Coop could be so sneaky," Grant chuckled. "I'll have to keep an eye on him from now on."

Grant studied Sam, thinking how rough it had been for him to grow up with Mort as a father. Sam was like a son to him, and he was worried about what he might do when he caught up with Mort. The Mort he had known was a weak, cowardly bastard, but that was no longer the case.

"Sam, watch your back."

"I'll watch Jake's back, too. He's helpless as a baby lamb but still roaring like a lion."

Grant laughed. "Are you staying the night?"

"I'd like to stay if you wouldn't mind."

"Why would I mind? It's your home. You're part of the family. I've always thought of you and Jake as my sons and often wished you were. I couldn't be any prouder of you or love you more if you were my own blood."

Sam stumbled over his words. "You've been like a father to me, and I can't tell you what that has meant. But sometimes it feels like, well, like I'm taking advantage of you."

"You never have, Sam. Look, I wasn't going to say anything about this. I don't enjoy discussing morbid things, like my death. But I think you need to hear it. This ranch was my father's dream and my legacy. There is only one thing more important to me than this land, and that's my family." Grant took a draw on his cigar. "I won't live forever, and when I'm gone, Winnie, Jake, and you will each inherit a third of the ranch and everything else I own. I know the three of you will care for it as I would. I cannot make it any clearer, Sam. You're my son, and don't you ever forget it."

"Grant, I—"

Grant cut him off. "I haven't talked to Winnie or Jake about any of this. I didn't feel they needed to know. This is between you and me. Now, go to your room—son, before this gets all maudlin."

"Yes, sir."

CHAPTER 77

I'LL NEVER TELL

The following morning, Jake tried to kiss Winnie goodbye but settled for a painful hug. Chris and Pete had saddled the horses and brought them along with a step stool for Jake to use. Jake scoffed, but after several unsuccessful attempts to mount his horse, he gave up and used it.

Halfway to town, Jake broke the silence. "Don't you ever tell anyone that I had to use a step stool?"

"My lips are sealed. By the way, when did you say Judge Taylor would be back?"

"Day after tomorrow, according to the wire," Jake replied.

"I'm glad Taylor will be here for the trial and not that lame-brained Judge Mitchell. That cabbage head might find a reason to release those men."

"Mitchell isn't well thought of by the law, but outlaws seem to like him well enough."

Sam smiled. "You aren't slurring your words quite as bad. I've understood almost every word."

"Still hurts to talk." Jake paused. "And to breathe. And to move."

"Be nice if you could heal yourself."

"Wouldn't it."

Sam removed his hat, poking his fingers through the two holes, glad he hadn't been killed. "You think the judge will send our prisoners to the gallows?"

"Can't imagine he could do anything else. Texas might attack if he doesn't."

"Speaking of Texas, what do you suppose happened to our Texas Ranger." Sam settled the damaged hat back on his head. He liked it and hated the thought of breaking in a new one.

"Hard to tell. I still can't believe he attacked you and tried to burn down the jail." Jake said, blinking his eyes, his vision clearing.

"He's determined. Got a fire burning in his gut to get those men back to Texas to hang."

"That powerhouse of a swing you laid on him nearly knocked him back to Texas."

"I wish it had," Sam said. "You know, breaking out our prisoners and getting them back to Texas is a tall order for one man. He could be holed up waiting for reinforcements."

It was a while before either spoke again. "Jake, if the ranger or anyone else is going to make a play for the prisoners, it'll likely be when we take them from jail down to the courthouse for the trial. That's when we'll be the most vulnerable."

Jake nodded.

"I was thinking—what if we move them to the courthouse the night before the trial? No one would be expecting it. We can keep them locked in one of the back rooms."

"I like the idea, Sam."

CHAPTER 78

A NEW HAT

The first stop in town was at the doctor's office. Sam watched Jake flinch every time Coop touched him. "Why don't you use a cattle prod on me?" Jake growled.

"I'll have one available for your next visit," Coop said, frowning at his frequent customer. "I was worried about your one eyeball, but it's healing nicely. Seriously, Jake, you need lots of rest, and for God's sake, take it easy for a few days."

Jake muttered something under his breath, then asked, "How's Red doing?"

"He'll live. Long enough to hang."

"Sam and I are headed out of town for the day," Jake said. Coop frowned, and Jake quickly continued before Coop could argue. "We'll ride easy."

"Do you ever listen to me?" Coop sighed. "Perhaps I should check your ears."

Jake ignored Coop's sarcasm. "If Red starts coming around, get Logan up here. Red may be weak but don't forget how dangerous he is. Doctor or not, I doubt he'd hesitate to kill you."

Coop watched them leave, shaking his head and muttering, "Why do they never listen to me?"

Steven scurried to meet Sam and Jake as soon as they crossed the threshold of the general store. He gasped at the sight of Jake's face.

"Coop says I'll be fine, and the swelling will be gone soon. It's already better than it was."

Jake answered a barrage of Steven's questions while Sam tried on hats. Sam liked the cream-colored hat he'd worn for years but found none in that color that set comfortably on his head. He tried on a dozen hats and narrowed it down to two. He tried on one and then the other, struggling to decide.

"For the love of God, Sam," Jake growled. "You're wearing out the mirror and my patience. It's a hat. Pick one."

"What do you think, Steven, light brown or black?"

"Black works for Jake, but it's too severe for you. That soft brown one accents your eyes. It's perfect."

Sam looked at Jake. "What do you think?"

"Oh, yes. Definitely, the brown one." Jake rolled his eyes. "It goes with those lovely eyes of yours. Let's go."

Sam pulled the braided leather band from his tattered John B. and slipped it over the crown of the new one. He settled it on his head and, checking the mirror one last time, tossed his old hat to Steven.

Jake grunted, trying to pick up a bag. Sam pushed him away, and Charlie followed Sam out the door with the last bag of supplies. Charlie warned, "My bones are guaranteein' a storm's a-comin'. Be sure to take your slickers."

Leaving the store, Jake turned to Sam. "We'd better stop by the jail and check with Logan before we head out. He's probably cranky at being left alone to guard the prisoners."

CHAPTER 79

JAILHOUSE FROLIC

They walked into the marshal's office to find Logan snoring, leaning back in the chair with his feet on the desk, his hat tipped over his face, and hands clasped across his belly. As Jake and Sam walked in, he pushed back his hat, squinting at them. "Everything's fine here, but thanks for stopping by. It's always nice to know you're on the job. I suppose you're here to tell me you'll be out of town for a week."

"Just today. How are the prisoners doing?" Jake asked, easing into one of the visitor's chairs.

"Oh, sure. All concerned about the prisoners. Not a care for me, eh? Well, I will tell you what, those prisoners are fine. They got a bit rowdy last night, but they're fine as gravy on a biscuit."

"What happened?"

"Ever since you brought in that Velasquez woman, Bob's been trying to get at her through the bars. Can you imagine him trying to do her through the cell bars?" Logan laughed. "It was quite a show you missed. Last night, she got real cooperative with old Bob. She squeezed those big tits of hers through the bars for him to play with, and he stuck his dick through the bars for her to play with. Then she pulled her britches down, backed her bare-assed hindquarters right up against them bars, and bent over, letting him take her from behind."

"You didn't stop it?" Jake said.

"Hell, no. I told you it was quite a show. Them cell cages were rattling and groaning, making near as much noise as Miss Velasquez. I ain't been so hard in years. Besides, once the show was over, they settled down. I reckon they had the trial on their minds."

Jake shook his head. "Logan, I don't know what to say."

"Aw, Jake, there was no harm done. They didn't hurt nothin', and it gave them something to do, some enjoyment. They'll be swinging soon enough." Logan grinned wickedly. "I asked Rachie to bring me supper tonight so we can spend some time spooning. Who knows, there might be another show, and I'd hate to waste an opportunity to impress my girl."

"Guess where there's a will, there's a way," Sam said with a chuckle as he and Jake left the marshal's office.

"Good morning, Marshal, Deputy," Quimby Beck said, "I can't seem to get into my building." Quimby cupped his hands around his face and pressed his nose against the dirty windowpane. "The bank manager said he doesn't know where the key is. I'd hate to break one of the windows, but it looks like I may have to."

"This is your building?"

"Yes, Marshal. It's my building, and it's perfect."

"Perfect for what?" Jake asked.

"For a newspaper, of course. A town this size needs one, and I'll bet you and the deputy have some stories to tell." Quimby knew this was his future. He would have the freedom he longed for. He would be the owner and editor of his own paper.

"No stories here, Mr. Beck, but it's fortunate we happened along when we did. We have your key in our office," Jake said, glaring at the dandified Easterner.

Sam stepped back through the office door. "Logan, get the key to the building next door. It's in the top desk drawer."

After considerable grumbling, Logan tossed the key in a high arc to Sam, who snagged it out of the air. Handing the key to Beck, Sam thought at least it wouldn't be another saloon.

Quimby's whole face smiled. "Yessiree, won't be long until you folks here in Grant's Crossing have yourselves a newspaper." Quimby saw the look of concern pass between the lawmen. "I'm an honest reporter, and my newspaper will be beneficial to you and the town. Let's talk tonight over supper."

"Mr. Beck, I..."

"Please, call me Quimby. Supper tonight, then." He unlocked the door and disappeared into what would soon be the office of the Grant's Crossing Clarion.

Sam and Jake stood on the boardwalk, staring at the closed door. "A newspaper office right next to us. Sam, what have I done to deserve this?"

They walked across the street and mounted their horses. Sam swung up effortlessly and watched Jake grunt and wince, using the pommel and stirrup to pull himself slowly into the saddle. Drach looked back as if doubting it was Jake.

Riding out of town, their conversation focused on what Quimby Beck had sprung on them. The previous newspaper had gone bust. The editor sold advertising that never appeared in the paper, and his reports were seldom in line with the truth. Events were dramatized to increase circulation, and if there wasn't any news, the editor created it. If the rumors were correct, the editor smeared the wrong man somewhere along the line and got run out of town, barely avoiding hot tar and feathers.

"I wonder how Quimby would report on what happened at the jail last night?" Sam asked with a smile.

CHAPTER 80

A STORM ROLLING IN

Riding easy, it took them over three hours to get to the Caldwell farm. They found the couple outside tending to their gardens. When they saw the riders, they dropped their hoes and hurried to greet them.

Sam unloaded the supplies, and at the couple's insistence, they stayed to chat for a bit and shared a light meal.

The Caldwells followed Sam and Jake to their horses. "We don't get many visitors out this way," Mrs. Caldwell said, looking up at Sam. "You boys are welcome anytime."

"Wouldn't mind staying a bit longer," Jake said, "but there's a storm moving in, and we have one more stop to make before we head back to town."

Riding north, they watched the sky grow darker by the minute as ominous-looking clouds roiled toward them. Thunder grumbled and growled nonstop in the distance. Close to the horizon, lightning sizzled and streaked across the sky. Dust devils swirled and danced frantically around the fields and across the road as if they knew their spinning lives were about to end. The sweet smell of rain permeated the air, guaranteeing they would get the rain they so badly needed.

There was a sudden electrifying change in the atmosphere, and the winds swirled, changing direction. The storm bore down on them, buffeting the men and their horses. Dust and debris pelted their hands and faces, forcing them to stop and don their slickers. Both tied their hats down with their wild rags and wrapped a second one around their faces.

Sam pointed back toward the southwest. "It's coming in fast," Sam shouted.

Behind them, in the distance, dark gray curtains of heavy rain could be seen. The unending rumble of thunder was louder, and flashes of blinding light lit the sky. *We're in for a humdinger.* Sam thought as he watched the sky turn an odd shade of yellowish-gray.

"This could get bad, Jake. You know any place nearby where we can shelter?"

"We can't be too far from Brownie's," Jake yelled against the wind.

CHAPTER 81

BROWNIE

Approaching the fork in the road that would take them the last half mile to Brownie's homestead and shelter, sheets of lightning split the sky. A boom of thunder loud enough to shake the ground startled the men and their horses.

Just as the horses were calming down, a dog, black as night, with a squawking chicken in its mouth, flew out of the timber and across the road in front of them. The horses reared and snorted, and a gunshot rang out, sending the dog head-over-paws, losing hold of the chicken.

The dog tried to get up but fell back to the ground with a whimper. Sam jumped from his horse, holding tight to the reins. Jake winced in pain as he slowly slid from his saddle, passing his reins to Sam. A farmer came charging out of the timber, gun raised.

Jake headed toward the farmer. "Drop your shotgun," Jake yelled, fighting off the pain in his ribs.

"This is my land. You ain't gonna tell me what to do. Now git. Git off my land. I'm gonna kill that thievin' varmint. He won't be gettin' anymore of my chickens." The farmer aimed his rifle at Jake. "I said, git."

Jake stood his ground and warned him again to drop his weapon, but the farmer moved his thumb up to the hammer. He wasn't fast enough and found himself staring down the barrel of Jake's Colt 45.

The man dropped the rifle. "Sorry, fella, guess I overreacted a mite, but that stinkin' dog's been stealin' my chickens, and you're trespassin'. I had you dead to rights. I could have shot you."

"Decent bluff, but you didn't have enough time to chamber another round in that old Sharps you were hoisting in my direction." Jake holstered his gun and slowly bent to pick up the rifle, checking the breach. He threw it back to the farmer with a grunt. "You Brownie?"

"Yeah, what of it?"

"Tom Grant asked us to stop by. I'm Marshal Jacobs, and that's Deputy Watkins. We have supplies for you, and we could use some shelter. Looks like a bad storm is blowing in."

"If I'd knowed you was law, I wouldn't have threatened you." Brownie pulled a knife from the scabbard on his belt and headed across the road to kill the chicken thief.

Sam sat on his haunches next to the dog. He'd wrapped a scarf tight around the dog's middle to stop the bleeding.

"What're you doin'? I mean to put an end to that varmint," Brownie yelled.

"Sorry, but I'm taking this dog into custody. He's under arrest."

"Under arrest?"

"For theft."

Brownie stomped back across the road, grabbed the bag of provisions, and continued into the timber. Without a nod or a thank you, he disappeared among the trees.

"Guess there'll be no shelter at Brownie's place." Jake shook his head, trying to remember. He could have sworn Grant said he tried to talk Brownie into coming to work at the ranch. *I must have heard wrong,* he thought.

Sam wrapped the dog tightly in a blanket and tucked him against his chest under the slicker. As they started toward town, the rain-bloated clouds opened up. It was a slow, wet, and windy ride to Grant's Crossing.

The men, the horses, and the dog were soaked to the bone by the time they rode into town. Sam headed straight for the vet's office and Jake to the marshal's office.

Jake found Logan in the same position as when they left, asleep with his feet on the desk.

Water gushed from the brim of Jake's hat, leaving a sizable puddle of water at his feet. He hung up his slicker and hat and sat gingerly in one of the wooden chairs in front of his desk. It hadn't been the easy ride he'd anticipated. He was wet and cold. He needed to change into dry clothes, but it would be painful, and he didn't know if he had the strength.

Logan got up quietly and poured a cup of hot coffee. He pulled a bottle of whiskey from the desk drawer and dumped a healthy dose in with the coffee. "Here, this will make you feel better. Where's Sam?"

"He took his dog to the vet."

"His dog?"

CHAPTER 82

TOWN VET

Sam hoped to find Dice in his office and sober. The town veterinarian had earned the nickname Dice because of his addiction to Chuck-A-Luck. Gambling and alcohol were his vices of choice.

When Sam entered the vet's office, he found him with his head on his desk, snoring and drooling. "Dice, wake up. I've got a customer for you."

Dice reluctantly opened one bloodshot eye, squinting up at his tormentor. "I'm not open for business," he said, closing his eyelid.

Sam pulled his head up by the scruff of his shirt collar. "Damn it, Dice. Come on. It's an emergency. Wake up."

Dice got up from his chair and stumbled to the stove. He picked up the cold coffee pot, poured a cup, and drank it down. "It ain't hot, but it'll get my blood circulating."

Sam tried to put the dog on the vet's table, but the dog clung desperately to Sam's shoulder. Sam finally pried him loose but held him securely against his side. Dice guzzled a second cup of cold coffee and approached the table. He looked at the dog and grunted. "What the hell is that?"

"It's a dog, Dice. How the hell did you ever get to be a vet?"

"I can see it's a dog, Sam. Why didn't you put him out of his misery?"

"He's been shot. Can you stitch him up or not?" Sam's voice rumbled. The dog's wound still oozed blood, and Sam's patience was growing thin.

Dice shook his head, looking at the filthy, bedraggled mess. "I can't see the wound for all the matted hair. I'll need to shave a spot. Is he a biter?"

Sam shrugged. "He hasn't bitten me."

The injured dog trembled and made a noise somewhere between a whimper and low growl, as the vet touched the tender area around the wound. He leaned harder against Sam, as Dice nervousely shaved away a small patch of fur.

"Hmmm, far as I can tell, the bullet went clean through. I can't be sure, but it doesn't appear to have done much damage, but he'd have bled to death. You saved his life, wrapping him up the way you did."

Sam held onto the dog, talking to him in a soothing voice while Dice closed the wound with stitches. The dog whimpered, melting into Sam's side.

"I've got the bleeding stopped. He's weak and full of ticks and fleas, but he'll survive."

"Now what?" Sam said.

Dice rolled down his sleeves and downed another cup of cold coffee. "I'll keep him here. I'll need to chop off most of his hair to get to all the ticks. And as for the fleas, he can't have a flea bath until the wound heals, but I do have some powder that'll do the trick." He looked at Sam, shaking his head. "I'll be up most of the night dealing with this creature. Come back tomorrow morning—late tomorrow morning. On second thought, make it afternoon."

"Do what you can," Sam said, scratching the dog's head and ears and whispering to him not to be afraid. "I'll be back for you," he said, turning toward the door.

Dice called after him. "What's his name?"

Sam hesitated with his hand on the doorknob and looked back at Dice. "Duke, his name's Duke."

CHAPTER 83

IT'S A DOG'S LIFE

Duke had forgotten how it felt to have a human scratch his ears and talk to him softly. He liked Sam and couldn't help but whine when he went out the door. He hoped Sam wouldn't leave him the way the other humans had.

It had been over a year since his people abandoned him, leaving him to fend for himself. He tried to follow the wagon that carried his family, but the scent got weaker and weaker, and so did he. Tired and hungry. Eventually, he gave up.

He learned fast how to take care of himself. He found shelter in a cluster of enormous boulders that rose out of nowhere on the otherwise flat prairie that stretched in all directions. A deep recess in one of the larger boulders served as his home. It wasn't deep enough to be called a cave, but it gave him protection from the worst of the weather. More than once, he fought to defend his home and had the scars to prove it.

A small stream that meandered past his rocky fortress provided a water source and brought animals to his doorstep. There was no shortage of food, but he missed his people, especially the children.

He didn't know why the stream dried up, but the water steadily slowed until only the slightest trickle meandered through the rocks. He hadn't caught a rabbit or anything else for days and was hungry and thirsty. As a last resort, he lowered himself to thievery. He should have waited for dark to raid the farmer's henhouse, but his hunger drove him to take desperate actions. Even now, his stomach grumbled for food.

Listening to the snip, snip, snip of clippers, Duke fell asleep.

CHAPTER 84

WHERE'D THEY ALL COME FROM

The clanging of the blacksmith's hammer stopped as Sam rode into the main alleyway of the livery, leading Drach behind him. John came to greet his friend with a handshake and took Drach's reins. They walked to the back stalls of the livery that were reserved for the marshal and his deputies.

"Looks like you got caught out in it," John said, stripping the saddle from Drach's back.

"For a fact."

"We need it. Thought it looked like it might hail there for a while."

"We ran into plenty of rain but no hail," Sam said, pulling the saddle from Pal's back. "Where'd all of these horses come from?"

"It's been getting busier by the minute," John said, tending to Drach. "Folks are arriving for the trial, all vying for a spot to camp, even in this rain. I don't think any of 'em has a lick of sense, but I can't complain. Their money's spendable."

"I didn't think the trial would be such a big deal, but I suppose people are curious."

John shook his head. "Hard to figure people. Any sign of Mort?"

"Not yet," Sam said.

"You worried about him?" John asked.

Sam frowned. "The man scares me. He's a back-shooter, and I won't see him coming." Sam chuckled, "I hope he's still a poor shot."

The horses bedded down, John walked out with Sam, pausing inside the livery door. Sam looked up and down Bridge Street. "It's a lot busier than usual."

John leaned back in a stretch. "Looks like the sky is lightening up some over in the west. Maybe the rain'll be letting up. See you later," John said, returning to his bellows.

Sam quick-stepped through the continuing downpour to the marshal's office. Jake was behind the desk, dry and looking at the day's mail. Logan was in the back checking on the prisoners.

Sam shook the water from his slicker and his new hat. "Why aren't you lying down? Coop said you need your rest."

"It hurts either way. At least sitting up, I don't feel like an invalid. What's the story on the chicken thief?"

"Dice says he'll be fine. Says we can pick him up tomorrow. We need to find him a proper home, Jake."

"We?"

"Yeah, we."

"And where are *we* going to keep him in the meantime?"

"Here at the jail. It's as good a place as any for a thief."

Jake figured they had themselves a dog. "Come on, let's go."

"Where? It's still raining like a son-of-a-gun."

"We're going to Kat's. Steven and Charlie are probably over there, and they'll know what we need for your pooch. Dog bowls, a blanket, and food. What do you feed a dog, anyway?"

"Well, we know he likes chicken."

CHAPTER 85

EXPRESS TRAINS

They left Logan with the prisoners and crossed the street, holding slickers over their heads and dodging horses and wagons. Kat's Place was standing room only.

"It's busier than Founder's Day," Jake said, looking from one end of the saloon to the other. "What the heck's going on?"

"John's livery is near full up. He says it's folks coming into town for the trial." Sam looked across the crowd. "If our friend, Ranger Hill, has called in additional men to help him, we'll never know it. Most everyone in here is a stranger."

Steven and Charlie had somehow managed to get a table, and Jake and Sam headed in their direction. They dodged servers carrying trays laden with drinks, trying to snake their way through the milling crowd. The sound of the Chuck-A-Luck dice and the clatter of the Roulette wheel never stopped. At least five poker games were going on, and Alex was dealing Faro. He shut down the game amid some colorfully threatening comments and weaved through the crowd to join them.

As a tray of drinks neared the table, Alex took it from the girl's hands with an apology. "Express trains started arriving this morning," Alex said, passing out the drinks. "Calvin says there are more headed our way. All of them packed with reporters and gawkers. Those four over there are from St. Louis papers, and the table over there is a mix of Philadelphia and Chicago reporters. The three men in the corner represent Kansas City, St. Joe, and Omaha. These yahoos are calling it *the trial of the century*."

"They got here fast," Jake said, his eyes scanning the room.

"It's been busy like this since noon." Alex saw the glint of a badge from under Jake's vest. "If I were you, I'd keep those badges under wraps unless you wanna be overrun by a herd of over-eager newspapermen."

"How come you're dealing Faro?" Sam asked.

"Kat caught that new girl, Stella Reeves, cheating. Guess she thought she could get away with it in all this commotion."

Jake took a drink of whiskey, wincing as it hit the still-tender split on his bottom lip. "I never expected anything like this for the trial. Wonder what it will be like by tomorrow night?"

"Worse. If you need me for anything, let me know. Otherwise, my guns are here, protecting Kat and her place." Alex smiled as he looked across the room to where Kat was pouring drinks. "I'd better get back to work before she catches me loafing."

Alex started toward the faro table, then turned back. "Jake, those are some serious-looking black eyes you're sporting."

Jake knew his face was still a mess, but at least his eyes and fingers were working. He looked across the table at Charlie and Steven. "How are you doing?"

"We've been busier than all get out. This is the first break we've had since ten this morning. We figure on having a nice supper and a tipple or two and then we'll reopen. I'd like to go home and put my feet up, but this crowd is making us nervous. I'm afraid they might break in and rob us." Steven looked at Charlie, who nodded in agreement.

When Sam told Steven about the dog, Steven told them not to worry. They'd make sure he had everything a law dog would need come morning.

"Charlie, you packing?" Jake asked.

Charlie pulled back his coat, showing off an 1860 Colt Army Revolver. "And I've got a Winchester and a shotgun stashed behind the counter. I know how to use 'em if need be."

CHAPTER 86

QUIMBY STANDS HIS GROUND

The rain let up as Jake and Sam splashed across the street back to the marshal's office.

Quimby and Logan were chatting comfortably like old friends.

Jake bristled. "I hope you told Logan you're a reporter."

Quimby scowled. "Of course I did. Look, I wouldn't try to trick anyone into divulging information. Like I said this morning, I'm a man of integrity. Unlike most of the reporters hanging out in the saloon over there, I want to report the news, not make it up. They want a juicy story and don't care how they get it. But if I can scoop them, it would put a stop to their lies. I know you don't believe me, but we have a lot to discuss. Let's go to supper."

Jake hurt from head to toe, and he couldn't remember ever being so tired. All he wanted was a soft, warm bed, but he did need to eat. He followed Sam and Quimby across the street to The Wishbone Cafe. The food at the Wishbone was as wholesome as Mother's, and if you needed a quiet spot to talk, this was usually the perfect spot—but not tonight.

Minnie, the owner, greeted them. She liked it when the marshal and his deputies came in for a meal and always gave them extra.

Like every place in town, the Wishbone was crammed. Sam leaned over the counter and kissed Minnie's cheek, making her blush.

"Sam Watkins. I remember a dozen times when I chased you out of here for being a foul-mouthed little tough."

Sam couldn't help but chuckle, "That was a long time ago, Minnie, and look at me now. Here I am, making you blush."

"You're still a rascal, Sam Watkins," Minnie said, brushing past him and surveying the tables. The men at one of the tables had finished eating but were hanging out chewing the fat. She chased them off and motioned to Jake and his companions as she cleared the table.

Minnie wiped her hands on her apron. "I don't know where all these folks came from, but my business is booming. You want breakfast or supper." She couldn't take her eyes off Jake's face. "Who won?"

"You should see the other guy," Jake said with a grin.

"You got him locked up?"

"No, he got away, but we'll find him."

"Well, I don't hold no sympathy for any man who beats up one of my boys."

"Fix us up a feast, Minnie. Sam hasn't eaten but three times today and he's feeling faint." Jake did his best to wink at her.

"You two boys are such flirts," she said as she finished clearing the table and bustled back to the kitchen.

By the time they finished the meal, Quimby had them convinced. His genuine exuberance and the promise to contribute to the community by printing reliable news was enticing. There were plenty of gossipmongers all over town spewing their version of events. Maybe it wasn't such a bad idea to have a paper legitimately reporting the news.

"This is a new start for my niece and me, and we're excited about our future here." The two lawmen looked at each other with raised eyebrows. They had assumed that Hannah and Quimby were married.

"I will always cooperate with the law in any way I can. I'll always come to you with anything suspicious or if there's something you need to know about. And I have something you might want to know about."

Sam had leaned back in his chair, stretching after a full meal, but sat forward, intent on what Quimby was saying.

"There is a large three-story house on the corner of South Jackson Street and New Street, or maybe First Street. There seems to be some uncertainty."

Sam rolled his eyes, wondering if the town council would ever decide on a name for the new street.

Quimby continued, "Regardless, you know what house I'm talking about. I take a walk every morning after breakfast and couldn't help but notice all the deliveries to that residence. Yesterday, three large mirrors and what appeared to be a small, rather ornate bar were delivered. A week ago, they hauled in a gleaming grand piano, and I've seen a number of—feathered girls going in and out. Something is going on there. If I had to guess, it looks like the makings of a saloon or, more likely, a parlor house."

Jake and Sam were silent, their faces masked with skepticism. He was talking about Miss Purdy's place, but there was no way Miss Purdy would turn her home into a house of sin. She was a staunch, proper, upright citizen who sat in the front pew at church and looked down her nose at everyone. She didn't drink or swear and was ramrod straight. She never married and, as far as anyone knew, had never been courted.

Jake poked Sam's arm. "She did take those young girls in when we raided the Stable Saloon and remember the delivery Steven told us about? The fancy corsets?"

Sam laughed out loud. "Oh. You have got to be kidding me. Miss Purdy a madame?"

Jake wanted to laugh but knew it would be painful. "Quimby, I think we're going to get along fine. When do you want to interview me?"

"Now, Marshal, right now. I can get the story out before any of those vultures in the saloons know what hit them. How late is the telegraph office open?"

Sam excused himself. "Jake, you can handle this, and I'll take care of the rounds. I'll catch up with you later."

CHAPTER 87

HELLO, PAPA

Sam started down Bridge Street, seeing no familiar faces in the crowd. Most townsfolk were home with their doors locked and barred. He couldn't say he blamed them. The press of people was overwhelming, and Sam figured the street was even more congested than when they'd left Kat's less than a couple of hours ago. Weaving in and out and around, he thought how lucky he was to stand far above most of the crowd. At least he could see where he was headed.

Nearing the river, the crowd thinned some, and he wasn't jostled from all directions. He passed the telegraph office and spotted Wade hunched over his desk. The flickering lamp light illuminating a face etched with concentration as he tapped out a message. It was most likely a reporter's story being sent to a newspaper.

Sam climbed the stairs to the train depot, stepping over men who were passed out or asleep on the steps. The station was dark. He checked the doors, each rattling noisily as he tested them. Everything was locked up tight. The train from Sioux Falls wouldn't roll in until late morning, and he hoped no more express trains would show up. He somehow doubted they would be so lucky.

He turned his attention to the freight office. The doors were closed and locked. Two massive freight wagons sat idle in the alley between the office and the stock pens. Sam stepped up on the wheel of one to look inside. He found them empty and stepped down.

Turning toward Washington Street, Sam caught sight of Mort. He was perched on the top rail of one of the cattle pens a cheroot clenched between his lips.

"Hello, son. I didn't expect to see you down here by the pens, but I'm glad you came by."

Sam answered calmly and steadily, "I'm not your son."

"Oh, you found out about that, huh?"

"Yeah." Sam's body began firing up for a fight. The rush of adrenaline and the bloodlust that went with it ignited the hate he felt for the man who called him son. He wanted to draw and kill him outright, but he could see that Mort wasn't packing.

"Well, my dear nephew," Mort sneered. "Come sit beside me, and we can have a nice friendly chat."

"We have nothing to talk about." Sam's jaw tightened, and he squared his shoulders. "Mort Watkins, you are under arrest."

Mort let out a hearty laugh. "I don't think so, Sam," he said, flicking his cigar into the cattle pen. He reached into his pants pocket, smiling as he slid his fingers into the brass knuckle duster. "I'm not one bit interested in hanging."

Before the words were out of his mouth, Mort launched himself at Sam. Mort was fast, and the move unexpected, but Sam was faster. He twisted away, clipping Mort's face with his elbow. Mort stumbled past Sam but remained on his feet. He spun around to face Sam, his lip curled. "I'm going to put you in the ground."

It was Sam's turn to laugh. "You can try, old man."

Mort charged at Sam, throwing punch after punch. Sam blocked them all but was so watchful of the brass wrapped around Mort's knuckles that he didn't have time to respond. But Mort was tiring or becoming careless, and as he pulled back to swing, Sam plowed into the opening with a rib-buster followed by a fist to Mort's jaw.

Mort fell back, grabbing one of the wagon wheels for support. Doubled over and gasping for air, he remembered another time when he had clung to a hitching rail. He pushed away from the wheel and, standing straight, wiped the blood from his mouth. He spat at Sam's feet. "I ain't drunk this time—son."

The fury of Mort's rage propelled him as he launched himself at Sam. His arms outstretched, he grabbed Sam around the hips and dragged him to the ground. Sam had the breath knocked out of his lungs, but he knew he couldn't quit moving. He quickly rolled to his side, avoiding the razor-sharp brass knuckles that Mort swung at his face. But he didn't avoid two solid jabs to his ribs. He'd clenched his muscles, but the sharp barbs of the enhanced knuckles did some damage, and Sam knew he had to get them away from Mort.

The growing crowd around the fight cheered and jeered as Mort jumped to his feet. He was about to slam his boot and spur into Sam's neck, but Sam grabbed Mort's foot and twisted it sharply, bringing Mort down on top of him with a grunt. Holding Mort, Sam grabbed his wrist and, bending it back, yanked the brass from his fingers. Mort elbowed Sam in the side and broke free. Rolling over, he pinned Sam beneath him. His eyes were wild with hate as he tried to slam his fists into Sam's face.

Sam blocked a left and then a right before gaining enough leverage to flip Mort onto his back. With his knee planted in Mort's belly, he delivered a powerful haymaker to his face.

"You broke my nose, you son-of-a-bitch," Mort roared, struggling to free himself.

Sam hit him again. "Let it go, Mort. You're done."

Still, Mort struggled. "I'll hate you till the day I die," he screamed, spitting blood.

"And that won't be long. You'll hang with the rest of your friends." Sam rose, breathless, rubbing his side where the knuckles had pierced his skin. "You're under arrest, Mort Watkins," Sam said, pulling Mort to his feet amidst a rousing cheer from the spectators.

Sam shoved Mort toward the jail as the cheering crowd parted to let them pass. The story of the fistfight and the capture of the fourth killer preceded Sam and his prisoner as they made their way to the jail. There were no significant incidents along the way. Mort received pokes and prods from the crowd, and one woman jabbed him repeatedly with a nasty-looking hatpin. Sam only smiled.

They entered the jail covered in a mixture of mud, blood, and cow manure.

Jake stood up and walked around his desk. "You got him."

"I did." Sam tossed the metal knuckles onto Jake's desk. "But I lost my hat," he added, pushing Mort toward the cell block as Jake unlocked the heavy wooden door.

"I need a bath," Sam said.

Jake pinched his nose. "For a fact, Sam. You could outstink an outhouse."

CHAPTER 88

JUDGE TAYLOR

The following morning, Jake and Sam stood in the doorway of the marshal's office, gazing out at the crush of people packing the boardwalks and milling about in the streets. An incessant hum of chatter and laughter filled the air as the mass of humanity shuffled from side to side and back and forth, going nowhere, waiting for the trial.

"Where did all these people come from?" Jake said, moving behind his desk and sitting down. He shifted, rubbing his side with a muffled groan.

"Both hotels and the boarding houses are full to the brim," Sam said, pouring two cups of coffee and taking one to Jake. "There's folks camping in the schoolyard and churchyards, and John says they're camped all along the roads for a mile on either side of town."

"Good thing the rain ended overnight. Too bad it didn't discourage the gawkers," Jake said, blowing the steam from his coffee.

"At least the town is peaceful. I hope it stays that way."

Judge Taylor entered the marshal's office through the side door. "Just got into town. I didn't expect anything like this. Where'd all these people come from?"

"They're coming in from everywhere," Sam said, shaking the judge's outstretched hand. "When the railroad execs heard about the trial, they started selling excursion tickets to what reporters have labeled *the trial of the century*."

Jake winced as he reached across the desk to shake hands with the judge. "And it's not only those special express trains," Jake said. "The stages and wagons are coming in loaded down with sightseers and reporters, too."

Judge Taylor glanced out the window, watching the logjam of people on the boardwalk and in the street. "You two worried?"

Sam rubbed his hand down his jaw. "We've got four deranged killers in our jail, a Texas Ranger who wants our prisoners to stretch hemp in Texas, and a restless crowd that could turn into a mob at any minute. Yeah, you could say we're worried."

Judge Taylor frowned and took a deep breath. "I can wire the fort for troops," he said, looking from Jake to Sam and back. "It's your decision, Jake."

"I've thought about it, Judge, but no soldiers," Jake got up slowly. "It could do more harm than good. Troopers riding into town might be all it takes to push these folks over the edge." Jake looked toward Sam and got a nod of agreement.

Judge Taylor eyed Jake, "Are you up to all of this, Jake? It makes me hurt just looking at you."

"As long as I don't get pulled into a fistfight, I'll be fine."

"He's never been a fighter," Sam confided to the Judge with a grin.

Judge Taylor scoffed quietly, shaking his head. "Listen, you two. I'll ask Kat if we can use her place tomorrow morning for the trial. We can get more people inside to see the proceedings, and you won't have to take the prisoners to the courthouse. What do you think?"

Quimby burst through the side door, startling the three men. "I saw Judge Taylor come in. I'd like an interview."

Sam chuckled. "Jake, we have got to start locking that door. Judge, I don't believe you've met Quimby Beck. He's editor of the Grant's Crossing Clarion."

"Newspaperman, huh?" the judge said, giving Quimby a long, assessing look. He turned to Sam and Jake. "You vouch for him?"

"Yeah, we'll vouch for him," Jake said grudgingly.

The judge extended his hand. "If you have their approval, you're all right in my book, but we'll have to wait on that interview. I've got bigger fish to fry." The judge turned to Jake, "If you and Sam have no issues with me using Kat's Place for the trial, I'll head over there right now."

"It's fine by us," Jake said.

Judge Taylor gave them a brusque nod and slipped out the side door, followed by Quimby, peppering the judge with questions. Sam locked the door behind them.

The judge pushed his way into the street, slowly gaining ground. A man holding a half-empty bottle of whiskey hung his arm around the judge's shoulders, offering him a drink. Startled, the judge ducked and did his best to hurry away. When he reached Kat's door, he breathed a sigh of relief, but the relief was short-lived. Bumped and jostled, he could barely hold his position. He tried to push through the batwings, but there was little give, only curses, and oaths from the men on the other side of the door. The judge shoved with all his strength, and the door opened enough for him to squeeze through as another man, pushing his way out, slipped past him.

A cloud of smoke hung in the hot, unmoving air, thick enough that the judge couldn't see the back wall of the saloon. The smell of whiskey, beer, and sweat permeated the air. The judge looked for Kat, trying to see over the shoulders of the men surrounding him and wishing he were as tall as Sam. The push and pull of the crowd moved him gradually toward the back of the room, but Kat would most likely be at the front of the saloon behind the bar. In stubborn determination, he raised his arms and hurled himself in that direction.

Somewhere out of the crowd, a hand grabbed hold of him and pulled him through the rabble. A sturdy, dark-haired man was clearing the way.

"Here you go, Judge," Bear said, lifting the flip-gate at the end of the bar and pushing him through to safety. Bear quickly dropped the gate behind them. "Looked like you needed a hand," Bear said, pulling a stool out of the corner and offering it to the judge. "Haven't had a chance to use this lately," he said with a tired smile.

"Thank you, Bear." The judge's racing heart was beginning to quiet. He understood the dangers of such a large crowd, and even though Sam did not use the term lynching, he knew it had to be on the minds of both lawmen. Most of the people here were harmless. They'd come to witness *the trial of the century*, but there were always troublemakers. If something set this crowd off, there'd be no reining it in. What could three lawmen do if a mob this size stormed the jail? There'd be bloodshed, and innocent people would be killed.

Kat's voice brought him out of his reverie. "Judge. Good to see you. Quite a celebration, isn't it?" The judge couldn't help but notice the tiredness in her voice and her eyes. Her dress was rumpled and stained, and her hair was in disarray, not her usual unruffled appearance. But her smile beamed as big and sincere as ever.

"It is something," the judge said with a chuckle. "Never knew so many people were interested in the law."

"I don't think they're interested in the law, Judge. They want someone to hang for those murders down in Texas. From what I hear, the bank robbery in Dallas was glorified in graphic detail in newspapers all across the country. Headlines demanding retribution for those who were murdered. They got everyone all riled up. When folks found out about the trial, they wanted to jump on the revenge bandwagon." While she talked, Kat was drawing beers and setting them on a tray for one of the servers. Taking a breath, Kat turned to the judge. "What can I do for you, Judge? I doubt you fought your way in here for a chat."

"You're right. That's not why I'm here, but I wouldn't turn down a drink. Kat, I want to use your place for the trial."

Kat set up a line of glasses and, grabbing a bottle of rye, poured her way down the line, filling each of them to the top. She handed one to Judge Taylor before the tray was swept away. "I'd be happy to let you use my place, but how do you figure on getting all of these people out of here?"

The judge wiped the sweat from his face with his handkerchief. "That's a job for Jake and his deputies."

Kat filled another line of glasses, and the tray was immediately whisked away by one of her girls. "Jake and Sam will love you for that."

"I expect they will."

At the rear of the saloon, an argument escalated into a shouting match with threats of gunplay. Alex, who was dealing Faro, stood and turned toward the disturbance. He assessed the situation and left the table, warning the punters not to touch anything on the board. Alex muscled his way through to the center of the argument.

"You men need to quiet down," he said, his voice calm, as he pulled his coat back, showing them the rig of a two-handed gunfighter. "I haven't shot anyone in weeks, but my guns are oiled and ready, and I could use some target practice." He paused, eyeing the two men who had been arguing, then swept his eyes to those who were intently watching.

"It wouldn't bother me none to shoot any one of you. It's what I get paid to do."

A man in a ragged, sweat-stained shirt stepped forward. "I don't care how tough you think you are or how fast you are, you can't take all of us." His red-rimmed eyes glared at Alex, and his rye-soaked words were received with drunken approval from his audience.

"You're right, but I will take five or six of you with me before I go down." A slow smile spread across his face. "You'll eat the first bullet. Any volunteers for the second?"

No one volunteered, and the two men who started the ruckus turned and disappeared into the crowd. They were in a hurry to get away from the man with steel-hard eyes, two guns, and no fear.

Kat felt relieved as Alex returned to the Faro table, where the players had remained unmoving. "That's not the first time Alex or Bear have had to put out a fire. I don't know how the rest of the businesses are doing, but we've kept things peaceful—for the most part. I hope we can keep it under control for another twenty-four hours."

"You don't think this will be over tomorrow morning after the trial?"

"There will be celebrations afterward. Most folks will head out with their curiosity satisfied, but some will need more whiskey and more fist fights. Those are the hardcore folks that worry me. The ones who won't want the party to end."

Judge Taylor nodded, letting out a sharp breath. "Well, Kat, we're in for a penny, in for a pound. The trial will begin promptly at seven a.m. Can you have this place set up for me by then?"

"You bet I can," Kat said, pouring the judge a glass of whiskey from her private stock. "This one should go down easy, and you look like you could use another drink."

The judge saluted her, downed the whiskey, and put the glass back on the bar.

"Bear," Kat shouted above the clamor. "Clear a path for the judge back to the marshal's office."

CHAPTER 89

SMASHED SANDWICHES

Earlier, Jake had sent Logan to the ranch with instructions to ride fast and warn his family not to come to town. Grant, Lorene, and Winnie would want to attend the trial, but he didn't want them anywhere near the madhouse Grant's Crossing had become. Jake thought it would be a good idea to have another experienced man standing with them, and Nate Daniels filled the bill. Daniels had been a high-ranking officer in the Confederate Army, and his training and expertise would come in handy. Jake left Sam to guard the prisoners and headed south to Daniel's Farm. Jake found him at his house, and Daniels agreed to help in any way he could.

Heading back to town, the closer Jake got to Grant's Crossing, the more crowded the roads became. There were campsites scattered all along the road for miles.

Taking the back alleys into town, he led Drach into the enclosed yard behind his office. Sam was waiting for him inside. "What'd he say?" Sam asked.

"He'll be here."

"Good. Judge Taylor just left. The trial is at Kat's Place and starts in the morning at seven sharp. He says we need to clear everyone out of Kat's to give her time to set up." Sam chuckled. "He had no suggestions as to how we could go about it."

Sam looked at Jake with a frown. "You look battered."

"The ride out and back was harder than I thought it'd be, but I'm all right. Go get something to eat while I lay down."

Sam left, and Jake stretched out on the cot, but he was too restless to sleep. He got up and paced, then sat behind his desk, trying to read the newspaper that Quimby had dropped off. He couldn't concentrate, couldn't get past the front-page headline, *The Trial of the Century*. He got up and paced. Hunger gnawed at his belly, exhaustion pulled at his shirttails, and he hurt all over. He was eager to check in with Kat to let her know about his plan to bring the prisoners over at midnight and to get something to eat. But he couldn't leave until Sam or Logan returned.

Jake sat with his elbows on the desktop. Balancing his face between his fists, he stared at the newspaper unseeing. Where were Sam and Logan? What was taking them so long?

Flexing his knuckles, he took stock of his men. Counting himself, there were eight. Would it be enough? He toyed with the thought that maybe he should have wired the fort. Maybe he'd been a fool not to ask for their help, but it was too late for second-guessing, and he stood by his earlier decision. A column of soldiers riding into town would be a mistake.

Jake rose from behind his desk and straightened slowly into a stretch before moving toward the window. Halfway to the window, he heard a tapping on the door. "It's me, John. Let me in."

"Sam said you could use some help tonight," John Miller said, coming through the doorway. He was followed by a dozen other men, all with guns strapped to their hips and rifles in hand. "We're all behind you, Jake." John and the rest of the men raised their rifles in agreement.

Jake shook his head. "This is an ugly situation that could turn deadly in a heartbeat. I can't ask you to get wrapped up in this mess."

Mal spoke. "We're already wrapped up in it, Jake. We live here, we have businesses here, and you aren't asking us; we're volunteering. We've got families to protect, and we want law and justice in Grant's Crossing as much as you do."

Jake was moved by their willingness to put their lives on the line. He deputized them, saying he would need them around midnight when he planned to move the prisoners across the street to Kat's.

"We'll be here," John said, nodding to Jake. Then he turned to the men behind him. "Come on, let's get back to our businesses. We'll meet here at midnight." John left, cutting his way through the crowd, making a path for the others.

Sam returned soon after the men left. "I've been making the rounds and doing some recruiting. Most everyone volunteered when I told them what we were doing. If they all show up, we'll have fifteen or twenty men on top of the others we've already got lined up."

"Some of your recruits were just here. Thanks, Sam," he said, grabbing his hat and moving to the door.

"Where are you off to?"

"I'm starving," Jake said, pushing open the door and shoving his way into the street.

Jake fought his way to Kat's. Every shove, nudge, and elbow sent pain shooting through his body. Bear saw him and opened the flip gate. "You look tired, Jake," he said, motioning to the stool in the corner.

Jake sat. "I've felt better. Is there any food left?"

"Yeah, Tank put food back. I'll get one of the girls to bring you something. Need anything else?"

"Yeah, I need to talk with Kat. It won't take long." He got up with a muffled groan and went to stand by her side.

"What do you need, handsome?" she said, continuing to fill whiskey glasses without missing a beat.

"We need to talk in private."

Kat laughed. "And where would that be?"

"I see your point, but step back from the bar for a moment. I don't want anyone hearing us."

She tossed an empty bottle into the trash bin. "You're serious. Sorry, Jake. What is it?"

Jake and Kat turned their backs to the bar and spoke in hushed tones. "I'm bringing the prisoners over tonight around midnight. We'll use the back door and take the prisoners to the cellar until it's time for the trial. If everything goes right, no one will be the wiser."

"That's fine by me, Jake. I'll make sure the door is unlocked." Kat looked at Jake with a frown. "How do you plan on clearing this place out? Judge Taylor said you'd handle it."

Jake looked around and shrugged, "I have no idea, but we'll think of something."

Kat returned to pouring drinks, and Bear handed Jake two wrapped sandwiches. "Marshal, you can't eat those here, or you'll cause a riot. Tuck them in your shirt and find a safe place before unwrapping them."

Jake nodded as he looked across the sea of brim-to-brim hats, dreading the pummeling he would take crossing back to his office. He shrugged and struggled into the crowd.

Closing his office door behind him, he leaned against it with a heavy sigh and looked at Sam. "I'm going to sleep for a week when this is over."

Sam watched him gimp to his desk and pull smashed sandwiches from his shirt. "Next time, I'll bring you food," Sam said with a grin. "You gotta quit pushing yourself. Why don't you lie down when you're done eating and get some shuteye? It looks like you could use it."

"I'll rest when this is over. Logan should be back anytime now," Jake said, washing down a bite of sandwich with leftover cold coffee.

"I think I'll take a walk and see what's going on around town, and I need to stop at the store for a new hat."

"Don't get the black one," Jake said, around a mouthful of sandwich.

CHAPTER 90

A RUCKUS AT THE SLIPPER

As Sam left the marshal's office, Zeke snaked his way to his side. "There's a big ruckus down at the Slipper. Pitt and Duck need your help."

Pitt and Duck were owners of the Scarlett Slipper Saloon and had been for some time. They didn't allow fighting or gunplay in their establishment, and both had the grit to back it up.

"Check to see if Alex can get away. Tell him I'd appreciate some backup."

Zeke nodded and headed for Kat's, poking and prodding his way across the street. Sam took off as fast as he could, weaving through the jostling bodies. Sometimes, the crowd carried him forward in the direction he was headed, and sometimes, he had to fight to stay on course. Oddly, it seemed no one besides him had a particular destination.

Sam muscled his way into the Slipper and found Pitt and Duck standing on the bottom step of the staircase with shotguns in hand, fending off a crush of men who wanted to get to the upper level and to the Slipper's women.

Sam surveyed the men gathered at the foot of the staircase, trying to identify the instigator. Pitt and Duck were keeping them back, but if one of those shotguns went off, it could turn into a bloodbath.

Alex came in as Sam homed in on the leader. "Who's the head of this snake?" Alex asked.

"I'm saying it's a two-headed snake. The one left of center with the checkered shirt and the whiskered one to his left."

After a quick assessment, Alex agreed. "How do you want to handle this?"

"Haven't got a clue. You?"

"No idea," Alex said with a smile that didn't reach his eyes.

"Well, let's get their attention for starters and see what happens," Sam said, pulling his gun and firing into the air. That gunshot was followed by two more sharp pops; one from each of the pearl-handled Colts now in Alex's hands.

Sam looked at Alex with a raised eyebrow.

"Thought I should leather two irons tonight. What with the way things are and all."

Sam and Alex holstered their guns, not wanting to ignite the situation. "Everyone, move away from the staircase," Sam shouted, stepping forward.

No one budged except the two men Sam had identified as the ringleaders. They shouldered their way forward to face Sam and Alex.

Sam held his hands up, signaling them to stay back. "Everyone needs to settle down. Go to your tables or go home."

Still, no one moved. "If you don't break this up, you'll all go to jail."

The whiskered man laughed drunkenly. "Lawman, your jail ain't big enough for all of us, and you wouldn't put us in with them killers anyway."

"Our cellar is big enough, and the rats won't mind. Sadly, there are no windows and no facilities. It might be crowded and stinky, but it'd only be for two days—that's the penalty for disorderly conduct."

"You can't take all of us," Whiskers growled. "Come on, men, let's rush them." The men muttered and shifted nervously, but no one moved forward.

Alex laughed, "That's what your kind always says. Hell, it's the second time I've heard it today. And now I say...but you and your friend are first. You're as good as dead."

"We've got your back, Deputy," Pitt yelled from the staircase, his timing perfect.

Everyone except Whiskers and the man in the checkered shirt began to back away. No one wanted to die for the women upstairs. Sam didn't know if it was whiskey or a broad streak of stubbornness that trumped their good senses, but the two instigators stood their ground. Pitt and Duck lowered their shotguns and moved behind the bar as the four men faced off. Everyone's attention was riveted on the outcome.

"We're not going to jail, not in this lifetime," Whiskers snarled. "Hook and draw, Deputy."

Sam widened his stance and turned slightly to the side. "Your choice, but there's no way this will be a fair fight. Back off and walk away."

"Looks to me like you got a yellow streak. Are you a coward, Deputy?"

Neither of the men moved, and Sam nodded to Alex. "Let's do it their way."

When Whiskers made his move, Sam and Alex drew. Alex, only a split-second faster. Neither of the men who faced them had a chance. Sam holstered his gun, and squatted on his haunches, checking the two men lying on the floor. They were dead.

Pitt came out from behind the bar. "Thanks, Deputy, Alex."

"What happened, Pitt?" Sam said, rising to face him.

"Everything was quiet, and then these two men started arguing about who was going upstairs next. Then fists started flying, and it got ugly fast. We didn't want to use our shotguns, but we couldn't let that mob get to the women. They'd have killed them."

"I'll let Bones know he's got customers," Sam said. "Come on, Alex. Let's go."

Word of the gunfight flew through the streets like a bolt of lightning. A rush of people descended on the Slipper, pushing and shoving to get inside. Everyone wanted to see the bodies and to get a look at the two men who survived.

"Thanks for the backup, Alex."

Alex nodded. "Any time."

The two men turned for the door, and the crowd of people parted to let them through. Sam smiled, feeling a bit like Moses.

CHAPTER 91

THE MILE-A-WAY

round ten o'clock, Kat began to worry about getting her place cleared out. She surveyed the crowded barroom with a sense of urgency. "They're going to have to do something soon," she complained to Bear.

"We need time to get things cleaned up," she said, an edge of panic in her voice. "We need to bring tarps from the cellar to cover the gaming tables, mirrors, and pictures, and cover all the liquor bottles, too. I hope we have enough tarps. We also need to set up tables and chairs for the judge, jury, and lawyers. It'll take some doing, and right now, it looks impossible."

She was about to send Bear across the street to fetch Jake or Sam when Clark came in, grumbling under his breath. He held a shiny silver spur in each hand, using them to poke and prod his way forward through the crowd.

He spat a stream of tobacco juice, hitting a brass spittoon with a twang, and wiped his shirt sleeve across his mouth. "I came to clear out your saloon," he said, climbing on top of the bar. "Alex. Get your hindquarters over here," he hollered. "Kat, you might want to get anyone you care about behind the bar and out of harm's way 'cause there's gonna be a stampede."

Kat didn't stop to ask questions. She gathered her girls and bartenders behind the bar. "Now what?" she said, looking up at Clark.

It was ten-forty-five when Clark bellowed at the top of his lungs, "Free drinks at the Mile Away." Clark's voice echoed across the swarm. "Free drinks at the Mile Away." There was some confusion about the location of the Mile Away, but they were working it out as they rushed and scrambled through the batwing doors, forcing themselves into the street. At eleven o'clock, Kat closed her doors behind the last of the revelers.

"What a brilliant idea," Kat said, smiling at Clark. "And no one deserves it more than that slimy Bert James."

The Mile Away Inn, located south and west of town, was the worst kind of saloon imaginable. Bert James, the owner of the two-story doggery, was a less-than-reputable man and had been on Jake's watch list for some time.

Only half a dozen patrons remained in Kat's Place, those who were inebriated to the point of being unable to move, and those who knew the Mile Away was best avoided. Alex escorted the last few out the door while Kat's staff prepared the saloon for the trial. All hands pitched in, and they quickly put together an acceptable courtroom. Kat sent everyone home for a night's rest. They would need it. Tomorrow morning would be wilder than anything they'd seen tonight.

Alex sat down at the piano and began to play. At first, it was a simple, childish ditty, and then more complicated music flowed effortlessly from his fingers. Kat sat beside him, wondering how she had ever survived without him.

CHAPTER 92

MIDNIGHT TRANSFER

Sam stood in the doorway of the marshal's office, watching the crowd. He was anxious about moving the prisoners and glad to see that the street had cleared some. Nate Daniels had arrived earlier, and he, Jake, Logan, and Clark sat around the desk. Sam closed the door and joined them.

"What worries me most is that any one of our prisoners could have friends or kin watching the jail, waiting for a chance to free them." Jake pushed the hair from his forehead. "And then there's Ranger Hill."

"If all your volunteers show up, you'll have enough men to take up all the strategic positions we've identified," Nate Daniels said with confidence. "You'll have good cover, and if we're quiet about it, we might not even be noticed. There's nothing more you can do, Marshal."

When midnight rolled around, a group of twenty-five businessmen, ranchers, and farmers showed up armed and ready. Jake and Sam both breathed a sigh of relief.

Quimby Beck stood on the boardwalk in front of the marshal's office, a notepad in hand and an ever-present pencil stuck behind his ear. He watched intently as preparations for the transfer of prisoners began. The deputies quietly cleared as many people as possible from the area and then took up their positions. Some were posted on street corners, and rifle barrels could be seen poking from rooftops and upstairs windows. The alleys beside the marshal's office and Kat's Place had been searched and blocked off.

Sam came out of the office and stood beside Quimby, his eyes scanning the street.

"You look concerned," Quimby said.

"I'd be less concerned if I knew where that Texas Ranger got to," Sam said, his eyes searching the faces. "And anyone one of these men could be here to make a try for the prisoners."

Sam and Quimby watched as they brought out the last prisoner. Nate tied up the Velazquez woman with the rest of the prisoners amid a mix of vile oaths and promises to service any man who released her. No one complained when Nate shoved a gag in her mouth.

Jake checked all the ropes and nodded to Daniels. "Let's get them across the street."

The street remained crowded, but some had returned to their camps, others were drinking in the saloons, and some were passed out. Sam, Jake, Logan, Alex, and Clark each escorted a prisoner, with Bear in front clearing the way and Nate bringing up the rear. If they were lucky, they would fade into what was left of the crowd.

Kat's Place was almost directly across from the jail, but tonight, it seemed like a mile. Halfway across the street, they heard the sharp crack of a rifle. Everyone hit the ground, pulling the prisoners down with them. Guns were drawn, and their eyes searched for the shooter.

"Anyone hit?" Jake said, cautiously getting up.

Quimby hollered, "I saw a flash on top of the General Store. John's up there."

Nate and Bear ran toward the General Store in time to see a short, heavyset man running through the crowd, up the street, and around the corner. They'd never be able to catch him and were more concerned about John. They charged up the steps to the roof.

John groaned as he sat up. "You hurt," Bear asked, extending him a hand.

"I'm mad as a hornet at being bushwhacked," John said, rubbing the back of his head.

"Good thing you're hard-headed," Bear joshed as all three hurried down the steps to rejoin the others.

"What's wrong with Quimby?" John asked, rushing to his side. Quimby was sitting on the boardwalk, leaning against the building. "He's been shot," John hollered as he pulled Quimby from the ground and headed to Coop's office.

The prisoners were taken the rest of the way across the street and into Kat's without further problems. Few people had taken any notice of the gunfire, and those who did were too drunk to care.

Alex and Bear remained in the saloon while Jake went outside to check with his deputies. They were gathered by the front door, waiting for instructions and John had returned from Coop's office reporting that Quimby had only been grazed by the bullet.

"Good to hear," Jake said with a nod. "The trial starts tomorrow at seven sharp. I'd appreciate any help you men can give me."

"We'll be here," John said.

Jake jostled his way up the street to Coop's office to check on Quimby. Poking his head in, he saw Quimby buttoning his shirt, a big smile lighting up his face. "I got shot, Jake."

Jake looked at Coop, who shrugged his shoulders. "I've never once had a patient excited about getting shot. The bullet barely grazed his arm, but at his request, I have stitched him up."

Still smiling, Quimby said, "Coop says I'll have a scar." He paused for a second, then, with newfound enthusiasm, he jumped to his feet. "Jake, teach me to shoot."

Coop laughed at the Easterner's unbridled enthusiasm. Jake scowled at him, "Not until you calm down some. But I agree. It isn't a bad idea for you and Hannah to know how to use a gun properly." Jake slapped him on the back. "You even became a part of the story out there tonight. I can see tomorrow's headline: *Newspaperman Wounded Guarding Prisoners*."

Relieved that Quimby hadn't been seriously wounded, Jake turned to leave.

"Jake, you need to slow down and get some rest before you fall over on your face." Coop's voice was edged with a sternness that Jake had never heard before.

"I'm fine, Coop, and this will be over tomorrow. Then I can rest."

When he got back to Kat's, two poker games were still in progress, including the one that had been going on for years. Everything else was buttoned down for the night. Jake walked to the piano, where Alex was playing a ballad. Jake had heard it before but couldn't quite place it. Kat sat beside Alex, looking as tired as he'd ever seen her.

Jake pushed his hat back. "Alex, your talents never cease to amaze me."

"How's Quimby?"

"Only a graze."

Alex continued playing softly. "Who is this Quimby fellow anyway? He came in yesterday snooping around. He seemed particularly interested in the reporters."

"He's editor and chief of The Clarion, our new town newspaper," Jake explained.

"You trust him?"

"I do. At least until he proves me wrong."

The one poker game broke up, and Jake escorted the men to the door and locked it behind them. "It looks like you're ready for tomorrow's trial. See you in the morning," Jake said, heading to the cellar to check on the prisoners."

Jake went through the back hallway to the cellar door, where Clark and Logan stood guard. "Any trouble?"

"None."

In the cellar, Sam was leaning against the wall, his hand close to his gun. "They're restless," Sam said, motioning toward the five hate-filled faces glaring at them.

"The trial starts in less than six hours. Think we can stay awake until then?"

"One of us has to. Why don't you stretch out and try to get some rest? You look like you're about to fall over."

"Coop shares that opinion." Jake said, slumping on a whiskey barrel. It was going to be a rough night. "Wish I knew who shot at us. From the description Bear and Alex gave, it could have been the ranger."

"I don't think so, Jake. If it was the ranger, he'd have been limping away."

CHAPTER 93

THE TRIAL

At six-fifty the following morning, the five prisoners were escorted up the cellar stairs and into the saloon. All the liquor behind the bar was covered with tarps, and all the tables had been covered and pushed to the side. The unending poker game had been moved to the furthest corner and surrounded by room-dividing screens. The judge paid a last-minute visit to the men at the poker table, warning them to keep it quiet or they'd be playing their final hand.

By dawn, before the prisoners were brought in, the barroom was packed. Those who couldn't find a seat had sandwiched in wherever they could. The boardwalks and streets were still crowded, but this morning, the crowd had a goal. Like sunflowers raising their blooms to the sun, all faces were turned toward Kat's Place.

At seven o'clock on the dot, Judge Taylor mounted the steps to where his desk had been set up. Jake, Sam, the prisoners, and their defense attorney, Charles Riehle, took their places. The prosecuting attorney sat alone. The judge pounded his gavel until the tumultuous din of voices fell silent, and the trial began.

The judge called the names of those men who had been chosen at random to act as the jury. They had been notified the previous day and were all present when they were called on to take their seats. When the jury was seated, the judge addressed the four men in cuffs. "Will the defendants please rise. Mort Watkins, Robert Jenkins, Robert (Patch) Lutker, and Paul (Red) Redenbaugh, you've been charged with murder, attempted murder, kidnapping, robbery, burglary, assault and battery, destruction of property, arson, and resisting arrest. How do you plead?"

Each man pleaded not guilty to a chorus of jeers from those seated in the public area. The judge pounded his gavel, silencing the courtroom. "Any additional outbursts and I'll clear the room."

The judge addressed the woman. "Margaret Velasquez, you are charged with accessory to murder, kidnapping, robbery, and resisting arrest. How do you plead?"

She pled not guilty with a wink and a suggestive wiggle for the judge, causing laughter to ripple through the crowd.

Judge Taylor banged his gavel and nodded to the prosecuting attorney, who gave a moving opening argument. He listed and briefly described each of the vicious crimes the men had committed. When he finished, the judge nodded to the defense attorney to begin.

The crowd booed the defending attorney from the moment he stood, but one bang from the gavel and all went quiet. No one wanted to be thrown out. Everyone wanted to hear.

The defense attorney approached the jury with a furrowed brow. The barrel-shaped man stood in front of them, his coat open and his thumbs hooked in his suspenders. "All the evidence against my clients is circumstantial," he proclaimed in a booming voice. "As a matter of fact," he looked toward the prosecuting attorney, "the prosecution has no factual proof or eyewitnesses to corroborate the outrageous charges brought against these fine, law-abiding men." He sighed dramatically and turned to each juror and looked them in the eye. His voice softened, "Some have called this the *trial of the century*, and maybe it is, but if these innocent men are convicted," he paused for effect. "It will be the *travesty of the century*, and no justice will have been served."

Waving his arms dramatically, he passionately responded to each of the prosecution's charges. His opening speech dragged on, and the spectators shifted in their seats, becoming restless. They wanted a verdict.

Despite the judge's repeated warnings, jeers and cat calls erupted, drowning out the attorney's voice. Unfazed, he pressed on. Then, a boot hit the stage, followed by a barrage of boots, one hitting its mark. Laughter rang out along with the jeers. The judge pounded his gavel, finally bringing order to his courtroom.

"Wrap it up, Chuck," the judge instructed with a warning glare at the attorney.

Witnesses were called and sworn in. Jake and Sam each had their turn in the witness chair. Their testimonies were factual and short. Then, Alex took the stand.

Alex recounted the bank robbery in Dallas and what happened to the kidnapped girl in graphic detail. He spoke elegantly, walking the jury and the crowd through what had transpired. As he told how the young boy had died at Mort's hands, Sam glared at his stepfather, and his fists clenched on his lap. He couldn't help but think that if he had killed him when he'd had the chance, that young boy might still be alive. And how many others, he wondered.

When Alex finished his testimony, there wasn't a dry eye in the courtroom, including the defense attorney.

"Mr. Scott, you may step down. Are there any more witnesses? If not, we can begin our closing arguments."

A voice from the back of the room interrupted. "I apologize to the court, Your Honor, but I have pertinent information to share. I'm Mark Hill, Texas Ranger."

"This is irregular, but I'd like to hear what you have to say." The judge asked the two attorneys if they had any objections and, finding none, he motioned Mark Hill to the witness stand.

Mark walked up the middle aisle limping, his arm in a sling. The bailiff swore him in, and each of the lawyers questioned him. He reiterated all the facts Alex had testified to. Then he asked the judge if he could speak his mind, and the judge gave an approving nod.

"I know it doesn't matter to the law here in Dakota Territory, but I want you to know for a fact that there are five reliable eyewitnesses in Texas who can identify these men: two bank employees and three surviving customers who were in the bank at the time of the robbery."

The attorney jumped to his feet. "I object. That's hearsay, Judge. It's not admissible. Why aren't those reliable witnesses here to testify so I can cross-examine them? All we have is this man's…"

A rumble of displeasure grew, and the judge raised his gavel, glaring at the crowd. Everyone stilled, waiting for his ruling.

"Sit down, Chuck. I'm interested in what this man has to say."

"But, your honor."

"Shut your mouth, Chuck," the judge warned and turned toward the witness. "Please continue, Ranger Hill."

"I guess it doesn't matter where they hang. But if you folks aren't going to hang them here, please, let me take them back to Texas. All I want is justice for the people they've killed—the lives they've destroyed."

The courtroom went wild as Texas Ranger Mark Hill left the witness stand. Screams for a guilty verdict and a hanging reverberated, and the crush of humanity melded into a mob, surging for the stage. The judge slammed his gavel frantically but to no avail. Jake fired two rounds into the ceiling as Sam, Alex, Logan, and fifteen sworn deputies moved to the front of the stage. Each armed with scatter guns pointed at the crowd. The crowd went quiet. The stillness rolled from the stage to the front of the saloon and into the street.

"My jail isn't big enough for all of you," Jake hollered. "But there are cattle cars sitting on the railroad tracks, and they'll do just fine.

People slowly began returning to their seats amid grumbling and the scuffing of boots and chair legs. Once everyone had settled down, the judge asked for closing arguments. Charles kept his remarks brief, with no posturing or arm waving. At nine-fifteen, Judge Taylor gave the jury instructions on the points of law to be considered and sent them to the billiards room to decide the prisoners' fate. The verdict came quickly and unanimously. The defendants were guilty as charged on all counts. Cheers erupted, and Texas Ranger Hill breathed a sigh of relief.

The judge gave a short speech to the spectators, praising them for their interest in seeing justice in action and scolding them for their unruliness. Then, he addressed the convicted men. "You've been found guilty of the aforementioned crimes. I sentence you to be hanged by the neck until dead."

A murmur grew into a cheer, but one stroke of the judge's gavel silenced them. Looking into the barrels of fifteen scatterguns had made everyone considerably more respectful of Judge Taylor and the law.

"The sentence will be carried out the day after tomorrow at nine o'clock a.m. here in Grant's Crossing." The buzzing of the crowd swelled as word spread to the people outside. The curious onlookers shifted their attention to the woman, eager to hear what would become of her.

"You have committed a string of serious crimes. If you were a man, I would see you hang along with the rest of these no-counts. But since you're a woman, I am sentencing you to life in prison at the women's correctional institute in Butte Point."

Sam and Jake barely heard the judge as he sentenced the woman. Had they heard him correctly? The hanging was to be here in Grant's Crossing.

"Open the bar, Kat," Judge Taylor hollered, banging his gavel on the desk. "We're done here. Court's adjourned."

CHAPTER 94

THE GAUNTLET

Sam and Jake hurried the prisoners out the side door. The men guarding them formed a path across the street to the jail. People pushed and jostled their way against the line of deputies, wanting a closer look at the prisoners. Cheers and boos followed the prisoners and their guards as they shoved through the crowd. They were splashed with beer and whiskey, and a rock whizzed by Nate's head, knocking the Velasquez woman to the ground.

The short distance to the marshal's office had become a violent gauntlet. The crowd was closing in, pushing harder against the deputies trying to get at the prisoners. Every step became a struggle. They were on the verge of losing control when two resounding gunshots from the direction of Kat's Place filled the air. The gunfire drew the attention of the converging mass of people long enough to give the guards time to get the prisoners into the jail and slam the door closed behind them.

Sam looked out the window and saw Alex standing on the boardwalk in front of Kat's Place. He gave him a quick salute and Alex acknowledged with a nod.

"That was Alex, saving our hides," Sam said, turning from the window. "Guess we should have waited until things calmed down before bringing our prisoners back across the street."

Nate watched Bear and the other volunteers leave through the side door, but he hung back. "Those men have businesses and families here in town to protect, but this mob is no threat to my place. If you're agreeable, Marshal, I'll stay to lend a hand."

"I'll take you up on that, Nate."

There was an insistent pounding on the side door, "Who is it?" Sam asked, approaching the door.

"It's me, Quimby."

Sam opened the door, and Quimby charged in. "I've already sent off my story. I have an arrangement with Wade. Since I'm local, my stories get first priority." Quimby paused to take a breath. "Marshal, do you think I could interview the prisoners? I want to find out how they feel about being sentenced to hang?"

Nate looked at him, shaking his head. "I doubt they're thrilled with the idea."

Jake frowned. "I don't know why I'm letting you do this, but yeah, go on back."

"Back there?" Quimby said, looking at the locked door between the office and the jail cells. "I thought you would bring them out here one at a time or something."

Jake shook his head. "Too dangerous. I don't want them leaving those cells until hanging time."

A deafening rattle and clanging, accompanied by loud grunts and raucous laughter, came from the cellblock. Quimby jumped, and Logan cackled, "Come on, Mr. Beck. You're about to get a real story. Don't know as you'll be able to print it, though."

Logan closed the door behind Quimby with a chuckle. He was in the midst of describing the source of the ruckus to Nate and Clark in colorful detail when a red-faced Quimby flew from the cellblock. He murmured a thank you to the marshal and hurried out the door. The flustered reporter had no questions for the five lawmen seated around the desk.

When the laughter quieted, Jake spoke. "We need to make our presence known. Folks need to see us and our badges on the street. They need to know there's law in Grant's Crossing,"

There was a knock on the side door. "It's me, Judge Taylor." Sam opened the door and stepped aside with a scowl, letting him enter. "Good job keeping things in hand during the trial. I thought for a minute there you were going to have to make a tough decision."

"It's what I get paid for," Jake said, scowling at the judge.

"Look, I know I've put you men on the spot, and I'm truly sorry. But think about how dangerous it would have been getting those men to Butte Point. I have total confidence that you can handle this, and I'll help with the details and any regulations that need to be adhered to."

Jake thanked the judge for his assistance, but there was a sharp twang of sarcasm in his voice.

Judge Taylor rose to leave. "You boys have a lot to do. I'll arrange for the lumber and carpenters, but you'll have to tell them where you want the gallows built. I'd recommend somewhere outside of town. When word gets out about the hanging, there'll be more people on their way."

Jake sighed. "Just what we need—more people."

CHAPTER 95

AN UNEXPECTED VOLUNTEER

As the judge left, Ranger Hill limped through the door with his hat in his hand. He spoke in a slow, Texas drawl, "I know we got no love lost between us, but I'd like to help. I can patrol the streets, and it looks like you can use all the help you can get."

Jake hesitated, wondering at the ranger's motives. "If you're serious, we could use your help." Jake looked at Sam, wondering if he held a grudge against Hill for the knifing. "Sam, you got any problem with the ranger joining us?"

Sam got up and opened a desk drawer. He pulled out the ranger's Bowie knife and tossed it to him. "No problem, Jake. None at all."

Hill saluted Sam with the knife and returned it to the empty sheath hanging from his belt. "Thought you should know some rabble-rouser at the Bent Ear is talking about a lynching."

"Nate, you and Clark stay here with the prisoners."

"I'll team up with Logan if he don't mind," Hill said. "You and Sam need to be seen together, and Logan and me, we're old-time lawmen." He looked at Logan. "You willing?"

"I've been paired with worse," Logan replied with a snort.

Jake nodded. "Well, then, let's hit the streets. Sam and I will go to the Bent Ear. Logan, take Hill and head to the east end of town."

Jake and Sam slipped into the Bent Ear. They nodded to Mal, who stood behind the bar with his hand on the hidden shotgun under the bar. The surly-looking rabble-rouser holding court at the bar didn't notice them, and if any of the rapt members of his audience had, they gave no indication. The man's beard was stiff with tobacco juice and rose comically up and down when he spoke, but what he said held no humor.

"What are we waiting for, men? Let's get down to that jail and get them killers. They've been found guilty. I don't see no need to wait."

"Yeah," a voice replied. "That big old oak up by the church will hold 'em all."

A chorus of "Yeah, let's go," accompanied his words.

"Break it up," Jake hollered, elbowing his way to the front of the crowd. Thirty men turned their eyes toward him. "Pipe down, mister. There'll be no lynching in Grant's Crossing." Then he turned to the mob. "And there are four men with shotguns inside the jail" he lied, "with orders to kill anyone who tries to take my prisoners."

The agitator turned his long, narrow face toward Jake. "No stinking lawman is going to tell me to pipe down or tell me what I can and can't say." The crowd murmured in agreement. "I got rights," he hollered, banging his beer mug on the bar. All the men at the bar and at tables began banging their glasses, and the chanting for a hanging grew louder and louder.

"Tone it down, mister. Stirring up trouble isn't one of your rights," Jake said.

The man who had been brazenly sarcastic suddenly turned deadly. "I told you, nobody muzzles me, not even a lawman. Your justice is taking too long. They've been convicted and sentenced." He spun toward the crowd, long white clumps of hair dragging across his shoulders as he turned. "What are we waiting for, men?" The crowd bristled and stirred, egging him on. "I say we give those killers a taste of Dakota justice."

"I say it's time to back off," Jake hollered as loud as his aching ribs would allow.

"I heard tell the marshal of Grant's Crossing is a tight-assed lawman and fast with his gun, but you wouldn't stand a chance against me." He turned to his audience and raised his beer mug. "Let's go, men, we'll storm the jail." He chugged down the last of the beer and slammed the mug on the bar.

In one fluid movement, Jake's gun was in his hand, the bullet shattering the empty mug. "Mister, you're going to jail."

The man scowled at Jake, pulling back his long, ragged coat and displaying a pair of well-used pistols. "You still want to play?"

"Two guns don't bother me. It only takes one bullet."

With his hand on the butt of his gun, Sam closely watched the crowd of bystanders who were drifting out of the way. Mal pulled the shotgun from under the bar and nodded to Sam.

The man riling up the crowd leaned one elbow casually against the bar. He shook his head and grinned. "Holster your gun, Marshal, and let's make this interesting." Before the last word was out of his mouth, he went for his guns. Jake shot him before either of his guns cleared leather.

The man hit the floor with a tremendous thud, his body convulsing, the hole in his chest pulsing blood. He finally stilled, but his beard continued bobbing up and down even as he took his last breath.

Jake surveyed the room. "There's law in this town, and there'll be no lynching in Grant's Crossing." Jake turned to Mal. "Set them up on me. I'll settle with you later."

As Jake and Sam left, they heard Mal asking some of the men to take the dead man to the undertaker. "Think that was wise?" Sam asked. "Buying them more alcohol."

"Maybe they'll pass out," Jake said with a groan, rubbing his side.

Quimby came running up the street, threading his way through the crowd. "I heard shots. What happened?"

Sam looked at Quimby with a smile. "You're getting to be a downright pest, Quim. Talk to Mal. He can give you the details." Sam motioned toward the Bent Ear, and Quimby took the hint, hurrying away.

"Thanks, Sam. I didn't want to talk about it."

"You mean how that idiot drew down on you while you had a gun in your hand?"

"There's that. I killed a man, Sam, and somehow having all the gory details in the newspaper doesn't seem right." Jake shrugged. "Guess, now that we have a newspaper, that's how it'll be."

"Quim will tell it how it happened," Sam said as they approached Bridge Street. "I think he's right. A newspaper will be good for Grant's Crossing."

"He's green as a pea," Jake said.

"He is that. But remember what a tinhorn Coop was when he first got here, and look how he's turned out."

"Heard gunfire—everything alright?"

They looked up at the sound of Charlie's voice. He was on the small landing at the top of the stairway behind the General Store. He was leaning casually against the weathered railing, a quirly hanging from his lips, and a shotgun balanced in the crook of his arm.

"There was a commotion at the Bent Ear," Sam said as people shuffled around them. "You?"

"I got a dandy view from up here," Charlie said, striking a match. "We hired one of the Wilkinson girls to help in the store so I can keep watch up here." Charlie looked up at the clearing sky. "It'll be hot and humid tomorrow. Might make folks a bit fussy."

Jake and Sam waved and turned the corner onto Bridge Street. They caught sight of Coop battling his way toward them through the press of bodies. Sam grabbed his arm to anchor him.

"Where you headed?"

"To find you. Mr. Terrance is in trouble, up at the schoolyard."

CHAPTER 96

MR. TERRANCE

Sam took the lead, bulling his way through the crowd. When they got to the schoolyard, they found Mr. Terrance in the middle of an altercation, trying to reason things out with his tormentor. His students were inside. Some were hanging out of the schoolhouse windows, waiting to see what would happen.

Usually, on a Monday afternoon, the children would be outside playing, but today, filthy campsites filled the playground. Folks who had come for the trial lingered to see the hanging, and the tents were crammed closer and closer together as additional curiosity seekers arrived in town.

Sam saw Mr. Terrance take a vicious punch to his midsection. As he doubled over, an uppercut to the jaw sent him to the ground. The man raised his leg to stomp on Mr. Terrance, but Sam rushed forward, shoving him back. Jake helped his former teacher to his feet, steadying him.

"Take him inside, Jake. I've got this," Sam said, his eyes fixed on the man stomping toward him.

The man's nostrils were flared, and his body swayed with aggression. "You may be wearing a badge, mister, but I'm the boss in this camp. These folks do what I say, or they move on, and now, you're the one who needs to move on."

"He's making us pay to camp here, Deputy," someone in the crowd yelled.

Sam scowled and shook his head, his voice steady. "You need to give any money you've collected to the man you were pounding on. It'll help pay for cleaning up this mess when you've all moved on. Fork it over."

The tormentor threw back his head, roaring with laughter. Sam cut the man's laughter short when he stepped forward, delivering a swift, explosive punch to his chest. The man's ribs cracked from the force of the blow, and he fell to the ground, doubled over, gasping for breath like a fish out of water.

The crowd surrounded them, cheering as Sam took the gun from the tormentor's holster. He pulled a Bowie knife from a sheath hidden in his boot and a derringer tucked behind his belt buckle. He removed a money poke from around the man's neck and weighed it in his hand. "Seems like you've collected quite a bit from these folks."

Sam looked with disgust at the man curled up in a fetal position at his feet. "Mister, the man you were beating on is a friend of mine. Consider yourself lucky that I'm wearing a badge." Sam grabbed the man by the collar, pulling him up to face him. The man, still choking and struggling for air, whimpered in pain.

"The badge stopped me this time, but if I see you again, this badge won't make a bit of difference, and you'll be staying on as a permanent resident—in Pauper's Field. Get out of Grant's Crossing tonight, and don't come back." Sam released the man, shoving him toward Bridge Street.

Sam walked into the schoolhouse to a cheering welcome from the children. Mr. Terrance accepted the poke of money. "Thanks, Sam. I hope you didn't hurt him too badly."

"He'll live."

For the next day and a half, it was relatively quiet, considering the number of people who had converged on the town. There were brawls and struggles, broken windows, furniture destroyed, gunfire and fireworks, and short-tempered boozy brawls all over town. But all dustups were quickly handled, and there was no more talk of lynching after the gunfight at the Bent Ear.

CHAPTER 97

THE HANGING

Quimby put down his pencil and reread the article he had just finished writing. It could be better, he thought, but he didn't have time to refine it. He had to get it on the wire before the other reporters beat him to it.

Grant's Crossing, Saturday, the twenty-second day of May.

At seven o'clock, the men condemned to hang for the robbery of the Atherton Bank of Dallas and the gruesome murders committed during that robbery were given a last breakfast of steak, eggs, biscuits and gravy, a cup of whiskey, and a cup of coffee. Two of the four prisoners took communion from Pastor Emil Larsen of Our Savior's Lutheran Church.

After breakfast, their pant legs were tied with twine at the knees and ankles. Then, their wrists and ankles were shackled. At seven forty-five, they shuffled, with chains rattling, from the jail to a large, open farm wagon modified for transporting the prisoners. Five lawmen and numerous members of the community, who had been deputized, guarded the prisoners as they were brought from the jail and helped into the back of the wagon. Once inside, they were seated on wooden benches.

I watched from the back of the wagon as their chains were attached to iron rings bolted into the sides and bottom of the wagon.

Marshal William Jacobs, Deputy Marshal Samuel Watkins, and Pastor Emil Larsen climbed into the wagon with the prisoners, closing the tailgate behind them. Deputy Marshal Clark mounted the wagon and took the driver's seat. He slapped the reins, and the wagon jolted as it pulled away from the jail. It rattled west on Bridge Street toward a large open field northwest of town where the gallows were located. Ten deputies on horseback rode alongside, forcing the crowd to stay behind the wagon. The street leading out of town turned into a river of the gruesomely curious. Heads bobbing and shoulders shifting, they followed behind the wagon like a herd of sheep.

Someone began singing "Shall We Gather at the River," and a chorus of voices joined in. The nearer they got to the gallows, the louder the singing became.

Shouting, singing, and laughter filled the air as the wagon carrying the condemned men bumped into the meadow, now known as Gallows Field.

The river of people from town merged with the crowd already gathered at the base of the grotesque wooden structure looming ominously against the morning sky. Families lounged on blankets, their picnic meals spread before them, while their children laughed and giggled, playing tag. Vendors set up makeshift stands selling popcorn, peanuts, and beer. An air of macabre celebration and merriment permeated Gallows Field.

When the wagon carrying the prisoners stopped at the foot of the gallows, Marshal Jacobs and Deputy Watkins escorted the four prisoners to the bottom of the stairs leading to the row of four nooses swaying in the breeze. The deputized guards surrounded them, all wearing somber faces and carrying rifles or shotguns.

Texas Ranger Mark Hill, who volunteered to serve as the hangman, was already on the platform. The prisoners climbed the stairs slowly, not eager to meet their fate. The prisoner known as Red had to be forced.

Judge Taylor moved to the front of the gallows and gave a brief speech regarding the need for law and order in the territory. He finished by saying, "I hope this hanging will deter any future murderous crimes. May God have mercy on their souls."

When the judge finished, each man was allowed to say his final words. Mort Watkins stepped brazenly to the railing. "I have no regrets. But if I had it to do over, I'd have drowned my bastard son before he let out his first cry."

Then Patch spoke, "I've killed over a dozen men since the war, but you can only hang me once." He laughed and spat at the crowd. Then he turned to the hangman, "A quick snap of the neck would be appreciated."

The man called Red was pale and quaking with fear. He hung onto the railing for support. "I ain't never killed anyone except in the war. I helped rob that bank, and I know it was wrong, but I didn't kill anyone. Please, I don't want to die. Sweet Jesus. I don't belong here. Please." His knees buckled, and Marshal Jacobs caught him, pulling him back until the trap door was under Red's feet.

Bob Jenkins was last. He threw back his head and howled like a wolf. "Tell the whores in hell that Bob is coming to—"

There was a gasp from the crowd as Deputy Watkins roughly pulled him back. I heard him tell Jenkins, "Watch what you say. There are women and children out there."

"You think I care?" Jenkins told him.

The men were moved to the middle of the drops. Marshal Jacobs slipped black hoods over their heads, and Deputy Watkins checked to see that the shackles were secure. He spoke whispered words to Mort and then stepped back to wait for nine o'clock. This reporter can only imagine what the deputy must have said to his father.

The hangman dropped the nooses over the heads of the condemned. He pulled them tight and adjusted their placement. Pastor Emil gave one final prayer, asking God to receive these sinners with pity and compassion. His voice boomed as he called on all those present to join in singing "Amazing Grace."

At precisely nine o'clock, the drops were triggered, and the four outlaws fell to their deaths. Cheers and singing from the crowd masked the sounds of their necks snapping as they hit the ends of the ropes. Ten minutes later, the bodies were cut down and carried to the undertaker's wagon, where four coffins awaited them. Doctor Franklin Cooper verified the death of each man before the wagon lumbered off, taking the corpses to Paupers Field for burial under wooden markers.

The singing faded, and the crowd began to disperse. The celebration was over, and the empty gallows stood abandoned, frayed ropes eerily swinging in the breeze. Justice had been served.

CHAPTER 98

BACK IN TOWN

Jake and Sam rode back to town alone on the wagon. It had been a hellacious week, and they were physically and mentally exhausted. Turning onto Bridge Street, they noticed most of the campsites by the school and churches were already abandoned, leaving a mess of horse and human waste behind. The smell was overpowering.

They stopped at John Miller's livery to return the wagon and team they'd borrowed to transport the prisoners. John had already mucked out part of his stable, and his corral was nearly empty. Sitting on a bale of hay, he leaned against the wall, a bottle beside him.

"Pull up a bale and have a drink." He tossed the bottle to Jake and sighed. "What a stinking mess. I haven't been home for a week, and I'm exhausted. When my helper gets here, I'll be hightailing it home to see my wife and my kids." John took a draw on the bottle Jake had returned to him. "Why in blue blazes did Judge Taylor decide to have the hanging here?"

"It makes sense. We were already torn up, Sam said. "Why tear up another town? Besides, getting the prisoners to Butte Point would have been a problem."

"Did you ever figure out who knocked me out and took a shot at the prisoners?"

"Nope. Never did. We were lucky you weren't hurt any worse than you were, and we're lucky Quimby was only wounded."

John scratched his head. "I had a thought this morning while shoveling out the back stalls. I know Quimby is new in town, but could the shooter have been after him and not the prisoners?"

Jake's eyebrows shot up. "We never considered Quimby as the target. It's something to think about."

Jake and Sam crossed the street to Coop's and caught him napping on one of his examination tables.

Sam laughed. "I thought this was a table for paying customers only."

Coop looked up at them. "Go Away. The office is closed, and the doctor is out." He rolled over and punched his pillow, looking for a comfortable position. "If you aren't injured, leave quietly and lock the door on your way out."

"I've never seen him this cranky," Jake said.

Coop sat up and threw the pillow at them. "What in thunder do you want?"

"Just checking and wondering if there was anything you needed us to do."

"I don't need anything. Could you please leave me alone? I've had people in and out of here at all hours non-stop. My supplies are depleted, I can barely keep my eyes open, and this morning, I was an official witness to the deaths of four men. I had to examine them and pronounce them dead before Bones carried them away in his body wagon. It was my first hanging, and I hope it's my last. It was barbaric."

Coop looked at the two men, his shoulders sagging. "I'm sorry. You were there, too."

"Yeah, and it was our first hanging."

"I'm sorry. Sam, Mort was—"

"A bastard," Sam finished for him. "And I have no grief for the man. After killing that little boy, he didn't deserve to live. He got what's been owed him for a long time."

Sam and Jake left the doctor's office and made their way through the town, lending a hand where needed. None of the businesses had suffered too much damage, and most agreed that the profits made up for the mess left behind. They also all agreed they never wanted to go through anything like it ever again.

It was late afternoon before they completed their rounds. They had gone up and down every street assessing the damage and putting their shoulders to the wheel when needed. They were proud of how the community had pitched in and how quickly things were returning to normal.

Sam went to the vet's office to pick up Duke, who he'd left with Dice during the pandemonium of the trial and hanging. The minute Sam set foot in Dice's office, the dog came charging at him. He jumped into his arms, frantically licking his neck. Sam scratched his ears and neck, trying to calm him.

Dice was sitting at his desk, grinning, a steaming cup of coffee in his hand. "That dog has been pining for you ever since you left. He sat and stared at the door for the longest time. Then he hid in the corner, moping. He hardly ate or drank a thing the whole time. But he's a fine-looking mutt now that he's cleaned up. I'd say he's not much more than a year old."

"He looks kind of ragged around the edges," Sam said with a frown.

"I'm a vet, not a barber," Dice growled. "If you don't like the way he looks, take him to the barbershop. I'm sure Angus would love to give him a proper haircut."

Sam snorted. "Not a bad idea. Maybe I will."

Sam scratched the dog's neck. "What do you think, Duke? How about a trip to the barbershop?" The dog barked and licked Sam's hand.

"Why'd you call him Duke?"

"I thought King might be a bit pretentious," Sam said with a smile. "How much do I owe you?"

"Buy me a drink next time you see me at Kat's."

Sam returned to the office to find Jake sound asleep on the cot and Logan with his feet up on the desk. A duet of snores filled the air as Sam turned to leave. "Come on Duke, let's go down to the butcher shop and get you a bone. Then I'll take you to meet Kat.

CHAPTER 99

HANNAH FLIRTS

Hannah noticed Deputy Watkins while she was still a block away. He was seated on the bench in front of the marshal's office, his long legs stretched out in front of him, his hat tilted low over his face. She'd been watching him for some time, which wasn't unpleasant. He was undeniably a very attractive man. Tall, well-muscled, and he seemed to possess an unshakable confidence. Perhaps it was because of the badge on his chest, but she doubted it.

Her Uncle Quimby frequently spoke of Sam's easy-going ways and often prattled on about his abilities. "He's got fists of iron," Quimby would say with admiration, "and a nail-driving accuracy with his Colt and Winchester that few can match."

She smiled, thinking he was perfect—strength, confidence, abilities, and the power of the law behind him. If she were his woman, he would protect her from her father.

Hannah held the package she was carrying in front of her and loosened the top two buttons of her blouse, exposing more skin than was respectable. She checked her reflection in the store window and smiled.

Sam heard light footfalls rapidly approaching and pulled his legs back out of the way. The footsteps stopped in front of him and when he pushed his new hat back on his head, he saw Hannah Beck standing directly in front of him. She was flawless.

Since her uncle, Quimby, had opened the newspaper office next door, he had often seen her coming and going, but it had always been from a distance or as she sailed past the windows of the marshal's office. He smiled at her, wondering if she looked as perfect without her clothes. Quickly burying such thoughts, he rose and tipped his hat.

Hannah stopped and smiled a most beguiling smile. "I'm a bit tired from carrying this package. May I?" She motioned to the bench where Sam had been sitting.

Duke, who was napping under the bench, got up and wandered over to get a closer sniff. He growled and returned to his spot, lying down with a grunt. He didn't like her.

It was only a few more steps to the newspaper office, but Sam smiled. "Absolutely," he said, brushing away imaginary dirt with the brim of his hat. "Please, join me."

Hannah sat close to Sam. *Closer than proper*, Sam thought.

They chatted easily about The Clarion and the disarray caused by the trial and hanging. Then, she asked if she could have a one-on-one interview with him.

Sam hesitated. "I don't know, Hannah. Quimby has already interviewed Jake. I doubt there's much left for me to say."

"But you will have a different viewpoint," she said, leaning forward and allowing her blouse to fall open. Her impressive cleavage promised hands full of softness hiding beneath her white blouse. "Please, Deputy Watkins, don't disappoint me."

Intrigued by the woman and her cleavage, Sam accepted.

"Meet me at the hotel dining room at seven o'clock for supper." Sam got up as Hannah rose to leave. She subtly brushed her breasts against his arm and, feigned a blush as she bustled into the newspaper office.

Sam looked after her with a shameless smile. She had flirted with him, bold as brass. She hadn't been the least bit subtle. She was enticing. But why was she so bent on getting his attention? She could have most any man in town. So why him? And why so blatant? Maybe it was because he had shown her no interest, and she thought he'd be a challenge. Whatever the case, he doubted an interview was what she wanted.

Sam had no trouble attracting women and could usually tell which ones to avoid. This one perplexed him. She had purposely given him a tantalizing peek, and he couldn't help but imagine what she would look like naked and sprawled across his bed. *Too young for me,* Sam thought, and his rational mind told him to cancel the interview. But an unexpected surge of desire told him not to pass up a sure thing.

Jake closed a folder on his desk and got up from behind his desk as Sam entered. "I'll be at the ranch for the rest of the week. Winnie sent word I'd better get my hindquarters home. We have things to discuss about the wedding. I didn't know there was anything to discuss. I planned on showing up at the church in my new suit, saying I do, and hauling my bride off to bed. Guess there's more to it than that."

"Always is."

"What are you doing tonight?" Jake said, buckling his gun belt around his waist and adjusting it.

"Hannah Beck asked me for an interview, and I'm meeting her for supper at the hotel."

Jake scoffed with a slight smile. "I wondered how long it would take before you were sniffing around her skirts."

"She was the one doing the sniffing. I wasn't interested in her—too young and innocent. At least that's what I thought." Sam smiled at

Jake. "I'm not so sure about the innocent part anymore. She gave me a tantalizing peek at a very inviting cleavage."

"Careful, Sam. All women are problems, and that goes double for a woman with her kind of looks."

"You're probably right, but she was making me an offer that is not easy to ignore."

"So, after one brief chat, you've come to the conclusion that she falls into your safe zone. She's unmarried and already been sullied."

"I don't want an angry husband with a shotgun trying to kill me for rustling his wife or an irate father wanting to make an honest woman of his virginal daughter."

"If you get Hannah all hot and naked tonight, I want to hear all the juicy details."

Sam chuckled, "I'll give it my best shot so as not to disappoint you. I wish I could shake the feeling that something isn't quite on the up and up with this interview thing."

Jake looked at Sam with a big grin. "Then don't go."

Sam looked back at him with a raised eyebrow. "That's exactly what my horse sense is telling me, but my body says different."

"I don't have to worry about such things anymore," Jake said with a smile. "I'm broke and saddled."

"You always were. Just took you a while to realize it."

Jake left, and Sam pondered the uneasy feeling in his gut. It wouldn't go away. He knew how he wanted the evening to end and decided to take it one step at a time.

CHAPTER 100

SAM AND ALEX

Duke followed Sam to Kat's Place for a late breakfast. It was still busier than usual, but Kat was back at her usual place at the far end of the bar.

He waved and met her at the bar. She gave him a big smile and bent down to scratch Duke's chin.

Sam gave her a hug and an affectionate kiss on the cheek before heading to his usual table. Sitting down, he threw his new hat in the chair next to him.

Kat started to follow him but raised voices and threatening shouts erupted, indicating that an argument was picking up steam. "I'll join you after I tend to these rowdies."

Sam watched as she approached the noisemakers. He knew she could handle all kinds of frays and did so daily.

Bear slid a steaming plate piled high with pancakes, bacon, eggs, and muffins in front of Sam. Setting a mug of steaming coffee next to the plate, he noticed the direction of Sam's gaze. "She wouldn't like it if you interfered," Bear said.

"I know," Sam said, his voice held a sense of unease. "But can't help worrying about her."

"I know you do," Bear said, giving Sam's shoulder a reassuring squeeze that acknowledged their friendship. "So do I."

Standing at the top of the staircase, Alex had been watching Kat and Sam. Amid the chaos of the trial and hanging, Alex had moved into the apartment next to Kat's to be available at the first sign of trouble. He was falling in love with Kat, and Sam's obvious affection and concern for her irked him. He felt a prick of jealousy whenever he saw them together. It was a new feeling that he didn't much care for.

He made his way down the stairs and went straight to Sam's table. "Good morning, Deputy."

"Good morning, Alex. Grab a chair. I wouldn't mind the company."

Alex sat across from Sam in silence, watching him eat.

Sam put his fork down. "What's on your mind, Alex? You're making me feel like a bug about to be squashed."

Alex looked at Sam for a moment. "What is your relationship with Kat? You two are extremely, uh, comfortable with each other, and you have a certain reputation with women."

"Oh," Sam said, leaning back in his chair. "Kat and I have had a long and complicated friendship. And as far as my reputation goes, it's like most reputations—far more imaginative than factual."

Alex glared at Sam but didn't speak.

"The first time I met up with Kat was when I was maybe nine or ten. I slipped in here trying to look up the skirts of one of the dance hall girls, and she chased me off, pounding me with a broom all the way back to my house." Sam couldn't help but chuckle at the memory.

"That must have been a sight," Alex said, his face stoic, no humor in his voice.

"I'm sure it was." Sam slipped Duke a piece of bacon. "Over the past five years, since I took on the job as deputy, Kat and I have become close. She's one of a kind, but I believe you already know that." Sam took the last bite of his breakfast. "Kat and I have had some moments, but we've never been together like you're imagining. We're friends, Alex, plain and simple."

"So, you and Kat don't have a relationship?"

"Not the kind you're thinking about." Sam contemplated the stern face in front of him. "Just friends, Alex, relax. I've never been called on to prove it, but I would eat a bullet for her. That's how much I care for her, but we have never shared a bed. And like I said before if you hurt her…"

Alex put up his hands in surrender, his face softening. "I know you'll kill me."

Sam grabbed his hat. "I'm riding out to do some target practice. Interested?"

"Yeah. Unless you're taking me out to shoot me? Are you?"

"No, but I would like to see what you can do with those fancy irons of yours."

Alex told Kat he was leaving with Sam, and the two men walked to the livery, followed by Duke. They talked about their preferences in horses and what had drawn them to their specific mounts. In both cases, it had been their spirit and beauty. Alex rode a Missouri Fox Trotter he called Mooch. He chose a trotter because of their stamina and agility, traits he needed when hunting down outlaws through all kinds of weather and terrain.

Alex had trained Mooch himself. For the first six months, Mooch contributed nothing to their partnership, which was how he earned the name. He balked, independent and unwilling to give up his freedom. Alex didn't want to break his spirit and persisted in gently persuading the horse's cooperation. It paid off. He'd never had a better mount than Mooch.

As they walked past the newspaper office, Hannah stepped out and waved, interrupting their conversation. "See you tonight, Sam."

Alex had a big grin on his face. "I didn't realize you were interested in Hannah. Although, with her looks and that body, what man wouldn't want to bed her?

"It's not like that," Sam said. "Looking and imagining, definitely. She wants an interview and has invited me to join her for supper. Hard to resist an offer of food and a gorgeous woman."

Alex smiled. "She could be a man-eater."

"I told Jake I was concerned that she might be up to something. I can't imagine what, but she's never paid me any mind, and now out of the clear blue…"

"Then don't go."

Sam laughed. "That's what Jake said."

"If there's a warning voice telling you no, then you should listen to it. But she is an eye-full, and any rational message could easily get garbled."

The rhythmic clanging of the blacksmith's hammer stopped as they strode into the livery. John Miller came to greet them, his muscled torso bare and glistening with sweat. "Good morning. Say, you two wouldn't have time to help me finish mucking out these stalls, would you?"

"Sorry, John. We have plans." Sam and Alex walked to the back of the livery where their horses were stabled. John followed and leaned against a supporting timber.

"Sam?"

"Yeah."

"Is there any truth to the rumor that you'll be taking over for the mayor? I would hate to lose you as a lawman, but the town needs a strong leader. One with a moral compass pointing true north."

"The mayor is still in office. He hasn't been ousted by the council or arrested for any of his misdeeds. I don't see any need in fretting over it until I'm officially asked."

John slapped his back. "I'd hate to lose you as a lawman, but you could do great things for Grant's Crossing as the mayor. I'm behind you either way, but it'd be odd not to see you and Jake prowling the streets together."

John disappeared through the side opening of the livery and into the blacksmith shop.

"Duke, go to the office," Sam commanded. Duke growled and looked at him with what Sam could only describe as indignation before he turned and trotted toward the marshal's office, his tail between his legs and his ears back.

The horses were restless, prancing, and eager to go. Sam and Alex mounted and held them to a spirited walk until they reached the outskirts of town. Then they let them run. Once the horses had burned off the pent-up energy, they slowed to a trot and then to a walk.

Sam turned onto an obscure path barely visible from the road and continued for about a mile. The scent of pine wafted to them on the breeze as they rode into a wide-open area. The meadow was blanketed with short prairie grass and colorful wildflowers. Majestic pine trees bordered two sides, and on the third side was a homemade frame for targets.

"This is where we usually do our target practice," Sam said, dismounting. "We're far enough from town that no one can hear the gunfire and get upset, and we can't shoot anyone by accident."

"What happened to the mayor? I've heard the rumors about you replacing him."

"Mayor Richards was running wild and over-spending. Some thought he was stealing from the town coffers, but we can find no proof.

Then, he got tangled up with the wrong person, and the town council put him on probation. Unless he does something rash, I don't think there's going to be an opening in the mayor's office any time soon."

Target practice turned into a friendly competition as they talked about different kinds of guns, their power, and their accuracy. Alex let Sam use his special-made, ivory-handled Colt.

Alex gave Sam some tips on improving his draw. "A split-second can save your life, Sam. Have Ross over at the harness shop adjust the slant and widen the top of your holster to keep the hammer and trigger free. It'll make a difference." Alex gave him a smug smile. "I like to think I just saved your life."

"Subtle save," Sam smirked, but he would make the changes. "Why don't you sign up for the turkey shoot this weekend and we'll get an official accounting of who's the best marksman. I've only been beaten twice. Both times by Winnie."

Alex laughed. "A girl, huh? Bested by a girl?"

"Yep, Winnie's a crack shot, and there is no shame in being bested by her. Jake's not bad, but he's no match against Winnie or me."

Alex had a smug smile on his face. "Perhaps I need to shake things up and show you how it's done."

"You're welcome to try, Pinkerton," Sam goaded as they walked back to their horses.

"I'm not a Pinkerton anymore," he said as he mounted. "I resigned yesterday."

Sam looked across his saddle at Alex in complete surprise. "Does Kat know?" he said as he mounted.

"Not yet. Only you and me, and Mr. Pinkerton, of course." They rode slowly, stirrup to stirrup, "I need some time to get used to the idea of being unemployed before I share the news with anyone else."

"Any idea what you're going to do?"

"Not the slightest, and to be honest, I'm lost. My life has always been planned for me. Another assignment always waited. That's been my life since I was a snot-nosed kid, but I'm tired of it. I want a life I can call my own." He paused and shifted in his saddle, looking at Sam. "There is one thing I'm sure of. Whatever I end up doing, I want Kat at my side."

"She has feelings for you. And the fact that she let you move into the room next to hers says it all."

"I've never cared for anyone like this. When I'm near her, my insides turn to mush. So does my brain. I fumble around like a love-sick dolt."

"A word to the wise. Don't let Kat think you quit Pinkerton because of her. She would not be happy, and that would not be in your best interests."

"Thanks, Sam." Alex chuckled. "That's solid advice coming from a man about to be eaten alive by the enticing Hannah Beck. I hope you survive the interview."

"I'll let you know tomorrow."

CHAPTER 101

HANNAH BECK, REPORTER

Hannah breezed into the hotel cafe, stopping just inside the door. The quiet hum of conversation faded as all eyes turned in her direction. She waited until she was sure all eyes were on her before walking gracefully to Sam's table. Sam figured she must be used to such scrutiny as he rose to pull out her chair. She sat with the gentle rustle of satin and lace.

Under the table Duke gave a small growl, not pleased with Sam's eating partner.

"Good evening, Deputy," she said, her warm and flirtatious voice wrapping Sam in a blanket of desire. "How about we get this interview out of the way, then we can have an enjoyable supper? I've prepared some questions."

"Fire away."

"What were you thinking, standing there on the gallows, watching your father fall to his death?"

He knew it was coming and had prepared for the question. "I performed the duties of an official witness to the execution. That's all. They were all killers and deserved to be hung. As for Mort Watkins,

I have no sorrow at his passing, only relief that he can't hurt anyone else."

Looking into Sam's soft brown eyes, she got a way down kind of shiver and had to admit an undeniable pull. It had started with a flutter in her stomach, or was it her heart? She wasn't sure. All she knew was she wanted him to take her in his arms.

"You and Marshal Jacobs are highly respected all across the Dakota and Montana Territories. I spoke with several law enforcement officers, and not one has a single bad thing to say about either of you. All say they'd be proud to ride with you. How did you inspire such loyalty from these men?"

"We did a bit of traveling over the years looking for the man who killed Jake's parents. We got to know a lot of the sheriffs and struck up some friendships. Thanks to Marshal Jacobs, we have a peaceful territory."

"You don't take any credit?" Hannah asked, wondering how his lips would feel on hers.

"I'm Jake's backup. He carries the weight on his badge."

What had she been thinking? Trying to seduce this man was a mistake. He was seducing her. This wasn't how she planned it. She intended to use him. She would sleep with him, and he would take her as his woman, and she'd be safe. But a longing for him pounded throughout her. She wanted him.

She cleared her throat and took a soft, trembling breath. "Word on the street is that the town council may ask you to take over the remaining term of the ousted mayor's term."

Sam smiled, displaying his dimples. "That wasn't a question, Hannah."

"But you know what I want," Hannah said, her eyes sparkling with a blaze of desire and an unspoken promise. A rush of heat surged through her as she held his gaze, her heart pounding. She had thought him to be an ignorant, gun-toting brute, but he was educated, articulate, and disturbingly attractive. Not at all what she had expected. But that was a good thing. The thought of being mauled nightly by some brutish heathen made her shudder.

"The town council hasn't ousted the mayor," Sam said. "So, there's no sense worrying about it."

Several additional questions followed before Hannah breathed a sigh. "All done, Sam. Let's have supper and talk." Under his gaze, she doubted she'd be able to eat a thing. She was losing control.

Despite the voice nagging him, Sam knew he wasn't mistaken. Her flagrant flirtations made her intentions perfectly clear.

Conversation over supper came easily. Sam told her how the town had started and grown, especially after the railroad came through. He told her about local ranchers and farmers and how he'd come by his dog Duke, who was curled up at his feet.

"You never talk about yourself," Hannah observed, light from the candle reflecting dreamily in her eyes. The flickering glow cast soft shadows on her features, accenting her captivating beauty. Sam wondered if there could be a more perfect face.

"I'm not all that interesting. I live a simple life. I love my friends, food, and books. That about sums me up," Sam said, his eyes drifting to her cleavage.

Hannah smiled, leaning forward seductively to give him a better view. "What about a woman, Sam? Is there anyone special in your life?"

Sam shrugged. "No." The heat between them was becoming palpable. "How'd you get into the newspaper business?" he asked, eager to redirect the conversation.

"I wasn't a reporter until Uncle Quimby brought me out West. I grew up in Chicago, a spoiled brat. My friends and I were always searching for something new and exciting." Hannah leaned forward as if sharing a secret. "One night, we went slumming in the poor parts of Chicago, pretending to be missionaries on a humanitarian errand. We saw all sorts of things. We even went into one of the Bawdy Houses. It was wonderfully scandalous."

Hannah sat back and studied Sam's face, wondering how he got the scar on his chin. "My father was furious when he found out. He sent me to Europe to separate me from my disreputable friends and to broaden my horizons. He hoped to change my ways." Hannah blushed innocently. "I'm sorry, Sam, I shouldn't be telling you all of this. You'll get the wrong impression of me."

Sam's impression was that she wanted a tumble, and he was eager to oblige. He shrugged and, with a smile, reached across the table, taking her hand in his. The warmth of his hand sent a shiver racing through her body. "Everyone has a history, Hannah. And most have disapproving fathers."

When the waiter came to the table to pour coffee and clear their empty plates, Sam hesitantly released her hand. "What does your father do?" he asked, making small talk, his heart racing with anticipation and restraint.

"He has one of the largest manufacturing companies in Chicago. He has dozens of repair shops and owns buildings in Chicago, New York, and Philadelphia. He has what he calls an empire, but he wants a legacy. Daddy was about to marry me off to an old man to seal a business deal, but Uncle Quimby hustled me off in the dead of night."

She hadn't planned on telling him as much as she did, but his big brown eyes told her she could confide in him. "I'm sorry, Sam. You didn't need to know about my father," she said, tugging at the linen napkin on her lap, subtly watching Sam through long, dark eyelashes. "I'm terrified of what he'll do when he finds me." She finished with a shaky sigh, blinking back tears. She hoped she sounded frightened enough to arouse Sam's protective nature.

Sam watched her intently as she spoke, trying to focus, but his thoughts were elsewhere. He longed to be alone with her, to cup her face in his hands and touch his lips to hers, and to feel her body against his. "You're safe in Grant's Crossing, Hannah," Sam said.

"Well, I should get you home." Sam was surprised by his own words. It was that persistent voice telling him she wanted more than a tumble.

Hannah was confused by his words. She could see the lust in his eyes and knew he wanted her. "Sam, I don't want to go home," she said, her voice holding a hint of desperation. "I don't want the evening to end." She looked across the table with a soft smile. "If it isn't too forward of me, I'd like to see where you live. My readers would be interested."

Sam's mind shot back to an earlier vision he had of her lying across his bed naked, and the fire he'd been fighting ignited. They would need to order dessert. The annoying voice was nagging, telling him to take her home. He ignored the voice.

Hand in hand, they walked slowly toward Sam's house, with Duke just a few steps behind. The night sky was sprinkled with stars, and the evening had turned cool, as spring evenings are prone to do. Sam slipped off his suit jacket and draped it over Hannah's shoulders. As the jacket enveloped her in his warmth, she felt a chill run down her spine. A chill that had nothing to do with the temperature outside but everything to do with the tall, desirable man at her side.

With a gentle tug and a warm smile, he drew the coat together in front of her. "It's a bit big on you," Sam said, his voice soft and teasing.

Holding onto the lapels of the jacket, he pulled her close. She could feel the warmth radiating from his body as he leaned down for a kiss.

Sam's lips were soft and persuasive, and she melted into his embrace. When they were both breathless, Sam pulled away with a smile. He tucked a strand of stray hair behind her ear, his fingers brushing against her cheek. The warmth and tenderness of his touch sent a ripple of desire crashing through her body.

He draped his arm around her shoulders, guiding her toward his house, once again envisioning her draped across his bed.

Hannah could hardly contain the longing, and with each step she took, all she could think about was Sam and what it would be like when he held her in his arms and made love to her.

CHAPTER 102

HANNAH'S DECLARATION

Sam opened the door to his home and followed Hannah inside. He lit a fancy lamp that sat in the center of an ornate table near the entrance. Duke went directly to his bed, circled several times, scratched furiously at the blankets, and circled again before settling with his chin on his paws. His eyes darted between Sam and the she-wolf, and he wondered how long Sam would allow the beast to remain in their house.

"What a beautiful lamp," Hannah remarked, her gaze wandering around the spacious room. The soft glow from the lamp illuminated oversized leather furniture and a wall of towering bookshelves crammed with books. Not what she expected.

"It was my mother's pride and joy—one of the few things her husband didn't destroy," Sam said as he slid his coat from her shoulders and tossed it over the back of a chair. Sam wrapped her in his arms, pressing his lips to hers. His kisses were gentle but urgent, and she could feel the heat and hardness of his body as she leaned into him.

"If this isn't what you want, tell me to stop," he breathed against her neck.

His warm breath sent shivers down her spine. "I want you, Sam," she said softly. Sam guided her into his bedroom and lit a single wall sconce. As he dimmed the flame, a warm, comforting glow surrounded them.

He turned to face her, his eyes dark with passion and a primal lust.

This was going to be easy, Hannah thought. After this he'll be wrapped around my little finger, and he'll do anything I want. He'll protect me with his life.

But she hadn't expected to feel the way she did. That wasn't part of the plan. He was meant to be a tool and nothing more. In her mind this was a business deal—she would let him take her, in exchange for his protection—but her body wasn't in agreement.

Sam folded her in his arms, his touch and each of his tender kisses ignited a spark deep within her that left her wanting more. His kisses deepened and she melted against him. She hadn't expected such gentleness.

Taking a deep breath and trying to gather her wits, she helped Sam with the buttons on her blouse. He ran his hands gently along her shoulders and down her arms letting the blouse fall to the floor. He eyed her corset and the impressive cleavage it created with a grin. Kissing her neck and shoulders, he unbuttoned her skirt, letting it fall around her ankles. He began undoing the snaps down the front of her corset, but she pushed his large, clumsy hands aside and quickly finished the job.

Sam tossed the corset aside. The sight of her body was intoxicating, and the anticipation was excruciating. He wanted one thing, and he didn't know how long he could hold off.

Hannah watched his eyes, taking in every inch of her. She knew she had a beautiful body and had no shame in her nakedness. Sam pulled her close, his mouth hungrily covering hers, his tongue exploring the sweet heat of her mouth. .

The roughness of Sam's clothes and the cold buckle of his gun belt pressing against her were oddly exciting, but she craved the feel of his bare skin against hers. With trembling fingers, she unbuttoned his shirt. She pushed it off his muscled shoulders, and he threw it off.

Wrapping her in his arms he lowered his lips to hers. Her breasts were warm and soft against his bare chest. He kissed and nibbled his way down her neck, his hot breath bringing soft moans from her throat as his mouth reached its destination.

She ran her hands over the firm muscles of his chest and linked her hands behind his neck, stretching on tiptoe to reach his lips. The heat she was feeling inside exploded into desire, and her body was begging Sam to ravage her—to possess her—and end the torment. Nothing else mattered. Nothing else was real.

Sam picked her up and laid her across his bed. His eyes never left her as he hung his gun belt on the bedpost and sat on the edge of the bed. Hannah watched his shoulder muscles ripple as he removed his boots and shucked his pants, dropping them beside his shirt. He stood for a moment, looking down at her. His eyes lingered on her body before slowly returning to her face. A smile spread slowly across his lips as he watched her evaluating him.

Her eyes lingered on the breadth of his shoulders, then drifted lower, tracing the firm lines of his chest and the taut plane of his stomach. The sculpted V of his hips drew her gaze like a magnet, and she didn't try to look away.

Sam chuckled, and suddenly Hannah jerked her eyes to his face. "I can't do this. I can't," she cried, rolling off the bed.

She stood shaking, her heart racing. She had failed. She could not go through with it. Her plan was ruined.

"Hannah? Sam said gently, as he approached her. She watched him; she didn't move. He pulled her into his arms, kissing the top of her head. "What is it?"

Hannah laid her cheek against his chest. "Sam, I've never been with a man."

"What do you mean; you're a virgin?" Sam growled and pushed her to arm's length. "You should have told me."

"I—I didn't know how. I was scared, that's all, but I want you. I want this. Please, Sam. I need this."

"I can't believe this. The way you talked, the way you flirted with me. I thought you were an experienced woman. I thought…"

"I should have told you. I'm so sorry." She was sorry—sorry she'd panicked, and sorry her plan to use Sam's bed as a safe haven was ruined.

Sam took a deep breath and raked a hand through his hair. "Why the deception?"

Tears rolled down her cheeks. "My father. He's ruthless, and I'm terrified of what he'll do to me. If I were your woman, you'd keep me safe, and I thought sleeping in your bed would be a small price to pay."

"A small price to pay," Sam repeated with a snort and a shake of his head.

"I didn't mean it like that, and it doesn't matter that I'm a virgin."

"It matters to me and this isn't gonna happen. No worthwhile man wants to marry a woman who's been broke by another rider. And I'm not gonna be that rider. All you had to do was ask, Hannah. I would have protected you."

"I know. I was wrong. I shouldn't have deceived you."

"I would have protected you."

Hannah's eyes glistened with tears. "I have feelings for you, Sam. At first, I was pretending, but now…" Something in the set of his jaw stopped her. He wasn't smiling, and no boyish dimples softened his face. Suddenly embarrassed by her nakedness, she wanted to run for her clothes, but his gaze held her pinned where she stood.

Her beauty taunted him, the lust still pounding through his body refused to give up. It whispered to him to throw her to the floor and give her what she wanted—what he wanted. He ignored it.

"I got a good look at the real Hannah, and I don't like her. And I don't appreciate being used. Funny thing, though. I'll protect you anyway. I won't let your father have you." Sam looked her up and down with contempt. "So flawlessly perfect on the outside, but on the inside..."

Hannah bristled. She had offered herself to him—how dare he? Her anger sparked, burning as hot as her desire had only moments before, and Sam saw her eyes turn to flint just before she slapped him.

"I don't deserve that," Sam said, rubbing his check. "I think you should go now. I'll walk you back to the boarding house."

Sam pulled on his pants as Hannah dressed.

"No need," Hannah snarled. "You'll pay for this, Sam Watkins. You'll pay," she said, rushing to the door and slamming it behind her.

I suppose somehow I will, he thought as he walked to the door. Duke, who had remained curled in his bed, came to stand by Sam with a rumble in his throat. He was glad she was gone. He didn't like the she-wolf. The two remained at the door, watching until Hannah disappeared inside Murphy's Boarding House.

CHAPTER 103

CATALOG WOMEN

Anna Marie Trask stepped onto the depot platform and took three shaky breaths, wondering what possessed her to leave home. She smoothed her skirt and tucked an unruly lock of hair behind her ear. Clutching her valise, she looked up and down the boardwalk. Surely, he didn't forget she was arriving today. But what if he hadn't received her letter? What would she do if he changed his mind? Lord in heaven, what would she do? She didn't have enough money to get back home. Why had she charged off to this uncivilized land to marry a total stranger?

On the verge of panic, her teary eyes settled on one of the tallest men she'd ever seen. Her face brightened with the beginnings of a smile. He was tall, broad-shouldered, and had an easy, confident gait as he strode toward her. Everyone greeted him as he passed them. A ragged black dog trotted along, panting happily at his heels. This was the man she'd come to meet, and he was positively perfect.

As he drew nearer, he tipped his hat to the woman who had been on the train with her. He squatted down to speak with her young daughter. Anna chewed her lip, straining to hear the conversation. He asked the child about her trip and smiled, listening intently to her answer. Then he picked her up and spun her around. The little girl's joyful squeals and giggles filled the air as he sat her down.

It wasn't him, after all. Anna's shoulders slumped as she shifted her valise to her other hand. It was getting heavy, but she was afraid to put it down. She looked over at the happy reunion, but the woman and the little girl were walking away, and the tall, handsome man walked toward her. She tucked the wisp of hair behind her ear again and nervously licked her lips.

He walked right past her, doffing his hat. He entered the train depot, ducking his head to avoid the top of the doorframe. Why didn't he recognize her? It had to be him. She pulled the picture from her purse. It was him. She'd had no picture to send him but had described herself in her letters. She cautiously moved to the depot door, shifting the valise to her other hand. She peeked into the depot.

"I have two letters here for you, Deputy, and one for the marshal."

Anna took a breath, her heart pounding. The letters hadn't mentioned anything about him being a lawman. Maybe her intended had a brother who looked like him. Had she been deceived? Panic grabbed her heart.

Sam shoved the letters in his shirt. "Thanks," he said, turning toward the door. He had noticed a woman at the door studying him, and then dart out of sight.

"Hey, Sam," the clerk yelled after him. "Tell Logan to get his rear end down here. We got a game of checkers to finish, and if you see Chris, let him know there's mail for Mr. Grant.

"I'll let him know."

As Sam exited, he saw the curious woman standing outside the depot door. She was leaning against the wall with wide, teary eyes, clutching her valise against her chest. Sam tipped his hat, smiling, and asked her if he could be of any help.

"No," she whispered. "He called you Sam. The man inside the depot called you Sam."

"Yes, ma'am, that's my name. I'm Deputy Marshal Sam Watkins. Can I be of any help?"

A slight blush climbed up her neck, and she stammered, "I'm sorry. I didn't mean to stare. I… I mistook you for someone else."

Sam laughed gently. "Ma'am, trust me when I say no one has ever told me that." A dimpled smile flickered across his face.

She couldn't imagine what was humorous about what she'd said, but looking up at him, she realized that his size and striking good looks would make it almost impossible to mistake him for anyone else. She couldn't help but smile back.

"What's your name, miss?"

"Anna Marie. Anna Marie Trask."

"Pleased to meet you, Miss Trask. Let's gather your belongings, and I'll escort you to the hotel. It's just across the street. You can freshen up, and then if you like, we can talk."

"Thank you. I'd like that." Anna smiled, a bit breathless, her heart racing erratically from the uncertainty of this horrid situation. What else could it be?

Neither Sam nor Miss Trask saw the two men stalking them as they strolled across the street and into the hotel. Sam took her to the front desk, where Sally smiled brightly in his direction.

"I have some errands to run," Sam said. "But I'll be back directly, Miss Trask. When you're ready, I'll be waiting for you in the cafe." Sam glanced at Sally, "Take care of her."

He left the hotel with Miss Trask on his mind. She must have been waiting for someone, he thought. He wanted to ask her who, but she was so upset that he was afraid she'd burst into tears. Taking her to the hotel would give her time to collect herself, and talking over a cup of coffee in the hotel cafe might be more comfortable. He suspected a story went along with this woman, and wanted to know what it was without the complication of tears or hysteria.

When he returned to the hotel, he was surprised to see Pete and Chris sitting at a table in the far corner, with pie and coffee in front of them. They were top hands at the Circle G Ranch and seldom came to town. He wondered what had brought them to the hotel. Normally, they would be at Kat's or the Bent Ear, hammering back whiskey and chowing down on pickled eggs and deer jerky.

He waved at them and said, "Hey Chris, there's mail down at the depot for Mr. Grant." Duke settled at Sam's feet, watching and hoping for scraps.

Chris nodded, and the two men darted glances between each other and Sam. Sam couldn't shake the feeling that they looked guilty of something. The more Sam thought about it, the more suspicious he became. Pete and Chris were not men who would dawdle over pastries in a hotel cafe. He was about to go to their table when Miss Trask came into the cafe looking composed and calm. Sam watched her approach the table, thinking how lovely she was. He rose to hold her chair, then sat down across from her. Sally put coffee in front of them, giving Sam a wink.

Anna Marie saw the wink and blushed. "Is she your girl?"

"Sally? No. She's married to Lars, the owner of the hotel."

Sam watched Anna intently. "What brought you to Grant's Crossing, and how can I help you?"

As she looked up into his piercing brown eyes, she felt herself blush. "I've come to meet my fiancé," she said, fiddling with her napkin. "We've been corresponding for some time, and I came to meet him. He sent me this picture so I'd recognize him. I should have known it was too good to be true."

"What do you mean?"

She blushed as she handed him the picture. "A man as kind and handsome as you wouldn't need to advertise for a wife."

Sam's head jerked back, and he sat bolt upright. He looked at the picture and back at Anna Marie. There was no mistake—it was him in the picture. He remembered the day it was taken. But who would have sent it to her, and how would they have gotten hold of it?

All at once, the pieces fell into place. He turned in his seat, looking across the room at the two ranch hands sitting with their heads down. Feeling Sam's eyes staring them down, they picked up their forks and started shoveling pie into their mouths. Sam remembered a previous conversation with Mr. Grant talking about catalog brides from back East. That conversation had taken place after Belle stomped on Pete's heart.

Anna Marie took a sip of her coffee and ran her fingers along the edge of the cup's rim. "I was so stupid, but the letters seemed sincere and they were so sweet. When I wrote saying I'd like to travel to Grant's Crossing to meet my intended in person, he sent train fare." A tear trickled down her cheek. "Now, I don't know what to do. I can't go back home."

"Who was supposed to meet you?"

"Peter Christensen."

"I see. Give me a minute, and I think I can sort this out." Sam excused himself and went to the corner table where Pete and Chris were seated. He threw the picture Miss Trask had given him on the table. "Any idea how this came to be in her possession…gentlemen?" Sam asked.

They looked up sheepishly. "It seemed clever at the time. Sorry, Sam."

"I'm not the one who needs an apology," Sam growled at the two men. "I can't believe you did this. Peter Christensen? Miss Trask says you were the one writing to her. The man she traveled across the country to meet today. Why weren't you there?"

"We were there. We were trying to figure out how to introduce ourselves, on account of the picture not looking like us, and then you got all tangled up with her. We followed you here."

"So, which one of you wrote the sweet, sincere letters to her?" Sam scowled.

"Uh, we, uh, sort of wrote the letters together, and then we sent the same letter to each of them."

"What do you mean—each of them?"

"Well, we've been writing to six of them women folk who want husbands, and we figured we'd sort out who got which one when they got here."

Sam lowered his head, his eyes intent on Chris. "You mean to tell me five more women are on their way to Grant's Crossing?"

"We didn't think they'd all want to come at the same time. We figured we'd be lucky if we could bamboozle two of them into coming out here to meet us. We must have some wicked letter-writing skills."

Sam took a breath and let it out. "Bamboozle, huh? That's how you want to get a wife?" He turned to look at Anna, who was watching them, her head tilted. Sam smiled at her and gave her a little wave. She was a fine-looking woman, and he wondered why she had any trouble finding a husband. Then, he had a sobering thought. He said, "These other women don't all have a picture of me, do they?"

"Oh no. We only had one picture of you and one of Jake."

"One of Jake?" Sam put his head down, his hand over his mouth to hide the smile. He fought to contain his laughter. Jake was gonna love this.

He wanted to laugh, but none of this was the least bit funny to Miss Trask and wouldn't be to the other ladies these cabbage heads had tricked into traveling to Grant's Crossing. When he regained his composure, he crossed his arms over his chest, giving the men a loud snort of disapproval.

"I'll introduce you to your intended, and you can explain yourselves. You both owe Miss Anna Marie an apology, and it better be sincere. You're a pair of lowdown, egg-sucking skunks for pulling a stunt like this." He glared at the two men. "Besides, what, in God's name, made you think you could sort them out after they got here? You can't cut a woman out of the herd like she's a calf to be branded." He saw the contrition on their faces but still couldn't believe what they had done. "You'll be lucky if she'll have anything to do with either of you after this."

Sam escorted them back to the table where Anna Marie was seated and introduced the two letter-writing knotheads. He politely excused himself and left them to work it out.

Sam had known Chris and Pete most of his life. They could be wild and a bit reckless at times, but they were both decent men worthy of a loving woman. He couldn't imagine them pulling such a stunt, but then again, he had seen them do plenty of idiotic things.

The following morning, Sam went to the depot to meet the ten o'clock train. He saw Miss Trask sitting on a bench with her satchel on her lap, waiting to board. He wasn't surprised to find her there, but he hoped he could talk her out of leaving. He sat next to her, removing his hat. She turned slightly to smile and nodded but didn't speak. She turned back, facing forward, waiting for the train to chug its way to the platform.

"I don't know where you're heading, Miss Trask, but if it's a new start you're looking for, this is a mighty fine town, and we could use more attractive young ladies like yourself."

A faint blush crawled up her neck, making him smile. "I don't mean to be forward, but if getting married is on your mind, I know of at least a dozen law-abiding, church-going men who are looking for wives. I can even tell you which of them to avoid."

"I'm so embarrassed," she started, but Sam held up his hand.

"You have no call being embarrassed over what those two cabbage heads did. You assumed the letters were on the level." Sam paused, admiring her easy way and quiet beauty. "Chris and Pete are good men. I'd trust them with my life, but sometimes, they just don't think things through.

Sam paused. "Listen, there's a festival the weekend after this. It's always quite a to-do. During the day, there's a three-legged race, a hogtying contest, pie judging, a turkey shoot, and lots of entertainment. Then the day ends with a dance." Sam smiled. "And knowing the men around here like I do, your dance card will be full. Why don't you stay till after the festival? Get to know Grant's Crossing and the people. I think you'll like it here, and if you don't, you can always leave."

She looked at Sam and smiled. "Is there a boarding house in town that isn't too expensive?"

Sam liked her smile and was pleased she was open to staying. "As soon as we see who gets off the train, I'll escort you to Murphy's Boarding House and introduce you to Rachael Murphy. I think you'll like it here."

"Please, Deputy, call me Anna."

"Only if you call me Sam."

"It's a deal, Sam."

***

Anna and Sam watched as at least a dozen people stepped from the train. Most travelers were met with smiles, hugs, or handshakes, but two women were left standing alone, looking lost. Anna and Sam looked at each other with knowing smiles and went to greet the two ladies.

"I think Mrs. Murphy is going to have a full house tonight," Anna Marie said with a musical laugh that Sam liked.

Sam escorted the three ladies to the boarding house, telling them there would be no shortage of eligible men vying for their attention and that he would help them make proper choices. As far as Anna Marie was concerned, he had already eliminated all the men from the potential husband list.

He turned the ladies over to Mrs. Murphy and hurried from the boarding house, late for the final fitting of his new suit. A suit Winnie had insisted upon him wearing for the wedding. He thought it made him look like a waiter in one of those fancy restaurants he'd read about, but at least Winnie hadn't insisted that he wear one of those silly swallow-tail coats. There were, after all, limits to what any man could endure, even for a friend.

CHAPTER 104

THE BODY BELOW

Isaac Beck leaned casually against the marble balustrade surrounding his private balcony. The double doors leading from his bedroom were open, and a cool evening breeze billowed through the light fabric curtains.

He had been ruthlessly persuasive, but despite his efforts, his wife hadn't revealed their whereabouts. She must not have known.

He lit a cigar, calmly puffing it to life. He glanced down at his wife's body, lying in a pool of blood in the courtyard beneath his second-story balcony. Such a terrible accident, but everyone knew how clumsy she was. Or perhaps it was suicide? Yes, she must have jumped. He was sure of it. She was, after all, a frail woman who had been steadily unraveling ever since Hannah's disappearance. Yes, poor thing, it had finally pushed her over the edge.

He smiled coldly, looking down at the broken body. He was finally rid of his useless wife. Tomorrow, he would call on the Pinkerton Agency. They would be able to find his treacherous brother and daughter; but tonight, he would have to deal with the authorities and act the part of a grieving husband.

Read what's next in the Grant's Crossing Series!
Here's the first chapter of *Marshal's Suspicion*

MARSHAL'S SUSPICION

CHAPTER 1

HADLEY EVERS

Immediately following his wife's tragic suicide and a somber day of mourning, Isaac Beck tossed his black armband into the trash bin and contacted the Pinkerton Agency. They told him no agent was available for at least another week. Isaac did not want to wait. He contacted the Smithers Detective Agency, which his lawyer recommended.

Eager to secure Beck's business, Mr. Smithers, the owner of the agency, quickly rearranged his schedule. He would meet with Isaac that afternoon. Adding someone as rich and powerful as Isaac Beck to his client list would be a feather in his cap and a great boost to the agency's reputation.

When Isaac arrived, the secretary greeted him with a smile and escorted him immediately into Smithers's office.

Smithers offered his hand; Isaac ignored it. "I need to find my brother and my daughter. Are you able to help me?"

Smithers smiled and leaned a hip against his desk. Right down to business. I've heard that about you, Mr. Beck. Yes, we can help you. Hadley Evers just wrapped up an assignment and is available. He's my best man—an ex-Pinkerton detective. Quite capable. He's skilled at finding what's been lost, whatever it may be. I should warn you, though, he's a dangerous man with few boundaries."

"Sounds perfect. When do I meet him?"

"You already have. He's waiting outside," Smithers said, going to the door and motioning for Evers to come in."

Isaac had noticed the man sitting in the waiting room and had been repulsed by the strong, unpleasant odor that emanated from his direction. When Hadley entered Smithers's office, he brought the stench of body odor, alcohol, and stale smoke with him. His shirt, which may have once been white, was now tea-brown. It hung loosely on his lean frame, the collar and cuffs frayed and stained a dull yellow. Over that was a filthy and tattered long coat that was clearly several sizes too large for him.

Evers's beard was a wild, tangle of matted hair, and his fingernails, long and jagged, were encrusted with dirt.

Isaac's first impression was not favorable.

Seeing the look of disgust on Isaac's face, Evers smiled arrogantly, tugging at the wild tangle of matted hair on his face. "Smithers sent word that he wanted me here immediately. And here I am. I didn't take the time to gussy up."

Evers removed his misshapen hat, revealing a retreating hairline that left behind a defiant patch—an island of red hair surrounded by bare scalp. He tossed his hat onto Smithers's desk, where it landed with a thud, sending up a cloud of dust and earning him a sharp, disapproving glare from Smithers.

The ex-Pinkerton smiled at Smithers and then turned to Isaac, returning Isaac's calculating stare with one of his own. "So, Mr. Beck, what can I do for you?"

"Find my daughter, Mr. Evers. My brother kidnapped her, and I want her back."

"And your brother?"

"Kill him."

GRANT'S CROSSING WESTERNS

MARSHAL'S OBSESSION

A WESTERN NOVEL

JM JOHNSEN

MARSHAL'S DILEMMA

A WESTERN NOVEL

JM JOHNSEN